HEAR THE WORD!

A Novel about Elijah and Elisha

This novel is about Old Testament characters who have already featured in modern fiction. Of course – here is one of the world's great stories. But you can make it either a gaudy epic (Jezebel, bloodbaths, etc.) or an imaginative achievement.

This book is in the more serious class. The Woman is in it; blood is in it; full of action, it ranges over Israel's life. But essentially it is a study of prophecy – its waiting, its weakness, its lonely ecstasy, its uncoil. Written by a citizen of modern Israel, it penetrates into the biblical mind.

It is about a word which comes to Elijah in his despair, which years after is fulfilled through Elisha, which even then is not fulfilled, for human passion conflicts with it. It is about the word of the Lord.

HEAR THE WORD!

A Novel about
Elijah and Elisha
by

HEINRICH ZADOR

SCM PRESS LTD
BLOOMSBURY STREET LONDON

Translated by Robert W. Fenn from the German
Die Erfüllung
published by Lucas Cranach Verlag,
Munich

FIRST PUBLISHED 1962

PRINTED IN GREAT BRITAIN BY
CHARLES BIRCHALL AND SONS LTD
LIVERPOOL AND LONDON

I

THAT morning Jochabed, the wife of Simon the potter, got up very early. She had not brought in enough water the evening before, so she had to go down to the well in the grey light of early dawn, and there against the steps she found a man lying asleep.

She rubbed her eyes and looked at him with growing suspicion. After a while she prodded him with her foot. When he did not move she became frightened. Perhaps he was dead. She crouched down beside him stiffly, for she was no longer young. He had pulled his cloak over his head, so she could not see his face, but now she could hear his slow rasping breathing. She put her hand on his shoulder and shook him. When that did not waken him, she got up painfully, stood with her hands on her hips and looked helplessly round.

The square around the well was deserted. Beersheba was still asleep. The brown houses and workshops, the people and the animals were silent. Then in the distance a cock crowed. Jochabed looked down at the sleeping man again. His cloak was black and coarse, much worn and covered with grey dust, which the dew had turned to a brittle crust. The shepherds in the north wore cloaks like that, made from the skins of their sheep and goats, roughly sewn together. Perhaps this sleeper came from the north. He must have travelled a long way, for the hard soles of his feet were flecked and streaked with dried blood, and his thin brown legs were badly cut and scratched. Jochabed bent down and shook him again. Still he did not wake, so she ventured to draw the cloak away from his face, but this did not tell her much more. It seemed a young face, brown and with a sparse soft beard, but it was so gaunt and thin, with such prominent bones, that in a queer and terrifying way it looked also very old. Jochabed kept wondering if he was really only asleep. He was breathing, so he was certainly alive, but she was sure that it was not a normal healthy sleep. She leaned over the wet edge of the well, drew a pail of water, and splashed a handful in his face. Nothing happened, and now she was really alarmed. She turned away reluctantly shaking her head, for she had already spent too much time over the poor fellow and she must go back home. She hurriedly filled her pitchers, straightened her head-pad, put one pitcher on her head, picked up the other carefully and left.

It was beginning to get light. She set down the pitchers in her little courtyard and went to milk the goats, wondering whether she should tell Simon about the sleeping man. What was there to tell after all? What did it matter that a stranger, a wandering beggar, an unknown man, lay sleeping by the well? It would be better to forget about him. A sudden bleat from the goat warned her that she was milking clumsily, and she only just saved the pail from being overturned. She had been thinking about the sleeper and had pulled the goat's udders too hard. She was sure it would be wiser not to say anything, and at the same time she knew that she could not keep quiet. This annoyed her and made her uneasy.

When she turned back to the house, she found Simon standing in the doorway. She fetched some olives, some bread and a piece of goat cheese, that she had prepared the day before, poured out some milk and remained standing by the table, while Simon ate his breakfast.

"The sky is overcast," she said at length. "Perhaps there's rain coming."

"And about time too!" Simon mumbled, with his mouth full.

"Yes . . . and listen, there's a man asleep on the steps of the well."

Simon did not answer.

"Did you hear? He's fast asleep, and I couldn't wake him."

"Why do you want to wake him? What business is it of yours, if there is a stranger asleep by the well?"

"He's sleeping so heavily. I could not wake him, even by shaking him or by splashing water in his face. He's alive, he is breathing, but I could not wake him."

Simon said nothing. He was a methodical man, who did things in proper order, and only one thing at a time. At the moment he was eating. However, once he had finished, and went to work, he would have even less time to listen to Jochabed, so she said irritably: "Why don't you say something? Perhaps he's ill and needs help?" She paused. She was worried about the young man. Why was she so anxious for Simon to answer her? Why not forget the whole thing? Simon went on eating, drank his milk, wiped his mouth carefully, and stood up. Jochabed knew what he was going to say before he spoke.

"I'll go and have a look at him," he said, and went out.

Jochabed began to clear the table. She drank some milk and made sure that there was enough left for another person—for the sleeper by the well, whom Simon would bring home. She knew that he was coming. Presently she heard footsteps, but she recognized them as only Simon's. Was he coming back alone after all? She pushed the door open.

Simon was half carrying the sleeper. The young man's legs were dangling on the ground, and if Simon had not held him up, he would have collapsed like a heap of rags. By now his eyes were half open, but he did not seem to see anything. Simon dragged him to the bed and laid him down.

"He's ill," he said. "Scarcely conscious. I couldn't get anything out of him. He's really ill. How did he find his way to the well in the dark? He wasn't there yesterday evening."

"Perhaps he was thirsty and wanted some water."

"As he was by the well, he'd probably had some water," said Simon smiling. "But however did he find his way to the town in the dark?" He looked more closely at the sleeping boy and said doubtfully: "He looks to me very much like one of those fanatics who call themselves Servants of the Lord."

"Oh, go on! He's little more than a child. How could he . . .?"

Jochabed paused. She had contradicted Simon only because she suspected that he was right. She went across to the table, poured out some milk, lifted the boy's head and tried to get him to drink. He took a mouthful and choked, tried another and managed to drink some. Then he opened his eyes. They were dark and filled with terror.

"The Woman!" he whispered hoarsely and sank back on the bed, his face twisted into a grimace that was perhaps meant for a smile and muttered:

"Too late! The Master is not here. We..."

He said no more. His eyes were closed. He was already asleep.

"The Woman!" Simon repeated. It sounded like a question, but there was no need to ask. They both knew what it meant. In Israel "the Woman" was Jezebel, the stranger, the daughter of Baal, the idolator, the dangerous irresistible beauty. It was rumoured here in Judea that forced labour had been widely imposed in Israel, for Jezebel was accustomed to luxury and splendour and had King Ahab completely under her thumb. That single word "the Woman" had brought her here into Judea, into this very house.

Simon stood deep in thought. "Let him sleep," he said presently. "Just let him sleep—but listen. Nobody must see him. Do you understand?" He glanced back at the bed, shaking his head, then turned away and went across to his workshop.

It was now broad daylight outside. The sky had cleared, the sun was warm and honey-gold. From the street and the neighbouring houses came voices and the sounds of activity. There was still not much light in the room where the boy lay sleeping. He had come out of the darkness and the cold, and his first words had betrayed his secret. He was a fugitive from the Woman!

Jochabed reckoned that he should be safe here in Judea, but she wondered anxiously whether he really would be safe. Jezebel was powerful and cunning. Who could tell how far her arm might reach, and if it reached the fugitive, what would happen to those who had helped him?

Simon did not seem particularly worried about it. Several times during the morning Jochabed peeped through the half-closed door and saw him busily at work as usual, but when he came in at mid-day, his first question was: "Is he still asleep?" Jochabed nodded. The boy was still sleeping, but he no longer seemed so alarmingly ill and exhausted. He was sleeping like a very tired child and breathing quietly. Simon kept glancing at him as he ate his meal, and presently said with decision: "Now I'm going to wake him up. I've got to talk to him."

Jochabed answered uncertainly: "Yes, I suppose you had better wake him. How long is he to stay here? He'll have to go. You heard what he said. The Woman! Who knows what he's done?"

"Nonsense! What do I care about the Woman? She can't do anything here in Judea—at least not yet. I want to talk to him, because I want to know who his master is and also where he is. That's what I want to find out."

He went over to the bed and took the sleeper by the shoulder. The boy turned with a moan and woke. At first his eyes were blank and expressionless, then gradually a look of surprise and suspicion came over his face. He tried to sit up, but fell back again, then took hold of the edge of the bed and pulled himself up till he was resting on his elbows. He stared at Simon without speaking.

"Who are you?" asked Simon gently.

The boy moved his lips once or twice and then repeated Simon's question in surprise: "Who are you?" His voice sounded hard and hoarse, as though he had been silent for so long that he found it difficult to speak.

"Don't be afraid," said Simon. "I found you at the well and brought you home here. I am Simon the potter, who are you?"

"Do you walk in the ways of the Lord?"

Simon smiled. "I try to. Why do you not answer my question? You need not be afraid. You are safe here. Who are you and what is your master's name?"

"I am the servant of my Master, Elijah."

The young boy spoke the name softly, diffidently and at the same time reverently, as though it were a talisman or a password. Simon stared at him and asked: "Where is your master?"

"He went on. I didn't leave him, he ordered me to stay. He didn't want ... Believe me, I was his servant and I should not have left him, even though my feet were bleeding and I was exhausted, if he had not ordered me to stay by the well."

"Where was he going to?"

"He was going on ... into ..."

"Into the desert?"

"Yes."

"Was he running away from the Woman?"

The young man burst out: "How do you know that? Has the news reached here?"

"No, no, nobody else knows about it."

The boy asked no further questions about the source of Simon's information. He hung his head in silence. Simon thought for a moment, then he turned to Jochabed, who was standing in the corner by the bed.

"Bring him some food. He has slept long enough."

Jochabed went somewhat reluctantly and returned quickly with some milk and bread. The boy broke off a piece of bread and ate it greedily. With his mouth still full he said: "Jezebel hated my Master. The Lord had shown his power through him. What could the hundreds of servants of Baal do against him? Nothing. The Lord defeated them by the hand of Elijah, and the brook was red with their blood. Elijah's bullock was consumed by the fire of the Lord. Elijah brought blessing to Israel after the long drought. The rain came and filled the brook. That made the Woman angry. She sought the life of Elijah in return for the useless lives of her useless priests, but . . ."

Simon interrupted him: "Slowly, slowly. I don't understand. Where have you come from now?"

"From Jezreel."

"You mean that Jezebel threatened Elijah's life?"

"Her messenger came to Obadiah's house in the night and said: 'These are the words of my mistress: the gods do so to me and more also, if I do not make your life like the life of one of them by this time tomorrow.' Elijah answered: 'I was with the King and he was witness of what happened.' Then the messenger laughed and said: 'O wise man, don't you know that the King is under Jezebel's thumb: She told the King what she intended to do and he did not object. I tell you, Jezebel has you in her power.' The Master made no reply. He staggered, and I had to hold him up, as you did me, and in the morning he fled for his life from Jezreel, and I went with him."

"Your life like the life of one of them! What did that mean?"

"Her servants, the priests of Baal, the gang! They are dead, executed, before the eyes of Elijah and the King! They are all dead!"

"What! Where is all this supposed to have happened?"

"At the brook, at the foot of the mountain, where the Lord sent his fire for Elijah in order to show his power."

Simon said impatiently: "Listen, crackpot! I can't make anything of all this nonsense. All I can understand is that your master is in danger and probably needs help. Haven't you thought of that? I'll ... Look! You must try to tell us clearly just what has happened."

The young man hung his head again and swallowed once or twice. Then he said peevishly: "This is what happened. The spirit of the Lord told my Master to go to Jezreel, to the King. I was afraid, but my Master said that that was what he had been told to do. On the way there we met some of the King's men. The drought had been severe in Israel. Year after year the harvests had been bad and the fields were bare. The cattle had been destroyed because there was no food for them. There was great misery among the people, so the King sent his men out to look for grass and water. It was very hot, a scorching wind was blowing from the desert. We were sitting by the roadside, when Obadiah came along."

"Who is Obadiah?"

"The King's steward. He walks in the way of the Lord."

"How do you know that?"

"My Master said so. When Jezebel tried to destroy all the prophets of the Lord, Obadiah hid them and supplied them with food. That's what the Master said ... and when Obadiah came up, the Master was sitting with his head between his knees, so that Obadiah would not recognize him, but Obadiah did recognize him and got off his horse and came up to him and fell on his knees before him and said: 'Is it you, my Lord Elijah?' And the Master laid his hand on Obadiah's shoulder and said: 'It is I. What are you doing here?' And Obadiah told him about the drought and the famine, and how they were being sent out everywhere. The Master just looked at him, and then looked from one of the King's men to another, and many of them lowered their eyes. Then the Master said: 'All right, just go back and tell your master that Elijah is here.'

"The King's men put their heads together and held a whispered consultation. At last Obadiah said: 'What have I done to you, my Lord Elijah, that you should send me to the King for him to kill me?' He told Elijah how the King had sought him everywhere, and not for any pleasant reason either, and now the Master was asking him to go and tell the King that he was here, and meanwhile the Spirit of the Lord might send him somewhere else, and then where would Obadiah be? When the King found the news was not true, he would vent his anger on Obadiah. I was afraid Obadiah would take the Master with him. The King's men suggested that, and what could I have done to prevent it?"

"Nothing," said Simon dryly.

"Nothing, could I? But the Master calmed Obadiah down and promised to wait there. Then Obadiah returned to tell King Ahab the news. I was terribly frightened, for Ahab is a very wicked man. The Master had often said that he has done more evil in the sight of the Lord than anyone else before him. Then some shepherds and farm people came along, and they must have spread the news, because the crowd round Elijah grew bigger and bigger, but the Master said nothing."

The young man paused, his head cupped in his hands, as though he were trying to show how Elijah had been sitting, silent and as if in a trance.

"He was listening," he said after a while. "The villagers gathered round him, hoping that he would speak to them or lay his hands upon them, but he sat still and said nothing. I told them that the King was coming. They did not all believe it, but they stayed with us and waited. We waited many hours before we saw the dust of the King's horses. The Master remained sitting on a stone by the roadside. I bowed down low before the King, but he took no notice. He went up to the Master alone, slowly and very pale. I could see the sweat on his brow. The Master stood up and went to meet him, and the King raised his hand, as if he were afraid that Elijah would come too close, or even touch him. His throat was dry after his dusty ride, and he cleared his throat once or twice and then said hoarsely: 'Is it you, destroyer of my people?'

"The Master raised his hand, just as the King had done, perhaps in mockery, as he answered: 'I'm not the one who is destroying Israel.' I noticed that his eyes were turned towards the King, but he did not seem to see him, nor Obadiah, nor the soldiers, nor the carriages. They might have been just thin air, through which he could see the whole land of Israel. So they stood in complete silence. The King passed his hand across his brow once or twice, as if tired by the heat of the day, and then asked a little unsteadily: 'Why have you come? Israel is suffering great misery, the drought has hit us badly, and now you come.' The Master nodded. He seemed to have expected the question, and said sternly: 'You are the destroyer of Israel, my Lord Ahab. The time has come for the Word of the Lord to be spoken to you publicly. You have disregarded the commandments of the Lord and his covenant, and have brought strange gods into the land. It is your sin that has brought misery and famine to Israel.'

"A horrified murmur ran through the crowd. Those on the outside asked what the Master had said, some drew back and others slipped away, thinking that the Master was certain to be killed. Obadiah was trembling, and some of the King's soldiers raised their lances, but the King gave no sign. It was difficult to tell whether he was afraid of the Master or was jeering at him, as he said with tight lips: 'What does your prophecy say is going to happen?' The Master answered without hesitation, as if he had expected the question and had long since considered the answer: 'This is the message that the Lord has given me. The rain will come, and the crops will grow when you cease to do evil in his sight. The rain will come and the crops will grow, as soon as the strange gods and their priests are driven from the land!' The King stamped his foot and shouted: 'Talk sense, you madman! Tell me what is to happen.' And then, believe me, the Master raised his hands and shouted back: 'I will prove to you their futility. Get them all together, all those whom Jezebel has brought into the land and who eat at her table, and all those who offer sacrifices to her gods. I will match myself against them, I alone, in the name of the God of Israel, so that he may show his power. And let the people see, so that they may be witnesses. That is what shall happen!'

"He lowered his arms and turned away. 'Where are you going

now?' asked the King. The master stopped, looked round at the dried up fields beside the road, and at the rocky slopes of the hills bordering the valley, rising bare and steep up to the ridge. Then, pointing to a rocky promontory high up near the crest of the mountain, he said: 'That is where I am going, and where you may come. There I will show you the power of the Lord.' The King replied angrily: 'Right, so shall it be!' And he announced his decree. In the evening the Master and I went across the fields and up the steep mountain side."

The boy reached for the jug of milk and drank. Jochabed leaned over to Simon, took his hand, and whispered: "Do you believe him?"

"What? What did you say?"

"Do you believe what he is telling us?"

"Yes. Such a thing could not be invented. He saw it right enough."

"Or dreamed it. Well, I don't believe it. Who could make the King of Israel come out to meet him somewhere on the high road, and then tell him that he was the destroyer of Israel? And then, would the King issue a decree at the insistence of this impudent fellow? I just don't believe it."

"Hush! Don't say any more. You don't know who Elijah is. He is not afraid of the King."

"Why did he run away then? The boy himself admitted that Elijah had fled. I suppose that was true?"

"I'm *not* lying!" the boy broke in angrily. "Mind what you say and beware of the anger of the Lord!"

Simon quickly intervened. "The Lord's name be praised! Go on. What happened next?"

"We went up the mountain. From below in the valley I couldn't see how we could climb it, but the Master knew a path that led us to the top. Here he took me to a cave and told me to get some sleep, but he stayed out on the open space in front of the cave. I quickly fell fast asleep, and when I woke it was getting light, and the Master was still sitting there, where I had left him the evening before, his eyes wide open.

"As the sun rose, the first group of people arrived, followed by more and more. They sat down under the trees and in the shade of the cliffs. Presently someone shouted from the edge of the clearing: 'Here they come! Here they come!' Then they all crowded round the edge of the promontory to see if the King and the priests were really coming. There was a long line of carriages and we had to wait a long time, while they made a wide detour to get to the top, but at last they arrived."

"And were the priests of Baal actually there?"

"Yes, masses of them. The Master stood up and looked at the King and his courtiers and the crowd of priests in their robes, with poles and stakes and implements, then he turned to the people who were crowding round, whispering and staring. His voice was so clear and loud that the rocks and trees seemed to shake as he called out: 'Children of Israel! How long will you halt between two beliefs?' And there was dead silence. Then the Master struck his staff on the ground and shouted: 'You shall decide! Today you shall decide! If the God whom I serve is the God of Israel, then turn to him and obey his commandments. If Baal be god, then follow him!' Nobody answered. It was so quiet that I could hear the horses pawing the ground and the tinkling of the ornaments on the vestments of the priests, who were impatient at having to stand still. The Master paused, his eyes swept over the lines of spectators, as if he were examining and memorizing every face, and challenging each one to decide and answer there and then. Then I thought he smiled and his voice became gentler. 'Look!' he said. 'I'm the only prophet of the Lord here, and there are hundreds of priests of the false gods. I will match myself against them. Let the King give us two bullocks, and let them choose one. Let them cut it up and prepare it for sacrifice, but put no fire under it. I will do the same with the other bullock.'

"There was a lot of uneasy consultation amongst the priests, and the Master called out to them: 'Listen! When your sacrifice is prepared, you call on the name of your god, and I will call on the name of the God whom I serve, and the one that answers by sending down fire let him be the true God!' And before the King or any of the foreigners could answer the people shouted: 'Good! Agreed!'

"Ahab said nothing, but I saw his eyes look from Elijah to the servants of Baal, and when Elijah had finished, I was surprised to see fear in his eyes. One of the foreigners, an old man in magnificent vestments, went up to him and bowed and said something to him. The King listened with a furrowed brow, but I could not hear what was said. Obadiah was standing there in silence smiling. The old man went back to his companions. Then the two bullocks were brought in and the priests crowded round them, examining them carefully before making their choice.

"While they were preparing their sacrifice the other bullock was brought to Elijah, but he had gone back to his stone and murmured without looking up: 'Not yet!' After a while he glanced at the priests, who were bustling about, preparing their sacrifice, chanting and calling out incantations. Then he lowered his eyes again."

The young man spread his arms in a wide gesture and said laughing: "I saw it all! I crept as close as I could. Everybody was watching them as though it were an entertainment, with a lot of shouting and dancing, singing, chanting and weeping, such as the hills had never witnessed before. The noise seemed to fill the air, but with all the noise there was another sort of silence, for they received no answer, no fire came down to burn their sacrifice. Nothing!

"At midday the Master got up, as though he were getting impatient. He strolled out into the middle of the clearing, to the empty space between the King's seat and the sacrificial altar and called out: 'Call him louder! Is he not a god? Perhaps he is meditating, or gone out, or is on a journey, or even asleep. Call him louder and wake him up!' The King bit his lip in anger and the people laughed. Ahab was sitting under a canopy to shield him from the sun, but his face was red and moist with sweat.

"As the afternoon wore on the priests of Baal made even more noise. They slashed their bodies with knives, so that the blood flowed down to the ground. They worked in relays. When one dropped exhausted another took his place. Yet there was no answer from the hot and pitiless sky.

"At last, when the sun was already sinking towards the sea, Elijah stood up before the King and said to the people: 'Now come over here.' And they came. The Master said: 'First I want twelve stones.' He carried them by himself: nobody was allowed to help him, and the King said: 'Why twelve, Elijah?' The Master answered: 'For the twelve sons of Jacob, of whom the Lord said: Israel shall be thy name.' With the twelve stones Elijah built an altar, and as he did so, the people could see his lips moving and they knew that he was praying. When the altar was finished the Master dug a trench round it, then piled the wood on it and cut the bullock in pieces and laid them on the wood. Then he turned to the King's servants, as if they were his own, and ordered them to bring four pails of water. They ran and fetched them, and the Master told them to pour the water over the sacrifice, and before they had got their breath, he said: 'Do it again!' After the second lot of water had been poured over the altar, we could see little trickles running down into the trench. Then Elijah said: 'Do it again!' and after twelve pailfuls of water had been poured over the twelve stones, the ditch was full. Meanwhile the servants of Baal stood in awed silence beside their altar, staring at Elijah and his sacrifice. The Master went up to his altar and raised his arms to heaven. His face looked strained and the veins stood out on his temples, as his voice rang out over the mountainside: 'Lord God of our fathers, let it be known this day that thou art the God of Israel and that I am thy servant, and that I have done all these things according to thy word. Hear and answer!' He took a deep breath and shouted again: 'Hear and answer, so that this people may know that thou art turning their hearts back to thee!'"

The young man sat up and shouted excitedly: "And then it happened! As Elijah stopped and fell on his knees, it happened! Before the dazzled eyes of the crowd fire came down and burned up the bullock and the wood, the stones of the altar became red hot and turned to black ashes, and the flames even licked up the water. The people fell on their knees, hardly daring to lift their heads, and shouted: 'He is God! He is God!' And when they saw that the blazing fire did not hurt them, they crowded round Elijah, but it seemed that he neither saw nor heard them. He continued to stare into the fire and his face shone like the stones, then suddenly he turned and went up to the King and shouted: 'Did you see his fire? Do you believe in him?' Ahab drew back, but Elijah held him by the arm. Then the King said in a trembling voice: 'I do believe in him. He is God.'

"Elijah let go of his arm. He turned to the crowd and pointed to the priests of Baal—they'd seized their implements and were about to leave: He cried: 'Don't let these unmasked deceivers escape—not one of them!' Then the crowd set upon them, and even some of the King's soldiers joined in. Their officers did not dare to stop them while the King looked on in silence. The crowd seized the foreigners, dragged them to the ground, stripped them, tied their hands and threw them down the hillside. As the victims fell, or rolled down the slope, the mob stabbed them or threw stones at them, till their dead bodies lay in heaps at the bottom of the hill, and the water of the brook was red with their blood. I saw it all with my own eyes.

"Up on the mountain the fire was still smouldering. Elijah was standing beside the trembling King. Obadiah and the few remaining courtiers did not dare to move, as though Elijah's very presence meant fire and death. After a long time the King murmured: 'You had them killed.' The Master was looking down into the valley. He was exhausted. I could tell that by his face and his voice. Without moving his eyes he answered: 'Not I. I am only a servant. The Lord, whose power you saw in the fire, he destroyed them.'

"Then the King said softly and bitterly: 'I suppose I did see it.' He leaned forward in order to see Elijah's face. 'Tell me,' he said. 'Does he only speak through you? I cannot read your secret thoughts. Does he not speak through me also? Supposing I announced that the spirit of the Lord had revealed to me that your magic with the fire was evil, and that your prophecy was false. Supposing in his name I made your life like that of those down there?'

" 'That would be a lie, and you know it,' the Master answered.

"The King stroked his chin with his hand for a while and then asked in a subdued voice: 'Tell me, all the same, Elijah, why is your God the only God of Israel?'

"The question startled me and I was afraid that Elijah would be angry, but he turned round slowly and spoke patiently and with pity, as though the King were sick or just a child who knew no better: 'Because he is the source and father of all things. The chaos and the ocean were subject to him and the earth and all that is in it or lives in it, for he created it. He chose Jacob to be his witness and gave his law to Israel to be the foundation of her faith. He led his people through the wilderness with a pillar of fire by night and a cloud by day. He drove out the other nations before Israel and divided the land among the tribes. He made a covenant with Israel to protect her, and his eye watches over her. And so you should fear him and worship him, for his word is always fulfilled.'

"Ahab was silent. After a long time it was Elijah who spoke again. He beckoned to Obadiah, bowed to the King, and said gently: 'It has been a long day and you are tired, King Ahab. Come and eat and drink, and cheer up, for I can hear the sound of heavy rain.'

"The King's servants brought him food, and while he was eating and drinking, the Master beckoned to me, and we slipped away. I found it hard to keep up with him, as he climbed higher up among the rocks without any pause, until he reached the further rim of the summit, from where we could see the sea. There he laid his hand on my shoulder and said: 'Leave me here to rest. You keep watch and tell me what you see.' He sat down a little way away with his back against a rock and closed his eyes. In the distance the sea looked dark; there was no sign of the white waves that were usually to be seen. I thought the Master had fallen asleep, but after a while he asked: 'What can you see?' I said: 'Nothing.' I did not know what to look for. From time to time the Master enquired again and each time I answered: 'Nothing.'

"Dusk fell and the sky turned a smoky grey, and then towards the north I saw a tiny cloud, that looked no bigger than my fist. When I told the Master, he looked up, jumped to his feet and called out: 'Run down to the King and tell him to get his carriages ready to leave at once so that he may not be overtaken by the storm.' I ran as fast as I could, but by the time I reached the clearing where the King was, the sky was already dark and the wind was getting up, shaking the trees and whistling round the rocks. The King's servants harnessed the horses, and the King was already standing in his carriage when the Master reached us. It was beginning to rain, and the King called out cheerfully: 'Come along, Elijah, get in, we are ready to start.' But the Master said: 'I'll go on ahead.' He led the way down the mountainside in front of the King's carriage. Obadiah took me in his.

"By the time we reached the valley the rain seemed to be coming at us in all directions, the trees were bending before the violence of the storm, and it was lightning and thundering overhead. The King called out again: 'Come up into the carriage, Elijah, so that we can drive faster.' But the Master just laughed, tucked up his cloak, snatched a torch from one of the servants and shouted: 'Drive fast, King Ahab, I will light your way!' And the spirit of the Lord seemed to come upon the Master, for he ran in front of the King's carriage all the way to Jezreel, and the King's horses could not overtake him."

The young man fell back and shut his eyes, as if he had finished, but he was only out of breath, and after a while he went on with his eyes still closed: "At Jezreel Obadiah took us home to his house. He washed the Master's feet and gave us food and drink. Elijah said: 'Now I am tired, my son Obadiah.' And Obadiah answered: 'My house is yours, my Lord Elijah. Rest and rejoice, for the One God has heard and answered your prayers, and now you are high in favour with the King.'

"A bed was prepared for us and we went to sleep. In the middle of the night I was awakened by the sound of voices and footsteps and the clatter of arms. The door was flung open, and a messenger from Jezebel pushed his way in, followed by an agitated Obadiah. The messenger asked: 'Is this the madman? Get up and listen to a message from the Queen.' When he had delivered his message and had gone away, Obadiah said horrified: 'I cannot make out what has happened, my Father. You'll have to get away, your life is not safe here. I sent the messenger away and bribed him with a purse of money not to arrest you at once, as he was disposed to do, but I cannot hide you in this house.'

"The Master was so distressed that he could hardly speak. I thought he would collapse. Then he demanded to be taken to the King. Had he not shown Ahab the power of the Lord only that very day, and had not Ahab professed to turn to the Lord? Obadiah answered sadly: 'O my Master, I think I can guess what has happened. The King is annoyed because your great victory humiliated him publicly, and Jezebel is angry too. Now he is back with her, and she has the power to do whatever she likes with you, for he is under her thumb. You understand? You have got to escape, my Lord.'

"The Master stood silent for a long time, and when he spoke his voice sounded weak and hollow: 'The spirit of the Lord came upon me, and I spoke his word and showed his power. What more could I do? It seems that I have not served him well enough, and he has forsaken me and delivered me into the hands of the foreigners.'

"With the first grey light of dawn Obadiah brought us food for our journey and led us out by a back door. The guard let us through, when Obadiah showed his seal of office. We travelled for three days and three nights, avoiding the main roads, and all the time the Master did not speak. In the evening of the third day we arrived here, and when we reached the well, he spoke for the first time: 'You stay here and rest. I am going on.' I tried to get him to stay and rest also. I begged him to let me go with him to look after him, but he shook his head and said: 'My way is no longer your way.' So he went, and you found me by the well."

Simon looked up as if waking from a dream. "Yes," he said, "I found you by the well."

He went to the window and opened the shutter. Dusk was falling. Outside in the street children were driving sheep and goats home. Now and then a neighbour came by, stopped and called out to Simon and seemed inclined to talk. Simon stood in the window so that nobody could see in, and answered shortly. Presently he pulled the shutter to, stood a moment in thought, and then turned back slowly into the room. Jochabed came up to him and asked softly: "What are we going to do?"

"I don't know . . . I'll seek advice. I'll have a sacrifice prepared and ask for guidance."

"And meanwhile he is to stay here?"

"Would you turn a needy stranger away from your door?"

Jochabed dropped her eyes. "It was I who told you about him. If

I had kept quiet, you would not have brought him home. I am afraid, Simon!"

Simon laid his hand on her shoulder. "You did well, and you have no need to be afraid." But as he went slowly out of the room, his shoulders were bowed, as if he were bearing a heavy burden.

2

CHANAN the priest was old and stern. Simon tried in vain to read an answer in his face, and asked uneasily: "Tell me definitely, is the Lord favourable to my plan?"

They were standing in the courtyard of the little temple. Chanan looked at him intently and answered cautiously: "You have not said what your plan is. What's in your mind?"

"I am very worried."

"Because of the stranger in your house?"

Simon was startled. "Do you know about it? Do other people know? I thought..."

"I know about it. Old people do not sleep very well, and I saw you at the well and I saw the stranger. I did not know that he was still in your house until you told me so."

"He's still in my house."

"Who is he?"

"I don't know what to do... That is why I came to you. The stranger is the servant of Elijah, the prophet of the Lord. Yesterday evening Elijah was in Beersheba, resting at the well."

"And where is he now?"

"He went on, out into..."

"I understand. What's worrying you now?"

"What the boy told me. I will tell you."

Simon tried to speak calmly, but by the time he reached the end of his story he was out of breath, and his voice was trembling. Chanan had listened without speaking. His thin wrinkled face showed no emotion as he asked coldly: "What is worrying you then?"

"Just think, Rabbi Chanan, what the Lord has done to Elijah! And now the prophet has gone out into the desert—into the desert! He is fleeing for his life and is exhausted with his journey, and he is old."

"Isn't he in God's hands even in the desert? He came out of the desert. . . . Supposing that now, if it is the Lord's will. . . ."

Chanan paused. He thought for a while, and then said in a more friendly tone: "Don't worry, my good fellow. I have listened to your story and this is my answer: There is no need for you to do anything further. Let Elijah go his way. It is better for him not to return here, or to any part of Israel."

Simon looked at him in surprise. "Will you explain! I don't understand what you mean."

"May the Lord enlighten you!" Chanan stroked his beard and thought for a while, then he said: "Elijah is fleeing from Jezebel's anger, as you say. I imagine that Ahab is just as angry as she is. Perhaps it was Ahab's anger in the first place. He can't have felt very happy, that day on Carmel. Now think what that means. Is not Ahab in fact Lord of Judea also? Our King Joshaphat was delighted that Ahab's daughter should marry his son, whom he had named after Ahab's firstborn, and does not Judea always have to carry out Ahab's demands? You understand? Ahab's emissary may already be on his way here, and our King will not hesitate to search for any man, whose head Ahab wishes to remove. Are you going to wait for that? Do you want to be questioned by the King's men? Are they to search all the houses here to see if Elijah is hidden in one of them, or has left any evidence of his presence? I don't want that to happen here."

"You do not mention, Rabbi, that King Ahab has done great evil in the Lord's sight, and that Elijah is a consecrated man, who by command of God turned the hearts of the people back to him, and the heart of Ahab also, who witnessed the sacrifice on Carmel?"

"I'm not discussing that. I agree that Ahab has done many things that we do not understand, and which are not easy to justify. Things are very different here, thank God, from what they are in

Israel. The courage and endurance of old Elijah are very estimable, but he is expecting too much. It is no longer possible nowadays, and therefore senseless."

"Forgive me, Rabbi, but I find it hard to understand. . . ."

"I will explain to you. When our fathers came into the land, they were desert nomads, fugitives, and it must be admitted few in number, and without much by way of culture or possessions, but the Lord was with them and they conquered the land that had been promised them and settled down in it and grew and prospered and have now become two kingdoms. They are no longer desert nomads, and consequently their way of life is different from that of their ancestors. Do you understand? It is quite simple, but Elijah refuses to see it. He insists that we should live according to the pattern of our forefathers."

"Elijah demands that God's people should return to his covenant and live according to his laws."

"That's a just demand."

"You're confusing me!"

"The people should live according to God's law, but what is the law? It is an ancient tradition and difficult to interpret. You cannot interpret it, nor can your neighbour. We, the servants of the Lord, have been given that duty, because it was to us that the scriptures were taught, and through us they have been handed down, and because we have studied the law and the rubric, and because we devote all our time to this and nothing else, and because this task has been given to us by the will of God, and to us alone, you understand? Not to those who for their own glorification claim that on this or that occasion the spirit of the Lord came upon them."

"The Lord has shown his approval of Elijah by many wonderful signs."

"Signs? Yes, of course. I ask you, was it not the will of God that his people occupied this land and settled here? That marked a great change in their former organization. It was his will also that the families of the patriarchs should grow into a nation with kings ruling over them. That was a further development. A new order needs new laws, or a new interpretation of the old ones. Those of us who have spent our lives from childhood in his service and doing his will know this interpretation. Look! Ahab allows the worship of strange gods and has even built places of worship for them. Nobody will deny that in this he has not acted well, but on the other hand these are Jezebel's gods, and she has brought wealth and power to the land of Israel. Moreover the temples of the Lord are still there, and Ahab brings rich offerings to them. Besides, is it not recorded that our own King David prayed to the gods of the Philistines, when he had taken refuge in their country? And did not the great Solomon marry Pharaoh's daughter and build her a magnificent temple in which to worship her gods? And he was the one who built the glorious temple of the Lord, even more beautiful than David had planned, and appointed priests according to the old ordinances, who should live in the temple and teach the law to the people."

"What *is* the law, then?"

"That knowledge is not easy to attain. Consider a moment whether Ahab's guilt is really as bad as Elijah says. Famine and misery came because of the sin of Ahab, he says. Well, it was a bad year, the harvest is poor, but the fact remains that Israel has prospered. Today it is more powerful than Judea, its cities are magnificent, and Ahab's power is feared everywhere. In Elijah's eyes splendour and greatness are sinful, because Israel did not live in luxury and power in our forefathers' time. Would all this prosperity have come, if it were contrary to the will of the Lord? Where then is the truth in Elijah's words?"

"The Lord sent down fire to prove the truth of his words."

"That is what you were told. You were told about the fire and the greatness of Elijah in the presence of the King. It is only hearsay, but Elijah's flight is not hearsay, it is fact. Otherwise the young man would not be in your house. What more evidence do we need?"

"The fire was not the first sign."

"We have to exercise caution in doubting and caution in believing, Simon. Many things have been reported, and who has seen them all? Rumour travels far and changes on the way."

"You are a scholar, Rabbi, and know best. How could I . . . ? Answer me one more question. What is to become of Elijah? He went away, and is in danger of dying from hunger and thirst."

"This is my answer: It is not your responsibility. You did not bring him here, and it is not your fault that he has gone. We want to live in peace here. I shall forget what you have told me, and you forget it also. Give the boy food and drink and send him away. Then if the King's men come asking questions, we shan't know anything. That's what you should do."

"And supposing the Lord puts into my heart this anxiety about what is happening to Elijah, so that I can find no peace till I know that he is safe?"

"You exaggerate your own importance. The story you have heard has confused your mind. You asked for advice and I have given it. Now go home and do what I have told you to do." When Simon did not answer, he asked more peremptorily: "Will you do so?"

Simon lowered his eyes and said sadly: "I shall go home."

Chanan laid his hand on Simon's shoulder and said gently: "Go in peace and be wise."

Simon bowed and took his leave. In the next street he stopped and leaned against the wall, deep in thought. It was getting dark and the street was deserted. After a long time he sighed and then walked quickly away, as though time were short.

Jochabed was in the courtyard preparing food for the animals. When Simon came in she stood up and asked: "What did he tell you?"

"The boy has got to go. Where is he?"

Jochabed pointed to a corner of the courtyard. The boy was squatting on his heels and gazing up at the stars. The moon was rising and the sky was getting lighter. Simon went up to the boy and said softly: "Get up!" The boy stood up.

"Are you rested enough to go on your way?" The boy nodded.

"What is your name?"

"My master Elijah calls me Micha."

"Micha," Simon repeated thoughtfully. He took the boy to the little stable, where he kept his two donkeys. He looked at the manger and water trough, stood up again and said to Jochabed, who was standing in the doorway: "Light the fire."

"What, now? In the night?"

"Yes, you must bake some bread."

Simon pulled the boy closer to him and said softly and gently: "Listen, Micha! Early tomorrow morning, at the same time as you arrived here, you will go away again, and I . . . I am going with you."

He raised his arm and waved it in the direction of the desert.

Elijah awoke. The angel was standing at his feet.

The moon was high in the sky, filling the night with a silvery radiance. Across the grey sand the dark shadow of a gorse bush lay sharply outlined, as if drawn by a human hand. Elijah's neck was stiff from resting on a knobbly root that had served him as a pillow.

The angel was standing at his feet—standing, or perhaps floating, it was hard to tell, because his feet were hidden. His long dark blue robe fell without line or fold, merging with the sand, and yet it seemed also to be part of the sky, visible and yet translucent, without outline. The angel was standing silent and patient. His face was brighter than the moonlit night, with a soft luminosity of its own.

Elijah was not at all alarmed, hardly even surprised. He had slept heavily. His one desire before sinking into the dark oblivion of utter exhaustion had been that he might never wake. Now he was awake and alive, and whatever fear or surprise he could still feel was connected with that miracle,—that and his sense of absolute peace. The torment that had pursued him over hill and dale and through the night, till at last he had collapsed here in the shade of the gorse bush, had gone. As he lay without moving, he was conscious only of peace. Awakening was like returning home, without hope, of course, but also without torment. There was peace within him and around him, the night, the moon, the wide stretch of sand and the withered bush all holding their breath and listening. He was listening too.

The angel spoke: "Eat and drink."

Elijah's eyes followed the direction of the angel's pointing finger. Beside the bush, half buried in the sand, was an earthenware pitcher, and beside it, wrapped in dry fig leaves, some little flat loaves of bread. Elijah tried to speak, but his lips were numb and cracked and had a bitter taste like leather. He raised his hand tentatively and saw the thin shadow of his arm against the sand and the curiously elongated and distorted shape of his hand as he reached for the pitcher and took it up. A shower of sand from the sides of the pitcher fell on his chest as he drank obediently. The water was cool and tasted wonderful. It ran down his throat and seemed to spread all over his body, refreshing every fibre, just as the rain soaks into the parched earth in autumn. He reached for the bread and tried to break off a piece and put it in his mouth, but the effort was too great. He was shivering, and the sky and the sand seemed to be shivering too. He closed his eyes, but he could still see the angel through his lowered lids.

The angel said again: "Eat and drink."

Elijah groaned. "I don't want to," he said.

"Why not?"

Elijah opened his eyes reluctantly. The great peace seemed to be at an end, his words sounded bitter, but the angel spoke with compelling gentleness. Elijah whispered imploringly: "Whoever you are, go away and leave me to die. I drank, as you told me to, and do not wish ..."

The angel smiled and said for the third time: "Eat and drink."

He said it very quietly but firmly, like a command. Elijah picked up the bread again, turned it over hesitantly once or twice, and finally began to break pieces off. The angel watched him and seemed satisfied. Presently he said quietly: "No matter what you wish, it is not for you to decide. You know that. Your journey is long, and you must go the way ordained for you."

Elijah looked up and answered querulously: "I have travelled ... Haven't I travelled unquestioningly long and far? Is this the first time that I have had to flee for my life? Not by any means! When I had nothing but the water of the brook and the food that the ravens brought, I asked no questions, and knew that the water and the food came from the Lord. When the brook dried up and the ravens did not return, I set off according to his word and was hidden by his spirit. What can I do now, when he has forsaken me? Why has he forsaken me? I was not afraid of the King and told him what the Lord had revealed to me, and the Lord showed me what he would do and finally answered me by fire to convince the King. Then that very night he gave me into the power of the great whore, and ignored her threats, and put fear into my heart, so that I ran away. Since he gave me no sign at that critical moment, and I am no longer able to divine his will, there is no course set for me. I seem to be going round in a circle like the camel on the threshing floor, ending up where I began. Perhaps all my visions were only hallucination and mirage."

"The Lord has not forsaken you."

Elijah sat up to listen. The angel was looking steadily at him, and to his great surprise he suddenly felt his pain and weakness going from him like mist before the rising sun. In some mysterious way the angel's eyes resting on him produced a soft warm glow, a gentle crystal-clear irradiation, freeing him from all sensation. He could hear and speak without being aware of his own breathing or the movement of his lips. He seemed to be talking in a wonderful enchanted dream and listening to someone at an infinite distance, distant and yet all round him, seeing everything, the angel, himself and every grain of sand. He could hear what was about to be spoken. Now Elijah knew too why he had not been afraid of the angel. The angel had been with him from the beginning and knew everything, and now also he had understood.

Elijah raised his eyes to the angel and said humbly: "Alas! I have not done my duty nor finished my task. I cannot do so. You know that. Look! I have sought him—not in the words spoken by human lips, nor in visible images, but in what he did and what he revealed to me, and I did not sit and wait for his word to be fulfilled. I tried to serve him and was ready to go wherever he wanted me to go and to do whatever he wanted me to do. I sought him as our fathers sought him, as Jacob did, in whom after a time of no rest the word of the Lord was fulfilled. I strove in solitude that I might see him. I knew that his power ruled the heavens and the earth, and recognized his hand in the fire on the mountains and the movements of the ocean and in the life that he has created, and I proclaimed him as the only God and declared his righteousness and faithfulness."

"Yes, you have done that," the angel agreed.

"No. I have done nothing, and he was right to forsake me. My voice was weaker than the rustling of this gorse bush, and what I achieved weighs less than this grain of sand in my hand. Again and again the Lord has smitten Israel because of her faithlessness, and I—I have done the same as Israel. I am no better than my fathers.

"Tell me, what was wrong with me, that my voice was no louder than the hiss of a tortoise, and that Israel's ears were as deaf as this sand? Did I not turn the hearts of the people so that they shouted: 'He is God'? And did not the King's arm tremble beneath my hand as he said: 'I believe'? Yet the King's heart eluded me like a snake and nothing happened. The graven images are still standing all over the country. Baal and Ashera are held up before the people as great gods for them to worship. The law is forgotten, justice is on the side of the powerful, and the widows are left helpless. Forced labour is imposed on Israel to provide the King with glory, and those who enjoy his favour live in exotic luxury in the magnificent houses he has built for them in the cities. They only remember their God as they might an aged slave. They throw him a crumb or two occasionally in case he might be useful sometime.

"That day on Carmel, as I stood alone, my sacrifice blazing in his fire, my heart rejoiced. I thought: 'Now at last I have been a good prophet of the Lord. Israel has come to her senses,' and then that same night I awoke to find that my efforts had been useless, and fear gripped me like a wild beast. The Lord did not speak to me, and my sense of desolation showed me that I am not as strong as the Woman, who has the King under her thumb."

The angel said nothing. After a while Elijah went on: "I am getting old. My beard is white and my legs are not as strong as they were. I am old, and have no longer any part in Israel's life. This people is no longer Israel. They do not live as their fathers lived, their eyes are greedy, their consciences are untroubled. They do not want to accept the discipline of the Lord."

The angel answered softly: "And has he ceased to exist because Israel has forgotten him?"

"He created them out of dust, and he will remain when they return to dust."

"That is true. Your wisdom did not create him, nor the wisdom of Israel. He is himself the source of all wisdom, and you know no more than he permits you to. He gave you his word to proclaim —his word, you understand, nothing else. Israel was not turned back to him by your message, so you imagine that it was not powerful enough. You should know that his word is the one thing that is eternal and sufficient. But do you really listen only for his word, or do you consult your own wishes as well? You say you wanted to be a good prophet of the Lord, but since nothing happens contrary to the Lord's will, the King's cowardice was also his will, just as much as his answer by fire was. Are you going to argue with him because the outcome was not as you wished? Did you not know that his will can neither be influenced nor coerced?"

"Surely it must be his will that Israel should return to her faith? Why else did he speak through me and send me his fire?"

"That is not the right question. Which of us can know both the means and the end that he plans for his creation and for his people? You are his creature, so is Israel. It is for you to live according to his word, and to admonish Israel, so that she may recognize her Lord in herself. That is your mission. His word is his spirit, but your understanding of it and your actions are subject to human error. It is his hand, not yours, that will fulfil his purpose for Israel."

"Yes, Sir," whispered Elijah. Then he asked timidly: "I am tired. Will the Lord speak to me again?"

The angel answered gently: "Rest here. You were wakened so that you might rest. Build up your strength, for you have a long journey before you."

The angel raised his hand in a friendly gesture of farewell. The moon passed behind a bank of clouds, and when it reappeared Elijah opened his eyes again. In the distance he thought he could see shadows, but soon not even these. All round him was deep and utter silence, unbroken like the desert sand. He fell back exhausted and slept.

The angel returned the following night. He had not said anything about coming back, but Elijah awaited his coming with the same anxiety and impatience as he used to feel when waiting for the spirit of the Lord to come upon him and his voice to speak to him. He would wait in fear, because the voice produced in him complete and frightening catalepsy, but mingled with the fear was a consuming desire, because it would be accompanied by indescribable happiness and release. Whatever it said, the voice meant light and wonderful contentment. Elijah did not fear it because of the magnitude of its demands, but only because of the overwhelming joy of being the chosen prophet of the Lord. He could not hear the voice whenever he wished to; it came when it chose to, but he knew by curious physical sensations when it was coming. It was like that now, before the coming of the angel.

Elijah lay beside the gorse bush all that day. Sometimes he watched the little clouds following the sun across the sky till they caught up with it at dusk. Sometimes he listened to little sounds in the stillness, the soft murmur of the occasional breeze that stirred the whispering sand, or the dry rustle of the gorse bush. He passed the daylight hours in dreamy contemplation, vaguely aware of great waves of weariness. At dusk he opened his eyes, conscious of a feeling of excitement. Night fell and the moon came up, and suddenly the angel was there again. He had eluded Elijah's watchfulness. There he stood, and Elijah was not sure whether he had really come back a second time, or whether the daylight hours since his first appearance had been nothing but an illusion of his distorted mind, for the angel was standing at his feet as before in the shadow of the gorse bush, and with exactly the same gesture said: "Eat and drink."

This time Elijah obeyed without protest. When he put the pitcher down he waited for the angel to speak, but the angel only looked at him in silence, till at last Elijah said humbly: "What message have you for me, and what do you want the servant of the Lord to do?"

The angel slowly turned his head and answered: "It is not I who have a message for you."

"Oh, I have been waiting for you, hoping you would return. I have been lying here by the gorse bush all day, half-covered with sand, because I did not want to move. I was waiting for your message."

"The message comes from within you."

"I can't hear anything."

The angel did not answer. After a while Elijah whispered: "What am I, if the Lord forsakes me? Did you not promise that he would speak to me? You said that he had not forsaken me."

"You will hear his voice, if you follow the truth in your heart."

"I asked you before to go away and let me die. That was all I wanted and is what I still want, since he will not speak. His silence can only mean that that is his will for me."

The angel answered gently: "He brought you here so that you would be safe. Do you think that this gorse bush was to be the end of the road? You must be dreaming!"

Elijah did not know what to say. The angel waited a little while, and then said in the same stern tone that had made Elijah eat and drink the night before: "Since you imagine yourself forsaken and want to die, why did you not stay and defy the Woman, instead of fleeing for your life? There may be reason behind your fear after all. Perhaps you went to find the voice that would not speak. Well, what are you grumbling at? Go on searching." And then the angel added softly: "You will go, and you will return."

"Where to?"

"To find the word of the Lord, and after that wherever it sends you."

Elijah put his head in his hands, and the angel went on: "Time is short." Then he bent over Elijah and whispered very gently: "Now that you are refreshed the voice will speak again."

"Where and when?"

"On the way." The angel's voice grew softer and fainter. "Eat and drink, for now that you are rested you must go."

"Will you stay with me?" asked Elijah timidly, but he found he was talking to the empty night. He called out, but the angel had gone. He stumbled to his feet and looked in despair, first at the shadow of the bush, and then at the pale expanse of sand. He was alone. Again he buried his face in his hands, his breath came in great sobs.

At last, after a long time, he dropped his hands. The wind was rising and blowing the sand into whirling eddies, the moon disappeared behind scudding clouds. Elijah seized the bread and water and ate and drank. Then he groped for and found a branch and broke it from the bush, removed the thorns and tried the staff through the air once or twice. He gathered up the cloak that he had been lying on and wrapped it round him, glanced at the heavy sky and set off.

How many days and nights he walked he did not know. The moon waned and the nights became dark, the wind tugged at his cloak and urged him on, the rain disturbed his sleep, the sun came out and made warm green shadows on the brown sand. He walked on. Some Kenite shepherds whom he encountered wondered where he was going. The time of the autumn rains had come, and they were driving their flocks to new pastures. As they sat round their camp fires in the evening they talked about the old man, who had passed them on his solitary journey. He had stopped and rested for a while now and then at one or two camp fires, and they were surprised to find what a lot he knew about the shepherd's life and its worries and dangers. He knew about the habits, ailments and seasonal movements of the sheep. Perhaps the old man had once been a shepherd himself. He was not afraid of the night or the desert. Others told a different story: they had seen him and called out to him, but he had avoided them and passed by in silence with a sad and bitter look. There was obviously something remarkable about him, because they remembered even his silence. Some had met him early, others late, he was evidently making a long journey.

Elijah knew nothing about all this. The days and nights came and went like the rhythmic breathing of time itself. He plodded on without objective, first eastwards then southwards, only because he knew that thus he would be leaving further and further behind all signs of human habitation. Often by the evening his legs would carry him no further. He thought of his talk with the angel, and imagined the angel was back again, for now he could think of many things to say to him, that he had not thought to say at the time. He called out into the darkness: "Give me peace!" Why should it worry him that Israel had forgotten the covenant and the law? Why should he go on tormenting himself, because his message had been so ineffective? And yet he knew that the real reason why he had cried out was because he was alone, and the angel had delivered his message and had not returned. Elijah had to go on.

Surely this apparently aimless wandering was just what his forefathers and the Hebrew tribes had done? Nobody really knew the full story of the tortuous journey they made. Perhaps it had been much the same with them as with him, searching for something without really knowing what, just because one of them, or a few of them, had heard the word of the Lord and its mysterious promise, and thereafter knew no peace.

Elijah was travelling without knowing whither, yet his journey was at once a flight and a returning home into the desert, beside which he had spent his childhood, a journey into the far distant childhood of Israel, when they were conscious of the presence of the Lord, and when he chose them and gave them the tabernacle and the covenant. When did they forsake his commandments? It was when their trials became too severe that they began to doubt the truth of his promise, and they forgot him also when in his great faithfulness the promise came true. He had appeared to them, he had chosen them, and they were too weak to bear the responsibility of being the chosen bearers of his word, too weak to live in his presence.

Elijah wondered whether he had continued to speak and prophesy because of his love for this weak and faithless people that he was leaving behind, and whose sin he hated, or because of his love for the invisible Lord who chastened him and let him suffer. He did not know the answer.

The desert was becoming more rocky, and he met no more shepherds. One day he saw mountains on the horizon, grey and hard like the heavens. He recognized them with surprise. That night he did not sleep, he walked on and on with quickening pace. Sometimes he looked up at the stars that he could pick out between the clouds, afraid lest he might lose his way in the darkness, and anxious because he knew that he had at last reached his destination. Dawn came up slowly, the mountains looked quite close, and yet seemed to get no nearer. Elijah walked steadily on till his legs gradually became numb with exhaustion. By dusk he was climbing amongst rocks and bushes, and at last the path faded out and he stopped.

He found that he had already climbed high up the mountainside. Far below him the plain lay in shadow beneath the brown cliffs. It began to get dark, and a cold wind whipped fine rain against his face. He clung to the bare face of the cliff and groped his way towards a crevice in the rock. It was the narrow entrance to a cave. He crawled in and crouched down in the shelter of the roof. His eyes were burning and he could hardly breathe. The darkness around him seemed solid and impenetrable, the rain grew heavier, and the cold chilled him right through. He drew his cloak over his head and shut his eyes.

The wind howled round the mouth of the cave, and amid the din he thought he heard a voice: "What are you doing here, Elijah?"

Elijah cried out, startled: "Lord, speak to me again. Israel has become faithless, and only I remain as thy prophet, and they are seeking my life to take it away."

He buried his face in his arms, and then through the noise of the storm he heard a voice saying: "Go out and stand before his face."

Elijah crawled to the mouth of the cave and stood up, half deafened, clinging to the rock. The rain was like a dark wall, as the invisible clouds hurled down angry masses of rushing water. The howling of the wind had risen to a despairing scream against the background of roaring floods. Above Elijah's head stones and pebbles, loosened from the mountain, came crashing down into the valley in an avalanche of stone, as though the mountain itself were disintegrating. Elijah stood motionless. Amidst the tumult of sky, night and mountain he felt as if he were just a part of the darkness, a drop of water, or a puff of air. The voice had aroused in him such eager expectation that he forgot his fear. He only knew that he had to wait still longer, that the answer had not yet come. From inside the mountain came a deep rumbling, the ground beneath Elijah's feet shook as though the very centre of the mountain were trying to burst its outer walls. Elijah cried out: "Lord, that is not thou!"

He probably imagined that he was shouting. His words were drowned in the thunder and the storm almost before they were uttered. Elijah no longer knew where he was. Was he still standing on the same ledge of rock, or had the mountain already engulfed him? He thought he was going to die. Jagged bursts of fire tore the sky apart, and thunder rolled unceasingly from everywhere at once, echoing from darkness to darkness. The bluish-yellow light revealed only the vertical walls of torrential rain with the tempestuous patch of sky overhead. Overcome with horror Elijah tried to hide his dazzled eyes, and whispered again: "Lord, my Lord, that is not thou!"

The words stuck in his throat. Fire and darkness forced him to open his eyes and made him close them again. Rain lashed his body, the lightning struck beside him and above his head. He lost consciousness and all sense of time.

Sometime or other the crashing thunder subsided and gradually gave place to a deep rumbling, becoming more and more distant, and answering the lightning more softly and at longer intervals. The jagged lightning grew paler and then died away, leaving only a blue veil of light glimmering through a widening expanse of darkness, till it vanished out of sight. The rustle of the rain grew softer, the mountain hushed its noise, the storm subsided. The wall of water thinned and became transparent and presently disappeared.

Elijah opened his drenched eyes hesitatingly. Earth and sky were peaceful again. Little streams were trickling between the rocks, otherwise all was quiet. The silence was painfully, terrifyingly sweet. The clouds dispersed and high above Elijah's head stars appeared. A soft breeze arose, gently feeling its way towards the morning. Elijah was engulfed in a vast choking overwhelming happiness. With trembling lips he whispered: "Oh, my Lord!"

Now in the gentle breeze that announced the coming dawn he heard again the question, which was also an answer: "What are you doing here, Elijah?"

He fell to his knees and bowed his head till his forehead touched the cold stone. With trembling hands he pulled the soaked and heavy cloak across his face, for he dared not meet the eyes, which now at last rested on him again. He cried out again, as he had done in the night in the cave, but now his voice was calmer, as though he were now beyond all suffering, little more than a murmur, and then silence.

Then the voice began to speak.

3

IT had been raining without stopping for three days, and the day before the sky had still been covered with dark clouds, with frequent showers and a cold wind. However, towards evening it had cleared up, the stars had come out, and now the morning was glorious.

Old Shaphat was sitting on the stone seat outside his house watching the men working in the yard, harnessing the oxen to the plough. He would have liked to go out into the fields with them today. He could tell, as if he were holding the plough, how the earth would feel beneath the ploughshare: softened by the rain, gently dried by the night wind, rich and heavy with the promise of a rich yield. It was time the ploughing was finished, for winter was nearly over.

Shaphat raised his eyes in gratitude to heaven and blinked in the sunlight. The morning sun warmed his limbs and filled him with a feeling of drowsy well-being. Everything was going well. The oxen were big and strong with shiny coats, the sheep in their enclosure had strong thick wool, the cows and goats were giving plenty of milk, there was labour enough for all the work of the farm and fields. Shaphat nodded in satisfaction: the Lord had certainly blessed him. His eyes grew heavy, and he might perhaps have gone to sleep, but just then one of the men came by and asked: "How many yokes of oxen shall we need today, Sir?"

"What? What's that? Oh, how many yokes? You'd better ask Elisha." He felt a little ashamed that he had almost nodded off, so he sat up and called out in a voice grown high and thin: "Elisha! Elisha!" He could see his son by the stable door, too far away to hear his shout, so he turned to the man again and said: "There he is over there. Why don't you ask him?"

"Yes, Sir. It's just that he is standing there silent, and I thought..."

Shaphat said sharply: "Go and ask him."

Secretly he was flattered that the man had turned to him, although Elisha had been standing near, but since he had once and for all decided that Elisha should have authority over the farm and its affairs, he was the one to ask, nobody else. The man knew that, but none the less he carried out the order reluctantly. Shaphat watched the man go across the courtyard, and as he looked at Elisha anxiously, impatiently and puzzled, the same words came into his mind that the servant had used: He is silent.

Elisha was standing in the doorway of the stable, leaning against the doorpost, holding a piece of harness in his hand, but he was not doing anything with it. Shaphat knew his son's face well enough and could understand the servant's hesitation. It was a heavy taciturn face, broad and bony, with bushy brows above the deepset eyes, firm lips and a thick beard that made him look older than he actually was, and gave his features an expression of stern and forbidding melancholy. They are afraid of him, thought Shaphat. He might have said: "They too are afraid of him," for Elisha produced in him also a sort of shyness that was almost fear. He had every reason to be proud of his son, for he got through as much work as two men would normally do, and since he had taken charge, the farm had been more prosperous than ever before. He was a good son, and yet in Shaphat's heart this shyness remained. Perhaps it had always been there, ever since Elisha was born. It was his reserve, thought Shaphat, or perhaps his voice, or maybe his eyes. Elisha's eyes could ask a question and yet seemed to know the answer at the same time. They seemed to look right through one, to read one's mind and one's secret thoughts, probing the truth unerringly. Often his voice seemed to come from far away, from some distant realm of his own thoughts, that nobody else could enter. He could remain silent for a long time, or sometimes he would answer quickly; in either case his words were calm, wise and conclusive. He gave the impression of calmness and of mysterious restlessness at the same time, as though his calmness was the result of iron self-control. Sometimes he would remain silent, as if he did not hear what someone quite close to him had said, and then one hardly dared to interrupt his absorption.

He is unhappy, Shaphat thought, and he looked across at him again anxiously. He did not want to admit even to himself that Elisha was unhappy. He wondered whether he had been out again during the previous night. During this last year Shaphat had often been wakened by the sound of Elisha's door creaking as he stole out into the night. Sometimes he was back again before dawn. Sometimes when the men went out to work in the morning, they found him already busy in the yard. Sometimes it was much later when he returned. Where did he go to at night? Why did he go? What did he lack? He had a prosperous farm and a comfortable life. A wife perhaps! It was time that Elisha married and raised a family. Not a few of the girls turned pale and then blushed if he just looked at them. He was popular with the girls in the valley, but he had never been seen playing around with them, and they spoke softly and respectfully to him as to an older man. After being out at night, he returned remote and abstracted, his brow furrowed in gloom, his eyes weary and sad, as after vain and exhausting toil.

Shaphat shook his head. He was worried. His mood of contentment had vanished. He found himself at last forced to face the question which arose in his mind when Elisha went out at night, which he had tried to avoid, but which kept him awake till dawn: will he come back? His heart was oppressed with fear, love and self-reproach. He knew that he would never dare to ask Elisha about his nocturnal excursions. Perhaps he is a king, thought Shaphat perplexed, but that was only a feeble attempt to explain Elisha's strangeness, the inexplicable cause of his own shyness and uneasiness.

"Twelve," he heard Elisha's answer to the servant. "And hurry! I will go with you."

Out there at the edge of the field red flowers were swaying gently in the breeze. The moist earth was steaming, as Elisha strode along behind his plough. Now and then the ploughshare stuck, and he would stoop down and pick up a stone, and balance its moist coolness in his hand before throwing it on to the little heap that was accumulating at the edge of the field. The oxen plodded on unhurried; the other teams drew their furrows at regular intervals. Sometimes the men called out to each other a question, a remark, or a joke. Elisha worked in silence. The fine morning had raised his spirits and he felt at peace. In the sunshine and the silence thoughts and pictures floated through his mind like the little clouds that drifted across the deep blue sky.

Towards noon he saw the man standing on the ridge above him.

Elisha was startled and checked his plough. It was only by chance that he had glanced up at the hill, and it suddenly seemed as if the figure had been standing there for a long time and had compelled him to look that way. Elisha looked away quickly, but was forced to look again. Perhaps his eyes had deceived him. He did not want to believe them, but already he felt the blood drain from his cheeks, his heart beat wildly, and the blood rushed back into his face. No, he was not mistaken. The tall lean figure stood out clear and dark against the brilliant sky. The man was leaning on his staff, shading his eyes with one hand, looking down over the field and the ploughing, and at the river in spate after the heavy rain, and at the houses and farmsteads of Abel-Mehola. There he stood, quite unmistakable. Elisha stopped his oxen. Then he dropped the reins, called out to one of the men in a hoarse and breathless voice, and ran.

Half-way up the hill he paused involuntarily again, for now he could distinguish the man's features quite clearly, and that increased his alarm. He was confused, as though he had been struck on the head, and hardly knew whether he was running towards the man or trying to get away from him, but that moment quickly passed, and he ran up the hill and gasped: "Elijah! Is it really you?"

Elijah answered quietly: "Yes, it is I."

"My Master, my dear Master!"

Elisha bent over Elijah's hand and kissed it. Elijah raised him up, took hold of his arms and looked searchingly at him. Elisha stood in confused silence, looking for some sign of joyful recognition in the piercing eyes of the old man, which held him spellbound. Gradually into the dark eyes came a look of wonder, yet without surprise, and then tenderness. Elijah nodded and released him, saying: "Yes, you must be the one."

"Does my Master not recognize me?"

"Yes, I recognized you."

Elijah sat down on a stone and gazed thoughtfully into the valley. "Spring is coming," he said. "The seeds will begin to grow."

"For me your coming is the spring. Now I know what I have been waiting for."

"Did you know that I was coming?"

"I was waiting. I have been waiting a long time and looking for a sign. Now you have come. That is the sign, though I do not know yet what it means. Where have you come from, and where are you going?"

"I went away because I had to go, and I have returned as I was told to return." He looked up, and his eyes rested sadly and mysteriously on Elisha. "I have come to you and to you alone, and I shall go away again."

"To me? Well then, come home to my father's house, and let me get you some refreshment."

"No, I'll stay here. You say you were waiting. Tell me, what sign were you waiting for?"

"A sign or an answer. My heart is restless, and I can find no peace."

"What makes you restless?"

"I suppose you are really the reason. You taught us the word of the Lord and its meaning. You also taught me to ask questions, and when I began to ask them, you went away."

"Did you not find an answer in your own heart?"

"I find too many. How can I venture to interpret my own feelings?"

"Elisha, have you heard what Ahab did to me?"

"Yes."

"Who told you?"

"Those who call themselves the Sons of the Prophets are uneasy.

They travel about a good deal. They know our house and when they visit us they talk to me. They told me about it."

"Has the King been looking for me?"

"Here? No."

"I fled for my life." Elijah sighed and looked hard at Elisha again. Then he said: "You did not dare to interpret your visions . . . so I will tell you. The house of Ahab will be destroyed, Elisha. That is the word I have received from the Lord."

"The word!" repeated Elisha bitterly. "I always believed the word you spoke. When I sat at your feet, you knew the answer before I asked. Then I was left alone with plenty of time to ask questions. Look, you taught me that every day is lived in the sight of the invisible Lord, and that his guidance should be sought in everything we do. I have indeed kept eyes and ears open, as I was taught, but I hear too many answers. How can I be sure which is the word of the Lord? What proof have I?"

"In its manifestation. The mystery of the true word of the Lord is that it needs no proof and permits of no question. When that word is spoken to you, you know that it is the true answer, but perhaps you have not yet had that experience. The word that I spoke to you was given to me."

"Perhaps I must wait a while longer, and perhaps the Lord has already spoken to me. I could not decide, and have been waiting for you. I know that what you say is always true."

Elisha raised his eyes to Elijah and said softly but resolutely: "What you are saying today does not answer my question." He leaned forward and pointed with outstretched arm to the valley. "Look there, my Master and Teacher, it is beautiful and peaceful here and life is good. The moist earth is awaiting the approach of spring, and they say that this is a time of anxiety, but do they know what there is to fear? Old superstitions and all sorts of silly nonsense are mixed up in their minds. They fear the wind, the rain and the drought, they are anxious for the crops and the corn. The fear in my mind is something quite different. When I am out walking at night, I am conscious of a menace in my breathing, in the wind, in every stone and tree and plant, in the call of animals and in the night itself. I cannot get away from it. There are arrows in the wind and fire in the darkness. The path beneath my feet is gay with flowers, and it seems as if the earth were being shaken by heavy feet. The sun is bright and cheerful and I hear thundering wheels. Is this just my fear or do I dread the answer?"

"What are you afraid of?"

"The Lord in his anger. You speak of the destruction of the House of Ahab. Who is Ahab? Just a man like myself. To me the voice speaks of the destruction of Israel."

"Israel! Israel will suffer, so that through suffering she may recognize the hand of her Lord. She will be restored in his covenant, for his anger is not greater than his love for his people."

"If only I could be as sure of his love as you are! When I was a child, sitting at your feet, you told me about the days gone by, about how our forefathers lived, about how the Lord led them by cloud and fire, how he built them into a nation and promised them this land. You told me how he punished them for their fear of Anak and Amalek after the report of the scouts, and how after their expiation he restored them and gave them victory over Sihon and Og, and how the resistance of the inhabitants collapsed and Israel conquered the country. Where are now Canaan and Heshbon and Medeba? The children of Anak and Ar of Moab are forgotten. Why, my father, why? I think it was because they had their day and according to the purpose of God their sun must set. All the nations are nothing but dust and are scattered in his good time. They lived here in this land and built cities, and prospered and became rich. You know, I hear a good deal and know what is going on in Israel these days. Israel is behaving exactly as they did. That is why I am afraid that soon the same thing will happen to Israel that happened to them, but Israel is too blind to see it. I can see that Israel has lost her youth and innocence. There are rich and poor in Israel now. The rich are greedy for more possessions, and the poor suffer oppression and injustice. The rich bring their offerings as bribes to buy themselves out of trouble, so that they can commit more injustices, and the poor live in hunger and distress. Israel is soft, like rotten fruit. Is she also to perish?"

Elisha paused. Elijah's eyes were fixed on him and presently he murmured hoarsely: "Why did you stop? Go on."

"I have said enough, dear Master. You know what I want to ask. I see the end of the day for Israel, a blood-red sunset, and a new day bringing new claimants for her land. Israel is surrounded by enemies. I see them advancing like a flood, just as Israel once overran Canaan and Amor and Bashan. Is this the time of trial? Is it the disaster that I fear?"

"Is that your question? The Lord exalts or humbles a nation according to his will, but Israel's covenant with him is eternal, because he is eternal."

"But is Israel also eternal?"

"Israel will endure as long as she acknowledges him, and it is her fate to return to him again and again."

"Again and again you say. How often did our fathers return to him, only to forget him again in their sin! What is the reason for this vacillation? Why this endlessly repeated story of blindness, faithlessness and repentance? Does the One God afflict his people just to raise them up again, and exalt them just to humble them again? That would be a cruel sort of game. Isn't it after all . . . ?"

"Trial and punishment perhaps, but not forgetting." Elijah sat with bowed head and murmured: "Listen, I could not help hating this people because of their blind wickedness. I deplored this and accused Israel to the Lord, but that is not what he wanted to hear. I was wrong not to remember this. It is his prerogative to judge. Our part is intercession. I did not know enough about his mystery and his mercy. Now I understand. My life was exposed to the fury of his storm. The deluge from his clouds drenched me and his lightning struck at my feet, but he protected me and afterwards spoke his word to me."

"Trial and punishment perhaps, you say. What can be done to avert it now?" Elisha jumped up and stood squarely with clenched fists. "What more can be done? Even your words and the fire that you called down did not turn their hearts. Who did anything to help you, when you had to flee for your life? What more can be done than you have done? That's the question that worries me day and night. How can I remain idle, when I see and know and feel in my bones the coming of trial and punishment? Tell me what to do. Who am I, to raise my voice and appeal to the whole people? What influence do I have over them? And yet how can I remain silent?"

Elijah was no longer looking at Elisha. His brow was furrowed and he just nodded, as if he had been waiting for this question, which had confirmed his own decision. He got up, untied the hempen cord that fastened his cloak, and threw it off. Holding the cloak in his hands he said: "Your question is a fair one: What is to be done? This is my answer: You shall be my successor. I am old and lonely and your task shall be to carry my work further."

He spread out the cloak and flung it round Elisha's shoulders.

Elisha exclaimed in horror: "Master! What are you doing?"

"What I was commanded to do. You have been chosen: it is your destiny."

"No! Do not make fun of me!"

"I am not making fun."

"Then take back your words. Try to understand. My dear Master, there are our fields, this is our farm. My father and mother live here and they are old and frail. I am responsible for the farm. How can I become your successor and carry on your work?"

"I have lived all my life in this way. You have had time enough. The Lord is your father and Israel shall be your house and farm."

"Who am I to proclaim the word of the Lord?"

Elijah shouted in sudden anger: "Is this just affectation, becaue you live so comfortably? I expect you know it is. What else did your question mean? You have known about this for a long time, admit it. You have no peace because you know your destiny. Are you now going to refuse it?"

Elisha stared at him wildly. With a voice broken by sobs he said: "My knowledge was the cause of my fear. Must my knowledge be true, if I don't want it to be true?"

"What has knowledge to do with what you want? You know that too."

Elisha turned away and hid his face in his hands. His shoulders were bowed as if aching beneath the weight of the cloak. He groaned and without turning back to Elijah said in a low voice: "What do I know? I know nothing. Give me time. Come home with me and rest before your journey, and let us celebrate your return."

"No, I will not stay in your house. Will you follow me?"

Elisha stood silent. After a long time he said wearily: "You are my Master and you leave me no choice. Give me then at least time to go and tell my father and mother and bid them goodbye. Then I will do as you bid me."

Elijah's voice became suddenly gentle and quiet. "Go," he said. "Remember what has been done to you, and come back."

Elisha stumbled down the slope. His legs moved by themselves as if in a dream. Perhaps the meeting with Elijah on the hill had also been a dream. He did not dare to turn round. He knew that Elijah was watching him, and that his eyes were stronger than he was.

The men had finished ploughing and were standing talking at the edge of the field. Elisha went stumbling past them faster and faster. He hardly knew whether he was running away from Elijah or was hurrying to get back to him, as he went over again the questions that were chasing wildly through his mind: What do I want to do? What is he doing to me? What have I done? And all the time at the back if his mind there was the terrifying knowledge that Elijah was waiting for him and he must hurry. The sun was setting and the air was cool. The night will be cold, he thought, and even the coldness of the night had now a different significance than before. In Ahab's kingdom Elijah was in danger, and no doubt it was better to travel by night. And Elijah had said that he did not want to wait longer here. His mantle is upon me, he thought to himself, what would that mean now? There was so much in himself, that he could not understand, and he found no answer to the questions in his own heart. Had Elijah's words really come as a surprise? Perhaps they had crystallized and put into words what he himself had guessed and even desired for a long time. That was why in his uncertainty his nights had been so restless and troubled, and yet now he was as if deaf and dumb, and frozen into astonished resistance. Then he ran.

The yard was empty. His mother Silpa was just coming out of the kitchen. She saw him at the gate and was about to come towards him, but when she saw his ravaged face she was alarmed and went back into the kitchen. Elisha stopped at the gate to get his breath. Tomorrow the oxen must rest, he thought absentmindedly, then the men will have time to mend the stable roof, where the rain was coming through, and then he suddenly thought: Where shall I be tomorrow? He strode across the yard.

Shaphat was sitting in an armchair beside the fireplace. He looked up in surprise when Elisha came in. There was not enough light in the room for him to see his son's face, but he knew at once that something had happened to bring Elisha home unusually early, but he was afraid to ask. Instead he began to talk about whatever came into his head, before Elisha could say anything.

"Ah, there you are! You are early. I suppose you have finished the ploughing, otherwise you would not be back yet, or are you ill? It must be wonderful today, with the earth soft after the rain, and easy going. I should have liked . . ." He stopped. He had forgotten what it was he would have liked, for Elisha was standing waiting patiently, and Shaphat's chatter was no match for Elisha's patience.

"Yes," said Elisha. "It was a beautiful day and the ploughing is finished. The men will be back soon. I came back early so that I could talk to you, Father."

"Good! Good!" Shaphat muttered uncertainly. "Well, what's the matter?"

"Elijah the teacher has come back, Father."

"Elijah! You call him the teacher? I have never asked you to be a pupil of his. Where is he?"

"Up on the hill. He is waiting there, for he has come to see me, and I have come to ask you to let me go, Father, for Elijah has cast his mantle upon me and I must go."

"What do you mean? Go where?"

"You know very well, Father! To go with Elijah." Elisha spoke slowly as if he could hardly trust his own words: "Elijah said to me, 'I am old and lonely, and it is for you to carry on my work. It is ordained.' And so now his mantle rests on my shoulders."

"No! No! No!" shouted Shaphat. He stared at Elisha openmouthed, then his face twisted and he burst into tears, and put his head down on his hands that were crossed over the handle of his stick. "No ! No ! No !" he whimpered, his whole body shaken with sobs.

Elisha waited. At last he laid his hand on Shaphat's shoulder and said: "Father, don't struggle against the will of God."

Shaphat sat up. He had stopped weeping and banged on the floor with his stick and shouted angrily. "Who is this restless Elijah, that you should regard his words as the command of God?"

"You know the answer, Father, without my telling you. It is I who am the restless one. Elijah is a prophet, blessed of the Lord. He speaks the word that is given to him."

Shaphat said plaintively: "What are you thinking about? You think too much. That is why you are restless. This is your home and your farm. Elijah comes and goes, wandering from place to place. That is his fate. The Lord has laid his hands on him and you call that blessing ! Your home is here. You have already taken over the farm, and who knows how long I shall live? All this is your property, and that is what the Lord really wills, for I have seen how he has blessed the work of your hands."

"Thank you. Father, I did not send for Elijah, but I have been waiting for him. I sat at his feet when he was teaching here, and his words remained in my heart when he went away. That was the Lord's doing, and I knew that one day he would call me. No, I did not know it. I feared it." And then he added softly: "I am the Lord's. You know that too, Father. I am the firstborn."

Shaphat sat silent. Elisha turned wearily and pulled a low seat towards him and sat down beside Shaphat. Shaphat shook his head from time to time and even seemed about to speak, but said nothing. It was gradually getting dark in the room. At last Elisha said tensely: "I do understand you, Father, and my heart is heavy. You are naturally surprised. I was no less so myself, and yet I wasn't. It is not the first time that I have heard the call. I tried to stop my ears, so that I should not hear it, but what can I do against the power of the Lord? Now I have to listen."

Shaphat muttered crossly: "Who can compel you if you do not want to? Can Elijah force you? You ought to be man enough not to let yourself be forced against your will."

"I have no argument against Elijah's words. I . . . I want to do as he says. What would you do, Father, if there were war in the land and the King summoned me to follow him?"

"Elijah isn't a king."

"The Lord is our king, and now Israel is in distress."

"And supposing the Lord decides to bring misery upon Israel, what do you intend to do about it? Are you going to oppose his will and make him change his mind?"

"Whatever I do will be his will. That is why he has called me. Don't ask me any more, for I do not know myself yet what he will have me do. My head is heavy and tired, it is all so much and so big! I only know that I have been called, and that knowing is not enough. The Lord demands obedience and action, and so I have to go."

Shaphat sat exhausted and dejected. "I've never questioned you," he complained. "Didn't I know when you crept out of the house? I never questioned you. Now my voice is weak and my arms have lost their strength. How can I stop you, and why all this fuss about asking me? You intend to forsake me? Well, you will go and do as you like. I shall not know whether you will ever come back, and shall probably not be here if you do come."

"Here is my home, where I belong. I'm not going out of the world."

From outside in the yard came the sound of voices. The men were coming back. They dragged the ploughs across the yard and began to untie the oxen. Elisha knelt down in front of Shaphat. "I came to talk to you because you are my father and a good man. For this reason it is not enough for you to let me go just because you cannot hold me back. I want you to lay your hands upon my head so that your blessing may go with me everywhere."

Shaphat put his trembling hands on Elisha's head and sobbed: "Because you want me to . . . Why do you need my hands to bless you, when you feel the Lord's hand upon you?"

His hands remained on Elisha's head. After a while Elisha raised a finger to Shaphat's lips. The old man's lips moved soundlessly, then he lowered his hands, leaned back in his chair and murmured hoarsely: "Fetch a light, and tell the men once more what they have to do."

Elisha got up and went out. In the dark passage he bumped into Silpa, who cried out and drew back against the wall.

"Is that you, Mother?"

"Yes."

"Have you heard?"

"Yes," and Silpa burst into tears.

Elisha put his arms round her without speaking, and held her to him. When she stopped crying, he kissed her on the brow and cheeks, and dropped his arms. Then he went out into the yard.

The night was clear and still with a full moon high in the sky. Elisha walked unhurriedly up towards the ridge, where Elijah was waiting motionless, as if he had not moved from the spot where Elisha had left him. His lean figure stood out clearly in the moonlight, as it had done when Elisha first saw him in the bright light of noonday. Elisha watched him as he climbed the hill, and when he reached the top he simply said: "Here I am."

Elijah asked: "What is that fire down in the valley?"

Elisha looked where he was pointing. Down below in the silvery mist of the hollow they could see a dull reddish fire, from which smoke was rising vertically through the mist into the sky.

"Down there is our farm, don't you remember? We have been sacrificing oxen to the glory of God and for his blessing on my travels. The whole village is holding a festival to bid me farewell. They are enjoying themselves, and did not notice when I slipped away. Perhaps they have not noticed my absence yet."

Elijah just nodded, turned away and motioned with his hand to start. Elisha had great difficulty in keeping up with him, for the path was stony, narrow and steep. Elijah walked in silence. When they came to the valley of the Wadi Yabes he stopped. A broad band of moonlight lay shining across the water. In its narrow bed the river was running high and swiftly with little eddies here and there, that splashed and gurgled in the quiet night.

"We're going across," said Elijah. "D'you know where there is a ford?"

"The river is too full here because of the rain, but it will be shallower lower down."

Elijah walked on in silence. After a while Elisha asked: "Where are we going?"

Elijah stopped again and answered quietly: "Back to the King."

Elisha thought for a while, then said cautiously: "Whatever you say! But you told me you were alone. Of course I am going with you wherever you go, but even with two of us we may need help and protection."

"If the hand of the Lord does not protect us, nobody else can."

"What about those who call themselves the Servants of the Lord, the Sons of the Prophets? Look, you are lonely because the Lord speaks through you. He speaks to very few and they must inevitably be lonely, but there are a considerable number of others, who will have nothing to do with the foreign idols and who follow your teaching."

"How can they help?"

"They pass on information about your movements. If you intend to go to Ahab, do not go in secret. Let all the people know about your return, and that you are not afraid of the King, or the Woman, and that you are back again. Then the King will be afraid of you. I have thought a lot about this. Let us tell the Sons of the Prophets and send them out to announce your coming. They're waiting for a word from you, so speak to them."

Elijah looked keenly at him and murmured without enthusiasm: "All right, we'll do as you say, Where shall we go?"

"No, Father, you decide and I will follow."

"You have been chosen, so you shall choose." Elijah paused, then said with suppressed violence: "Can't you understand? I did not choose you, or maybe I did. I was not very pleased about it. Let me tell you what happened to me."

"I am listening, Master."

"I was fleeing for my life, and yet I wanted to die, and when I was alone I cried to the Lord to let me die, since his voice no longer spoke to me, and I could not endure to live without his word. I dared not shut my eyes, and for a long time I could not understand this. Are you listening?"

"I'm listening."

"I walked and walked, till at last I came to the mountain where his voice had spoken to me for the first time. There I was back again. I climbed high up into the mountain and heard the storm—thunder, torrential rain and an earthquake and then silence. The voice spoke to me again in the silence. It gave me my answer and I discovered that I had been wrong to run away. I have not served him well enough, because I confused my own will with his. How could I fear the Woman's threats while I was in his hands? I had been wrong. I had not trusted him enough, and so I shall not be allowed to finish my task. Are you listening?"

"I am listening."

"You are to do it. That is not my decision. I am only his messenger. You are my punishment."

"Oh, my dear Master! Can you not love your punishment? I want your love, not your hate. I will serve you in love, that is why I obeyed your summons."

"You cannot serve me, you do not follow me. It is his commands that you obey. Believe me, I feel no anger towards you. I laid my mantle upon your shoulders with my own hands. I will advise you as long as I can and I have told you everything, because nothing may be hidden from you from now on. Listen, many others claim to speak in the name of the Lord, and they believe themselves to be called by him, but I have seen none like you, and I love you, because you accept your responsibility."

"I have always believed what you told me, Master."

Elijah walked on in silence. After a long time he asked: "How many Sons of the Prophets are there?"

"I don't know exactly. Many of them came to our house, and they all said that there were a lot of them, and that their number was growing."

"Where are they living now?"

"Here and there, wherever they can get together."

"Where do you suggest that we should look for them?"

"We shall find some outside the gates of Jericho. They won't go into the city, because the King rebuilt it in defiance of the curse. They camp in the gardens outside the city." Elisha smiled affectionately. "Don't you remember them? Don't you know that you are their guiding star and that they live by your teaching? That is why we should speak to them. They will pass your words on."

Elijah said with sudden impatience: "Come along! It will soon be daylight, and we have a long way to go. We had better hurry."

4

THE King was sitting with his head leaning on the back of the throne. His chin, with its thick square-trimmed beard, rested on his chest and was half concealed in the folds of his dark blue mantle. His arms were folded and he seemed to be listening, but not even Obadiah, his steward and friend, who was standing at the foot of the throne, could be sure whether the King really heard what was being said. Ahab's eyes were half hidden beneath the heavy lids and his face was without expression.

Baana, the Commander-in-chief, leaned over to Obadiah and whispered: "It is not yet midday, but the King is already tired."

Obadiah pretended not to hear. A little later he stole a cautious glance round. Had the other officials noticed the King's weariness? He hoped not. Anyway they gave no sign that they had noticed. Beside Baana was old Ahinoam on a low seat. He had been a member of the Council since the King was a boy and had once been Ahab's tutor. Because of his age he was allowed to remain seated even in the presence of the King. In the middle of the circle Ahaziah the King's son, sat staring fixedly at the ceiling, as though he did not want to see, and possibly not to hear, what was going on. Next to him was Adna, the collector of the King's revenue, who had turned sideways, and with tight and angry lips was watching Jehu, who was speaking. Adna was very ambitious and was envious of Jehu, who was addressing the King's Council for the first time, and had immediately become the focus of attention. Jehu himself was probably too excited to be really conscious of the attitude of the King.

Obadiah's eyes turned back to Ahab. He is getting old, he thought. The King's broad bony face had thickened in the last few years. His cheeks were bloated, round his mouth and nose were puffy folds, and his skin was pale. Obadiah was conscious of a feeling of helpless fear, as though the ageing of his master inevitably weakened his servants and made them helpless too. While Jehu was speaking Obadiah thought irritably: the King must not be tired. He must listen to every word and know everything. At the same time he wished that Jehu would stop talking. Jehu went on, with pauses between his short sentences, which his sharp high-pitched voice made to sound like excited commands.

The King suddenly sat up, leaned forward listening, and said softly: "The Queen!"

Jehu stopped and even Ahinoam and Ahaziah stood up. From the anteroom came the sound of the approaching guard and the rattle of their spears on the tiles. The curtain over the doorway was drawn back. Jezebel came in.

She entered with slow almost soundless steps, taking her time. She raised her arm in greeting and her broad golden bracelets jingled softly. She bowed to Ahab, but smiled as she did so. The formal gesture was just a joke, a gay exaggerated game, that pleased her and the King. Ahab's face brightened. He extended his hand to her, raised her from her curtsy and drew her to the seat by his side. She sat down and carefully arranged the heavy folds of her robe, unconcerned that the whole Council was waiting in silence. At last she raised her eyes, glanced along the waiting assembly and smiled. The smile caused an almost imperceptible sigh of relief among the members of the Council. Their faces relaxed.

Obadiah involuntarily lowered his eyes as Jezebel glanced at him. She is still beautiful, he thought with angry discomfort. He is getting old and she is still beautiful—the most beautiful of all. Today Jezebel had put on a saffron-yellow dress, close fitting down to the kness and reaching to the ground. It was made of soft and heavy material and yet revealed the outline of her body with provoking and embarrassing frankness. On her small feet were pink sandals with broad leather straps ornamented with gold, Obadiah's breathing quickened. It seemed to have become brighter and warmer in the room since Jezebel came in, but it was an evil warmth. The perfume of her body, which had come straight from some mysterious evil and enchanted bath, the perfume of her jet black hair, that she wore falling smoothly, with a fringe over her forehead, the perfume of her delicate and finely drawn face with its soft scarlet lips, pervaded the whole room even to the farthest corner.

"Why, there's Jehu!" Jezebel's voice was surprisingly deep and penetrating. Now it sounded confidential, intimate, and tinged with gentle mockery. "Why were we not told about the return of our brave spy, so that he could be suitably honoured? Or don't you deserve honour, Jehu?"

Jehu answered hoarsely: "Your Majesty knows that I went away in secret, and it was considered advisable that my return should be kept secret."

Ahab added affably: "He arrived today at dawn. He has earned our commendation, and his services will not go unrewarded."

"And what has our spy to report?"

Jehu did not reply, and the King answered for him: "What we expected."

Ahab's eyes suddenly seemed alert, and Obadiah discovered to his great relief that the King had heard and taken in every word.

"Jehu is cunning and fearless. He has visited Syria and seen Benhadad's preparations. He reports that Benhadad is only waiting for the end of the rainy season before he attacks Israel. The fool! The blind, arrogant fool! Anyone would have thought that last summer had been a lesson to him. He still cannot see where the danger lies for all of us."

Jehu said sharply: "If you will allow me, Sir, and if the Queen will grant me the favour of her attention ... I travelled through the land of Syria without being recognized. The Lord opened my eyes and protected me. I wore Syrian clothes and spoke their language and pretended to be looking for work. Benhadad needs soldiers and takes anyone with sound limbs, without asking questions. The army that he is now raising is to be three times as big as the force that attacked us last year. This time he is going to make sure."

Jehu's face twisted into a half-suppressed contemptuous and malicious sneer. "I was for several months in Benhadad's army, and by that means learned about his organization and strategy and perhaps something of his plans. I should explain, Ma'am, that Syria is confident, very wealthy and very strong. Their fields are well cultivated. It is a long time since they suffered invasion, and they live in wicked luxury. Their towns are magnificent, their warehouses and shops are bursting with goods, they have gold, precious stones, cloth and ornaments, all sorts of spices and wood and copper. Their markets are crowded with merchants from every land, and there are numerous festivals, that are celebrated with such dazzling splendour that it took my breath away."

Jehu paused with an expansive gesture and then went on in a different tone: "Benhadad has long since made up what he lost last year. He has soldiers and chariots and an enormous number of animals. He exacts tribute from all his vassals. Now he has let it be known that the reason why he did not defeat us last year was because we had fortified ourselves here in the hills. Israel, he says, is a people of the hills, and so Israel's god helped them. Out in the open country he would have annihilated us. That is what is being said. Benhadad is making no secret of his preparations for a new war against Israel. This time he intends to force us to fight in the open. He is not going to besiege the city of Samaria. His armies will spread out over the land like locusts and if we do oppose them, he will despoil Israel's fields and meadows, destroy her villages, steal her cattle and take her people captive. Then Samaria and whatever else remains will starve." Jehu raised his head and said vehemently: "That is his intention, if we let him, if we don't defend ourselves."

Jezebel was still watching Jehu. Round her eyes there were still faint traces of a smile, but it was difficult to tell whether it was caused by Jehu himself or his news, but her face was now intent and hard—curiously bleak and hard—and seemed older than when she came in.

"As you say," she said softly, "if we let him. We certainly will not let him."

Jehu bowed and stepped back. He turned impatiently to his neighbours, as if he expected them to speak. He probably did not yet know that members of the King's council only spoke when

Ahab invited them to. It was suddenly absolutely quiet, till the King said in a low voice: "Well, Adna?"

Adna bowed low, beginning to speak at the same time.

"The captain's report is depressing, but the Queen has already given the answer. You will not allow Benhadad to conquer Israel. Let the King tell his ministers what they are to do."

Ahab snapped with sudden anger: "You know quite well what is to be done. What I want to hear is what measures have been taken, what has been achieved and what is being done."

"We are doing all we can. The royal storehouses and depots are gradually filling. Progress is slow but encouraging. The King in his wisdom will be well aware that the last harvest was bad, and how much of its scanty yield was stolen or destroyed by Benhadad's troops. The King's overseer and his officials are working ceaselessly. The people contribute very unwillingly. They ask for time to pay and for tax relief, and it is difficult to disregard their appeal because of public opinion. The people are grumbling and are against another war. That is why our valiant Jehu's report is so depressing. With respect, Sir, the people are complaining that they cannot pay the taxes and that they are hungry. They are afraid of another war, and some here and there even have the impudence to ask if it makes any difference whether they die from the King's starvation or Benhadad's sword. I assure you that your servant and those under his control are doing all they can. We collect the taxes with the utmost severity according to your instructions, but in fact Israel cannot boast of the wealth that so impressed Jehu in Syria. Perhaps, therefore, Sir, you will consider also in your wisdom what I have said."

Ahab's eyes flashed as he answered angrily:

"I will not grant any relief, for I will not jeopardize the future of Israel. Listen, Adna, you will answer with your life that your officials do not forget my orders. Now is the time for sacrifice. When we have defeated Benhadad the cupboards and the stomachs of the people can be filled again."

Ahaziah took his eyes off the ceiling and said in a thin nasal voice:

"Tell me, Father! It is all very fine what this man Jehu has reported. I mean it is pretty dismal, and what Adna said also. Has it really got to come to war? Isn't it possible to negotiate with Ben-hadad? Perhaps he is only threatening us to get what he wants by bluff. Well then, perhaps we should listen and consider. We are pretty hard up these days, and with what a war would cost we might buy him off. I mean. . . ."

Ahab interrupted him. "If we negotiate now we shall not get peace. The only way to talk to him is after we have beaten him."

"And if we don't beat him?"

"We shall beat him!" Jehu broke in. "And he will no longer have any say in the matter. He will be dead."

The King glanced sharply at him. Ahinoam, the old man, raised his hand and tried to get up, but sat down again at a sign from Ahab. Breathing asthmatically he said sternly: "May I offer you my advice, Sir? In your wisdom you spoke of sacrifice. That is the right word. I suggest that you offer to the God of Israel a great and special sacrifice, so that we can make sure of his favour and protection."

Ahab glanced at Jezebel and answered: "Thank you for your advice. Sacrifices will be offered to all the gods, so that they may help us."

Ahinoam went on as though he had not heard the King: "I suggest that you should offer this sacrifice in the presence of all the elders and priests of Israel. I suggest that you summon the elders to be witnesses of the great sacrifice, and that you should tell them about the spy's report and what it means. Look, Sir, the people are complaining. Can we deny that they have some grounds for complaint? Remember that Israel has to contribute not only corn and cattle and fruit, but also soldiers. Let the fathers in Israel see your sacrifice and spread the King's words among the people. Then they will co-operate more willingly."

Jezebel said softly: "The King must not tolerate disaffection and opposition at a time like this. What are these old men suggesting? We know quite well who is grumbling and stirring up opposition. Tell me, Ahinoam, where is Elijah?"

Ahinoam answered quietly: "I don't know."

Jezebel's eyes looked sharply round the circle. "Where is Elijah? Which of you knows where Elijah is?"

Obadiah cleared his throat and said deferentially: "Nobody knows where the Master Elijah is. He comes and goes as the word of the Lord tells him."

"I guess I made him hear the true word of the Lord, when I threatened him and drove him away! We know who helped him at that time, too. For a long time he has not dared to come into the royal city, but he is still alive and stirring up trouble. Where is he?"

"I hear what the Queen says. The Master has not come to Samaria for a long time. I am afraid that is our punishment and not due to his fear. If he decides to return here, all the gates should be flung open and a banquet prepared for him, for he brings the blessing of the Lord."

Ahab hurriedly interposed: "Enough! I have no quarrel with Elijah." Turning to the Queen he said gently: "My love, you are as wise as the serpent and I understand your anxiety, but time is passing and Elijah's days are running out. He is an old man. Let him go where he likes. We have other things to worry about today."

"My dear Lord is too kind. Elijah is the centre of discontent and disobedience. I have heard that the number of his disciples is increasing steadily. He goes about collecting them. Has my Lord not yet heard of Elisha, Elijah's right hand man? The old man appoints his successor like a king, and it is a bad choice. Elisha is a man, they tell me. Perhaps, my dear, you would like to send one of your men to Gilgal, or Beth-El, or Jericho to report on the number of disciples sitting at the feet of Elijah and Elisha. Then, haven't you got one of the old man's followers among your own entourage? And you allow expressions of insubordination in your Council Chamber!"

"Listen! I don't want any new dispute with Elijah just now." Ahab passed his hand across his brow and said firmly: "I will keep your warning in mind, my dear. Meanwhile there is another form of help that you can give us. We must let your father, the great Ethbaal, know at once what Jehu has reported. We need his loyal friendship and help. I hope Ethbaal may be willing to deny

Benhadad the use of his harbours and put a bar on trade with him."

"I will send an envoy to my father. The news will not give him much pleasure. Whether or not he will be able to accede to your request I don't know."

"Let the envoy convey the King's special love and gratitude." Ahab turned with an impatient gesture to his courtiers and said: "Enough! Time is short and we have a lot to do. Ahinoam, you will talk to the assembly of elders. Send out messengers with a summons over our seal. Then, Baana! Recruiting! No, don't argue. You must guarantee that the captains everywhere have their troops within a month, particularly the young men who have not served before, and the bowmen and the charioteers. Are all the chariots ready?"

Baana said loudly: "As you ordered, but we have not got enough chariots yet. If we are to fight in the open country we have not got enough chariots, and we need more horses."

"You talk to Adna. He will see about the horses. Do you hear Adna? And you Obadiah! From now on the carpenters will work only for the army day and night."

Baana raised his hand again. "Will you decide where the headquarters camp is to be, Sir?"

"Why do you ask? In Jezreel."

"And this meeting of elders—if I may make a suggestion—must it take place? Must they be told everything? It is a breach of secrecy and security. Let the King order recruitment and his captains will see that the order is carried out."

Ahab said quietly: "The elders will agree with the King. Ahinoam is right. That is the ancient custom in Israel, and I do not want to break it."

Baana had something more to say, but the King went on: "The frontier guards are to be doubled. You have men enough for that, Baana. See to it at once. And you, Jehu . . ." The King paused with a quick smile, for Jehu had stepped forward as if he had been waiting long and impatiently for a summons.

"You go back to the frontier and organise a network of spies, so that we shall know in good time when Benhadad makes a move.

Then come back here. You shall have your reward. If it really comes to the battle that Benhadad wants, you shall have an important command. You shall help me."

"Yes, Sir."

Obadiah closed his eyes involuntarily. This honour had brought no look of joy to Jehu' face, not even of pride. His thin dark face was distorted with greedy and murderous cruelty.

The King nodded and turned to Jezebel, but she did not notice. She was looking at Jehu with half-closed eyes. Again she smiled, and her smile was in a curious way the response to Jehu's cruel sternness, as if the scowl and the smile had a similar origin, mortally opposed to each other, and yet mysteriously akin.

"You may go," said the King.

Jezebel left first. She curtsied to the King, just as she had done when she came in, then walked past the courtiers and disappeared behind the curtain that invisible hands held open for her. Then the others bowed too and left. Obadiah was about to follow them, but the King said sharply: "You stay, Obadiah!"

He waited till they were alone, then walked with heavy steps to the window. Obadiah remained standing by the throne waiting. Without turning round the King asked: "Where is Elijah?"

Startled, Obadiah answered: "I don't know."

"Don't you really know?"

"No."

Ahab turned round and came up close to Obadiah and looked at him with an angrily wrinkled brow. Obadiah drew back a step, but did not avoid Ahab's eyes. He stammered: "The Master comes and goes. How should I know? I told the Queen so, and you know that you have never had to question the truth of what I say. You know that the night when Elijah ran before your chariot was the same night when he fled for his life because of the Queen's threats. In all the years since then Elijah has never returned to the royal city. He was going to on one occasion, but he did not do so."

"Is it true what they say about him and his disciples?"

"The Master Elijah talks to his disciples about the word of the God of Israel and obedience to him. Is that wrong? I do not know what else is being said about him."

"You can be surprisingly ignorant when you want to. Are you blind too, Obadiah?"

"I don't understand your question."

"You don't know where Elijah is. Haven't you seen him either during these years?"

"Yes, I've seen him."

"Where?"

"Outside the gates of the city. A messenger came to fetch me."

"What did he say to you?"

Obadiah was silent. He hung his head, then fell on his knees and remained prostrate before the King. Ahab said angrily: "A lot of things are being said about you, and I have protected you and kept you with me. Actually I ought to have your head cut off, because you are betraying me."

Obadiah answered flatly without raising his head from the stones: "You know my love for you. I am not betraying you. Neither in my heart nor with my tongue have I ever said anything against you and I have stayed at your side in spite of everything."

Ahab climbed the steps to the throne and sat down. He leaned his head on his hand and after a long silence said: "Get up!" Obadiah got up stiffly. The King looked past him, sighed and muttered: "I want Elijah to come and see me."

Obadiah looked up in astonishment.

"You don't believe me. I tell you I have no quarrel with Elijah. Have I ever lifted a finger against him or his disciples? Do I not offer sacrifices to his God? I have no quarrel with him. It is he that quarrels with me."

Now at last Ahab turned back to Obadiah: "Listen, my servant and friend, I still believe in your loyalty. Can you see how great our danger is? Do you dare to face it? You heard Jehu's report. Israel has become strong during my reign. Perhaps for that reason we cannot expect peace from our neighbours. Now the people are grumbling because they have to make sacrifices and do military service. I know that the people are suffering privations, but how dare they grumble at me and refuse payments and service? Today I alone am Israel's hand and will. I am Israel, and if this kingdom survives its danger, it will be through my will, my resolution, my action, my severity. No, don't say anything yet. I know that Elijah is always attacking me. What he says is reported from many sources, and his disciples repeat what he says. Now answer me, Obadiah! Is that right? Is my will and my action not good and pleasing to the God of Israel? Should not my action be pleasing to your Master Elijah?"

"My dear Lord!" Obadiah murmured. "Your servant believes in you because he loves you, and because he loves you, he does not ask whether you do right or wrong. Is it my business to find fault with you? Elijah the Teacher, however, requires not only deeds but fidelity. According to his teaching the God of Israel is the only God and a jealous God."

"Is the jealousy God's or Elijah's?"

"I don't know how to answer that, but the God whom he proclaims has often shown him his power." Obadiah hesitated, then said resolutely: "You saw it with your own eyes."

"I saw his fire. I also saw the blood bath to which he incited the mob." Ahab shook his head arrogantly. "The hand of the Lord, you say! God has also shown his hand in my dynasty. What was Israel when my father was chosen king, and what is she today? My father Omri slew Tibni, who rose up against him. He subdued Moab. Judah had to make peace with Israel and today obeys my will. Sidon is our ally and friend, because my father and I wished it, and did we not resist even Benhadad last year? This city which my father built defied him. I have also rebuilt the accursed city and it is still standing. There is no longer a curse on Jericho and it is a strong fortress for our defence. Do you think that all this has happened to Israel contrary to the will of God? Does Elijah dare to say so, since God has shown his favour so clearly?"

"The King's glory is great. Why do you ask me? You know the answer. Elijah sees the worship of Baal and Ashera and all the other idols as a horror and an abomination. Elijah looks into the future, for he knows the patience of God and also his relentlessness. Israel has sworn a covenant with her God, and the covenant and the law cannot be broken without retribution."

"Obadiah, my friend, it is all very well for you to dream beautiful dreams and for Elijah to live in a world of fantasy. The King has to look at reality—Israel's isolation and her many enemies. It is easy for Elijah to make a fuss about Baal and Ashera, but the Queen is devoted to them and worships them, and she is not only the joy of my life, but she is also the daughter of Ethbaal. You know what that means, and you know also that Ethbaal has no time for your petty strictures. He did not object to building an altar to the God of Israel in his own city, and the fact that sacrifices are offered to the God of Israel in Tyre has not affected his prosperity."

Obadiah did not answer. The King leaned back and said pensively:

"I am not Elijah. I do not know all the secrets of his God, but I call to mind that there were ancient gods in this land when Israel came and settled here, and who knows all the mysteries of those gods? Look, Obadiah, Israel wandered about in the wilderness and found her God there. Did she really find him? Did he appear and speak to them? That is what they said later, but perhaps it was not like that, perhaps their misery and danger were so great that they needed a very big promise in order not to despair, and they regarded their deliverance as such a great miracle that only a God could have performed it, and so they found him ... and he preserved them and brought them into a fertile land and they conquered it. Israel's God had overcome the Gods of the land. Did he also destroy them? I defeated Benhadad, and he is still there and going to attack me again. The people of Israel are no longer desert nomads, they have become the people of this land. Must not their God change also? He was the God of the wanderings. And another thing, if he is the only God, as Elijah insists, then perhaps Baal is only another name for him, and he conquers Baal by becoming Baal. Is Baal to be identified with him? Is it only a question of name? Cannot everyone worship him under the name that he knows?"

Obadiah drew back and exclaimed in horror: "You must not say such terrible things to me, Sir. How could the God of Israel be worshipped as Baal, and what has he to do with Ashera? The sacrifices made to them are offensive to the One God, like putrid carrion."

"So now you are afraid that his displeasure and judgment will fall on you! Why do you stay with me?"

"If you think as you say, why do you want Elijah to come here?"

HTW 3

"Because I do not want him to remain a barrier between me and the God of Israel. It is easy for you, my dear Obadiah! You believe what Elijah says without daring to think or ask questions. But I do dare, and do you think on that account that the God of Israel is not my God also? I am the King and the Lord's anointed. Nobody has the right to speak against me in the name of the Lord. Does Elijah by any chance want to be King, since he presumes to speak in the name of the Lord against me? My father Omri had the rebel Tibni beheaded. Shall I perhaps do the same to Elijah?"

"If you will forgive my saying so, Sir, you are blinded by your anger. Does Elijah do nothing else than condemn you? Even in his condemnation there is no personal hatred against you. He condemns what you have done, your apostasy, your violation of the law, your negligence. Sir, Sir! Elijah lives his whole life in the conscious presence of his God. He despises wealth and luxury, he heals the sick, comforts the poor, settles disputes, and is a consolation and a father to all those who listen to him. They love him, Sir! He exhorts them and teaches them the law, and proves by his own life that it is possible to live in obedience to it. Perhaps they are a little in awe of him for that reason. Perhaps you should feel the same, but you should love him too."

"I tell you I have done no harm to Elijah, nor to his followers. He did once offend Jezebel very deeply, so that she threatened him so seriously. However, I should like him to come back here, so that he can serve me with his advice. Then he would be serving the people of Israel, and also his God, unless Elijah sees Israel's downfall as the will of the Lord. Just think, Obadiah, my downfall means Israel's downfall. I am not willing to believe that Elijah wants that. So tell me, you who know nothing, and who swear your love to me, do you still insist that you do not know where Elijah is? Or will you go and take a message from me that he shall come here and make peace with me?"

Ahab bowed his head and said almost humbly: "There will soon be no other peace for Israel than the peace between us, so let Elijah forget what has happened and think of what is soon going to happen to Israel. Will you do this for me?"

Obadiah answered with trembling voice: "As surely as I am

standing here and am your servant, I do not know where he is, but I will go and look for him, and give him your message, and I will not rest till I find him. Only you must understand that I have no authority as to his coming and going or as to what he says."

"I know that. I believe you. And listen! The Queen is not to know about your errand."

"As you say."

"Nobody is to know about it. You will go alone. So now go with my blessing and try to persuade him to come with you. Go!"

The King held out his hand and Obadiah came up to him, and bowed to kiss it.

The Sons of the Prophets lived in the lower part of the city in the narrow streets beneath the city walls. Obadiah immediately sent out servants to make inquiries, but they came back without success. Nobody knew where Elijah was at the moment. When Obadiah left the city at dawn next day, he did not know which way to go.

He had discarded his court dress and all evidence of his official position and was wearing a simple robe of rough wool, such as travelling merchants wore in winter, with a headdress of coarse linen, that concealed most of his face. He took with him a mule laden with bales of cloth, and a single servant on whose discretion he could rely.

When he started out the sky was still grey and the scanty grass by the roadside white with frost, but as the sun rose higher, dust soon began to rise beneath the feet, for there had been no rain for several weeks. Farmers were already complaining about the drought and the loss of autumn-sown crops. They are grumbling, thought Obadiah dejectedly. The King knows about their misery. He knows a lot, and yet he does not know enough. 'I am Israel,' the King had said. He will not believe that Elijah intends his downfall, but in that nocturnal meeting, which the King had forced him to admit, this downfall had been expressly prophesied by Elijah. 'The House of Ahab will be destroyed, Obadiah'—that was what he had said. Obadiah remembered the prophecy. The following year, when Ben-hadad invaded the land and besieged Samaria, Obadiah had awaited the fulfilment in silence and despair. When the city held out longer than was expected, and Ahab's last reckless sortie was so successful that Benhadad was forced to withdraw his troops in disorder and with heavy losses, Obadiah's belief in Elijah was not shaken, nor his anxiety assuaged. In his experience the Master's words were often obscure in their simplicity, and their full meaning only became clear after a considerable time. Was it not already clear that the suffering and victory of the previous year had been in vain, and was not the house of Ahab menaced more than ever by downfall and ruin? Obadiah never doubted for a moment that Elijah's words had been the sentence passed on Ahab, which only he could withdraw or mitigate. That was Ahab's only hope. Obadiah loved the King, and for that reason he had not told him yesterday about Elijah's fatal words. Now the King himself realized the necessity for making peace with Elijah, but was such a peace possible? Obadiah knew that Elijah's condemnation did not refer to the King alone. The King was only a sign and a token. Jezebel and Samaria, the splendour and luxury of the capital and the courtiers, the misery of the people and their idolatry were all signs and tokens, fatal signs and tokens of the degeneration and alienation of Israel, and her disregard of the covenant and the law. Could Elijah forget that, as the King wished? And where could he, Obadiah, find the Master?

The day turned out clear and still. Here and there people were working in the fields, travellers, caravans, cattle and carts began to appear on the roads. Obadiah raised his head and peered at every passing face in the vain hope that he might find Elijah in the same unexpected way as had happened years ago by the wayside. He was making for the north, for Elijah liked the heights and caves of Carmel, and so he would look for him first there.

In the evening of the following day he reached Jokneam. While his servant was unloading and watering the animals Obadiah strolled back a little way. The square inside the gate was swarming with people, merchants were busy packing up their wares. Through the arches of the gate farmers were bringing in their cows, sheep and goats. Little groups were standing about talking outside the houses, or sitting on stones and on steps. As Obadiah walked past he tried to pick out a word or two from their conversation. So far he had not found any trace of Elijah, and he was very tired. After a while he sat down on a stone seat and bought a drink of spiced wine from one of the sellers of sweets and drinks. The wine was dark red and tasted bitter. The first mouthful made him twist his mouth awry, but it quenched his thirst and warmed him. Obadiah drank deeply. An old man beside him said mockingly: "Be careful, stranger, don't overburden your legs with too much of our wine, or maybe you will not be able to find your way home to bed, and the curbstones in our streets are hard!"

Obadiah put his drink down. He was glad to have someone to talk to and answered amiably: "I was not drinking to cloud my senses, but because I was thirsty after a long journey."

"There's plenty of water in our wells. Would not a jug of water have quenched your thirst just as well?"

"Perhaps! But as you are so strict, Sir, tell me! Is the moderate enjoyment of wine displeasing to the Lord? I get about a good deal in the course of my business, and wherever I go in the land of Israel I find people enjoy wine, and not only the fools either, who want to drown their sorrows by getting drunk."

"Many things are happening in the land of Israel that are displeasing to the Lord. Israel's God is patient, but one day his patience will give out and the punishment will be bitter. That has been truly predicted."

Obadiah forgot his weariness. He leaned forward and lowered his voice. "You worship the Lord, Sir, and are well informed, as I see. Will you give me some advice?"

"What sort of advice do you need?"

"I'm looking for Elijah, the Master and teacher. Do you happen to know, Sir, where I can find him?"

The old man stroked his beard for a minute and answered very cautiously: "You ask for my advice. Tell me first who you are, where you come from, and why you want to find Elijah."

"I am Obadiah, the son of Chanan, of blessed memory. In my youth I listened to the teaching of the Master, and now I am anxious to see him again."

"There are all sorts of people anxious to see the teacher, some in order to find comfort in his words, and others pretending to be his friends and wishing to do him harm. If you are his servant, Obadiah, you know who they are who wish to harm him. Besides, who can tell where he is? The Master travels all over the country, wherever the spirit sends him. That's how it is. Perhaps you do not know that. You don't really look much like a disciple of Elijah."

"Don't judge me by my stoutness. The fact that the Lord has blessed me with some prosperity does not affect the devotion of my heart."

"You are modest, Obadiah."

"And now I'm in urgent need to find my Master. Do you really not know how to help me?"

"I can tell you nothing at the moment. It's evening. Have you arranged lodging for the night? My house is at your disposal, Obadiah, although you are probably accustomed to something better."

"Thank you, my father. My servant is at the moment watering my animals at the well belonging to the inn. I plan to sleep there tonight before continuing my journey tomorrow."

"That is wise. Stay at the inn, and you will probably hear more." The old man got up, looked at Obadiah again, as if he wanted to fix his face in his mind, then he smiled gently and said politely: "The Lord be with you, my Lord Obadiah, and grant you a safe journey."

Obadiah smiled happily as he watched him go. He assumed from the old man's last words that he had recognized him, and Obadiah had no longer any doubt that he knew where Elijah was. Probably some information would reach him at the inn. He walked back satisfied.

After a good meal he sat outside the inn and waited in spite of the darkness and the cold. Later on the innkeeper joined him and stood shivering and rubbing his hands, trying to start a conversation. Obadiah answered him curtly. After a while the innkeeper told him it was time to close for the night. Disappointed, Obadiah got up, took a light, went to his room and lay down fully dressed on the bed. He tried to stay awake, but as soon as he lay down he fell into an uneasy sleep, full of confused and restless dreams.

Mixed up with these dreams he heard knocking, that did not wake him until it had been repeated several times. He listened drowsily. Someone was tapping at the window. He got up and opened it and saw a half-veiled figure.

"Are you the man who is looking for the Master?"

Obadiah was suddenly wide awake. "Yes, I am."

"Come then! Hurry! You can get through the window."

With some difficulty Obadiah climbed out. The stranger seized his hand and drew him along.

"Where are you taking me?"

"To him. Hurry!"

In the darkness Obadiah could not make out which way they were going, but it seemed to be in the direction of the city wall. Presently they came to a little house, the stranger opened a half-closed door, and led Obadiah along a dark passage. They went down a few steps to a second door, narrow and low. The stranger unlocked it and then locked it again carefully from the outside. Obadiah looked up and saw above him the sky and the stars and behind him the dark outline of the wall. They were standing in the dry moat that ran along outside the wall. They scrambled up the slope and once in the open the stranger seemed no longer in a hurry. He stopped and said softly: "We have an hour's journey. Are you the Obadiah who is the King's steward?"

Obadiah thought a minute and answered simply: "Yes."

"My father thought so, when he heard your name. He asks you, Sir, not to try to find out who we are. I will take you to the Master."

Obadiah answered crossly: "I will not ask, but tell me, nameless one, why all this mystery? Elijah is not afraid, and who is molesting the Sons of the Prophets?"

"The Master is not afraid, but we, his followers, are afraid for him, even if at the moment nobody is molesting him. You know best about that, Sir. Did you yourself not have to hide the Sons of the Prophets because their lives were in danger, and was it not from your house that the Master was driven by the threats of the Woman?"

"Well, yes, but you exaggerate. You do not know the whole story. You have nothing to be afraid of now. Elijah's God is still the God of Israel. His disciples can speak freely everywhere. Perhaps they speak too much!"

"We go wherever he sends us and we do and say what he tells us to. It is not only that! You must not be alarmed, but Elijah is old and weary. He needs to rest. His vision is clear and he hears the word of the Lord, but his body is exhausted. We are very worried about him, for what would Israel be without our father Elijah?"

Obadiah breathed more quickly. He seized the stranger's hand and urged him: "Come, let us hurry. I have important news for Elijah and I am in a hurry for him to get it in time."

The entrance of the cave was by a narrow path, winding between two rocks, which concealed any light coming from the cave itself. As Obadiah and his companion approached, a young man who had been crouching in the bushes outside the cave, rose to his feet, looked hard at them and then murmured: "Here you are!"

He stayed with Obadiah's guide by the entrance while Obadiah went in. In the middle of the floor of the cave a fire was burning in a rough hearth of stones. It gave a dim yellowish light with flickering shadows. Elijah was half reclining on a ledge of rock that was covered with rough blankets. Beside him on a low slab of stone sat Elisha.

Obadiah saw at once that Elijah had aged considerably. His face had got thinner, his cheeks had fallen in, the lines on his face had deepened and his beard was now quite white, but his eyes, which had awakened awe and love in Obadiah, were unchanged. They were still large, sparkling and very much alive.

"Well, here you are, my son Obadiah!"

Elijah showed no surprise, and Obadiah guessed that he had had to wait so long earlier in the evening because the Master was being informed and asked for instructions. He bowed over Elijah's hand.

"O my beloved Master, how wonderful to hear your voice again!"

He turned and bowed to Elisha, who greeted him: "God be with you, friend!"

"Sit down and rest," said Elijah. "You have come a long way, no doubt."

"I was impatient to see my Master's face. I did not know where to look. The Lord must have helped me so that I found you so quickly."

"What message have you brought? What does King Ahab want from his enemy?"

"You already know that I am bringing a message?"

"You would hardly come without a message."

Obadiah answered cautiously: "Sir, you are not the enemy of the King, not in his opinion. He said to me: 'I have no quarrel with Elijah,' and he sent me out to look for you."

Elisha glanced up at Elijah. Neither spoke. After a pause Obadiah went on hesitantly: "The King's heart is heavy. He is worried and longs to make peace with you, for Israel is in great distress."

"What sort of distress is worrying the King?"

"Israel's. He has reliable information that Syria is arming against us again." Obadiah paused again, then as no comment or question was forthcoming, he went on plaintively: "It is not yet a year since Benhadad demanded submission and tribute from Ahab and besieged Samaria. It was only by the great mercy of God that we escaped Benhadad's sword at the cost of blood and sacrifice. It was not enough. Benhadad intends to return with greater power to lay waste the land, plunder Samaria and take the people into slavery so that Israel may never defy Syria again."

Elisha glanced up again and asked: "Where does your information come from?"

"The King sent out his servant Jehu to find out Syria's plans. He was away for many months. He is cunning and brave and saw everything. It was he who brought the news."

"Is that Jehu, the son of Jehoshaphat?"

"Yes."

"Jehoshaphat was a good man and a strict observer of the law. How can his son serve the King and Baal?"

"My good Master! Must the King's service inevitably be regarded as the service of Baal? What Jehu has bravely accomplished at the King's bidding may well be the salvation of Israel. Jehu certainly does not worship Baal, I can assure you. He has not forgotten the teaching of his father and hates the foreign gods. I imagine . . ."

"Go on! What do you imagine?"

"Jehu serves the King, but I imagine that he dislikes the Woman."

"Indeed! Jehu is young, isn't he?"

"One of the youngest of the captains. He will go far. He is hard and clever and does not know the meaning of fear."

"You do not like him, do you?"

Obadiah hesitated, then said frankly: "No."

"Why?"

"I don't know. He is rather to be feared than liked."

Suddenly Obadiah could see Jehu's face distorted with cruelty as he answered the King. He added quickly: "But what does it matter what I think of him?"

Elisha said softly and pensively: "Yes, yes, Jehu . . ."

Suddenly Elijah asked: "What then is the King's request?"

"I have told you already, Master! He has no quarrel with you and wants to make peace with you. Israel is in distress. There has been war, then the harvest was bad, taxation and the demands of military service are heavy, and the people are grumbling. Oh yes, my Master, those who have listened to your words know that the King has sinned grieviously against the Lord, and his covenant. You have said that Ahab's perfidy will bring ruin upon Israel, but tell me again. Benhadad mocks the God of Israel. He says he is only a God of the hills, and in the plains he would leave Israel defenceless, because he has no power there. That is what Benhadad says, and Ahab intends to defy him. Tell me, is not the King's intention good? If it is good, should stones be put in his path so that he falls? The people are grumbling—they do not yet know their danger. Is it wise to listen to their grumbling and encourage it? The King wants to divert the peril from Israel. He can only do that if all the people are behind him."

Elijah looked at him fixedly in silence. Obadiah felt his throat tighten, and went on with difficulty: "It is reported to the King that my Master's disciples are talking of resistance and refusal of military service. They profess to be speaking in your name. That distresses the King. It is his wish that his intentions and his actions meet with your approval and that you yourself, Master, express your approval publicly."

Elijah still remained silent. Obadiah looked at him in embarrassment and cried desperately: "You say nothing! That night you spoke of the downfall of the King. Does that mean also the downfall of Israel? I believe you. I believe your words. I have said nothing about it to the King. Take back your words, so that they may not be fulfilled, and give Israel your help."

Elijah sat up and said softly: "How do my words, that he does not know about, matter to the King? My message was spoken to him and he did not hear, and what he heard he disregarded. You speak of distress. But I know that the King lives in luxury, and even more magnificent is the temple that he has built to Baal. The servants of Baal feast in luxury at the Woman's table. She jeers at me and makes me flee for my life. Ahab and his favourites know nothing about want. If the King is so concerned about the starvation of the people, let him economise on the sacrifices and open his storehouses and treasury and the purses of his nobles to appease the hunger of the poor, and if he fears the future, let him bow down to Baal and ask him for blessing and protection."

"The King said to me: 'Is not Israel's God my God also?' He intends to offer a special sacrifice to the Lord, so that his enterprise may be blessed."

"And I said years ago: 'How long will you halt between two beliefs?' The King heard but did not heed. Let him destroy the temples of Baal and the stone images in the high places. That is the sacrifice required of him."

"Dear Master, the King cannot do that. I have always lived as in the sight of God, but I understand that the King cannot do what you ask, not at present. The Woman has treated you badly, and she will not go unpunished—but how can the King risk offending her and her father at a time like this? Israel has few allies and Ethbaal is powerful."

"Then let Ahab appeal to Ethbaal for help and forget about making his peace with God."

Elijah leaned back and closed his eyes. Obadiah turned away helplessly and caught sight of Elisha, who was sitting tight-lipped staring with furrowed brow into the fire. Perhaps he had not heard what they had been saying. Obadiah was completely exhausted.

Time was passing, and he did not know what to say or do. Elijah and Elisha seemed to have forgotten him.

Suddenly Elijah raised his hand and said tensely: "You wish to hear my verdict, my son Obadiah? Don't you already know it? The King may well promise now to offer a sacrifice to the God of Israel; he probably has his reasons for tolerating the worship of Baal, even for offering sacrifices to him. But the God of Israel is not a dealer. He never makes bargains. Look! I have demanded a decision from the King, but his heart is cunning and also timid and stupid. He avoids making a decision and prefers to take a short view rather than to look into the future. Necessity alone makes him turn to me. Yet I am only the mouthpiece of the Lord. I have to be stern, because the word of the Lord is stern. I know that your path is difficult, Obadiah, for you love the King, although you abhor his sins. You know that my prophecy will be fulfilled and you are afraid for Ahab's sake, because you love him. Isn't that so?"

"Yes, that's true."

"That's why he chose you as his messenger. He knows that you love me also. I suppose he imagines that for the sake of your love I shall forget my love to God. You are asking me to change my prophecy. Do you think I practise magic and can change the King's fate as I like? I see what the Lord in his mercy and faithfulness reveals to me. I say what I am told to say. The King's fate is sealed, and the seal bears the stamp of his own misdeeds. You will return to the King without my blessing."

"And Israel? What about the poor people of Israel?"

Elijah did not answer. Obadiah covered his face with his hands and staggered back. Elisha went up to him and drew him to the stone on which he had himself been sitting. Obadiah followed meekly. After a long time Elisha suddenly said: "Listen, Obadiah!" Obadiah looked up hesitantly. The words were addressed to him, but Elisha was not looking at him but at Elijah, who had sat up and fixed his eyes searchingly on Elisha. Perhaps Elisha did not see the Master either, for his eyes were wide open and staring, with a strange blind look, and a shy almost childishly astonished smile, and now he said in his deep soft voice: "You have heard the Master's words. Now I have one simple thing to add. The time that you are afraid of has not yet come. Israel will come through the trials that now threaten her, and if the King does right, Benhadad will be delivered into his hands."

Obadiah tried to jump up, but his legs were too weak. He stared at Elisha, incredulous and confused. Elisha went on quietly: "Not yet, I said. Benhadad scorns the God of Israel, and for that reason the God of Israel will show his power and forget for a while Ahab's sin. The Lord is very patient, and what is a year or a lifetime to him? Perhaps there may be another chance. It may happen that the King's heart will really be changed, when he sees his wonderful deliverance."

"Are you just saying this to comfort me, or may I tell your words to the King? Are you going to tell the people of Israel that they must support the King, because Israel is fighting for her life?"

Obadiah paused, glanced shyly at Elijah and stammered: "And will the Master confirm the word that you have spoken?"

Elisha was still looking towards Elijah. The smile on the Master's face was a mixture of sadness, secret mockery and surprise. He spoke softly as if he only intended Elisha to hear: "You have been called, you shall decide. It seems that you see . . ."

"That is what I see," whispered Elisha almost inaudibly. He passed his hand across his brow, turned away, laid his hand on Obadiah's shoulder and said kindly: "Ask no more questions. You have done everything in your power. Do not be afraid. I will go with you and tell the King what must be said. Your errand is done."

Obadiah was still staring at him in bewilderment. He struggled to his feet and looked inquiringly at Elijah. The Master had leaned back again, his eyes were closed, and his face sad and sunken. Obadiah realized that the final answer had been given, and he must not ask any more questions. Elisha waited awhile and then said: "Now you must rest. We will set out at dawn."

He led Obadiah deeper into the cave, where there was a second bed made with stones, skins, and blankets. Obadiah lay down. He was shivering as he wrapped the blankets round him. It was quiet. As he was falling asleep he could still hear the occasional chanting of the boy at the mouth of the cave. He opened his eyes again and saw that Elisha was back in his former place, sitting at the feet of Elijah and smiling the same shy surprised smile again, as he stared motionless into the slowly dying fire.

5

FROM the top of the hill the flat roofs of Samaria fell in steep steps down into the valley to meet the great stone blocks of the encircling city walls. Below the royal palace lay the gardens that Ahab had laid out with elegant terraces, steps, clumps of trees and ornamental pavilions. It was early evening, the sky was suffused with pink, the trees were casting long sharp shadows.

Elisha was standing at a window in the palace looking pensively down on the city. He was tired and impatient, and the garish ostentation of the room bewildered him and made him suspicious and uneasy. The walls were panelled with precious hardwood and decorated with ivory carvings. The hanging chandeliers were of solid gold, and so apparently were the legs of the round table with its dark polished marble top, and the throne on its raised dais. The floor was covered with soft fur that muffled any footstep and over the door and above the King's throne hung gathered purple curtains of heavy material embroidered with gold thread. The window was open, but still the air in the room was heavy with strong sweet scent, that caught the throat.

Elisha's fingers were playing absent-mindedly with the seal that the King had given him as a pass at the end of his first visit. At that time Elisha was not sure whether Ahab really wanted to see him again, and so had felt little confidence in the efficacy of the seal, but today it had been enough just to show it. The captain of the palace guard in person had ushered him in with every sign of respect, and had then hurried away to announce his arrival. Could he perhaps have been making fun of him? The King had not yet come. Outside in the corridor the guard were patrolling up and down. Elisha could hear their footsteps and the rattle, when they halted at the end of the prescribed seven paces and grounded their lances and turned about. Apart from that it was absolutely quiet and this silence too had a depressing and uncanny effect. Elisha began to wish that the King would not come at all. He had forgotten what else he had to say. He longed to go to sleep, and struggled in vain against the listlessness that had been gradually increasing during his long wait. At last he turned and was about to leave, but before he reached the door the curtain was raised. Elisha drew back, expecting the King. Jezebel was standing in the doorway.

He had not seen her before, but he guessed immediately that the woman facing him was Jezebel and he felt annoyed. Then she confirmed it by saying: "You know who I am, don't you, man of Jahweh?"

She seemed to be enjoying his embarrassment. She dropped the curtain that she had been holding with one hand, went over to the throne and sat down. She took out a little mirror, looked at herself with satisfaction, and said into the mirror: "I was told about your return. This time you have even come in the daytime. You are a brave man! I want to talk to you."

Elisha said hoarsely and with annoyance: "That is the King's throne."

"That's right. It is also mine. The King has not yet been told that you are here. The news was brought to me and I gave other orders." Now Jezebel looked at him. Her eyes were dark and piercing, cunningly shaded with cosmetics. "Look at me. Don't be afraid!" she said with a smile, and added after a pause: "So you were not afraid to come back?"

Elisha tried to avoid meeting her eyes.

"The King wanted me to come back. Whom should I be afraid of?"

Jezebel answered softly and with cool disdain: "Me!"

"No, I'm not afraid of you."

"And yet you know about me and my power. The first time you came at night and in secret. Now you have come in broad daylight."

"Yes."

"I am surprised. Your master Elijah was afraid. He ran away so that I should not kill him, and since then he has not dared to set foot in the royal city, but you dare to come and here you are. Did he not warn you, or do you no longer heed his words? I have heard. . . ."

"I came the first time with his full knowledge, as I do today. He has not warned me."

"Why does he not come himself? You realize that the King has no secrets from me. He cannot have. So he told me that it was Elijah he wanted to see, not you."

Elisha's face was flushed. "That is no concern of yours, and you should not wish him to come, daughter of Ethbaal, or are you so very anxious to hear from his lips the prophecy of your death?"

"Maybe, maybe not," Jezebel laughed. "You forget that I am not in the least afraid of his prophecy. To me it is just childish nonsense. Now and then it may even be amusing, but as to fear . . . He has no power over me."

"No. It is quite true that he has no power, nor have I. The power belongs to the God whose prophets we are. His will is fulfilled when the time comes. You can blaspheme him and mock him! The death that he will bring upon you will be a miserable one, and the dogs will eat your body outside the city walls. Those are Elijah's words and also mine."

Jezebel answered insolently: "You are mad, man of Jahweh! The King's summons seems to have gone to your head. Do you imagine that my threat to Elijah was just idle words? One word from me and your insolent tongue would be cut out immediately. Don't you realize that? And before your head was cut off I would give you time to think over who wields the power here."

"Then give the word here and now!" Elisha felt anger boiling up inside him like a fierce, savage joy. It cleared away his confusion. "You will not give the word," he said scornfully. "You do not want to kill me just yet. You said you wanted to talk to me. How could I talk without a tongue, and how could you answer the other tongues that would ask about me?"

Jezebel looked at him with flashing eyes and furrowed brow, but after a while she nodded as if to confirm what he had said, as if his answer had pleased her. She spoke quietly. Her voice was soft as silk.

"Yes, I do want to talk to you. I like you. You have courage. I have not found many with courage to stand up to me. Enough! You came the first time in the darkness. Of course, I heard about it the same night. You came when the King sent for Elijah, and now you have come back to the palace. That means your word counts as the word of Elijah. Tell me then what you said to the King, and what message you bring today."

"What I have to say is only for the ear of the King."

Jezebel laughed. Her voice was gay and seductive. "You are horribly rude, man of Jahweh. I find you difficult. Are you really so stupid, or is it just your inexperience? I warn you, I am not always as patient as I am being at the moment. Your rudeness may not always amuse me." She leaned back with lowered eyelids and asked him: "Aren't you glad that I like you?"

Elisha did not answer. Jezebel murmured sweetly: "You can ask your own reward. I will give you whatever you ask, as soon as you tell me what you said to the King."

"You cannot bribe me, daughter of Ethbaal. My words concern the King alone. I will speak to you when your time comes."

"You obstinate fool! What are you thinking about? Did I not tell you that the King can have no secrets from me? I hear everything. To me he is as open as my flat hand. Perhaps he has already told me what you said. No, he has not told me, because I have not asked him. I want to hear it from you. I have good reasons why I want to hear it from you. I'll tell you. Do you want to know?"

Elisha did not answer. Jezebel went on, as if he had said yes: "If your words are to make sense and be effective, you will have to make peace with me—more than that, a pact."

Elisha thought for a while and then said hoarsely: "Go on."

"The King sent for Elijah without my knowledge. I should not have done so. I know a better way of stopping the mouth of trouble-makers. I am no friend of yours, you might as well know that, but perhaps I should forget the past in view of the present. War has broken out. Tomorrow Ahab is joining his troops and Ahaziah is going with him. I am staying here in his place. Didn't you know that? I am the King's regent while he is away on the battlefield, and who knows what will happen there? Are you beginning to understand why you should talk to me? But perhaps I understand your silence, too, and that even helps me to forget unpleasant things. You obeyed the King's summons and talked to him. Now you have come back again. That is enough for me, even if you will not talk. It is an answer. It tells me that you want what the King wants, and so what I want also. That is good. Just now you said some horrid things to me, my dear man, and in your heart you hate me. Your hatred will melt like snow in the spring sunshine as you look at me and get to know me better. You probably realize already in your heart of hearts that there must not be any quarrel between us, and because you cannot bring yourself to admit it, I will help you and speak for you, not only for this present emergency, but for all the future. Look! I don't intend to bother any more about your God, and I do not mind if you and people like you offer sacrifices to him, as long as you just adopt the same attitude yourself. Why should you be always attacking my gods? Worship your own and see which helps the most. I am told that your followers have recently adopted a more friendly attitude. All right! The King and I, and you also are concerned about the land of Israel that is in danger. All quarrels must be forgotten."

Jezebel's smile became more amiable.

"Have I guessed rightly the purpose of your visit? Well then, this shall be a real peace, you will have a position of honour, and I will keep our pact. Do you understand?"

"I understand perfectly well."

"I am glad. Then you can at last be more friendly and not threaten me any more. Do you never smile, man of Jahweh—or would you rather be called by your own name, Elisha? Is there no smile in your heart to make your eyes more kindly and your lips less stern?"

"I am smiling, indeed I am, because you are as blind as a newly born kitten, daughter of Ethbaal. Do you really imagine that there can ever be peace between you and me? You want to know what I have to say? Then I will tell you. I find your gods ridiculous, and to the God of Israel they are an abomination. I will not rest till they are stamped out, because I really care about Israel. Who made you, a stranger, ruler over the people of God? It is you who are destroying Israel. What have I to do with you, and why should I speak one word from the Lord to you, since you profane his law with every breath you draw?"

Jezebel rested her hands on the arms of the throne and leaned far forward.

"Be sensible!" she hissed between her clenched teeth. "I am warning you for the last time. You are talking to the Queen, and she remembers every word you say. You will pay for this yet, when the time comes. Enough! You are talking nonsense. I am surprised that you meddle so childishly with things you cannot appreciate and which you do not understand. I offer sacrifices to the veiled goddess, who loves me. What do you know of her sweet love? I offer sacrifices to the great god. What do you know of his power? He inflames my senses. But you worship a God who is to be feared, as a child fears his father, and like a child you want to play the father and threaten with a big stick. You can believe what you like, what do I care? I just laugh. I am not of your people and am not obliged to fear your God. One day perhaps Israel will grow up and forget childish fears, and learn at last how to enjoy life, but do you know how to do that? All you can do is to shout and threaten, always trying to impose gloom and discipline on your poor people, poisoning their hearts with fear and guilt. Did you threaten the King again? Did you threaten him with ruin, destruction and punishment?"

Elisha shouted with angry scorn: "No! Now I will tell you. I cheered him up. I told him that he can overcome all his difficulties, and that my God will deliver his enemy into his hands so that he can destroy him, if only the King will do his duty and obey the word of the Lord. That is what I told him, for I know it is true."

Jezebel looked at him for a long time. Then she said with undisguised satisfaction:

"At last! Why did you refuse so long to tell me? Now you have told me after all what you said to the King. Your message is unexpected and I am all the more pleased to hear it. Now you may go back to your cave, or wherever you want to go. I have nothing more to ask you today, but I advise you to keep in mind what I have said to you, even if you are not willing to make a pact with me. I shall be here, so guard your tongue, and see to it that you do not alter your prophecy."

Elisha gasped. Infuriated he said: "I am not going back to my cave. I am going with the King and I shall stay at his side."

"You have courage, as I said before, and you have shown it today."

"You see, I must tell you this. The word that I have spoken is given by our God in his great patience. It has its price. I intend to to see that Ahab pays the price honestly."

"How could a God like yours grant favours without payment and reward? Now I can understand why the King kept quiet, and why he looked so gloomy in spite of your promise. Oh well, I shall be there when the time comes to pay the price, and I will see that you do not cheat the King."

Jezebel got up and asked indifferently, almost absentmindedly: "And do you still want to see the King now?"

Elisha stared at her in amazement. He tried to speak, but could not say a word. Jezebel waited, and at last he whispered with great difficulty:

"No, not any longer, not here."

"All right! Then I will tell him what you have said."

Jezebel clapped her hands. The curtain over the door was drawn aside by invisible hands.

"Farewell, my dear Elisha!" she said, and swept past him and out of the room.

Amongst the crowd that gathered at nightfall in the great square outside the palace, growing bigger every minute, Elisha felt in a strange way concealed. He did not remember how he got there. He had been wandering about in the narrow darkening streets, and the crowd had carried him along whether he would or not. He stood staring, jostled this way and that, occasionally taking an aimless step, only to sink back into his bruised and exhausted lethargy, in which he was conscious only that nobody noticed him in this hot and fragrant darkness, and that no one in this surging noisy crowd knew what he had been through. The night and the crowd were like the cave. In its dark recesses he hid.

Up there behind the long rows of open lighted windows the King was celebrating his departure with a great banquet for the more important courtiers. Shadows moved across the windows and occasionally the sound of voices and laughter drifted down to the people below. Elisha imagined that he could hear their words, as they laughed at him, and ridiculed him. The King was no longer expecting him. The Woman had no doubt reported their conversation and his prophecy. Now they were laughing. His message and promise were being sullied and debased. They were not afraid of him, whatever he said. They might well laugh.

Down below in the great square the whole town had turned out to share in the farewell celebrations. The crowd were chattering and singing, and perhaps the King wanted it that way. Perhaps he had deliberately arranged this festival in the great square so that the people should forget that next morning the entire garrison would be going with him to the camp of Jezreel, leaving Samaria to the protection of a handful of elderly foot soldiers; and perhaps also so that the town might forget the fugitives that had been arriving from the north in growing numbers, telling of murder and pillage by roving Syrian patrols.

The warm night air was heavy with the smoke of the many torches, flares and hanging lamps, the sweet fragrance of incense and burning bay leaves, the smell of cooking scallops, roasting meat and sizzling oil, and the hundreds of mingled odours of the surging crowds. Here and there groups of onlookers were crowding round open fires, where calves and sheep were roasting on gridirons or spits. In brightly lit tents wine was being dispensed. Eating houses had been set up in which sweet pastries were frying in spluttering pans and being offered for sale by the shouting, sweating cooks. Groups of soldiers, who were leaving nex day for the war, were pushing their way singing through the mob, calling out to the women and girls, getting laughing answers and going on their way arm in arm.

Elisha stood bewildered. He was seeing at first hand what he had only known by hearsay, and so had not really known at all. It seemed to him as if he were seeing in a nightmare the sultry world of sin and horrifying temptation. Then he started. A warm hand touched his arm.

"The night of the great goddess!"

Elisha found himself staring into two sparkling, smiling dark eyes.

"Look at the full moon! Won't you come with me and make offering to the veiled goddess, stranger? My couch is soft."

Jezebel's lips, Jezebel's eyes. All the women here looked like Jezebel. Or was Jezebel herself the veiled goddess? He pushed the inviting hand aside and tried to escape, but found himself wedged in, without any way out. He could only turn his head away angrily.

The woman shouted:

"Look at the coward who insults Ashera, because he can't do anything else!"

The crowd yelled with laughter. Someone caught hold of her and shouted, "Take me instead! Take me instead!" and was immediately carried away in the crowd. Elisha heard only the yells of laughter. Desperately and angrily he raised his fists and struck out at shoulders, chests and backs, at the damp warm flesh all round him, without heeding the blows and kicks aimed at him. He shouted hoarsely:

"No! No! Listen! Listen to me, Israel!"

He was jostled along further and further, a source of amusement to them. He reeled, stumbled, scrambled wearily up again, listening open-mouthed. They were not paying any attention to him, probably because he had never really shouted at all. How could he shout anyway, when he had no voice? His voice had failed, because Jezebel had got his message out of him with guile—the message that he decided to speak, when Elijah had refused. Elijah had not objected. He had not tried to stop him from going, but he had not changed his decision. Elijah had known better and had remained firm. Elisha grasped his throat as though he would squeeze the sound out of it. He gasped and sobbed as he struggled for breath, and would have fallen, if the crowd around him had not been so dense. Then he was carried further forwards, for suddenly the crowd surged, pushing and shouting, towards the palace railings.

From the roof of the palace came a long, loud note of a trumpet answered by calls from all sides. From the palace and the adjoining guard rooms and the royal mews the palace guards, mounted troops and torch bearers came streaming forth. The gates of the palace courtyard were opened and a troop of beautifully caparisoned lancers with pennons on their lances moved slowly and solemnly out. They carried their lances levelled and made a gradually widening lane through the spectators. After them came the trumpeters blowing continuous blaring trumpet-calls that drowned all the shouting and noise. Behind them came a solitary horseman bearing the King's pennon, then a mounted group of officers and finally another troop of foot soldiers. The procession moved into the centre of the square. There the palace guard formed a wide circle with the officers in the middle facing north, east, south and west. The officer bearing the King's pennon stood upright in his stirrups and shouted above the murmuring voices of the crowd:

"A message from the King! A proclamation before the campaign!"

There was silence. The herald took a deep breath and shouted:

"Any man who has built a new house and not yet blessed it, go home and stay there. Any man who has planted a vineyard and not yet gathered the harvest, go home and stay there. Any man who has contracted to marry and has not yet brought his bride home, go home and stay there."

He stood up higher in his stirrups and shouted:

"Any man who is afraid and faint-hearted, go home and stay there."

Then he resumed his seat in the saddle.

Elisha listened incensed. That was not a message from the King, but the ancient formula required by Hebrew law to be spoken before a campaign. The King was obeying the law and yet violating it. The sacred proclamation was to be made to the men who were actually about to go forth to battle, not to an idle mob such as was eating and drinking and celebrating here. It was a solemn heart-searching test, not an exhibition and a joke. Of course the proclamation was simply greeted as the climax of the evening's festival. The crowd responded with delighted cheering that went on and on. Suddenly amidst the deafening uproar the unexpected blare of a trumpet sounded. A solitary horseman detached himself from the group of officers, raised a copper tube to his lips, and shouted.

"That's enough! Quiet there!"

The crowd stopped shouting in surprise. The horseman went on:

"Attention, Jehu's troop! Attention, all men in Jehu's troop! Report at once to the assembly points! All men of Jehu's troop, report to the assembly points! We march before midnight."

He rode on beside the other officers and then repeated:

"Jehu's troop to march before midnight!"

Elisha had never seen Jehu before. The group of horsemen passed close to him. Jehu was sitting upright in the saddle. In contrast with the other officers he was not in full dress. He was wearing the ordinary soldiers' tunic of undyed drill, with a belt for his short broad sword. His shield was hanging from the pommel of his saddle and his helmet hung by its strap from his arm.

The crowd were pushing forward and the lancers had great difficulty in keeping a lane clear. Elisha bent down and drew back. He was shivering and felt a sudden terror, like that caused by being violently wakened early in the morning. Jehu looked at the crowd at his feet with tight lips and a peculiar expression of close attention and bored disdain. He seemed to see everybody and nobody. He even glanced at Elisha without particular notice, but Elisha was conscious of a feeling of terror and shame, as though Jehu had discovered his confusion and humiliation and weakness. He wanted to escape from the keen, cruel eyes, and yet could not take his eyes off the man who was riding past.

The crowd closed in as the soldiers rode away and the noise immediately broke out again. Elisha succeeded in reaching the edge of the square, where the crowd was a little thinner. There he looked back again as if seeing everything for the first time, the palace, the lights of the square, the enormous mass of heads and bodies. Then as though he had at last taken it all in clearly, he pulled his cloak around him, turned away and went down the steep street towards the lower town and the gates.

His footsteps echoed among the deserted houses. The air here was cool and fresh and he filled his lungs. Now in the darkness he could see the stars again. In the distance he could still hear the call of the trumpets. He quickened his steps as though the trumpet call was meant for him alone, bringing deliverance.

Baana, the officer commanding the camp at Jezreel, was wakened at dawn by the sentry outside his tent. A man had been brought in who was suspected of being a spy.

The sky was still dark and a thick mist lay over the plain, but the camp was already awake. From all around came the sounds of neighing horses, weapons rattling, people going to and fro, bugle calls and shouting. Here and there fires were already sending up white plumes of smoke and casting a reddish glow into the grey dawn light. Outside Baana's tent a horseman was standing, and beside his horse a man with shoulders bent and bowed head. His hands were tied and he was gasping for breath. As Baana came out, he raised his head feebly and let it sink again. Baana rapped out at the horseman, "What's all this about? Have you lost your tongue?"

"By your leave, Sir! We were on guard last night outside the camp, Sir, and captured this man. He says he has some information. He says that he comes from Kinnereth,* but we picked him up a long way from the lake. We think he is a Syrian spy."

Baana had been very late to bed. His head was heavy and his eyes burned. He looked at the man angrily. The man raised his head and whimpered: "Won't you let my cords be untied, Sir? I have really done nothing, that I should be brought here like an animal for slaughter."

"I'll ask the questions and you answer!" said Baana roughly. "Who are you and where do you come from? Mind you tell the truth!"

"I come from Kinnereth. Haven't I told you ten times already? I am a fisherman on the lake, as my father was before me."

"Tell me what you were doing at night so far from the lake."

"I was on my way to the King's camp to bring information, and hoping for a good reward, as the King's men promised us, if we stayed in the village and kept our eyes open. And now I have been made to run alongside this horse as though I were a

*Kinnereth—ancient name of the Sea of Galilee.

horse myself, and have had to suffer insults like a criminal."

The horseman interrupted him. "He says he has seen Benhadad's army. He says they went along the shore of the lake. That is why I asked them to wake you, Sir."

Baana was suddenly wide awake. "You fool! Why didn't you say so at once?"

"Because we didn't believe him. He speaks in such a peculiar way, and when we caught him he tried to escape."

"Because I thought you were Syrians!" shouted the fisherman breathlessly.

"Untie him!" Baana ordered. He went closer to the man and said in a more friendly tone: "Tell me what you saw."

"My boat was caught by the wind, and when it died down it was too late to row back. The lake is very wide, so I tied up my boat in the reeds and went to sleep there. Towards morning I was awakened by the sound of chariot wheels, horses and the clanking of marching men. Then I saw them. The sun was rising as they came past. You couldn't see any end to their lines. They went along the lake shore and then turned eastwards, foot soldiers, chariots, cavalry, store wagons and animals. About noon, when they had all gone past, I rowed back, spread the news of their coming, and ran."

"Where did you spread the news?"

"In the village."

"Are people still there?"

"The men who had to join the army have left, but the old men, the women and the children stayed."

"Why?"

"The lake is wide, Sir. We did not think they would come into our part of the country. We saw fires down in the plain and we heard of attacks by the enemy, but they did not come near us. Where could we go anyway? Our livelihood is there."

"And why are you running away now?"

"I was looking for the King's army. As I told you, we had been promised a good reward if we gave information quickly. Besides all our men have gone, and who else is to protect us but the King?"

Baana muttered impatiently: "Enough! Enough! Come with me."

On the way he paused once again, and said, sternly:
"Pull yourself together, fisherman, and mind how you speak."
"Where are you taking me, Sir?"
"To the King."

Ahab's tent stood on a little hill that commanded a view of the whole camp. Outside the tent the King's pennon had been hoisted on a pole. The guards, who had been huddled together to keep warm, jumped up quickly when they saw Baana.

"An urgent personal message for the King!"

While the King was being informed inside the tent, Baana turned to the fisherman again and said threateningly:

"If you are telling the truth, you need not worry about your reward, but heaven help you if you are lying! For my part I don't believe you."

The messenger came back and admitted them. Baana beckoned to the fisherman and went into the tent.

The walls of the King's tent were hung with heavy tapestry and the floor was covered with skins. Torches were burning in copper sconces fastened to one of the tent poles. Ahab was standing in the middle of the tent while two attendants dressed him. A couple of paces away Obadiah was reading out figures from a tablet: "Eighty sheep, twenty-five mules from Thirza. Fifteen yearling calves from Thaanach . . ."

Baana waited uneasily. The King's face was turned away from the light, but the unbroken silence in which he listened to Obadiah and ignored Baana, while the attendants got on with their work, indicated that he was in no better temper than on the previous day. He would have done better to stay in Samaria, Baana thought. The King did not like being in camp, and since his arrival he had not had a good word for any of his staff. He would spend hours walking round the camp, inspecting the smallest and least important details, grumbling and bullying. Then he would come back and disappear for hours, sitting silent and gloomy in his tent and seeing nobody. Nobody knew that better than Baana, for he was responsible for the whole camp and had to bear the brunt of the King's displeasure.

Obadiah's voice went on: "Sixty goats, five cartloads of corn from Janoah, ten cartloads from Jokneam. Good! That is more than we expected."

"Jokneam!" the King interrupted. "That was where you heard from him before. Have you still heard no word from him?"

"No, Sir."

"And you know of no fresh message? There are some of his followers in the camp. Has none of them any fresh message?"

"No."

"Now you see what your Elisha's promise is worth! He promised to come back. I suppose he is afraid now that he would be risking his neck, and so prefers to hide."

"He kept his first promise, Sir. His followers are supporting you in the camp. He will come presently. He gave you his promise and he will come."

"He comes and goes as he chooses. Do you imagine that Ben-hadad also has to fall in with his wishes? How long am I to wait? How much longer can we wait?"

"He has given you the message and the promise. What more are you waiting for, Sir? His word stands."

"I want a sign from him. We must march at a propitious time."

Baana cleared his throat with ill-concealed impatience. "I am here, Sir."

Ahab turned furiously and went for him: "Look here, Baana! It is a good thing that you have come. I am most dissatisfied. I went round the camp last night. Everything is in a frightful mess. Nobody is paying the least attention to my orders. Your sentries are playing dice or going after women instead of keeping watch. I found one fast asleep and took his spear out of his hand before he woke. Where are your eyes? Or are you doing the same as they?"

Baana flushed. "I cannot be everywhere at once, Sir. I did not go to bed till dawn. As for the sentry, I will have his hands cut off."

"That has been done already. The next one to be caught will be beheaded. However, that does not absolve you from responsibility. I am sorry I let Jehu go. He would have done better than you. What have you come for?"

"My men have brought in a fisherman from Kinnereth. He says he saw Benhadad's army."

"What? Where?"

"A large force passed along the lake side yesterday, going eastwards, infantry, cavalry and chariots."

"Along the lake?"

"That's what the fisherman says."

Ahab stepped forward and stood in front of Baana with legs astride and hands on hips.

"Have you questioned him?"

"Yes."

"Is he reliable?"

"You can question him. He is here."

"I am asking you, do you believe him?"

"Yes."

"And what about the messengers who reported yesterday that they had seen cavalry and chariots up in the Jarmuk valley, and the spies who say they saw Benhadad's camp being set up at the mouth of the valley? Which of them is lying, Baana? Or did the spies and the fisherman see the same army, and Benhadad can work miracles and be in two places at once?"

"Sir, perhaps none of them is lying. Benhadad has a large army. He may perhaps be advancing in two sections."

"And what about Jehu, whom we sent out on reconnaissance?"

"We have no news from him, Sir. His last communication was two days ago."

Ahab turned away without a word and went up to the fisherman, who was standing in the shadow by the entrance. He looked hard at him and was about to speak, but changed his mind and came wearily back.

"Give him his reward, Baana. I don't suppose he is lying. What more is there to ask him? It is a pity we have wasted so much time. I waited ... I wanted to wait until ... We ought to have been on our way long ago. How soon can we start, Baana?"

Baana's face lit up. "As soon as you give the order, Sir. There is no point in hanging about. Just say the word. Your men are eager to obey."

"Good! Here is the word. Have all the captains assemble here in one hour. Let the priests prepare a sacrifice. If the omens are not against us, we will start."

"Very good, Sir!"

"Wait!" Ahab smiled maliciously. "You agree completely, don't you, Baana? You have no further advice to give? Tell me, why have we received no further news from Jehu? Has he and his party been wiped out? Do you know what I am wondering, Baana?"

"I cannot read your thoughts, Sir."

"You precious simpleton! Hasn't the same question occurred to you? I was going to say—Or could it be that Jehu has left me in the lurch?"

"It was you, Sir, who in your wisdom put your confidence in Jehu."

"Yes, and now I am asking you what you in your wisdom are thinking. Look! We ought to find out what has happened to Jehu, for if he has the same ideas as I have, and if he has not been wiped out, it would be very clever of him to take cover and let the Syrians through. Then Benhadad would be between two of our armies, which could close in at the right moment. But if Jehu is no longer in Benhadad's rear ... Do you understand now, Baana? What is your opinion? Do you think Jehu has the same idea as I have and is acting accordingly?" Then, before Baana had time to answer, the King said abruptly: "I did not ask you. Don't answer! Forget it! You may go."

Baana went out. The King paced up and down for a while, then stopped in front of Obadiah, who had been waiting against the wall of the tent.

"You heard everything. Now I have got to take the decision on my own responsibility. Remember that, Obadiah. Your teacher has let me down. Now I have made the decision by myself."

Obadiah said humbly: "Will you give me leave to go? I have a lot to do before we start."

The King's only answer was a contemptuous gesture.

The sky had cleared. The morning was fresh and fine, with dew-drops sparkling in the sun. Obadiah paused outside the tent. The strong light dazzled him. Blinking, he looked down over the bustling camp. In the open spaces between the rows of tents platoons were being drilled. Further away archers were practising at huge targets. Beyond the tents chariots were being driven up and down in clouds of dust.

Obadiah's hands were clenched. He was badly scared. It was hardly a year since he had seen Benhadad's chariots and horsemen and foot-soldiers outside Samaria. He had had time enough to see them and to learn to fear them. Now they were coming back down the Jarmuk valley and along the Lake of Kinnereth. How long would it take them to reach the capital and the heart of the country? Four or five days, if there were no opposition. Could they be held back? This camp here and the men with Jehu represented the entire strength of the King's army, Israel's only protection. What about Benhadad's army? According to Jehu's report it was to be three times as big as before. Now the King was wondering whether Jehu could be trusted. Who would know, if the King did not?

Obadiah could no longer be sure, and horrified by this uncertainty, he began to wonder whether it was not madness to face Benhadad in open battle and risk everything in one venture. Had not the long delay made it too late anyway? Benhadad had moved very slowly, but now he was established in the country with his whole army and Elisha had not come. The King had waited for him, but he had not kept his word.

Obadiah shook his head in helpless despair. He was about to walk on, when his attention was suddenly drawn to the main gateway, and he stopped. He could not see very clearly what was happening, but he suddenly felt his heart beat faster. He hardly dared to believe in the wonderful surprise. A crowd of shouting people was milling round the entrance. They came slowly nearer towards the hill, hopping, dancing and leaping, with their black cloaks flying. Their singing and shouting grew louder. Now Obadiah could see the man in their midst, who was coming nearer amid all the noise, with immobile face and weary step. Obadiah ran with both arms raised and cried breathlessly: "Elisha! My Lord Elisha! What a happy day! We have been waiting so long for you!"

He bent over Elisha's hand and said hurriedly:

"The King has been asking for you every hour."

Elisha answered hoarsely: "No doubt the King had detailed reports about me."

"We knew nothing, dear Master, nothing, and were very worried."

"You're sure of that?"

"Since the night when I brought you to him the first time, Ahab has been waiting for your return. You promised to come and did not come, and the King's heart grew heavy, and he doubted your word."

"Strange, very strange! I should have thought . . . Never mind, take me to the King."

"Won't you let me get you some refreshment and bathe your feet? You're exhausted."

"Take me to the King."

"As you wish, dear Master."

Obadiah had not seen Elisha since their journey together to Samaria. Now, as he stole a glance at him, he wondered at the change that had taken place in him. His face was lined and drawn, as though he had been very ill, his lips seemed narrower, his eyes were sunk deeper into their sockets and they were cold and hard, as if they had forgotten how to smile. He was covered with dust and dirt. Obadiah ran on ahead up the hill past the sentries and burst into the King's tent, gasping: "Sir, Sir, Elisha the prophet has come!"

Baana and the other captains were already assembled in the King's tent. Ahab looked up, rose and asked briefly: "Where is he?"

"He is on his way to you."

Ahab went out and stood in the entrance to the tent. Elisha was coming slowly up the hill alone. He stopped a few paces from the King and bowed. Ahab said reproachfully:

"You have been a long time. Did you not promise that you would come back soon?"

Elisha came a step nearer and answered quietly:

"I went to the palace and could not see you, so I went away on an errand on your behalf. I have arrived at the right time. I have been with Jehu the last few days, Sir, and have come straight from him."

"You . . ."

"Yes, I was with him, and we have seen the enemy. They marched along the lake and did not see us up in the hills. We saw them and Jehu is now waiting for his opportunity. He will do what you tell him to do. Listen! I have seen them and have again been given a word from the Lord. Fulfil what Israel's God demands and the invaders will be delivered into your hands so that you can destroy them. Will you do so?"

Ahab said in a hard voice: "Yes."

"Then gather the men together, so that I can give them this message and encourage them."

Ahab's eyes lit up. He stretched both hands out, as if to call the others present to witness, and said: "Thanks! The King thanks you! You shall speak to them all with my authority. Now come in and stay with me."

Elisha answered very quietly: "Indeed I will stay with you." He followed the King into the tent.

The army reached the Jordan late in the evening. The outposts could see from the hills above the river long lines of glowing fires in the distance. They guessed that these were Benhadad's camp fires. The troops made their way down to the river with great caution, but when they got there they found the fords unguarded. Patrols and bowmen waded across at once and disappeared into the darkness. The rest of the army remained on the near bank in the shelter of the escarpment, without light or fires.

The King was sitting with his chin in his hands staring into the darkness. He had sent all his attendants away, keeping only Elisha. The hours passed, and at last Elisha said: "Why don't you rest, my Lord Ahab?"

"This is no night for resting, my friend."

They sat in silence for a long time. Then the King asked: "What do you see now Elisha?"

"Do you want me to give you a new prophecy every hour, Sir? I see what you see—the confirmation of what I have already said."

"What do you see?"

"I see that the Lord has blinded the eyes of your enemy. He is taking things easily, encamped in the same place as he was yesterday. He thinks he is safe. He has not placed a watch on the fords, and has no idea that we are so close. Tomorrow morning at dawn you can attack him and defeat him before he is awake."

"Is that your advice, Elisha?"

"You asked me what I could see. Don't you see it also?"

The King thought a while and then answered:

"Yes, I see . . . and is it enough? Is there nothing more to see? You do not see enough. I shall not act on this advice."

Elisha got up and came to the King and asked in friendly mockery: "Tell me frankly what you are afraid of and why you hesitate. We are alone."

Ahab glanced up trying to see Elisha's face in the darkness and answered scornfully: "The King is not afraid."

"Then what else is the matter? This morning you welcomed me joyfully and believed my word unquestioningly. Now you keep on asking questions, but you will not trust my advice."

"I don't find it easy to trust you. How can I understand you? You proclaim the word of the Lord, you say, and you see more than we can. Now, however, when you see what I can see, and ought to see more than I do, you make out that you see nothing, and you speak lightly, as if in a dream. What is obviously a light matter to you like a breath of wind, is to me a matter of grave doubt and anxiety, for the fate of Israel is at stake. How can I be sure that you are giving good advice and not planning the ruin of us all?"

"Have you ever heard from my lips anything other than the good of Israel? Then you must know that you can trust me and act on my advice, for I serve only Israel and Israel's God."

"Do you serve me, Elisha?"

"I give you my advice and tell you what is revealed to me. That is my service to you."

"You are very clever, my friend! But you should be at least clever enough to know that your tricks do not fool me. Your answer is no answer. You know that as well as I. Do you serve me?"

"Understand me once and for all, Sir. I do not serve you, and why do you demand service from me? Your Obadiah serves you and his job is to look after your household and see that your men and animals are fed. Do you by any chance expect me to serve you by dispensing courage and confidence each day to you and your men like your steward distributes food and drink? There is one Lord over Israel and I serve him and him alone. Why should you demand service from me, when you ought yourself to be only a servant, as I am? For you are in his hands like the least of your slaves."

"I am the King of Israel. Am I to obey your word without question? If I accept your word, then you are the King and I am your slave. It is my job to rule Israel."

"My word will be as yours, my Lord Ahab, and yours will be as mine, as long as you submit to the will of God. Why are you quarrelling with me? You waited impatiently for me to come, and now you will not trust me, because in fact you are unwilling to trust his will and follow it. You are afraid of my advice because it reminds you of your duty. Now, however, you have to decide, Sir, because Israel is threatened and the hour of deliverance comes and goes. Without confidence you cannot undertake any venture. Why do you distrust me and hesitate to act on what I have told you?"

"You are only the voice, the command. I do indeed need your insight, but I have to deal with the facts."

The King got up, pointed down into the valley and said proudly:

"What do you reproach me for? I have done my duty, my friend Elisha. Look down there. That army would not exist, if my will and my orders had not created it, and created it in the face of violent opposition from your followers. Have you forgotten that? I am indeed Israel's fist, and while you were hesitating I took decisions. This army is here by my orders. Do you blame me if I hesitate to risk everything in one hazard, just because you say so? I know something about the art of warfare, Elisha. How many campaigns have you directed? Are you going to blame me if I see more than you do, and my instincts suggest a different path of duty?"

"Last year, my Lord Ahab, you raised Benhadad's siege by a night sortie that took him by surprise. You did not hesitate then and you won."

"How long did my triumph last? Hardly a year. What is the use of a victory, if it does not bring peace?"

"Can you see a better way, Sir? What other way can you see?"

The King considered a moment then answered cautiously:

"Benhadad is still encamped where he was yesterday. He is waiting. Last year he did not wait, and yet he is stronger now than he was then. A night attack is unlikely to destroy him. Why is he waiting? Perhaps he is not waiting, but merely giving himself time, since he has not yet seen us. Maybe he is waiting, because the omens are unfavourable, and he hesitates to strike. I want him to know first that we are here, to see that his way is barred and that Israel is prepared to defy him."

"And then?"

"Then he may be ready to listen to me, and to hear what he would not hear before. I have indeed some very serious things to say to him, and if he will not listen, if the Lord has made him blind, as you say, I can wait still longer. Then he may attack after all, so that the Lord's will may be fulfilled by my hand."

"Those are idle fancies, Sir, produced by your fear. Do you imagine that it is still possible for Benhadad to turn back? Do you imagine that he has raised this huge army and brought it all this way in order to accept what you choose to say? Open your eyes, my Lord Ahab! You are much weaker in arms and men than your opponent, so why not obey the word of the Lord, so that you can defeat your enemy in spite of that? Your task is not hesitation and idle hopes, but to strike."

The King answered through clenched teeth:

"I am very patient my friend and enemy! Now I ask you to trust me and accept my judgment. Can you do otherwise? Remember that only this morning you supported me publicly before all the men, and so you are allied with me, whether you like it or not. I want to strike at the right moment, but not in obedience to your advice, and I want you to understand what is in my mind. Today the enemy is encamped in the shelter of the mountains with his rear protected by my town of Aphek, which he captured by surprise, and that valley over there, at the mouth of which he has set up his camp, is deep and narrow, and easy to defend. I want him to come out into the open plain. Did not he deride Israel as a people of the hills that cannot fight in the plains? I intend therefore to await him in the plain, far enough away from Jehu, who is waiting in his rear, to cut off his retreat and drive him into my hands. It is a difficult plan, I know, but you will understand that I want to achieve more than you asked and promised. What use would it be to drive the Syrians back once more, as I did last year? This time I intend to do more, so let me wait and be cautious."

"What more do you intend to do, Sir?"

"I want to show him the might of Israel so clearly and definitely, that I can talk to the great Benhadad as I am talking to you and make him do as I wish."

Elisha drew back and said breathlessly: "The Lord's command is not to talk but to act. What he demands of you is nothing less than to destroy Benhadad." Elisha took a deep breath and asked sternly: "What do you intend to say to him, and whose will is he to obey?"

The King answered with gentle mockery:

"I don't claim to be a seer or prophet, my friend. My spies have not yet returned from their first reconnaissance. Your question is a little premature. I have my plans, and it will be some time before I know the outcome. How then can I answer your question now? However, since you know the will of the Lord and have proclaimed it publicly, you can be patient. It must be fulfilled, mustn't it, in your way or mine?"

Elisha was silent for a considerable time, and when he spoke his voice was quiet and controlled again.

"The Master Elijah refused to come when you sent for him, but I came and I promised to remain at your side, because you wished it, Sir. I hope you will not regret your wish and change it. The promise that I gave you was not unconditional. The time will come when you will have to give an answer to my question. I will not ask any more questions or give you further advice, for I want your own mind and heart to decide what you must do in order to fulfill those conditions, and because I know the will of the Lord and his command, I will be patient until then, as you wish."

The King answered calmly:

"I know what you said. There is no need to threaten me, my Elisha! Are you so sure that we shall both survive until the day of reckoning? Don't forget that it will not be till after the battle that you are urging on me. Can you really tell the path of every arrow?"

Elisha did not answer. The King smiled.

6

EARLY in the morning the King's scouts returned. During the night they had crawled as far as the earthworks that the Syrians had thrown up round the camp, and in the pale dawn light they had seen the watchtowers and the chariot park, the officers' tents with their gay pennons, and Benhadad's magnificent pavilion, standing on a slight eminence in the middle for all to see.

As the sun rose they could all see the Syrian camp in the distance. The morning breeze carried the sounds of the vast army and in the ranks of Israel many a man turned pale, so close and so powerful did the enemy seem, but when evening came and still nothing had happened, their spirits began to rise. The army of Israel lay encamped on one side of the plain and the enemy on the other. Someone said that evening that they were lying there like two great flocks of goats. So they remained day after day for seven days.

Nobody knew what the delay meant. Away back in Jezreel the Sons of the Prophets had been pressing for an immediate attack. Now they were going round the camp from morning till night saying that Elisha was in favour of an attack, but the King would not give the order. Someone had heard a rumour about a message that had been sent secretly to Benhadad and had remained unanswered. They were asking questions angrily and insistently. Who had lost his nerve? What they were still waiting for? Why was nothing happening?

When they at last ventured to ask Elisha himself, he only answered:

"I don't know."

"You're in the King's confidence and you don't know?"

"I know no more than you do."

"Then I suppose you don't know what is in his mind. You're obeying his will rather than the word of the Lord. Are you also trying to forget what you yourself prophesied before the people?"

Elisha looked the questioner up and down and said scornfully: "Who are you and where do you come from, that you should have a right to call me to account and accuse me of treason and cowardice?"

The other drew himself up and answered proudly: "The Master Elijah, whom I once had the privilege of serving, called me Micha. And I did as he did. I kept silent for a long time, listening to the spirit of the Lord. That is why I dare to speak."

Elisha's expression softened and he said in a more kindly tone: "So you are Micha! The Master told me about you, but you did not come back to listen to his word. Why didn't you?"

"To be silent you must be alone: to prophesy even more so."

"And do you see things differently from the way I do? Can the prophet of the Lord speak, just because his followers demand that he should?"

"The Lord spoke to me as he did to you, and I know that it is time to demand again and again that his word should at last be obeyed. I agree with you. We did not come out here to wait about, or for useless exercises, but to defend Israel and destroy the enemy, and if the King has lost his courage and does not dare to lead Israel to battle, can you keep silent and pretend you don't know it?"

Elisha stamped his foot.

"Look here, you new prophet, who were once Elijah's servant, this cloak is the Master's cloak, and his hand put it round my shoulders, because he trusted me and chose me for that reason. Won't you trust me as much? How dare you in your youthful impatience rebuke me, if I keep silent because I must do so? Believe me, I must."

He went away, taking no notice of the eyes that stared after him in bewilderment and astonishment. He walked down the slope and on and on in the gathering twilight without pause or objective.

The countryside was deserted, but Elisha's solitude was peopled by curious creatures, coming and going, in the shape of creeping animals and strange shadows, that pursued him and jostled him and disappeared like magic into the darkness, as soon as he opened his mouth to ask the questions that had been asked of him. Down there in the camp he could get rid of the questioners with angry words, but their questions rang in his own heart more loudly than when asked by human lips. Had he done right? He had had no sleep for days, wandering about racked and tormented in this desert of rocks and scrubs.

"Answer, shadows, answer!" He shouted, tearing his nails on the hard rocks that dispelled the phantoms of his imaginations. "Did I do right to keep quiet and demand no further decision from the King, or was my prophecy mistaken, and so I am being punished by having my mistake revealed?" The night gave no answer, but as soon as he hid his face in his hands, the phantoms returned, towering above his head and groping towards him with strangling arms. "Answer! Give me a message! Or are you trying to blind me, so that Israel's punishment may be fulfilled more surely?" The only answer was the rustling of the wind in the grass and the bushes. There was no voice.

From time to time he sat and stared with weary eyes down into the valley, at the camp, and the river shining in the pale moonlight, as it wound amongst the sandbanks and the green tangle of vegetation. The hills looked black and blue. Amongst them, many miles away, the village and fields of Abel-Meholah lay sleeping. One or two men from the village had joined the King's army and had brought him news and greetings. Supposing he set off now back to the farmstead, back to the animals and the plough? It had all seemed so far behind him as to be almost forgotten, but now the longing to go back home had returned. That was where Elijah had found him and had constrained him by laying his own mantle upon his shoulders. The mantle was so heavy. Would Elijah try to prevent him from going back now? Elisha shivered. His desire to see Elijah and his longing to return home were in sad and jealous conflict. Elijah knew so much more than he did. He had said nothing when Elisha gave the promise that he himself had refused to give. Perhaps he knew that the promise only revealed Elisha's weakness. Elisha had given a comforting message, because he shrank from the severity of the judgment and did not want to believe in the disaster that the punishment involved. How had Elisha dared to speak, when the Master was silent? What childish presumption to believe that it was his task to turn the King's fickle heart, that Elijah himself had been unable to influence! Just think! After running away he had returned to the King's camp, and the King had known nothing about his meeting with the Woman and his humiliation. The King had welcomed him and had made him repeat his promise to the people. Then they had set out immediately, obviously to implement the promise. That was what he imagined and he had felt so glad about it. Now, when the time had come to obey the command of the Lord and strike, the King had set the prophecy aside, and even pretended lightheartedly to see in Elisha's words a veiled threat. And the Almighty remained silent!

Was this the time to be silent, as he had decided, or to make an appeal, as his followers demanded? Had his prophecy been wrong, or his advice in the night? Had the Lord smitten the King with blindness, or did the King really know better how the promise was to be fulfilled? His answers had been confusing and dangerously clever, so it was difficult to guess what was in his mind. The prophecies had been ambiguous, and hidden in them was the fate of Israel. Elisha wondered with misgiving and despair what this fate would be. If only he had gone away after that first evening! He had stayed to find out the truth.

The King remained silent, but Elisha knew that he was not idle. Messengers had been sent to Jehu and had got back safely. Dispatches were also passing daily between the camp and Samaria. Inside the camp itself no one was idle. On the second day Ahab moved the whole army across the river, deliberately foregoing its protection, as if to offer a clearer challenge to Benhadad. Then he ordered earthworks and trenches to be dug, and when these were completed, ploughs were sent out to cut great furrows in the fields in front of the camp, leaving only narrow lanes for the chariots. Arrowsmiths, wheelwrights and lancemakers were working round the clock. Once or twice during the day small Syrian mounted patrols had come out to just within arrow shot, only to dash back again. Once three of them had been captured and questioned by the King for hours. Since their conversation on the first evening Ahab had not asked Elisha for advice. He gave him accommodation in his own tent and treated him with due respect, but did not seek his company. He did not seem surprised that Elisha did not appear very often and not for long, and sometimes it seemed to Elisha as if the King was aware of his distress and depression, and was secretly glad about it.

In the evening of the sixth day scouts reported unusual activity in Benhadad's camp. The King held a long council of war, and had the priests stay awake all night offering sacrifices. While it was still dark, foot soldiers and archers moved out in front of the camp. At dawn on the seventh day the sound of bugles and trumpets and general shouting made it clear that the King had rightly interpreted the movement of the enemy. Benhadad had at last given his troops the order to attack.

The sun had not yet appeared above the ridge, and the morning mist over the plain cut down visibility. The King and his staff officers up on the slope outside the royal pavilion could scarcely make out what was going on at the edge of the plain. Behind them chariots and a host of runners were waiting all ready to move. They were whispering among themselves and playing with their weapons or busying themselves with their horses' armour. All through the camp there were preparations for the advance, orders and trumpet calls. Couriers kept arriving with information and vanishing again.

The little group around the King was standing silent, because the King was silent, but presently Baana turned abruptly to Ahab and asked hoarsely: "Do you see what I see, Sir? Whatever does it mean? Surely they are not withdrawing?"

Elisha was standing a little aside. He had been awake all night and was tired out. He shivered in the keen morning air as he strained his eyes to see what Baana saw. He could hardly believe his eyes. Beyond the veil of mist it looked as if Benhadad's camp, which had been crouched there so long like a great spider, was now putting out arms like brown feelers growing longer and longer, spreading out from the fortifications to right and left. In the distance their movement seemed uncannily slow. The unbroken line of troops did not seem to be moving towards the camp of Israel, but along the line of hills, one arm towards Kinnereth and the other towards the plain.

The King's face looked pale and hard in the grey light of dawn, his eyes were narrow slits, his cheeks, which were usually slack and puffy, were now tense and the muscles of his jaw were working.

"Don't worry, Baana!" he said sneering. "They are not withdrawing. They are trying to encircle us!"

He stretched his arms out slowly, then folded them across his chest. Elisha understood. No doubt the King was right. Benhadad was using his superior strength. He had seen that Ahab was expecting a frontal attack, and indeed that might actually be his main blow, but meanwhile he was sending out strong bodies of troops in a wide circle towards the north and south in order to threaten Israel's flanks. To avoid this pincer movement the King would have either to withdraw or follow the enemy's pattern and extend his defence line on both sides. Elisha knew that it was almost impossible for the King to withdraw, with the river dangerously close in his rear, nor could he risk extending his defences, for that would mean weakening his centre. That was presumably Benhadad's object before making a frontal attack.

"Baana!" shouted the King. "Send two groups of chariots out to the flanks. Tell them to remain behind the infantry and not to advance until the enemy are quite close."

"Would you send out chariots yet, before we know?"

"Make haste! They're advancing without chariots, and don't expect to find any on the flanks. Quick! Quick!"

Baana beckoned to the runners and gave the order. The King stood looking towards the valley, as the mist lifted to reveal a bright and sunny morning. By now the distant horns and trumpets were silent, and silence brooded over the camp of Israel too. Elisha stood staring over the quiet landscape, completely absorbed by the profound peace of the blue and golden summer day, the dewy fields and shining mountains, and the breathless anxiety of the awful threat that was slowly developing. He closed his eyes and suddenly felt to his astonishment that all his doubts and torments had vanished. There was peace within him also—a strange and thrilling peace like that which preceded the coming of the word of the Lord. He heard no voice, he needed no voice, he knew that the voice was silent, because the will of the Lord was being fulfilled. He opened his eyes again.

The brown tentacles had completed their sideways movement and were now swinging slowly inwards. Israel's battle line was in the form of a shallow wedge with the point towards the camp. In this way the King planned to break the force of the attack and turn it inwards towards the centre, where he had concentrated his horsemen and chariots. These were clearly visible, but the foot soldiers were concealed behind bushes, shrubs, earthworks and rocks. They too could be seen from the slope in front of the pavilion, the occasional flash of a sword or lance-head, the bright piles of arrows and javelins on the ground, but from the front the line was invisible. Benhadad's troops advancing shoulder to shoulder across the plain could of course see the earthworks and the tents of the empty camp, but not the defence that awaited them.

The King left his companions and came across to Elisha and said softly: "Well, this is it, my friend! Your mistrust was unfounded. I did not withdraw, and Israel will fight. Will you repeat your prophecy to cheer me up?"

Elisha looked at him vaguely surprised at the humility of his reply.

"The word of the Lord stands, Sir. Be of good cheer, have faith, and it will be fulfilled."

The King seemed about to speak, but instead compressed his lips in silence. He looked back over the battlefield. Presently he asked roughly: "Where are you going to be, Elisha?"

"With you."

"You must not fight. I will give you a chariot and driver, but be careful."

Elisha merely nodded. The King shouted: "The signal! Now!"

Suddenly the air was filled with a sinister hissing, whistling sound. Benhadad's men had advanced to within range on the right flank and had discharged their first arrows. Elisha heard the single shrill note of a horn. The whole army of Israel answered with their battle cry. The archers stood up with drawn bows and behind them the javelin throwers with weapons poised, waiting for the oncoming attack.

The King rushed to his chariot, took his seat and dashed off almost in one movement, his officers close behind him. Elisha following was soon far behind, but he saw that Ahab was making for the group of chariots waiting behind the footmen. The King waved both hands, the chariot drivers whipped up their horses and followed, without the King slackening speed. The Syrians were now quite close. The foremost lines were already fighting with lances, swords, and daggers. The chariots wheeled in a tight circle and charged their flank. The men in the front ranks did not notice them at first and continued to attack until the rain of arrows which had covered them suddenly ceased, and was followed by shouts of rage and terror, that soon became deafening. The chariots bumped and ploughed their way forward through screaming, struggling, twisting bodies, bringing deadly devastation. The Syrian ranks broke, checked in confusion and then drew back, slowly at first and then in full flight.

Suddenly the King appeared beside Elisha in an ordinary chariot. He was almost unrecognizable, his face already encrusted with sweat and dust. He had driven past before Elisha's driver could turn after him and follow behind the tumult, bumping and swaying over the churned up ruts.

The King was making for the left flank, where Benhadad's foot soldiers had succeeded in breaching Israel's ranks in several places. Elisha found himself surrounded by grotesque, yelling, murderous figures, arms and fists and weapons crowding in upon him. His driver pressed on, his horse rearing, and screaming men going down beneath the hoofs and wheels, with a grinding, shattering, groaning noise. In the tumult it was difficult to tell friend from foe, for the ranks had become so confused. The air was filled with crashing, clattering, and moaning. A loud voice rang out above the din: "The King! The King!" That was the signal for the chariots of Israel to charge on this flank also. They met with stubborn resistance, but here also their intervention halted the attack. While the scattered remnants of the Syrian front ranks were being wiped out by the infantry, the main army began to withdraw, fighting a desperate rearguard action.

Elisha's chariot stopped. His horse, transfixed by spears, had collapsed. The ground all round was littered with bodies, some still twitching, some struggling to get up, only to fall back and lie contorted and still. Clouds of billowing dust caught the sunlight, the hot air was heavy with the sickly-sweet smell of blood.

As the advancing chariots drove the Syrians back, Israel's front line of infantry started off in pursuit without waiting for orders. Elisha, too, shouted: "Forward, forward!" All discipline was forgotten. Elisha had lost contact with the King, but all at once he caught sight of Baana covered with dirt and blood, standing on one of the half-destroyed earthworks and driving his men back at the point of the sword. Elisha ran towards him. He could not understand why Baana was trying to stop the pursuit and the destruction of the Syrians, but before he reached Baana he caught sight of the King's pennon right forward in the middle of the battlefield. The pennon was still. The King also seemed to have broken off the pursuit. Elisha tried to reach him, but after a few steps he felt himself dragged back. As he stood staggering and struggling the cavalry roared past. Then his vision cleared and his heart missed a beat, as he realized with horror why the King had broken off the pursuit. During the fighting on the flanks Benhadad's chariots and horsemen had been advancing in the centre. They were about a hundred yards or so away, waiting. The failure of his first attack had upset Benhadad's plans and given time for Ahab to bring up his chariots. The battlefield was still full of fleeing Syrian troops, but the discipline of their horsemen and chariots was unshaken. Their ranks extended as far as the eye could see, and they were unlikely to delay much longer. By the time Elisha caught sight of Ahab they were already moving forward. Elisha saw Ahab raise his sword in his right hand and wave it in the air as if to encourage his chariot driver on with a whip, and then he heard the King gasp out the order: "The signal! The signal for Jehu!"

"The signal!" Jehu roared.

He was lying on a rocky promontory, where he or his look-out had been keeping watch for several days and nights, consumed by impatience and afraid all the time too that they might be spotted from the formidable force encamped in the valley below. Jehu was staring with eyes aflame down at the plain, at the swaying masses of chariots locked in combat, at the brown blobs of madly charging foot soldiers, at the flashing rows of horsemen appearing here and there out of the clouds of dust and clashing fiercely together, and at the thin column of black smoke rising straight up into the quivering air from the camp of Israel. The smoke was the prearranged signal.

Jehu smiled with satisfaction. Only a few of his officers were still with him, but these at least would see that he had assessed the situation better than the King. When he saw the smoke he had shouted involuntarily, but no words were necessary, for he had already given his orders before the signal appeared. He had calculated long since that inevitably some considerable time must elapse between the issuing of the King's order and the appearance of the smoke, and that his troops could not get down the mountain in a matter of five minutes, so he had ordered them to start as soon as he saw that the King was in danger. He had probably seen this before the King himself had. Now a multitude of little bushes and shrubs, widely dispersed amongst the sun-drenched rocks and stones, were creeping down the slope. They were Jehu's men. During the last few days and nights he had made them collect leafy branches in the woods where they were hiding and fasten them to their shields and on their backs. In this green disguise, holding their shields over their heads, they were now creeping down towards the Syrian camp. Had they been seen? Jehu scanned the scene carefully. As far as he could see the camp was empty. There was no sign of movement. Clearly Benhadad had not bothered to protect his rear and had left only a very few men on guard.

After one more glance down at the plain Jehu sprang up quickly. He had seen the Syrian chariots and horsemen waiting, and had watched the first charge that had got alarmingly close to the camp of Israel before being held and driven back—not very far, only far enough to regroup and attack again. So far Israel had stood firm, and that showed that the King was fighting with great skill. He had not let himself be carried away by his first success. He waited for the Syrians to advance and resisted their attack until its first impetus was checked and then drew back, quickly striking at the enemy's flanks causing confusion and destruction, presumably without heavy losses. That was very wise and very right, but could the battle be won in that way? Now the two sides were once more heavily engaged, and this time the struggle seemed endless. Seen from the mountain it looked like a strange silent game, for very little of the noise of battle reached them, just a faint murmur rising and falling here and there, monotonous in spite of its ever-changing timbre and colour.

"Forward!" shouted Jehu, jumping up. Perhaps it would really be more sensible to stay here, because once he had started out, he would no longer be able to keep his eyes on what was happening down in the plain, but now he was seized with impatience, like a sort of fever, and he was angrily aware that this impatience was not due solely to lust for battle, but also to suffocating, over-mastering fear, that urged him into action.

How long could the King hold out? If his resistance collapsed too soon, before Jehu and his men had set fire to the Syrian camp and attacked their army in the rear, then it was all up with Jehu and his troops. At the same time he was afraid that the King might actually achieve the miracle of a victory by himself. Where would that leave him, Jehu, who had been waiting and scheming for so long for this opportunity to deliver a decisive blow? Perhaps if he had been in the King's place, he might have brought off this miracle, he thought with a sudden surge of envy.

"I'll do it!" Jehu said to himself. Taking a firmer grip on his sword he ran scrambling down the steep slope without bothering about concealment, till he reached the front line, where his torchbearers were. "Forward!" he shouted. "Faster! Forward!" Seizing a torch, he ran at the head of his men out into the open and up to the first line of earthworks. Suddenly figures appeared behind the fortifications and arrows came whistling through the air and there was shouting and noise in the camp. Were there more men there than they had expected? Had they been seen and enticed into a trap? Jehu saw red. In front of him appeared a raised fist, flashing eyes, a gaping mouth. His temples throbbing with rage, he pushed his flaming torch into the savage face, hardly noticing the cry of pain, and ran on slashing and stabbing. All round him there was hand-to-hand fighting in pairs or small groups, but at last they reached the tents. Gasping for breath Jehu held his torch to the tent cloth and waited, trembling with excitement, till it caught fire and the first tongues of flame broke out. Then to his great relief he saw here and there among the tents little columns and billows of smoke rising, thickening and forming into a cloud dyed red by the remorselessly spreading conflagration.

There was a roaring sound in Jehu's ears, his legs would hardly carry him, and the smoke stung his eyes, but he did not notice it. Suddenly his mind and vision cleared completely. They had pushed into the camp on three sides, and he had given his men clear and repeated instructions what to do, but now the fire was spreading with unexpected and terrifying speed. The men must get out of the camp before it was too late. Jehu put his horn to his lips and with bursting lungs blew so that his signal would be heard above the crackling and shouting and noise. He repeated it several times until a small group had gathered round him. He led them away. A few arrows and javelins were still whistling through the air. One or two watchtowers were holding out, but that would not last long. Already the camp was a sea of flames. The men in the watchtowers would be roasted alive.

Jehu ran with his men to the outer earthworks and jumped up to get a view of the plain and the battle that was still raging as fiercely as ever, and although the noise of it was closer and louder, yet it was an incredible and alarming distance away. Jehu realized with horror that the distance he would have to cover had greatly increased, because the Syrians had pushed on in spite of all resistance, and were now fighting immediately in front of Israel's camp. Jehu's men were running up from all sides, stumbling, shouting, sweating and blackened with smoke. He realized at once that he must give them time to rest and regroup, before he dare lead them across the wide plain into another battle. He collected a few officers and sent them off to halt and re-form the ranks, then looked along the lines. Their numbers had been considerably reduced. Was it possible to achieve anything with this small band? All he had done so far was to create an insignificant disturbance far in the rear of the main battle, which would continue over there to its horrible end. Jehu's throat tightened in furious helplessness. He raised his hand to give the next order without knowing what to say. He looked at the battlefield again—and suddenly paused, breathless, excited, incredulous and glad.

Away in the distance confusion had broken out in the struggling ranks. They were falling apart as if some giant fist had come down between them. Waves of infantry came racing back in flight. The chariots were making a wide circle in an attempt to get away. Jehu stood stock still. Now it had happened, after all! Now the Syrians had seen in the distance the smoke and flames from their burning camp. They little knew how pitifully small the attacking force in their rear actually was. They could only see the fire and scent the danger. They had broken off the battle and were running away.

It was victory—the great victory that Jehu and his men had decisively brought about! But the King's orders had involved more than this. He was definitely to attack the enemy in the rear and drive them into the King's hands. Jehu realized at once that he was no longer able to carry out this order. He and his band were now in greater danger than ever, for now the vast Syrian army would come flooding back in disorder, without any kind of discipline, a wild terrified horde, and by their sheer weight of numbers they would overrun and annihilate him and his band, if he tried to bar their way. He did not dare to deliver the blow that the King had ordered,—and then suddenly thrilled by violent, malicious joy he decided not to obey the King's order at all. Once again he knew better than the King what to do. The burning camp was a big enough obstacle in Benhadad's way and no doubt the King would be following hard on the heels of the fugitives. If Jehu were to withdraw his men now and wait until the Syrians and their pursuers arrived, he himself could be in the van of the pursuit and carry out the plan of destruction much better than he could here, where he would be overwhelmed by the human flood. Before his men had recovered and got their breath, Jehu pointed to the mountainside, whence they had come, and shouted: "Back up the slope and then after them into the valley!"

He led the first group, avoiding the burning camp, and disappeared behind the dense cloud of smoke.

By climbing on to a mound of earth Elisha escaped the charging vanguard of chariots and horsemen. He had no idea where he was, only a dim recollection of running. The king and his army were far away in the distance. Elisha was trembling all over. What he had seen of battle, and the despairing thought of what he would still have to see, filled him with a dreadful numbing sense of helplessness and fear. Involuntarily he cringed, as if to avoid the death blow, which would inevitably follow such a defeat, either immediately or before long. All round him forces had been let loose, of whose existence and strength he had never dreamed. They were strangely and horribly real and close. They were more cruel and deadly than he could ever have imagined. Perhaps the earth would open and swallow him up, or an eagle come and carry him off in the air, or a great hand reach out and snatch him away. Confused ideas like these passed through his mind in the darkness of his fear, as though his last hour had come. In the midst of the mêlée he was nevertheless alone, in desert solitude, a grain of sand in the lashing wind, abandoned, helpless and defenceless, to blind chance. Flinging up his arms he shouted shrilly: "Father! Father of Israel! Help!"

Then the miracle! It was so unexpected, so wonderful, so thrilling, that he could not understand what was happening to him. In the midst of the turmoil he suddenly seemed to be standing in a radiant flood of bright light. The fear that had been gnawing at his vitals, and had forced the shrill cry from his lips, was gradually being transformed into a blessed and soothing ecstasy. His cry of fear had been drowned by the deafening uproar, but now he felt as if his voice had become a hundred times stronger, and his words had found wings, as he shouted: "Israel! The hour of victory, Israel!" He shouted, because he had learned in this one instant of illumination that only now the great moment of trial had come, which he should welcome, and not fear. Death and destruction must be near and imminent so that the grace of the Lord's deliverance should be manifested clearly and irrefutably. Israel had to earn her deliverance. She must go through the ordeal of sacrifice without hesitation and reluctance, and so be worthy of God's mercy. It was to learn this that the Lord had sent him here. His defenceless commitment, endangering his own life, was just a symbol and example of this trial, the part allotted to him. His own vindication would be that he should forget himself and his fear, and if God decided to sacrifice him, it would be in order to attest still further the necessity for the sacrifice and the reality of his grace. That was the reason for his terror and all the horrors around him now.

The whole battlefield, as far as the eye could reach, had become one single murderous confusion. It was every man for himself, the air was quivering with the sound of spears, lances, arrows, swords, and knives. Elisha saw the men of Israel rushing at the Syrian armoured horsemen and charioteers with bare fists, dragging them to the ground from their horses and chariots, and others armed with knives crawling under the bellies of the horses, only to be crushed beneath the mortally wounded animals, but bringing their opponents down with them. Heads and bodies appeared and fell, slashed by the sickles of the turning wheels, trampled by the savage heels and hoofs, or torn by stab or blow. Elisha had not seen the King for a long time, he had no idea of plan or objective, only the radiant intoxication within him, the deep knowledge of the great purpose that demanded endurance from Israel, so that God could reveal and fulfil himself. The ground was strewn with débris and corpses and slippery with blood. Beside him Elisha saw a man stagger and fall. He snatched the spear from his hand, held it in front of him and shouted: "For the Lord! Fight for the Lord, Israel!"

Nevertheless, in spite of stubborn resistance Israel was still being slowly driven back. The casualties were heavy, the camp was already close and the river behind it, barring any escape. Elisha was reeling and he could hardly breathe. When would the ordeal be over and the judgment decided? Suddenly it seemed as if the sun were growing dark. He looked up in bewilderment. Above the heavy and revolting reek of blood, sweat and dust, he noticed the sharp bitter smell of smoke carried down the wind. Half dazed he heard somewhere on the battlefield the sound of shouting growing louder and louder and spreading rapidly like the fire itself that his streaming eyes could now at last see—the fire at the edge of the plain, the holocaust of the burning enemy camp, the dark cloud of smoke rising in great billows and darkening the sky and rolling slowly towards them. That was the sign marking the end of the ordeal. That was victory! Jehu!

Elisha was conscious of a great wave of relief, mingled with a feeling of jealousy and disappointment, which he fought down, for was not the King also just a servant, an instrument? Who put the plan into his mind? Who gave him the strength to hold out, if it were not the mighty God whose hand was protecting Israel? Now the King would fulfil the Lord's command. He could not do otherwise. Elisha laughed happily and his weary throat repeated the exhortation again and again: "For the Lord! Forward for the Lord, Israel!"

Impelled by exulting impatience he rushed into the thickest part of the fighting. The same emotion seemed to have gripped the whole army. The thinned and weary ranks charged the enemy as if they were only just beginning the battle, and the assailants, who had driven them to the verge of destruction, now stopped uncertain, turned in confusion, began at last to fall back, and were soon in wild, disorderly and desperate retreat, back to the edge of the plain, back to the burning camp, back to the mouth of the valley from whence they had come, and where they now hoped to find shelter, back to the death that Elisha knew was awaiting them. Where were Jehu's men who would cut off their retreat? Elisha shaded his eyes with his hand, but he could not see anything, the dust and smoke and mist were too dense. He caught sight of a chariot that had been brought to a standstill in the crush. He ran to it, jumped in, seized the reins and whip from the driver's hands and whipped up the horse and urged it on, flourishing his whip as though it were a spear or a torch and shouting: "After them! After them! For the victory of the Lord!"

At nightfall the King broke off the pursuit. His exhausted army of chariots had remained behind in the plain and the horsemen and the weary infantry could only make slow and difficult progress up the narrow steep ascent into the Jarmuk valley. Jehu and his troop led the pursuit. The King had sent him an order to follow the retreating enemy, while he himself returned to the camp with the remainder of the army. Thus a part of Benhadad's retreating forces succeeded in eluding pursuit for a time, and reached the town of Aphek, which they had captured during their advance. The advancing patrols of Israel saw the light of torches on the walls, where small parties were busy here and there repairing the fortifications. The gates of the town were barricaded with rocks and tree trunks.

Jehu drew a cordon of outposts round the town and ordered his men to bivouac. During the night he sent a message to the King asking for reinforcements. He was afraid of a sortie in greater strength than he could cope with. However, at the first light of dawn the barricade was removed from the gate, and the startled guard saw a solitary unarmed man coming slowly towards them. He was wearing only a sack round his loins and had a rope round his neck. He advanced to within shouting distance and stood with his hands above his head. He asked to be taken to the King of Israel. In spite of his miserable appearance his voice and bearing were so imperious that the guard brought him immediately and unfettered to Jehu.

Jehu was warming his hands as he crouched over the fire burning on a hearth of stones. Elisha was sitting beside him wrapped in his cloak and staring into the flames. They were silent. The men around them were asleep. At the sound of approaching footsteps Jehu got up and muttered: "The messenger! Can he be back already?" The guard brought the prisoner in and one of them said: "A message from the enemy, Sir."

Elisha looked up. Jehu stepped forward and stood in front of the fire with legs apart and arms folded. When he caught sight of the man whom the guard had brought in, he leaned forward as if unable to believe his eyes and whistled in surprise.

"Well, Sir," he said, "I should not have expected to see you in such disguise!"

The prisoner answered with an effort:

"I don't know you. You're not the King."

"Certainly not. And of course you don't know me, for when I saw you last you were in a position of honour, while I was just one among many, without even my own name."

"I asked to be taken to the King."

Jehu yawned and answered with contempt:

"What business is it of yours to ask favours, when your life is forfeit and you have a rope round your neck instead of your chain of office, and are wearing a sack instead of armour? What is your message and from whom does it come?"

"My message is to the King of Israel."

"The King is no longer here. He is searching the battlefield for the scoundrel who attacked him. It will take a long time, for the Syrian losses are enormous. At daybreak he will return to complete his victory. You can deliver your message or keep it. Your life and the lives of the rest of you are forfeit in any case."

The messenger said calmly:

"King Ahab's search will be vain. King Benhadad is alive and is with us."

Elisha came up and asked sharply:

"Who is this man, Jehu?"

"This miserable wretch, whom you see, my Father, in sackcloth and with a rope round his neck, was yesterday Benhadad's Commander-in-chief. His name is Hazael. You must make up your mind at once, Hazael, whether you are going to speak or not."

Hazael thought for awhile and at last answered sadly: "My master's courage cannot be broken by misfortune, and for a long time he would not listen to us. We argued all night and praised the clemency of the King of Israel. In the early dawn he said: 'Go to King Ahab in sackcloth and with a rope round your neck and ask him to spare my life'."

Jehu laughed, quietly at first and then in a loud guffaw. "You dare to bring this message!" he burst out breathlessly at last. "All of you have sought to destroy us for long enough. Now every one of you has forfeited his life, whatever Benhadad may say now. That's your fate."

Elisha came up to Jehu and laid his hand on his shoulder and said gently: "You ought not to laugh, Jehu."

Jehu stopped and looked angrily at Elisha, who repeated: "You ought not to laugh or to sneer at him. You are not his judge. He is only saying what he was told to say. Send his message to the King."

"Are they not condemned already? Did you not say yourself only last night that the Lord had destroyed those who had attacked his people, and that they were delivered into our hands so that we might slay them?"

"That is what I said, but those who have escaped the sword should be judged publicly by the King."

"If I sent the King Benhadad's head and those of his leaders, that would be more fitting, and believe me the people would approve."

Elisha sighed. "Do what I say, because that is the word I have received. Syria is beaten, but Benhadad is alive, so now the Lord demands a further response from the King. He must give judgment, and in doing so, make his own position clear."

Jehu looked at him and presently lowered his eyes.

"Whatever you say! It is not what I would do, but I will accept your advice."

He glanced up again and said haughtily to Hazael:

"I am in command here. Tell your Master to come here with all his surviving princes and captains to await the King's answer. All arms and war material of all sorts are to be collected and handed over. Whatever troops are now in Aphek are to remain there. They are prisoners. Do you understand?"

Hazael nodded without speaking. Jehu repeated more sharply: "Do you understand?"

"Yes, I understand," said Hazael quietly. Then he went up to Elisha, bowed to him and said respectfully: "Who are you, Sir, who have spoken so justly and on my behalf?"

Elisha answered in surprised protest:

"I was not speaking for you. I spoke for my Lord. My name is Elisha."

"Your name is not unknown to me. If I survive this day, let me return and talk to you."

Elisha looked at him thoughtfully. After a pause he answered with curiously mingled sadness and pride:

"Perhaps you will return and talk to me."

Hazael bowed again, turned to Jehu and said: "I await your further commands." The submissive words sounded so haughty that they might actually have been a command to Jehu.

Dawn came. Jehu's troops occupied the town, led the prisoners away, collected the spoil and carried out makeshift repairs to the walls. Benhadad and his officers were sitting in a little hollow under strict guard. Nobody was allowed to go near them.

Elisha was still sitting on his stone. He was consumed with impatience, but he felt more exhausted in body and mind than ever before. Every now and then he struggled to his feet and went to the edge of the hillside to look down into the valley, as though by sheer will power he would force his eyes to penetrate the distance and compel the King's messenger—indeed the King himself—to appear.

Before him the valley and the plain lay empty and deserted. The only movement he could see was the shimmering of the hot air. Israel's battle was over, but the real decision was still to come. Who else realized that besides himself? He returned wearily to his seat. Occasionally he looked across at the prisoners in the hollow, sitting motionless with their head-shawls pulled over their heads. They had to endure heat and thirst and doubtless also uncertainty and apprehension. Beyond the line of outposts there was a great deal of activity. Provisions, arms and supplies were being brought out of the town and stacked up in heaps. The men were sweating and grunting, but were noisy and cheerful. From time to time little groups would stop to stare at the prisoners and shout insults and abuse at them. The guards did not attempt to stop them and merely laughed. Elisha turned away. They sat there dolefully and had to put up with the insults. Only yesterday they had been threatening death and destruction, and then the Lord smote them. Elisha tried to find words of gratitude and praise. In the hour of supreme danger he had received grace and illumination, but now he was conscious only of gloom and disappointment, mingled with a vague and anxious impatience.

In the late afternoon, just as Jehu was preparing to move off, they caught sight of a cavalcade down in the valley. Cries of astonishment arose on all sides. Instead of chariots or lorries the King had sent his state carriages escorted by the mounted palace guard in full uniform. Jehu hurriedly ordered his troops to parade. At last the brilliant cavalcade came up the slope, drove slowly past the dusty, dirty, unkempt men and stopped. Elisha was shocked when he saw the occupant of the state carriage. Ahab had sent his son as envoy. Jehu too recognized him, hurried to the carriage and bowed low.

Ahaziah got out awkwardly and stood beside the carriage. He looked round and said:

"Praise and thanks to you, Jehu, from the King, my father, from my mother and from all the people of Israel. Congratulations also to all those who fought with you."

He spoke with a nasal tone and without any real expression, as though he had rather unwillingly learned his speech by heart and was now reciting it casually.

Jehu answered loudly: "I thank you on behalf of my men. What instructions has the King sent?"

"Where are your prisoners, Jehu?"

Jehu pointed to the hollow. Ahaziah gave it a brief glance. His face showed ill-concealed embarrassment as he said haughtily:

"My father has received King Benhadad's request, and after considering it, he said to me: 'As he is alive, let him come to me, for he is my brother'. That is the message I am to give him. Take me to him so that I may do so."

Elisha was standing a few yards behind Jehu. Now he rushed forward and shouted loudly:

"What do you mean? His brother? How can that be, my Lord Ahaziah? Did you understand what your father said? Benhadad, his brother?"

Ahaziah hardly looked at him and answered angrily:

"Do you dare to question it? That is what my father said."

"A wicked message! An ominous message, that will bring

punishment and disaster to Israel! Listen everybody! This is a wicked message, that will bring severe punishment!"

Ahaziah stepped back and said crossly and abruptly to Jehu: "That was the message, do you understand? It is my father's wish that King Benhadad should be accorded the honours due to his position. He sent his carriage, so that I might bring the princes to the King's camp."

Elisha raised his fist and shouted, his face contorted with rage.

"You are witnesses that I have spoken, you who have been through the battle. You are my witnesses. The King has sent evil instructions. He will bring ruin upon Israel. His order is contrary to the will of God. You are witnesses that I have spoken in warning!"

There was some muttering among the troops. Ahaziah stamped his foot and his voice rose in excitement:

"Mind what you say, wretched fellow! My father's patience is almost exhausted!"

Jehu stepped in front of Elisha, pushing him aside and ordered sternly:

"Quiet! Who dares to raise his voice? The King's command shall be obeyed. Benhadad shall receive due honours, now that he has become the King's brother."

Elisha stared at him in furious indignation. Softly, so that only Elisha could hear him, Jehu whispered as he turned away:

"Be sensible! Why are you protesting now, after preventing me from doing what should have been done, and what I wanted to do?"

Elisha detained him and gasped out:

"Don't you understand? The decision had to be left to him. I stopped you because I wanted him to prove his humility and honesty. I wanted his obedience to the Lord's will, not this cowardly and presumptuous message. That was the only reason!"

Jehu paused again, then whispered guardedly:

"Are you so sure? I remember well what you said last night. Perhaps the King's treachery will be of more value to you and to the Lord's purpose than his obedience, so let things take their course."

Elisha released his arm and drew back. He was staring at Jehu as if he were really seeing him for the first time and unwilling to believe his eyes and ears.

The town of Jokneam was already asleep when Elisha arrived outside its walls late in the evening of the third day. The moon was rising, the crickets were chirping in the dry grass, a night bird flew up on soundless wings and disappeared. Otherwise it was quiet, the streets and fields were asleep.

Elisha was glad of the silence. He had been travelling almost without a pause, avoiding contacts and questions, and with only one desire, to return home to Elijah and the cave. He was afraid too about this meeting, for it would inevitably expose his defeat. Nevertheless he felt impatient, for now more than ever Elijah was for him a solace and a haven of refuge.

He climbed wearily up the path amongst the rocks and low bushes. The nearer he got to the cave, the more it seemed to him as if he had never left it, and that the long and crowded period of his absence had been nothing but an unpleasant dream. Nothing had changed, the rocks and bushes on the hillside were as blue as in the moonlight in spring. Outside the entrance to the cave, between the rocks, a fire was burning, and some of the Master's disciples were sitting by it. As Elisha approached, one of them got up and came to meet him, greeting him without surprise, as if he were merely returning from a short walk.

"Peace be with you, Sir!"

"Were you expecting me?"

"The Master said today that we might expect you soon."

"What is the Master doing?"

"Waiting for you and meditating. He seldom speaks."

They had reached the fire. Elisha raised his hand in a brief greeting and went into the cave. There was a fire burning here too. Elijah was lying on his rock bed, and stretched out his hand in greeting. "Here you are, my son."

Elisha dropped to his knees beside the bed and kissed Elijah's hand.

"It's good to see you again."

"You have had a long journey, and I don't suppose you rested much. Now bathe your feet and sit down here and eat and drink."

A bowl of water was standing ready on the ground. Beside it on a slab of rock were some little flat loaves, a dish of grapes and wild berries and an earthen pitcher. While Elisha was washing and eating, Elijah did not speak. He might have been asleep. Elisha did not look up. It was very quiet in the cave, just the crackling of the fire. Once one of the disciples came in, put fresh wood on and went out again without speaking. Elisha ate slowly. As soon as he had taken a last drink and put the pitcher down, Elijah said: "Your prophecy was right. The King has triumphed over his enemy."

Elisha turned aside so that his face was in the shadow.

"Don't make fun of me. My prophecy was wrong and you were right."

"Have I been misinformed then? Isn't it true that the Syrian army fled before Israel and Benhadad was taken prisoner?"

"Yes, quite true. Ahab defeated his enemy, as the Lord intended he should, but in the hour of victory he spared his opponent and welcomed him, calling him his brother. He made a pact with Benhadad and sent him home in state. Didn't you know that?"

Elijah raised himself up and looked at Elisha with furrowed brow and said hoarsely: "No, I did not know that."

Elisha waited for the Master to go on, but Elijah hung his head and said nothing. They sat like that, still and silent, and at last Elijah said: "It is not the first time that Ahab has betrayed the God of Israel. It is not the first time that he has opposed his will. Your prophecy was right, the treachery was the King's. Did you condemn his treachery publicly?"

"Yes."

"And to him personally?"

"No."

"Why not?"

"I wasn't with him when he issued the order. He was already back in the camp. I was with Jehu who was leading the pursuit. I was with him when Benhadad and his princes surrendered at Aphek. When the King's son came with the order to bring back the prisoners in royal state, because Benhadad was the King's brother, I shouted in protest and warning. The King's son went so far as to threaten me, but when we got back to the camp in the evening, the people had been celebrating and were drinking, dancing, shouting and cheering. The King had had the camp decorated, and the battle and the dead were forgotten. Wine was flowing from countless barrels, a great number of sheep and oxen had been slaughtered, the women were dancing and making up to the men. Who would have listened to me then?"

Elisha paused and then continued unwillingly: "And the King was no longer alone. I wanted to speak to him but couldn't. On the morning after the battle he had sent for Jezebel."

"And you were afraid of the Woman?"

"No . . . no."

"Don't deny it, Elisha. I can understand your fear. Did not I too run away from her? That was my great failure, and maybe you have a still greater fear. Listen! You need not be afraid of the Woman. Her power is just a feeble illusion, just as her gods are. The Woman's days are numbered, they will pass like the water in a brook. The Lord is your father, and is all powerful. The Woman can do nothing more against him."

"I believe you. King Ahab would not hear me. He was sitting in his pavilion in great splendour entertaining his friend at a magnificent banquet, but only his officials and courtiers were allowed in. Guards with lances and spears barred the way to all others. They sat there eating and drinking and talking till dawn, but nobody outside the tent knew what they were talking about. The next afternoon when the people were gradually recovering from their carousal, the King drove in state through the camp with the Woman beside him, and Ahab's heralds proclaimed that the King's victory was complete, for Benhadad had sworn not only peace but also a treaty of friendship, returning the towns he had taken and granting rights of free trading to the merchants of Israel. And now there was nothing but universal rejoicing and praise for the King's power and wisdom. One of your disciples did indeed burst out angrily shouting: 'Because you have let the condemned man go, it will be your life for his life and your people for his people.' King Ahab was furious, but the Woman only laughed. The man who shouted had to stop, because no one in the crowd would listen to him, and the guards were going to arrest him."

"Why did you say nothing? It was for you to speak."

"Ah, my father, I can't speak any more. Let me go back to my farm, because I am not worthy to wear your mantle. You laid it upon me in spite of my protests. When I started off with you I was diffident, and yet believed I should hear the word of the Lord. I feared the word and yet wanted to obey it, but even in my fear there was presumption. My mind is confused, and what men say can reduce me to silence, because I am no longer sure of my wisdom."

"Tell me anyone who is wiser than you."

"When I protested against the King's message, it was Jehu. He asked whether the King's treachery might not perhaps serve God's will better than his obedience. I had left the King to make his decision alone, because I wanted his obedience to come freely from his own heart, and then came Jehu's question. He is clever, my father, and he knows how to keep his own counsel. After his question I kept quiet."

Elisha sighed and went on quietly as though talking in his sleep:

"The next morning Obadiah came to see me and told me about the King's plans and what he had done. I knew it before the people in the camp did. And Obadiah said that the alliance with Benhadad would be more useful to the King than his death. It was not Benhadad who was the danger, he said, but Assyria, that was already threatening the borders of Syria and was a hundred times stronger. The King's victory was important, but the death of Benhadad and his princes, and the destruction of his military power, would only further Assyria's plans and open the way to a direct attack on Israel. Who could stand up to the power of Shalmanezer single-handed? Nobody. Only an alliance of all the threatened powers could possibly save them. Ethbaal had given his daughter the same advice and he was ready to join such an alliance himself. The King had taken his advice. That is what Obadiah told me, and he suggested that I should keep quiet . . . and I kept quiet."

Elisha put his head in his hands and whispered almost inaudibly:

"I went away to turn the King's heart, to avert the punishment that his sin and obstinacy were bringing upon him. He listened to my counsel and concealed his difficulties and his plans. I suspected his duplicity, but did not want to believe it. Or did he act rightly? Look! I can understand his fear and I share it, so I kept quiet. King Ahab fought the battle differently from the way I advised and he won! He made peace contrary to my demands, and may it not be best for Israel? I am no longer sure, so I kept quiet. Was I not right to keep quiet? Tell me, my father, did I not have to keep quiet?"

"How blind you are!" muttered Elijah bitterly. Then presently he said more gently: "Yes, my poor boy, you had to keep quiet."

"Are you going back on your own words just to comfort me?"

Elisha looked up and was shocked at the merciless severity in Elijah's eyes.

"I have no comfort for you! You had to keep quiet, because your weakness was also part of the divine purpose. He leaves even his prophets their weakness and faults, for how else could they learn his greatness? You have asked me, so I will answer. You have not done what you were bidden to do. You allowed the Lord's word to be disregarded. You spoke when you should have remained silent, and you kept quiet when you should have spoken. Are you looking for comfort? The comfort I can give you is bitter. I let you go, because I knew that what you thought and did could not alter the Lord's purpose one iota, and would not hinder what he intends to do. His power is yours, when you do his will. When you forsake him and follow human wisdom, you carry no more weight than a spider's web. You ask me to approve what you have done. You know yourself that you have failed."

"I know. That is why I want to go home."

"You must stay!"

"Why?"

"You are the Lord's chosen servant."

"Am I still chosen, though I have failed so badly?"

Elijah laughed bitterly and yet kindly. "He has laid his hands upon you. That means for ever. When I failed my Lord it was from fear. Perhaps you failed from your love for Israel."

"What will happen, now that I have failed?"

"Just what I said. No victory will help Ahab and no ingeniously contrived alliance. His house will perish and he will suffer at the hand of his friend."

"I thought I knew better. I was wrong, and now I will keep quiet until his hour comes."

"You will speak when you are told to. I too will speak to him, if I am told to. Whether he is willing to listen or not, the word of the Lord stands."

Elisha nodded, but after a while he repeated with quiet persistence: "And what about Israel?"

"Israel will be punished for her blindness and apostasy. She will rise again, when she returns to her Lord. What are kings to him? They come and go. The God of Israel must be her real King. Whoever calls himself King of Israel must be anointed by his hand. The King is only a regent and may only rule by serving him. That is the will of God that will be fulfilled—fulfilled by your words and your deeds."

"What must I do? Tell me what I must do."

Elijah smiled again. "Do not ask. He will show you, if you remain faithful and trust his great patience."

Elisha fell on his knees and cried between sobs: "I will do as you say. Stay with me, so that I may always have your counsel."

Elijah answered calmly:

"I will stay with you as long as I am permitted to, but you must not fear my departure. My word will be within you, when I am gone."

7

THE years went by. Just how many nobody knows. Probably Elijah himself had lost count.

He was asleep and was suddenly wakened by the call. Above his head his drowsy eyes could see the wide starry sky and around him the bushes, grass and rocks were bathed in a mysterious light. The wind whispered in the branches of the oaks and terebinth trees standing sombre at the edge of the clearing.

Elijah murmured: "Did you call me, Angel of the Lord?"
A faint breath of air stirred above him.
"I called."
"What is your message?"
"Your hour is near. Get ready."
"I have been ready for a long time."
Elijah tried to get up, but his legs would not obey him. Suddenly he felt frightened, and with trembling lips he stammered:
"Can't I have a little longer? I am indeed ready. But how shall I face my Lord? I have lived a hard and yet worthless life. He will look at me . . . and I have not done enough."
The whispering air answered gently: "Go without fear. You have spoken for the Lord and that was your mission."
"I can hear you, but I cannot see you. Where are you?"
"Within you."
Elijah's eyes closed again. He whispered plaintively:
"You are trying to comfort me, but I dare not trust what you say. Look back over the years and what has happened. Is it not true that my lips did not speak the word of the Lord aright?"
"Yet you conveyed his meaning."
"I did not understand his will. Think of Naboth. Did I do right there? He would not give up the vineyard he had inherited from his fathers, and Ahab by cunning and violence caused his death. Then after the King had taken from him the garden and vineyard for his own enjoyment, the Lord sent me to him to warn him of his punishment. I said terrible things to the King, and yet, when he repented, I pitied him and promised reprieve instead of the fatal curse. But no repentance nor mercy could bring Naboth, the innocent victim, back to life. Did I interpret the Lord's will correctly?"
"Have you not always insisted that nothing happens contrary to his will? You knew that his wrath is always tempered by mercy, for he is our father. What he allows to happen remains, and all that happens only serves his purpose."
"And so Ahab remained unpunished all his life, because he gave lip service to repentance. Israel soon forgot her anger over Naboth, and to this day extols the King for his firmness and skill in dealing with his problems and his enemies."

"Israel will remember her anger. It was not any single action that brought punishment upon Ahab, but his whole life. Did not your prophecy concerning him come true? Neither disguise nor concealment availed when his time came. A chance arrow struck him, and the dogs licked his blood that the harlots washed from his chariot outside the gates."

"Yes, I prophesied his downfall. The reprieve I gave him was only a postponement, but I prophesied not only his downfall but also that of his whole house, and how much of that came true? His son now occupies his father's throne and follows in his footsteps. The Woman of Baal, his mother, at his side is accorded royal honour and is allowed to provoke Israel to further sin."

"You have lived a long time and yet you forget the patience of the Lord, which is even longer? Ahab had two sons, and what happened to Ahaziah the firstborn? The hand of the Lord smote him as you foretold, and after he had fallen from his upper window, he never left his bed again. Joram may remain King for a little while, but he will be the last of his line."

"Even if this be true, how can I be satisfied? Could I be content to foretell the future from the stars and entrails like the priests of Baal, and boast as they do when their blind guesses come true? I wanted more. I called for obedience to the Lord's covenant and commandments. What is my prophecy worth, as long as Israel remains stubborn in her sin? Israel is deaf and heedless. The Lord's stern demands are too much for their voluptuous tastes. They mix with foreign peoples and readily adopt their customs. Groves and sacred stones still stand on the hill tops. The Lord's people still sacrifice to the bull and give thanks to the horned woman for the dew and the crops. They can see nothing but themselves and their appetites, their hunger and their fear of the thunderstorm. They make gods out of them, and I have to look helplessly on."

"You have lived in his mercy and have heard his word. He permits evil so that his purity may be made known."

"I have scolded them, I have even prayed that the Lord would punish them in his anger, so that at last their eyes would be opened. I have cursed Israel! Do you hear? I have cursed Israel! And yet do I not love my people even in their sin? How hard it is to have your heart thus torn in two at the hand of the Lord! Then I think to myself, how could they in their dullness recognize their Lord, when I myself fail to understand his will? Speak to me, Angel of the Lord. He showed himself to our forefathers in the cloud and the pillar of fire. They saw him. Tell me, when I pass into his presence, shall I at last see his face?"

"He is not the pillar and the cloud, and you will not see him, for he is beyond sight."

"When I seek him, how shall I recognize him?"

"You won't recognize him. You will live in his light and will know him. You will be in him and he in you, for he can also be you, and you a part of him. That is the miracle that he has ordained."

"How shall I find my way to him? I am eager to go and yet afraid."

"He has put both fear and eagerness into your heart, so that you may seek him and find him."

"Show me the way. Stay with me and show me the way."

"I cannot do that, you alone . . ."

The voice died away. Elijah listened, but all he could hear was the dull laboured beating of his own heart and the sound of his gasping breathing. He lay still, shivering alternately with cold and heat. Every breath seemed a farewell and at the same time a blind ecstatic welcome. After a long time he groped for his staff and got up on to his feet. He was not conscious of the exhaustion of his limbs, only of an increasing restless excitement, a deep, sweet yearning, that enveloped him with a sort of dreamy radiance and would not let him rest any longer.

The wind had freshened, dawn was near, branches, leaves and grass were stirring. Elisha was asleep at the edge of the clearing in the shadow of the rock. He had pulled his heavy cloak over his face and pressed close against the hard rock, as though seeking protection and warmth. Elijah walked with shuffling steps up to the sleeper, looked at him with trembling head, and at last touched him on the shoulder with his staff. Elisha stirred, pushed back his cloak and began to get up. Smiling Elijah said softly, for his words and his smile came also out of his dream: "I must go now, my child." He turned away and had started off down towards the valley before Elisha was fully awake and had jumped up.

Down in the valley the mist was still lying over the fields and cottages of Gilgal. Elijah's knees were weak and his shoulders sagged. He stumbled as he walked, and grasped his staff with tightly clenched fist. It was this gnarled hand, with its prominent bones, veins and sinews, and its leathery wrinkled skin that alarmed Elisha much more than being wakened by the mysteriously gentle words of Elijah. He walked a pace behind the Master. Several times he tried to speak, but could not, because his throat was dry and constricted. Elijah's hand was now so tired that it almost seemed as if it were no longer guiding the staff, but just following it towards some mysterious destination that Elisha found deeply disturbing.

How often it had happened in the past that Elijah had set off suddenly on a journey, late at night or in the early dawn, sometimes after weeks or even months, and always with the same urgency that would listen to no protest or argument. Looking back it was clear that Elijah had always been right. Sometimes it had happened that Elijah had lain for a long time so exhausted that he had hardly strength to talk, and then one day to their surprise he would get up, causing his disciples to rejoice at the visible sign of the power of the Lord, who gave his prophet inexhaustible life. During this last summer, however, Elijah had hardly ever left his couch. His disciples, who called themselves his sons, his children, came up from Gilgal, and sat watching by his bedside, waiting for his words and his teaching. Elijah's failing health had become more and more evident with every passing day. He seldom spoke, and then in obscure mutterings that they scarcely understood—and now this morning he had got up and walked!

"Let me be blind and believe it is a miracle!" Elisha prayed. "Let it be a miracle and not parting for ever!"

He looked again at the hand on the staff, groping step by step down the steep and stony path, and he knew that this time his prayer was in vain.

Elijah's head was bent as if listening. From time to time he muttered a few hurried and disjointed words. Elisha could not understand them, and suddenly he felt that his own words could not reach the Master any more, even if he dared to open his lips. There he was. Elisha could touch him, and yet he was far away, shrouded in a curious isolation that filled his disciple with awe. How had this isolation become overnight so profound and impenetrable as to exclude him, who had for so long shared every silence, every dream and every utterance? Elisha did not know the answer, so he followed Elijah in silence and with a heavy heart, with one hand half raised ready to support his stumbling master. Not until they reached the cross-roads outside Gilgal did he step forward and touch Elijah's arm, asking hesitantly: "Dear Master, won't you rest a while? You are so tired."

He did not know whether Elijah had heard him or not, but a few yards farther on Elijah turned his head and said:

"You stay here. The Lord is sending me to Beth-El."

Elisha stared at him horrified. Obviously the Master was delirious. They had struggled as far as here, and Beth-El was many hours away, but even in Elijah's scarcely audible murmur there was such unquestionable authority that Elisha could only stammer in awe: "As you say, but do not send me away, for as surely as the Lord lives, I will not leave you."

Elijah tottered on in silence. He did not speak during the whole journey, which seemed endless, because their progress was so difficult. The sun climbed higher, but the sky remained overcast and grey. The wind rose and whirled sand and dust into dancing eddies. As time went on Elijah had to stop more and more often. Then he would raise his hand to his chest and move it up and down once or twice as if to urge on his failing lungs and heart. Elisha stood by with burning eyes, looking round helplessly for somewhere for the suffering man to rest and be cared for, but as far as his eyes could reach there were only stony hills and slopes, dry and deserted. There was no house anywhere, no shelter from wind and sun.

They reached Beth-El in the late afternoon. Outside the first of the houses they met a group of the Sons of the Prophets, who had been living here for a considerable time, proclaiming the word of the Lord as they received it. Elijah himself had lived here for a while and had often stayed here on his travels. When the Sons of the

Prophets saw the two men approaching, they came running to meet them, and then stood still in awed surprise when they saw Elijah more clearly. Elijah's head was still bent as if listening. His breathing was stertorous and his face grey and streaked with sweat. The disciples surrounded him shyly, and their whispered greetings froze on their lips. One or two of them turned inquiringly to Elisha but got no answer. Others ran and with skins and cloaks hurriedly prepared a place for Elijah to rest. Elijah let Elisha lead him to it and lay down in silence. He refused the water and bread and berries that they offered him. Soon he fell into a restless sleep. Elisha sat by his head. He asked for a soft cloth and gently wiped the sweat from the sleeper's face. The news of their arrival spread quickly and the circle round Elijah's couch grew bigger and bigger.

Hours passed, but to Elisha time seemed to stand still, for nothing happened. The only thing that gave it content and meaning was this bewildering end that was approaching more and more clearly before his eyes. Sometimes he felt as if it must mean his own end too. How could he live without Elijah, without his presence and his word? The answer filled him with still greater terror, because he knew in his heart that this end only meant a beginning for him. For the first time he would learn the full meaning of his appointed mission. It could not be stopped, it was only held in suspense as long as the sleeper still breathed.

One of the disciples got up and came over to Elisha and said sobbing: "D'you know the Lord is taking your Master away today?"

Elisha looked up as if waking from a dream. The profound sadness in his face answered the question before he spoke. He raised his hand in warning and laid it on Elijah's head as if to hide his face and whispered: "Hush! Yes, I know."

They asked no more questions and sat still until Elijah moved. He was still asleep, but his limbs were twitching restlessly as though he were having unpleasant dreams, and at last he opened his eyes. Elisha bent over him and saw with breathless wonder that the eyes were clear and definitely recognized him.

"Help me," whispered Elijah urgently, "We must go on," and as Elisha hesitated. "Put my feet on the ground."

Elisha did as he asked. Elijah sat on the edge of the bed breathing heavily, his hands groping for something to hold on to in order to pull himself up. After a while he muttered: "I must go."

Elisha fell on his knees before him, put his arms round him, leaned closer to his ear and said pleadingly: "Let us rest a little longer here. It's late, and where should we go to now?"

"I must go!" Elijah repeated. He bent his head again as if he were listening and he said sadly but with a strange pride: "You stay here—he is sending me on—to Jericho."

Still on his knees, Elisha cried out beseechingly: "Did I speak in vain this morning? I'm not deserting you, but how can you go so far?"

"Help me!"

Elisha stood up and helped him gently to his feet. Elijah stretched out his hand for his staff, grasped it and stood up. The disciples, who had listened to the conversation with bated breath, now crowded round with good wishes and blessings, trying to touch him or kiss the hem of his cloak. They begged him to stay, and drew back in awe when he took no notice of them. He raised his eyes and looked at the bright evening sky and then looked back wearily at Elisha, whose arm was still round his shoulders. Leaning on this arm and clinging to his staff, Elijah took the first step forward.

The news of their coming reached Jericho the same evening. The isolation in which the old man and his companion moved was so awesome and forbidding that no one ventured to follow them, but without asking for Elisha's consent, one of the disciples from Beth-El hurried on ahead to carry the news to Jericho. The Sons of the Prophets prepared a couch and food and drink. Later they went out, anxious and excited, to watch and wait at the edge of the orchards, where the road from Beth-El came out into the valley.

The night was warm. The moon high above was surrounded by a corona of shining haze. In response to questions and shocked exclamations the messenger from Beth-El had to repeat his account of Elijah's appearance, his illness and weakness, his marvellous recovery and departure. They waited a long time and their anxiety increased. They went further up the slope. At last when the moon was almost down, they caught sight of a dark shadow coming wearily towards them down the hillside. They hesitated, because they only saw one man, then some of them ran forward to meet him. It was Elisha carrying his master in his arms. Somewhere along the road Elijah had collapsed and had been unconscious ever since. Elisha must have carried him a long way, for he seemed utterly exhausted, but he would not relinquish his burden. He answered the horrified questions by silently shaking his head, and only when Elijah had been made comfortable on the couch did he sigh with relief and wipe his brow. He listened to Elijah's rasping breathing, stooped down and took some water from a pitcher, raised the unconscious man, moistened his lips carefully, and tried to get him to swallow a few drops. Then he sat down beside the couch, pulled his cloak over his head, and sat with his face half hidden. Someone asked him shyly: "May we offer you some refreshment, Teacher? There is food and drink ready."

Elisha looked up sadly: "No."

For a long time no one dared to speak to him. Only the gasping of the unconscious man could be heard, and now and then quiet whispering and weeping amongst the watchers. Once one of the disciples jumped up and cried sadly and angrily:

"Tell us, Master, why did you let him take this dreadful journey, that used up his last remaining strength?"

The others pulled him down in alarm. Elisha's drawn face relaxed for a moment in a contemptuous smile.

"He goes his own way and visits those whom his words have stirred. Who can forbid him when he hears the call?"

The man who had called out beat his breast in despair.

"Never again! Never again! His coming was always our great joy, now it is only sorrow. Do you not realize that the Lord is taking your Master away?"

Elisha bent forward as though he could not believe his ears and answered dully: "Hush! Yes, I know."

The question and the answer were spoken almost in the same words as at Beth-El, and Elisha's exhausted senses resented the repetition. Again he had a feeling that time had stopped and was waiting in motionless suspense. Perhaps it was still afternoon and this was still the tent at Beth-El and the question had just been asked for the first time. Perhaps it was just his fear that had conjured up the gloomy and agonizing horror of this evening and night. Then suddenly he understood that the repetition of the question and answer contained a hidden sign that he had to interpret, and that he knew what it meant. The words were repeated because the journey was not yet over, its mysterious circle not yet complete, and so Elijah would wake again. Elisha's heart nearly stopped beating as he watched the sleeper intently, waiting for the movement that would surely come, if his understanding were correct. Nobody saw that he was waiting. They just accepted his answer and wept aloud. But when the sky began to lighten over the tree-tops, Elisha jumped up from his seat, and the watchers crowded round overwhelmed, for they saw in the dawnlight Elijah's eyes opening and his lips moving. Now he raised his hand, groped blindly in the air, put his hand unsteadily to his forehead as if in greeting, and those standing near heard him whisper: "To the river! I must go to the river!"

Leaning over him Elisha groaned: "Master! Oh, my dear Master!"

Elijah's hand dropped, but his eyes rested on Elisha anxiously and yet with unwavering childlike confidence. Perhaps he also knew the secret meaning of the repetition, for just a fleeting moment his suffering face bore the shadow of a smile as he whispered: "You stay here. The Lord is sending me to the river."

This time Elisha did not answer. He put his arm under Elijah's shoulder and raised him up. He waited till Elijah had got his breath and a little strength, and suddenly he too seemed to become conscious of the same compelling urgency as Elijah, for with his free hand he motioned away the disciples, who were anxiously protesting, and said softly, comforting and encouraging Elijah: "Yes, I am staying with you. Let us go."

The morning dawned sultry and grey. It brought a hot wind from the east that raised clouds of dust and mist, veiling from time to time the opposite bank of the river. There had been no rain yet this autumn. All along the road the fields showed nothing but clods of baked earth and strawlike tufts of scorched weeds. Elijah walked as if he had gone to sleep again. His steps had become still shorter. After every ten or twenty shuffling steps he had to stop. Then he would stand gasping for breath, his head leaning on his trembling hands, that still grasped his staff. And yet he walked with the mysterious certainty of a sleepwalker and found unerringly the path to the river and the ford by which to cross it.

Elisha kept close to him. His heart was heavy with sorrow, and yet he too felt a sense of quiet serene thankfulness. Since the revelation the previous evening, Elijah's strange impenetrable isolation had vanished. He felt close to his Master in a new and wonderfully sweet way, beyond all physical separation, enabling him to share Elijah's rapture. He was no longer surprised that Elijah could find his way in spite of his dazed weakness. He realized now that this journey was a homecoming. The river and the valley meant home to Elijah, remembered in every detail through all his life and journeyings. Elisha was not conscious of fear or any fresh doubts until they had crossed the shallow water and Elijah did not stop. Elisha turned and looked across at the shadowy group of disciples, who had followed them at some distance down to the river and were now waiting helplessly on the farther bank. He had not wanted them to follow, but had said nothing when they set out, because he knew that he could not stop them. Now he was almost glad to know that they were there, in case they could help, and yet he knew that such a hope was vain. When they had scrambled up the bank, he asked desperately: "Where are you going, now that we've crossed the river?"

Elijah had his eyes fixed on a little hill, on the top of which was a stone slab resting on two huge rocks and affording some slight shade. He hesitated a little and seemed to be pondering whether he was at the right place, then nodded feebly and murmured hoarsely: "There!"

Elisha helped him up and waited. Elijah leaned against the rock and said loudly: "As I've not been told to go any farther . . ."

Elisha stroked his hand soothingly, then clasped it firmly.

"Don't worry. We are at the river, as you were told. Now you may rest."

Elijah looked at the hand covering his. It was impossible to say whether he knew whose hand it was or not. After a while he said plaintively: "The angel said 'Not I, only you,' but I do not know where to go now."

Then he seemed slowly to recognize Elisha and he went on softly, as if he were revealing a secret to prove his love:

"He consoled me too, because my intention was so good and my deeds so small."

"Speak to me once again," cried Elisha, "so that I may know your will now and for ever!"

"You know what my purpose was—that the Lord should rule over Israel."

"And you think you have done little? Think how they love you. You were stern and spoke of punishment, and yet they love you as their father. Who has done more than you?"

Elijah did not answer, but after a time he seemed to breathe more easily, and then suddenly he said quite clearly and quietly:

"You see now what you dreaded to see, my son . . . and there is nothing new to say. Or are you trying to hide something from me? Soon I shall be leaving you, so ask me what I shall do for you before I am taken away."

Elisha burst into tears, because the Master's last thought was of giving, and through the veil of his tears he saw Elijah's calm and peaceful face flooded with light, that seemed to come partly from within and partly from above them, and in this light he could see with heartbreaking humility and wonder Elijah's hard and splendid life as he had never seen it before.

"What am I without you, and what shall I do without you? I want to do what you have told me to do, and so that I can do this, grant me a double share of your spirit."

Elijah's voice was clear and wonderfully happy:

"You have indeed asked a hard thing. If you see me when I am taken from you, then it shall be as you ask. If not, then it will not be so."

Elisha whispered, choking: "Master, I shall see you. I cannot leave you."

Elijah said no more. The quiet happiness still showed in his face, but his eyes closed and his shoulders sagged, as sleep and weakness overcame him again. It took all Elisha's strength to hold him up. Presently he laid him down and tried to make him comfortable by propping up his head. From time to time he went down to the river, moistened a piece of cloth and laid it on Elijah's forehead. The heat was becoming more and more oppressive. The sky was yellow, the wind dropped, and the air was leaden and still in the dry heat. Now and then Elijah's face twisted as though he were in pain, his eyelids fluttered and his eyes opened, but their expression was empty and blind. The hours passed. Elijah lay with his mouth open, his breathing shallow and rapid. Once or twice he raised his hand as if for help. Elisha propped him up again and after a while lifted him right up in his arms so that he was standing leaning against the rock. Some time or other Elijah began to speak—odd syllables and unintelligible fragments of words that mingled with his stertorous breathing into a strange wandering sort of singsong. His eyes were now wide open, staring up into the sky in agonized, impatient expectation. His whole body shook convulsively and Elisha had great difficulty in holding him, for Elijah's muscles tensed almost as if he were trying to struggle free from the supporting arms.

Towards sundown the wind got up again, gentle and soft at first, then in gusts of rapidly increasing violence. The sky grew dark and heavy and thunder rumbled in the distance. Elijah's singsong stopped and then started again. The trembling of his limbs increased, and now it seemed that his poor body was nothing but a bit of earth and sand and stone, its trembling reflecting the tension in the hot circling air. Suddenly he cried out. From the blackness above them a flash of lightning, an enormous burst of fire, zigzagged fiercely across the whole mass of cloud and struck the earth right in front of their dazzled eyes. Elisha staggered back, trying to find some support to cling to in his confusion and terror. His senses reeled as Elijah cried: "His chariot and horses for me! At last! D'you see them?"

He raised his arms, swayed towards the slope and over the edge and disappeared from sight. Elisha tried to catch hold of him, shouting: "My father! O my father!" but his voice was drowned by the thunder. The howling wind and the torrential rain pouring down from the bursting clouds forced him to the ground. There he lay, overwhelmed by sorrow and called out once again:

"O my father, you charioteer of Israel!"

Then he seized his cloak in despair, and sobbing tore it in two pieces.

The wind dropped and the rain ceased after sunset, and the evening became silvery bright and cool. Raindrops still glistened here an there on leaves and branches in the bushes on the bank, and the moonlight shone on the wet rocks and the rippled surface of the river.

The disciples, who had waited all day by the river, were still sitting there, hungry and thirsty and soaked to the skin. They had not seen much of what had happened on the opposite bank, for they had been dazzled by the lightning, and after that the heavy rain had blotted out everything like a thick curtain. So they waited there shivering and bewildered, impatient and frightened. The other bank was now deserted apart from the occasional rustling in the undergrowth or the shadow of some animal prowling by the water's edge to disappear among the rocks. An owl on a swaying branch uttered a plaintive call and flew off on soft wings. Once they heard hyenas howling in the distance, and all was quiet again. Then at last to their great relief they caught sight of Elisha's dark bent figure standing motionless down by the water, as if he had been there for a long time. Now he was coming across the ford. They could hear the splashing of his steps. He was alone.

He was alone. Soon they were able to see in the pale moonlight the stark sorrow in the face of the man who was coming towards them as if he did not see them. Now they knew what had happened, and instead of running to meet him they drew back trembling and apprehensive as if the terrible thing that they had already surmised would only become real and irrevocable when he reached them and spoke to them.

When he stood before them with bowed head, one of them managed to whisper: "You are alone?" Elisha looked up. He had already seen them when he got down to the river, but he had immediately turned away. He did not want to see them, and tried to banish from his mind even this brief glimpse. In these last few hours he had received a wonderful gift from the Lord's hand. His grief and terror had been indescribably transfigured, so that he was enfolded in a quiet rapture, that shut out ordinary pain, but he knew that the first word, the first question, would tear this ecstasy apart. That is why he had stopped on the river bank and was about to turn back, but suddenly his reluctance turned to impatience and he came on. All at once he felt anxious to hear their questions, for his answer would be his first utterance about the mysterious events he had witnessed and shared.

"I am alone," he said, and after a pause he added more gently: "We are alone."

"What about the Master?"

Elisha took another step forward.

"He went up in the flaming chariot of the Lord. Do you mean to say that you were waiting here and did not see it?"

And as they stared at him in silence, he said harshly and with an air of authority: "I saw it, right to the end!"

He hid his face in his torn cloak in uncontrollable terror at his own words, but those to whom he had spoken paid no further attention to him. They fell back as though he had struck them and cried: "Oh, Master, how terrible!"

They bent down, beating their foreheads and breasts, tearing their clothes, and crouched weeping on the ground. Elisha lowered his cloak again and looked at them with contempt and yet with envy. They had not understood what he had said. They only knew what had happened to themselves, and so they wept. He said nothing. After a while one of them came up to him and asked in a choking voice: "Are you quite sure that he has gone for ever?"

Elisha answered in exasperation: "I told you and you heard. Why have you waited here all day, if you won't now believe?"

"We do not doubt your words, but perhaps the spirit of the Lord has come upon him and carried him away somewhere. Please let us go and look for him. There are strong men here among us who will go."

"You must not go. You will look in vain."

"Let us go none the less, so that we needn't give up hope."

Elisha said sternly:

"What children you are! I tell you that, as surely as I was with him at the end, you will look for him in vain, and why should you go, since the Lord's will for him has been fulfilled, and I could not hold him back?"

They went down on their knees and implored him:

"Don't be angry with us. We know that his spirit rests upon you. We want to go because our grief will not let us be idle."

Then Elisha bent his head and said reluctantly:

"Go then. I will not try to stop you any longer."

They jumped up and seized their cloaks and staves. Those who wished to go hurriedly drew up a plan, split up into groups and disappeared quickly into the night. A few remained with Elisha and asked him:

"Where are you going to now?"

Elisha raised his hand vaguely and let it fall again and answered indifferently: "Back the way we came."

They realized that the question had been unnecessary, there was hardly any other way to go. They waited in silence while Elisha wrapped his cloak round his shoulders more closely, looked once more across the river and then turned at last to go.

The search party returned three days later to Jericho. They admitted sadly and ashamed to Elisha that the search had been in vain. He hardly moved when they came and told him. Those who had stayed with him told them in a whisper that during these few days Elisha had sat silent by himself and had eaten only a few mouthfuls of dry bread and a little water. After a while he muttered to the searchers: "I told you that you should not go."

They nodded and sat down in a circle at his feet. Elisha knew that they were waiting for him to speak, but he still kept silent. He had no word for them. For three days and nights he had struggled fiercely and desperately to recapture the wonder of that first evening, but without avail. He could recall nothing except visions of the last few days and hours with his master and the words he had spoken. He could not rid himself of the curious and profoundly disturbing notion that he had not really accompanied his master on this last journey at all, but had been identified with him and had travelled the road himself right till the end. The Master had taken him with him, leaving behind only his insensitive body, which could not find its way back to life.

His nights were spent in torment. While others slept, he stared into the darkness, listening and struggling, longing for a word, a sign that was not just a recollection, but came from within himself. It did not come. Was the Lord preventing him from returning to life, or was he going to repudiate the succession that the Master had promised him? Wherever Elisha looked he felt only cold and emptiness. The Lord had obviously afflicted him with complete insensitivity. He could not even find words of supplication or sorrow.

The only things he was conscious of with tormenting and mocking clarity were his own physical feelings, hunger and thirst, his back aching from sitting too long in a cramped position, the blisters and cuts on his feet that were so slow to heal, the irritation of his dry dust-grimed skin, and the exhaustion of every muscle. These he could not forget, they kept crowding into his consciousness, but the words with which to ask the Lord for guidance would not come.

Now and then when he looked up he became aware of the disciples sitting round, but he scarcely saw them. He could only make out their features indistinctly in the dusk, and he had no idea whether they were the same ones that had been sitting there three days ago or different ones, one of those odd groups of young men and youths who always appeared and sat round like that whenever he arrived with Elijah. The way they sat silently waiting increased Elisha's agony of mind till it became unbearable. They thought that he was sitting there mourning and absorbed in communion with his Lord, whereas in fact he was just wandering round in a cage built of memories and words associated with Elijah, from which he could not escape.

At last towards evening he got up and looked uncertainly round him. The nights were already cool, but here between the gardens and in the shelter of the trees the air was mild and soft. Elisha stretched himself. His limbs were stiff and cramped through sitting still so long. He said softly: "Now I'm going."

The disciples asked in surprise: "Where are you going, Master? It's already late."

Elisha wrapped his torn cloak more closely round his shoulders and answered hesitantly, as though afraid that they would understand and see his weakness: "I'm going to look for him!"

"What do you mean? Haven't we searched in vain? Didn't you say yourself that we should not go to look for him?"

They crowded round him, and as he felt their warmth and their breath it seemed as if something awoke in him at last.

"Not in that way," he murmured. "Listen! While I was walking with him that day, his last question was what he should give me. I asked for a double share of his spirit. He promised it to me if I should see him at the last, and I did see him go. So now I shall go, and because I must do so, I shall try to live his life over again in mine. My step will be his step, his way my way. I will speak as he spoke and do what he did, so that I shall find him again in myself, and myself in him. That is the way I must go."

When he had finished there was silence, for they did not know what to say, but as he turned to leave one of them stepped forward, a half-grown youth whose cheeks had hardly even down on them, and whose voice was shrill and breaking. He seized Elisha's hand and cried: "Let me go with you, Father, and be your servant."

Elisha asked in surprise and discouragingly:

"What do you mean, child? What would I do with you?"

The boy held out his arm and said: "Just feel my arm and look at my legs. I am no longer a child and I am strong. I want to go with you and work for you."

"Stay with your father and work for him."

Someone standing near said quietly: "Gehazi has lost his father."

Elisha turned back to the boy, who was standing with arms hanging down, biting his lips and with tears in his eyes. Elisha laid his hands on his head and asked quietly: "Is that your name, Gehazi?"

The boy nodded in silence.

"And you have no father?"

"That is so."

Elisha's hand was still resting on Gehazi's head. He leaned heavily on it, but the boy did not move. At last Elisha said roughly: "All right then. You shall come with me, so that you will not be fatherless."

He looked round, curiously surprised at his own words. In spite of the gloom he could now see clearly for the first time the faces of the people standing round, face by face, feature by feature, this one and that one, as he had seen and known them for so long. They looked more cheerful. They were smiling as they asked:

"When shall we see you again, dear Master?"

Elisha's face relaxed. With a shy smile he answered quietly:

"You will hear of me. You will also see me."

8

As time went by, the people of Israel began to talk more and more about Elisha, on whom the spirit of Elijah now rested, as he travelled up and down the country following his Master's footsteps. Someone would tell how he had met him and had seen what he had done. Someone else who heard the story would eagerly spread it farther. The shepherds sitting round their fires beneath the starry sky talked of him. The old men by the fireside, who had leisure to listen to travellers' tales, were glad to hear new stories and to pass them on. Others had heard how somewhere or other he had put right some injustice or settled a dispute, and the women waiting their turn at the well spread the news. As the stories passed from mouth to mouth they were changed a bit, rounded off like pebbles in the river bed, one narrator would leave out something that did not seem to him important, another saw the incident through his own vivid imagination, and as he saw it, so it must have happened. Gradually fantasy, desire and wish-fulfilment crept into the stories, and although accounts did not agree, although what really happened may well have been very different, either simpler or more complicated, more important or trivial, and with an altogether different meaning, the eventual form of the story was accepted as true, for that is how it ought to have happened.

The people of Israel had always needed miracles, so much so that their whole life and character had been formed by them. Their emergence as the chosen people of God, the covenant, the wonderful promise and its faithful fulfilment—these things had happened to Israel and to Israel only. Twice the choice and the promise had been repeated, as though once was not enough for them to be understood and believed, and through all the years, and in spite of all Israel's wavering, these things had never been forgotten. So it came that many later incidents that seemed miraculous to them were related as having happened twice. When they began to tell stories about Elisha, who wore his Master's mantle and spoke the word of the Lord in his stead, and whom the Master himself had chosen and called according to the word of the Lord, and who had told his disciples that he would follow in the Master's footsteps so that his life would be his Master's life, his word the Master's word, and his actions his Master's actions—was it not perfectly natural that confusion should soon arise as to whether the stories referred to Elijah or Elisha? They told things about one that had really happened to the other, and so achieved a double satisfaction. They made the miracles happen a second time, and confirmed and authenticated the Master's successor. And because the miracles had happened twice they became really true, and proved themselves to be genuine miracles.

They told the story of the widow who came to Elisha complaining that her creditor was going to take her sons for slaves, because she could not pay her late husband's debts, and Elisha had pity on her and asked gently: "What can I do? Tell me what you have in the house?" And she said: "Your servant has nothing but a pot of oil." And Elisha told her to go and borrow empty vessels from all her neighbours. "Go indoors with your sons and shut the door and pour the oil into all the vessels, and when they are full offer them in payment." Next day the widow came back and fell on her knees before the man of God and kissed his hand, because all the vessels were full of oil and it was more than enough, and he told her to go and sell as much oil as was needed to pay the debt and keep the rest for herself and her sons.

And had they not told a similar story about Elijah also, how he increased the oil for the widow of Zarephath, when there was famine in the land and she and her children were starving?

They told the story about the man who came to Elisha in Gilgal during the famine and brought twenty barley loaves and some young corn in the ear, and Elisha said: "Give it to the people to eat." And the man said: "What is the use of twenty loaves for a hundred hungry people?" And Elisha answered by the word of the Lord: "Give them to the people. They will eat and there will be some left over." And he set the bread before the people, and they ate and there was some left over according to the word of the Lord.

Had they not told a similar story about Elijah, who increased the flour in the widow's barrel, when he was staying in her house, and she fed him and her whole household with bread?

They told also of the boys playing outside the walls of Beth-El when Elisha came past. They did not know who he was and shouted from the hillside: "Baldhead! Baldhead! Come up here!" and when Elisha would have gone on they crowded round him. Then Elisha stood still, and when they would not stop shouting, he threatened them in the name of the Lord, and when the boys continued to mock him, he cursed them, and bears came out of the wood and ate them.

But was it not also told of Elijah that he called down fire from heaven twice to consume the officers and their fifty men who were going to arrest him?

They told the story of the widow's son whom Elijah had awakened to new life in response to her pleading. Later on when they heard about Elisha's visit to Shunem, and how he returned and stayed a long time in the house of the woman who provided him with food and lodging, they soon began to tell of the kindness he had shown her, and in their minds it took the same form as the familiar story told of Elijah. What had really happened there they did not know.

Elisha arrived at Shunem the first time one winter evening. It had been raining most of the day with a strong cold wind. In the early evening the rain stopped at last and the wind dropped, but the sky remained covered with heavy clouds and it got dark early. The smell of sodden grass and rain-soaked earth was everywhere. As darkness fell the countryside seemed desolate and dismal.

Elisha came down the hill with Gehazi. His cloak was wrapped closely round him, but he was still cold, for he was wet through. They had been walking all day and had not found much protection from the weather. Now at last they saw lights in the distance. Gehazi asked dolefully:

"Father, when shall we find somewhere to rest and dry ourselves?"

"Are you very tired, lad?"

"Tired and hungry and cold."

"We haven't much farther to go. Down there we will find somewhere to stay."

They walked on. After a while Gehazi said with a mixture of flattery and peevishness: "Everybody knows about my Master. If he happens to visit the King, Joram receives him with the honours befitting a royal guest, and then a little later my Master travels about like a homeless beggar, and we are hungry and cold in the wind and the rain. Why?"

"I do not care for the King's honours. He treats me so because he can't help it and because he is afraid of me."

"If he is afraid of you, why do you not take advantage of it? You could get anything you want out of him."

"You poor stupid!" Elisha answered brusquely. "I do not need the things Joram would give me, and what he would like to buy from me he cannot have. He would gladly pay me to stay with him and give my approval to his actions. It's easy for him to offer lavish entertainment and amiable words or make a show of good intentions, imagining that I don't know what he's really doing. If I stayed with him, perhaps I really might not know—but as we travel round like beggars, as you say, then I hear what the people of Israel have to put up with, and I see what evil he and his servants are doing in Israel."

"Don't be angry with me," said Gehazi dejectedly. "How am I to know? He's afraid of you and your disapproval, and yet he sends for you and asks for your advice, and then goes on doing evil. How am I to know?"

"Remember this. He's afraid of me because he is a coward and because he knows that I don't forget. Maybe he would like to do what I tell him to, but at the same time he wants to go on doing evil because it's comfortable and profitable at the moment. He's just like his father; he'll go on doing evil to the end."

"How long will that be?"

"That's not for us to ask."

They had reached the first houses. From up on the hill they had seen lights, but now they could see only the dim shadows of the low roofs. The house on the right looked bigger than the others, and was obviously carefully whitewashed, for it showed up more clearly in the moonlight. Along the front of the house was a covered veranda with one or two steps leading up to it. They could see light shining through the half-open door. Elisha went up the steps and was just going to knock, when a voice from inside called : "Is that you, dear?"

Elisha paused and listened. It was a very pleasant voice. He answered with embarrassment : "We are strangers."

They heard footsteps coming to the door, and the woman who had spoken drew it open. She had an oil lamp in her hand and held it so that the light fell on Elisha and Gehazi. "We've been walking all day in the rain. Will you give us shelter for the night?"

The woman raised her lamp and looked closely at Elisha. Now he could see her face. She was beautiful. He tried to look away but could not. Her expression was serious, gentle and strangely confiding. He felt unaccountably thrilled.

"My husband's not home yet," she said, "but do come in." She looked at Elisha again and added hesitantly: "His house shall be your house."

She led them along a short passage into the living room. Elisha looked round. The walls were smoothed, and washed in light blue, the floor was paved with flat stones with little mats here and there, a warm fire was burning in a wide fireplace built into the side wall. Near it was a long heavy table surrounded by low backless stools. There were copper vessels and earthen pitchers on shelves along the walls. The whole room suggested prosperity and comfort. The air was warm and dry, smelling of pine logs. The woman rang a little metal bell and a maid came in, looked in surprise at the visitors, and at a word from her mistress fetched a basin of water and dry towels.

"Bathe your feet and dry yourselves." The woman looked at Elisha again and said with hesitation: "Give me your cloak, Sir." And to Gehazi: "And yours too." She hung the soaked cloaks over her arm and went out.

"You knocked at the right door, Master," whispered Gehazi excitedly. "These people are well off. It's a good place to stay."

Elisha just nodded. Gehazi washed and dried his feet. The warm water and the soft, dry towels were wonderfully soothing. Gehazi remained sitting at Elisha's feet by the fire, his eyes glancing inquisitively round the room. Suddenly Elisha said: "Listen! She didn't ask our name. If nobody asks us, don't tell them."

"Yes, Sir."

They sat silent. Elisha's eyes were heavy. He was only just beginning to realize how tired he was, and yet at the same time he was strangely restless and impatient. Once he felt like getting up and leaving, but he stayed, and only got up when the woman returned with a man who was obviously her husband. He looked much older than she was. His beard was grey and so were the hard eyes that were rather too close together. He was broad shouldered and thick set, his movements heavy and slow. He merely glanced at the two visitors.

"Bless your coming!" he said indifferently and turned immediately to his wife. "Let's eat."

While they were waiting he walked about the room, touching this and that, picking up a pitcher critically, putting it down again, poking the fire and straightening a mat with his foot. In between he asked casually: "Where have you come from and where are you going?"

Elisha answered quietly: "We are travelling through the country proclaiming the word of the Lord."

"Do you belong to those who call themselves Sons of the Prophets?"

"Yes."

"And who is there to hear your words?"

"We speak. Those who listen, hear."

"I see."

The man sat down at the table and asked no more questions. The woman came back with the maid and two farmhands. The men sat down at the table, and the woman took the food from the maid and served it. Only when they were all eating did she sit down herself. Nobody spoke. From time to time the woman got up to fetch something and sat down again. Elisha tried to keep his eyes lowered and not to see the easy grace of her movements. He was glad when the meal was over. His appetite had gone. When the table was cleared, the farm hands left and the woman fetched some sewing. She did not look up until her husband got up and went out. Her eyes followed him and she listened. He soon came back and she lowered her eyes again. He had brought a wooden peg and began to smooth it with a knife and a piece of stone. From time to time he ran a critical hand over it. The peg was already smooth enough. It was probably a hobby. Elisha watched him without speaking. Gehazi had already fallen asleep by the fire. After a time the old man said: "Well stranger, have you nothing to say? You seem a silent sort of prophet."

Elisha woke from his reverie with a start and asked evasively:

"What would you like to know, Sir?"

"Your message. You say that you preach the word of the Lord. I want to know whether that word offers comfort to your hearers."

"To some it is comfort, to others a warning."

"Which is more needed, comfort or warning?"

"What does that question mean, Sir?"

"Nothing more or less than what I said. Do not be afraid. You can speak freely. I have not asked your name. I don't want to know it. I know you and your sort and your restlessness. Still I think you mean well, better than so many who are comfortably off. I want to hear what you have seen, and what in your opinion is more needed, comfort or warning."

"How can I tell? The people probably need comfort and warning equally."

"I thought you would say that. Well, what have you to say to those in distress and in need of comfort? What do you say to soothe their suffering? And what do you say to those who really need warning?"

"Whom do you mean, Sir? Who needs warning?"

The old man went on rubbing his peg. He said crossly and scornfully: "Who else but the King? Surely you should know that."

"I have spoken to the King, too."

The woman raised her eyes and looked gently and wonderingly at him. The old man laughed.

"What you and your sort call speaking! Listen! I have actually been in the King's palace. I have sat at his table. I saw that many came into the courtyard and shouted. Sometimes one or two people stop and listen, and if the shouting goes on long enough and is loud enough, a crowd gathers. That is what you call speaking to the King. The King doesn't hear anything. He lets you shout—what does he care? If the shouting gets too loud, he sends for the guard and someone is arrested and is not seen again. I have seen his magnificence, the arrogance of his courtiers, the painted ladies, the foreigners, the many graven images, the splendour. I know why the people of Israel have to pay tribute and do forced labour and become poorer and poorer, and why the King's men go round registering everybody, and collect tribute and tithe, and take away the harvest and drive off the cattle, as though they were plundering a foreign country. I have not been to the royal banquets for a long time. If you could stop these goings on, that would indeed be something."

The old man swung his fist in the air and continued scornfully: "What good is your warning to the poor and humble folk? Let them do what they still can do. What comfort can you offer them? Does it make it any easier for them to tell them that they are being unjustly treated? Does your word provide them with milk and bread? It is all just a waste of breath."

"You grumble and make accusations, Sir, but in spite of all the hardships you seem to be not so badly off. Your house is warm and strong. Your workpeople seem content. Your food is good and you can dress well, and yet you are not one of the King's courtiers."

"I live with my family on the land inherited from my fathers. I am not grumbling on my own behalf or talking of myself. I am talking about the suffering of the poor people, and about the uselessness of what you are doing."

"You call it useless, but the poor may need a healer just as much as the rich. Isn't it possible that you yourself in your prosperity may be in distress and in need of consolation or even warning?"

The old man laid his peg down and gave Elisha a sharp glance. The woman lowered her head over her work, but her hands were still as if she were listening. The old man asked suspiciously:

"What d'you mean? What d'you think you know?"

"Nothing," answered Elisha evasively, and went on quietly: "Many a man may be living on his family lands, as his forefathers have done, and may have everything he desires, or almost everything, till sooner or later he begins to feel afraid, because he recognizes that he has been on the wrong road and that he has not done all that he should do. Then all he has achieved seems suddenly useless, and he is only conscious of his fear, for he is not yet willing to face his real duty. He only knows that he has to make a decision, that time is passing and cannot be recalled, and that he will be to blame, if he puts off the decision to do his duty. That means great anxiety for him. And where can he find help except from the word of the Lord."

He glanced up. The old man was sitting quite still and staring at him. He did not speak. Elisha waited and then said wearily:

"Indeed you spoke truly, Sir. There is great suffering in Israel, and how little my word can avail against it, and yet the fact that I listen to the complaint of the widow and give her advice and comfort, and that I help the orphan, that I do not keep silent in the face of injustice, but protest, so that it may be prevented, that I threaten those who plunder and enrich themselves from the tribute of the poor, and that I speak what the Lord commands and what is in accordance with his law—may not that be some help?"

The old man began to work at his peg again. "Words, mere words! What's the use of words to the poor man, when he sees that in this world things do not go according to the Lord's will? What's the use of Israel's covenant and the uniqueness of her God? Are you absolutely sure you are right and can you prove it? King Joram worships him and other gods too, just as his father did, and he does not do so badly out of it. Perhaps those other gods are not so false and powerless as you say. Perhaps they do exist. Listen! I have always lived according to the teaching of my fathers and have never had anything to do with sacrifices or idols, but what is it to me if my workpeople like to worship other gods? Can I say with certainty that my God is definitely superior? Only the priests and fanatics say that, and everybody would like to think his own God is the true one, of course."

The old man laughed hoarsely, leaned closer to Elisha and asked: "Are you going to find fault with me and threaten me with punishment? You say nothing, but I don't want you to remain silent. You must answer. What is the great message that you proclaim and that presumably brings consolation and help?"

Elisha smiled and said quietly: "Why are you getting so angry, Sir? What are you trying to defend yourself against? I'm not asking you to tell me something you would rather not talk about, nor am I telling you what to do or threatening you. The word that I proclaim is that justice shall be done. That's the essence of God's will. Israel's covenant with God—the facts that she's the chosen people of God—means that she has to live in the presence of the Lord. Her life and conduct must be decided by his will."

The old man pushed his knife and stone aside and muttered: "And if things turn out quite differently, what then?"

"You must be patient, Sir. The patience of God is beyond our understanding. His will does prevail, I say, and Israel will again recognize that God is her King. That will be both her penitence and her fulfilment."

The old man did not answer. Elisha glanced at him and then slowly turned his head as if someone had spoken to him. His eyes met those of the woman. She did not look away. Her lips were parted as though about to smile at some happy thought, but her eyes remained sad and wondering. Elisha caught his breath and waited nervously for her to look away. He suddenly found his hands trembling and was filled with foreboding. He felt that something was about to happen, something that he had been waiting for ever since they first arrived, without realizing that he was waiting, or what he was waiting for. It was he who first looked away in sudden confusion, as if their eyes had betrayed a secret that he must call back.

The old man did not notice anything, and went on:

"You certainly know how to put things. Listening to you, one could believe that what you say were true. Don't be offended. No doubt you honestly believe it *is* true. Now listen to my advice, for I'm older than you. Be careful where you repeat all these things. One day they may cost you your head, and anyway, what's the use of all the talk? Words alone never accomplished anything. If you want your words to come true, you have got to turn them into deeds, d'you understand? If you can't do anything, then keep quiet."

He got up awkwardly, shook the sawdust from his apron and leaned on the peg that he had been working at all evening.

"We have talked long enough," he muttered with gruff candour, "Your boy is already asleep. You can make your bed here by the fire, and if you are cold, put some more logs on. We have plenty. Good night!"

He went out. The woman too got up at once, put her work away, and followed him. At the door she turned round and said slowly: "I will send you some blankets, to keep you warm." She took a deep breath and whispered: "You are indeed a man of God." She seemed to be about to say more, but only shook her head and went out.

Elisha followed her with his eyes, heard her footsteps in the passage, and then the creaking of a door being closed. Then he seemed to wake up. He was shivering as if with ague, and covered his face with his hands.

He woke Gehazi in the early dawn. The fire had gone out during the night and it was cold and dark in the room. The household were still asleep as they crept on tiptoe across the passage, but the front door was open and they found the old man standing on the steps. He had a thick sheep-skin round him and was looking at the sky with narrowed eyes. When he saw them he growled sullenly: "I was going to do some ploughing today, but it will not be possible. You would do better to wait a bit. There's more rain coming."

Elisha stood beside him and sniffed the air as though he were testing it before he answered hurriedly: "No, we have to go on." After a pause he added: "Many thanks for your hospitality. The Lord be with you and with your whole house."

"Oh, well! You're welcome any time you care to come back."

Elisha turned away and drew Gehazi with him. He walked with his head down and his eyes on the ground until they reached the ridge overlooking the village. Then he stopped and took a long look back.

"There's the house!" exclaimed Gehazi eagerly. "The lovely house! Why could we not stay there longer?"

He looked up as he asked the question, but Elisha did not answer, and his face was so hard and forbidding that the boy just shrugged his shoulders and asked no more questions. It was not unusual for his master to remain silent for hours at a time, and on such occasions his thoughts were not to be disturbed. This time it seemed somewhat different and Gehazi became more and more alarmed for Elisha's gloomy silence lasted all through the long day, as they walked on through the wind and the rain, and during the following days also he remained taciturn and restless. For a long time he avoided meeting people and kept away from human habitations. They slept in caves and under the trees, enduring cold, storm, and flood. Often when Gehazi woke up in the night cold and hungry, he would see his master staring into the stormy darkness, or he would hear him walking about restlessly amongst the trees, and once Gehazi was wakened by the sound of groaning that seemed to indicate such intense suffering that the terrified boy hid his face in his hands and pulled his cloak over his head so that he might not hear it. It was a long time, almost spring, before Elisha's eyes began to look more kind, and Gehazi plucked up courage to ask: "Are we being pursued, Father, that we are wandering round without rest, like fugitives?"

Elisha stopped and his eyes grew hard again.

"You can leave me, if you are tired of travelling."

"No, no!" Gehazi cried in terror. "I want to stay with you." As

Elisha did not answer he asked timidly: "May I?"

Elisha could scarcely breathe. He said sadly: "Yes, yes! Let's go."

That day and through the days that followed he at last began to talk to Gehazi again, as if he were trying to make up for his harshness, for now he often spoke with the greatest patience and kindness. He began to tell him about his experiences and the things and places he had seen, about his childhood, about the animals he had watched in the woods and fields and by the riverside, and he talked more and more frequently about Elijah, whose pupil he had been as a boy and who had later called him. He spoke about Elijah's sayings and teaching. To the boy these were often obscure and alarming, but he did not dare to ask what they meant, for when Elisha was talking about these things, his voice became tense and rapt, as though he were talking to himself, and trying with passionate concentration to revive and recapture for himself the words and incidents. After a while he began to visit people again and to stay in their homes, and talk to people as he used to. He seemed to exert a new and mysterious attraction. Wherever he went people flocked round him, men and women, old and young, healthy and sick. They brought to him their troubles, worries and sorrows, their needs and problems, their doubts and disputes, and sought his help, advice and blessing. His sympathy, the touch of his hand, the words he spoke, possessed wonderful power and gave comfort, help and healing. Often he would sit surrounded by children or join in their games, and now and then he would lay his hand on a child's head, and the dark fire in his eyes would give place to a gentle dreamy smile.

Spring turned to summer. The evening at Shunem seemed a long time ago. Gehazi had ceased to be surprised that they never talked about it. Since then they had visited many places. That night had been just one among many. He did notice once, when he happened to mention the name, that Elisha's lips tightened and his face suddenly became stern and forbidding as on the morning when they left Shunem. This made Gehazi curious, and so he deliberately turned the conversation to the lovely house at Shunem. Each time Elisha either did not hear what he had said or evaded it with an impatient gesture and became silent. Once Gehazi asked straight out:

"When are we going back to Shunem, Father?"

"What have we to do there?"

"They were kind to us, and didn't the master of the house invite you to go back?"

"You shouldn't pay too much attention to that sort of remark. People say these things and don't really mean them." And he added: "We mustn't go to Shunem."

That day they walked far into the night and at last camped by the roadside. Gehazi asked no more questions, and only remembered the conversation much later, and then he was surprised and bewildered. Slowly Elisha's restlessness seemed to subside. They stayed for weeks with the disciples beyond Gilgal, and then in the olive groves below Megiddo. When they travelled on, they only walked short distances with long periods of rest between, and then one evening they crossed the ridge again and found themselves looking down into the valley lying peacefully in the light of the setting sun. Gehazi uttered a cry of surprise and was about to hurry on, but Elisha stopped him, and seized his hand as though he needed support. Gehazi could feel his Master trembling. They stood thus for a long time, till at last Elisha sighed and walked slowly down the path towards Shunem.

He could hardly conceal the disturbing and yet painfully sweet feeling of delight that overwhelmed him when he caught sight of the woman. He turned pale and broke out in a sudden sweat, and trembled violently. Nobody had seen them yet. They were standing in the dimly lit passage, the door into the garden was open, and framed in this bright doorway he saw her standing amongst the green fruit-laden trees. She had a half-filled basket of apples on her arm, and was standing with legs slightly astride reaching upwards. The upper part of her body was bent backwards and beneath the thin linen overall the graceful form of her body was clearly outlined. He took in everything, every little wonderful detail. She stretched one arm up with effortless grace, picked an apple, balanced it lovingly and critically on the palm of her hand, and laid it with a smile with the others in the basket.

Gehazi moved to go to her, but Elisha held him back with a tight grip. He could hardly breathe. This first dazzling moment made it clear that the torment and struggle of the past months had been in vain. What he imagined he had exorcised and killed was as much alive as on the first day, even more so, and had only put forth fresh and stronger roots in the darkness of his struggle to suppress and forget it. He suddenly felt as if he had been with this woman all the time. She had been close to him and he had talked to her about everything. There was no veil of secrecy between them. Of course it was only a dream and an illusion, but how ever could he go back to being just the stranger who had spent one winter night beneath this roof, and whom she had certainly long since forgotten. He had fought his silent, passionate and sinful emotion with mortification and severity. In his terror no penance had seemed hard or long enough, until at last he had attained peace. In this peace the suffering was not forgotten, and so he had felt serene, believing that he had overcome temptation. Now in this first infinite moment before they actually met again, he realized in terror that his trial was still to come, and that it was harder than he had feared or imagined. It was too late now to escape, for the basket was full, and the woman was turning back towards the house, where she would inevitably see him and the boy at once. Perhaps she would not recognize him and would turn him away. Perhaps, on that other evening, she was only taking pity on the traveller who was without shelter in the storm and the cold. Today the air was warm and filled with the scent of flowers. The sky was radiant and peaceful, and the nights were soft and mild. Then, because he could not endure any longer the delight and apprehension of waiting, he managed at last to subdue the trembling of his limbs and stepped forward slowly. He knew that now he could speak again: he had got his voice under control. He wanted to speak without betraying the hope that she had not forgotten him, but when she came up to him there was scarcely a moment's hesitation in her joyful recognition. Her face lit up as she greeted him with surprised pleasure:

"Dear Master, how glad I am that you have come back to us!"

She bent over his hand and kissed it before he could stop her, stood up again and said with a shy smile: "We soon learned who our guest was, and Ohad, my husband, was very much ashamed that he had not asked your name."

Elisha managed to return her smile. "You have no need to feel ashamed, since you have not forgotten me."

"How could I? I have prayed that you would come back, and now here you are."

She took his hand and led him along the garden path to a little annexe and said with modest pride:

"I said to my husband: 'Now we know that the man of God has come to our house, let's build a little room for him, where he can stay whenever he comes along,' and this is what we have built for you." She turned to face him and said with a gentle smile: "Are you going to stay this time, or is it to be again only for one night? Do stay with us!"

Elisha could only look at her, and saw her face become serious, her eyes grow bigger and more insistent, and suddenly he saw in them the appealing sadness that he had noticed on that first winter evening. He said bitterly, almost challengingly: "I will stay," and then immediately, as if to deny the challenge, he forced a smile and asked: "Now that you have found out who I am and have told me your husband's name, tell me what I am to call you."

She lowered her eyes at last and answered: "My name is Achsa, like the daughter of the Caleb in the book. My father wished it, because his name was Caleb. Come, let's go inside, so that I can show you your room and you can rest."

She pushed the door open. Inside there was a low wide bed with a table and chair. There was clean linen on the bed and across the foot lay a gaily coloured blanket. On the table there was a lamp filled with oil. The window was open and looked out on to the trees and bushes of the garden, the clear sky with the first stars, and in the background the gently sloping fields and meadows. Achsa said softly:

"The room was always ready for you, whenever you came."

He went to the window and looked out and said without turn-

ing round: "You are very kind. How am I to thank you?"
"We should thank you for coming. You bring a blessing."
Elisha did not reply. After a while she said shyly:
"I'll leave you now. Have a rest till Ohad my husband comes in. I expect he will be here soon."
Elisha stayed by the window deep in thought, how long he did not know. He stood quite still, as though that were his only defence, his only safety. He was staring out of the window, but he hardly noticed the evening descending over the hill and the valley, the fading of the shadows, the outlines of the hills dissolving and the sky becoming velvety and shining. From inside the house he heard footsteps and voices, but took no notice of them, and started violently when Gehazi came to the door and shouted: "Ohad has come home, and supper is just going to be served."
Then he turned and said quietly: "I'm coming."
Ohad was waiting for him at the front door. Elisha was afraid that the man would feel embarrassed, and so he held out his hand as he came nearer and said cordially:
"See, I did not forget the kind words you spoke when I went away, and now I have come back."
Ohad bowed low and answered eagerly: "Welcome! Welcome, Sir! I expect you had a good laugh at me, after I tried to give you advice as if you were a vagabond."
"I did not laugh. You were kind to me without asking who I was. That was more important."
"It was nothing, nothing at all. Now come and let us show you how glad we are to see you."
A long table had been laid on the verandah outside the house. There were flowers in earthen vases on the white tablecloth, dishes containing meat, bowls of fruit and salad, white cheese and bread, jugs of milk and bowls of cream. This time all Ohad's household were present and Elisha noticed that he had got not just two farm workers, as he had thought in the winter, but six, together with young farm lads and maids, who were standing round the table whispering in expectation. There were torches in copper sconces fixed to the supporting posts and fires were burning in two iron braziers by the steps. Spices and scented herbs had obviously been

thrown on to the fires, for the air was filled with a sweet and heavy fragrance that floated like a veil over the table and the balcony in the warm summer evening. The street and houses and the hillside in the background were bathed in clear bluish light from the moon and the stars, but the table was lit by a reddish-yellow glow from the torches and fires. When Ohad and Elisha appeared everyone crowded round to kiss the prophet's hand or at least to touch his cloak, casting sharp flickering shadows on the table and the white wall of the house.

Achsa was standing at the head of the table holding a broad heavy chair for Elisha. She was dressed festively in a long full-length robe, that fell in ample folds from the hips downwards, and was woven in a gay pattern. Her hair was oiled and done in a knot behind her neck. Over it she wore a white veil. Round her neck hung long chains of drawn silver and jewels, and in her ears she wore heavy gold earrings. The reflection of the torches and fire in her dark eyes made them appear to have a light of their own. She held her head high and on her lips was a happy and excited smile. Ohad set the chair for Elisha, and when he had sat down the other men took their places also. There were still one or two empty chairs, and Ohad went to the railing and shouted:

"Anyone who wants to share our joy come along and welcome."

Only then did Elisha notice that the street was full of people crowding round the house and stretching their necks to see the festivities. Only one or two accepted Ohad's invitation and came up the steps shyly and clumsily, bowed respectfully towards the head of the table, and found room amongst the others, murmuring grave shy words of admiration. Now Achsa clapped her hands, the maids placed plates and dishes on the table and poured out milk from the jugs. Achsa herself stayed close to Elisha. When he looked up he could see her proud head, her eyes watching the serving, the soft play of her lips as she occasionally gave a whispered order or just smiled. At last she too sat down. A seat beside Ohad had been kept for her, and they began to eat.

They ate with silent concentration. The only sounds were the soft clatter of jugs and dishes, and from the street the shouts and laughter of children, to whom Achsa had sent out some sweets, and here and there the bark of a dog, the neighing of a horse, or the complaining cry of a bird alarmed by the light and noise.

Elisha could eat little. In the midst of all the festive rejoicing he was conscious of a strange entrancing sadness, as though his watchful eyes took in all the colours and details of the lovely picture, and yet he knew beyond all doubt that it was only a dream. Ohad ate heartily and with relish and kept pressing Elisha to eat. He passed him dish after dish and kept offering him fresh helpings of food or drink. Achsa soon noticed that Elisha only took the food so as not to offend Ohad, and the next time she gently restrained him with a smile at Elisha.

When the meal was over, Ohad leaned back satisfied and said loudly:

"Look, Sir, what a lot of people have come to do you honour and to hear your words. Won't you please them by speaking a few words to them?"

Elisha raised his eyes and glanced at the circle of expectant faces in the dim light of the street, and back again to meet the eyes of the woman, and said quietly:

"Let me stay with you for a while, so that everyone who needs my help may come to me and I will speak to him. Today let there be only joy, and may there be always joy in your house."

He flung his arms wide in an expansive gesture, beckoned to the guests and the people standing round, and shouted:

"Come along and sing, and if you want to dance, then do so. Don't be ashamed of happiness."

For a moment there was a surprised silence, then a sudden and growing babel of voices. So quietly that only his nearest neighbours and perhaps Ohad and Achsa could hear him he said:

"When Elijah called me and I left my father's homestead, he arranged a farewell feast for me. The whole village turned out to celebrate my departure. I feel that today is a home-coming and you have arranged a feast for it, so let it be a joyful feast."

Ohad said dubiously: "I'm surprised you went away leaving your own farm and fields."

Elisha looked at him in astonishment: "The Master called me."

There was a deeper, warmer note in Achsa's voice and it trembled a little as she said: "Your coming is indeed a reason for rejoicing, especially as you are going to stay." And she added almost inaudibly: "It's a long time since we were gay in this house."

Then she quickly shook her head as if she wanted her last words to be forgotten. She got up and pointed to the end of the table, where Gehazi was sitting between the farm lads. They had moved closer together, and with their arms locked round each other's shoulders, they were swaying from side to side in time to the song that Gehazi was singing. Soon they joined in, a little hesitantly at first and then more and more loudly. Then here and there someone began to clap, keeping time with the singing, and one by one they came nearer to listen and then joined in, or began a new song, beckoning to the others. The singing, clapping and stamping grew louder and spread amongst the crowd like a slow irresistible fire, till groups formed here and there, linking arms and swaying to and fro, slowly circling round in the dance that the singing suggested.

Presently Ohad gave a loud laugh, got up clumsily and made his way among the dancers. Occasionally someone would glance at the table where Elisha and the woman were sitting with Ohad's empty chair between them. They were brief glances, just to make sure that the Master was still there, and that he really permitted, and, in fact, encouraged, these goings on, which were getting more and more noisy and unrestrained. Probably no one noticed that they were sitting there quite still, as if they saw and heard nothing, and felt nothing except their nearness, the unbelievable reality of their being together, and yet as if they were far away from each other, in a loneliness across which there was no bridge.

"These are for your room, dear Master," said Achsa, showing him a bunch of flowers in her hands. "Since you came the flowers in my garden have been blooming marvellously. Do you perform miracles with buds and blossoms too?"

Elisha was sitting on the stone bench outside the house. He looked at the flowers and then very slowly raised his eyes to the woman standing in front of him.

"It is the season for fruit and flowers," he said at last. "You look after them with such tender care, no wonder they grow well! I have nothing to do with it."

"You bring blessing," Achsa answered quietly. "I know that. Many people have come here recently and I have seen none go away without comfort and help. I will put the flowers in your room. You will enjoy them there."

Elisha watched her go, then closed his eyes and bent his head. She came and went, and it always seemed that she went away without saying what she really wanted to say, that she came intending at last to say something vitally important, and then could not get the words out. What did she want to say? He dreaded to hear it and yet longed to, just as he feared her nearness and was restless and depressed when she did not come. Her presence meant both fear and terrifying happiness.

"What are you doing here?" he asked himself in his hours of solitude. He was often alone for long periods. The news that he was staying there quickly spread and many came to see him, men and women, young and old, and also the disciples, the Sons of the Prophets, but they often sought him in vain, for he had set off at dawn, trying to persuade himself that he had heard a call, the voice that sent him now here, now there, and then he would walk aimlessly about the countryside. "What are you doing here? What are you waiting for?"

He tried to think about all sorts of things, in order not to have to think of this one thing, and all the time the question remained. How could he avoid answering it? How could he deny the truth? How was he to destroy this evil thing that was growing with such appalling vigour in his heart, like a malignant weed? All this had to find expression. It showed itself in the light of his eyes, that lit up when he saw her, and in the strength of his arms, that he wanted to hold out to her, when she came near, and in the trembling of his lips, parched with the fire of unspoken words. She was Ohad's wife, and denied to him for ever. She must not even be the dream that tempted and tormented the nights of a lonely man, only to vanish at daybreak. She did not vanish—she came back.

"Did you not know that, Elisha, and did you not impose on yourself penance and mortification, to atone for your sin, and then did you not after all give in and come back?" Sometimes he toyed with the awful idea that his penance and mortification had actually been payment, payment in advance, and that all the past, all the renunciation, all the discipline and courage of his life, had already paid for the present, and so it could have its way. And all the time he knew the depravity, the lie, the abysmal danger of such an answer. He knew beyond all doubt that time was passing and that he must sooner or later run away and escape, and yet he stayed on day after day and could not go, and time stood still in trembling expectation.

What had happened then? What was happening? No word nor deed, nothing. The summer lay hot and radiant over the land. During the day the air vibrated as though with fever, but the evenings were mild—a summer like many others. The homestead and its inhabitants lived as they had always lived and Achsa too worked as usual in the house and garden. She did not ask about his coming and going, but she did not forget him at any time. She looked after him, tried with tender solicitude to guess what he liked. When he found her at work, she invited him with a smile to stay, and she guessed, too, without asking when he wished to be alone. On many evenings they were alone together, and then she sat beside him, and if he did not speak, she too kept silent, and seemed content to know that he was there. She sat there gazing dreamily through half-closed eyes into the darkness, and seemed unconscious of the eyes that watched her shyly and then remained staring spellbound at the half-averted face.

What are you doing here, Elisha? I am waiting. What are you waiting for? For these lips to speak at last, for the dreamy sadness of these eyes to lighten, for this heart at last to open to me, so that I may find release and fulfilment in her, and my loneliness reach out to her and find communion. Could he still imagine that she did not know his secret? It was both inconceivable and unendurable that she knew it, and that her silence concealed answer, reciprocation and response. Was it inconceivable and unendurable? It was the most glorious fulfilment, that he longed for with every fibre of his being, a gift beyond all dreams, and yet at the same time death and utter destruction.

What are you doing, Elisha? I am waiting. See, I am behaving quite normally and doing what I can. Do I not speak the word, and do they not come to me as they do everywhere else and ask me for help, and do I disappoint or refuse them? I give what I can, and why not here?

Oh Elisha, you are lying and you must know the answer. It is all lies. That is why all is silence. The evening is coming, the leaves are whispering, for a soft breeze is caressing the trees and the grass, the flowers and fruit, but it is only wind, empty air. Your heart is silent, you do not hear the Lord's voice any more. The loneliness of his silence is the wilderness in which you must wander, and your passion is the desert heat which consumes you and which you cannot escape. This woman.... The room and the bed are tokens of her kindness, the fruit and the flowers are her tenderness, the food and drink are her solicitude, the quiet of the evening and the kindly words are her caress. The delight and torment of your eyes, the happiness and fear in your heart, the blindness, the dream, the forgetting and despair, are her curse and enchantment. She exercises them by an intuition, silently, without sign or word.

What are you doing, Elisha? I am waiting. What are you waiting for? Oh, do not ask. Yes, go on asking, and get up at last and flee with averted eyes, for time is running out and you are falling. Oh, shut the questioning eyes and listen and stay!

When at last the word of the Lord came and shook him out of his state of anxious waiting, he did not want to hear it and strove not to understand. His whole mind resisted, because he knew at once quite certainly what the message meant: the exhausted patience of time and its command.

The sky was dark on this evening and there was a hint of autumn in the coolness of the air. Ohad said anxiously:

"I had bad news today. War is coming again. The Syrians are making raids here and there and plundering and burning."

Elisha asked, unwilling to believe it: "Where did the news come from?"

"A merchant was passing through today and told us. In one or two places there was actual fighting with the frontier guards, and there are refugees coming down from the north. It looks like war again."

"War!" Achsa repeated in fear.

Elisha said bitterly:

"It probably is war again. It has been like that since my childhood, fighting and raids again and again. There has never been real peace with Syria."

Ohad got up ill-humouredly:

"That's how it is. I must go to the cow shed. One of the cows is due to calve tonight." He stretched and rubbed his arms.

"It's getting cool. Autumn is coming. You go indoors."

He turned and disappeared in the direction of the outbuildings. Achsa sat motionless. On the table in front of her was a little bowl containing bright stones and glass beads, that she was going to thread on a string. But now her hands lay idle in her lap holding the half-finished necklace, and she just stared into the darkness where Ohad had disappeared. She started when Elisha said:

"Achsa, I shall have to go now."

His voice was sad and hesitant, as though he could not believe his own words. He had expected protest, but Achsa lowered her eyes and simply said: "Yes, dear Master."

"Now I shall go to the King's palace to talk to him. You have been so kind to me. Tell me, have you any request to make to the King or his ministers? I will see that your wish is granted."

Achsa murmured softly: "I live among my own people on our own land, Sir, and have no request to the King."

"Then tell me something else that I can do in return for your great kindness."

She shook her head in silence and turned away. Elisha sat silent and depressed. Suddenly he noticed that her shoulders were shaking. He leaned forward and asked with a dry throat:

"Achsa, are you crying?"

She covered her face with her hands, but still no sound came from her lips. Elisha stretched his hands out, but did not dare complete the gesture, and waited trembling. Achsa suddenly turned round and said breathlessly:

"You asked me a question? Well, I will ask you one, and you

must answer me. What have I done that I do not find favour in your eyes?"

"What? Whatever are you saying?"

"What have I done that you should scorn me? Answer me, since you are going away."

"You ... you don't know what you are saying. You of all people!"

"I, I alone. Is it possible then that you do not see and understand? You are said to be able to see into all hearts and have comfort for everyone. Should you not know what is in my heart? I was waiting for you to ask, to speak to me. I dared not. I hoped that the time would come when you would be kind to me, but now you are going."

Achsa sat up and cried passionately: "Are you blind, prophet? Have you seen nothing during these months?"

Elisha cried in joy and despair: "Tell me what I am supposed to see?"

"Me! Me! You have seen me day after day. Is my body deformed, am I sick or repulsive? Look at me at last, and see my grief and hope. Am I really no longer attractive, and must I wither into old age?"

"You are beautiful, you are so beautiful, my dear. Was I not aware of it from the very first, and should I have said so?"

"Yes," Achsa breathed, "Yes. Speak to me at last and tell me what I should do."

Elisha jumped up. He raised his hand involuntarily, held it over Achsa's head and lowered it with trembling tenderness and he trembled still more as he felt the soft luxuriance of her hair, the warmth of her skin and the longing that drew him towards her. Dear fire, sweet consuming death, let me fall at last! Then he met her eyes. His hand remained still and he shut his burning eyes in terrified surprise. In Achsa's wide open eyes was a great enchanted light, boundless trust, the most profound and childlike trust and entreaty, so radiant and happy that it pierced even his dark and burning infatuation, as she whispered:

"Look, Father, here I am despised by all women, for I have no son. My womb is shut up and I have no son. What shall I do?"

She did not see him, did not notice his trembling hand, did not feel the sudden convulsive grip of his hand, that slipped from her head and held her by the shoulder to keep him from falling.

"O man of God, from the day you arrived I have been waiting for your help, for you spoke to my husband as if you knew all secrets. Who should help me if not you? And you came back and brought help to everyone, and I waited."

She stopped, leaned forward and let her head fall on her arms folded on the table. Elisha hardly noticed. There was a roaring in his ears, burning bands constricted his chest as if to strangle his desperate heart. Then suddenly it seemed as if a great hand took hold of him and shook him and set him on his feet. He felt himself floating in icy pitiless light that suddenly engulfed him. His lips opened and he heard himself speaking and his own voice was unrecognizable. It was suddenly glass-clear and so exhausted that it seemed to be coming after endless time from another shore:

"Don't be afraid, my dear. Don't torment yourself. This is my word to you. In a year's time you will be nursing a son."

She looked up. The shadow of a smile came over the suffering face now at last open to him. "No, please, do not lie to your servant from pity. What a long time I have waited! My husband is tired of me and has not found pleasure in me for a long time."

"I am not lying," whispered Elisha, and as she did not speak he leaned forward and took the beloved face in both his hands and with his face close to hers said: "Believe me! Believe me! Forget everything that may have happened and believe me. Go and do as I say. Open the door of your room and call your husband to you again, and make yourself beautiful for him as though it were a festival, and think of me. And it shall happen as I have said. Do you hear? Believe my word and when he comes to you, think of me and what I have said to you."

He stopped, overwhelmed by the grateful, confident joy that spread over her face as she listened, becoming brighter and brighter like the sunrise. He hardly heard the whisper of the happy lips: "Yes, yes, dear Master. How am I to thank you?"

He lowered his hands and stood there in front of her and murmured:

"As truly as I am standing here the Lord will bless you. May his peace remain with you always!"

He turned and went away.

9

THE night was dark and restless. A passing breeze disturbed the trees, prowling animals rustled here and there among the leaves, a branch creaked in the thicket, a stone rolled down the slope, hyenas began to howl, and in between an uneasy silence.

Elisha groped his way step by step up the steep slope. He walked as if stunned, and hardly knew himself why he had set off. Far away in the darkness he could still hear Ohad's voice telling him the bad news, and his own answering words: "Now I have to go." Why? His eyes could still see the play of light and shadow on the beloved face, his trembling limbs could still recall the shattering thrill, his hands still felt the touch of her skin, his ears still heard every word they had spoken. And then had come the terrible awakening. But at the time when he had first spoken of going nothing had yet happened. A moment before his illusion and desire were still strong, and he had known nothing. Why then had he to go? He did not know. Dark and silent emptiness had spread over his passion, like a heavy pall to cover his nakedness, the wicked nakedness of his desire, the memory of which was shocking and horrifying and must be wiped out and banished for ever from his sight.

He groped his way step by step up the path. This was the road he had come down to Shunem the first time. Here he had stopped, overcome with excitement, when he returned. Since then he had passed this way many times on his walks, for no other road led to the valley. He wanted to hurry, to run away with averted face, and could not. He walked slowly with dragging step and bowed shoulders, breathing hurriedly and with difficulty. Half way up he even stopped, perhaps to get his breath, perhaps to look back. Ah, lovely dream! Beloved, vanished vision! The valley and the village were lost in the darkness of the night. Elisha turned quickly away, struggled on, and after a long time looked up. Some distance ahead, on the top of the ridge he saw a shining light, a vague translucent veil of brighter cloud that melted into the surrounding darkness, and within the cloud the waiting shadows.

Elijah was standing there. He was leaning on his staff and looking down into the valley, his body tall and dark against the silvery light. Elisha recognized him without surprise. It had happened before, Elijah standing waiting for him on the top of the hill, at the beginning of his journey, at the beginning of his remembered life. In the next shattering breath-taking moment he was seized with terror—heart-rending joy at his Master's appearance and heart-rending fear. Elijah was waiting, he knew everything and was calling him to account. That was the meaning of his return, and how could Elisha face him? He raised his hand in greeting and defence, but Elijah took no notice. He probably could not see the gesture, because Elisha was still in the shadow of the slope. Should he turn back, creep away in the darkness and flee? He knew at once that he had to hurry forward. He could not hide from Elijah. Elijah was waiting.

"Elijah, Elijah, wait! I am coming!" he shouted breathlessly.

He listened in consternation and looked in horror, for his shout, borne on the wind, echoed in the silence, and yet the Master had not heard. He was standing motionless, yet when Elisha at last reached the summit it was deserted. When had Elijah gone away? The light was now shining on the edge of the wood and Elijah was standing there. Elisha held out his arms towards him in despair.

"Wait, please wait! Do you not want to see me and listen to me?"

Now he heard a gentle answer in the whispering breeze. It did not seem to be in any spoken language. Elisha could not repeat it, but in some strange way he was able to understand it. It was like a sigh close to his ear.

"Do you want to see me and listen to me, Elisha?"

"Yes, Father! Oh, my Father!'

"You did see me and wanted to hide from me."

"Is it surprising that I was afraid of your word and your eyes? Oh why did you ever leave me and let me go astray?"

"You asked for a double portion of my spirit. I promised it, so that in that way I would remain with you, but you forgot and have betrayed my spirit."

"No, Father! No, No! Your word. . . ."

"The word I spoke is not my word. Do you serve me only or the Lord?"

"The Lord, whose word you spoke."

"And you forgot, and served only yourself."

"I know! I know! But look, I have overcome temptation. Isn't that enough? Father! Answer me. What I did and what I did not do . . . wasn't that enough?"

"Not enough! Not enough!"

"Then let me go! Release me for ever! I have been asking for so long. I am not worthy to bear your mantle. I cannot go on."

"You cannot go on? You cannot do anything else. Do you wish to forget the word of the Lord?"

"No . . ."

"Then remain faithful. You yourself are the way, the will, and you cannot be anything else. Just the will. Give up everything, everything, only the will remains for you and its fulfilment."

The wind began to increase, singing over the trees. The light by the edge of the wood rose and faded. The figure of Elijah was just a shadow, and now that also rose, and Elisha heard the beating of great wings.

"Go! Go! You alone, always alone." And once more from far away: "Go!"

Elisha lay stretched on the ground and stammered in terror:

"I will go. Yes, I will go."

He listened trembling, but heard no more. There was nothing but the night, the rustle of leaves and the whisper of the grass, and in his ears the beating of his heart. His throat and chest were choked with suppressed sobs, that found no outlet. He was filled with infinite pitiless sadness, as though he realized for the first time the guilt and death within him, and also the way of loneliness that lay before him. After a while he got up with a groan, seized his staff, and staggered on.

When he opened his eyes it was daylight. He looked round reluctantly and puzzled. Sometime or other during the night he had collapsed and fallen asleep. Now he did not know where he was. He remained lying there, still exhausted and half asleep.

It was a lovely morning. The sun was already high in the sky and had warmed the stone beneath his head. The leaves and branches were still. Now and then birds twittered, otherwise all was quiet. Elisha's eyes closed again. Beetles crawled over his hands and face, the noonday breeze blew dust and fallen leaves over him, but he slept on. The sun went down, the dew fell, night came, and he still slept on and did not wake till the following dawn.

He stretched himself, still weak but refreshed, as after a long illness, but at last his eyes were clear again. His throat was parched and swollen. When he tried to speak, he was appalled by the flat hoarse croak that came from his lips. He got up, stood with legs apart, rubbed his body, and tried to remember what had happened and how he got there. He soon remembered everything, but it seemed so far away, so long ago, as though he had since been walking for ages.

Suddenly out of the infinite distance of long ago came a consuming sense of negligence and guilt. He was conscious of tormenting hunger and thirst and at the same time driving impatience and haunting fear. There were trees all round him and he had no sense of direction. He waited, noticed the wind, which always blew from the east in the morning, and saw at last the sun breaking through the trees. Now he knew more or less the way he had to go. Presently, he came to a little stream, where he drank and washed, and found some bushes with sweet sun-warmed berries to eat.

Towards noon he reached the edge of the wood and found that he had been walking along the ridge, and had travelled farther northwards than he had thought. Only then did it occur to him that he had met nobody the whole time, no hunter, no woodcutter, no charcoal burner. Here and there he had seen kilns, but they were burnt out and cold. Now he saw in the distance brownish fields and a pale wisp of smoke rising. He turned and walked more quickly down towards the valley. He was not surprised that the fields were empty. It was the end of the summer and the harvest was over, but when he got nearer he had a shock. He reached the smoke and saw that it was rising from bare earth. The fields all round were not brown, but charred and blackened, they were not reaped but burned, and here and there little heaps of ashes were still smouldering. Thin smoke was rising from them and the earth was still warm. This fire had only recently burned out. As he walked on faster and faster, till he was almost running, he came across field after field burned and charred, like wounds that had just stopped bleeding, and above them the sun, the clear sky, the mild air. He came round a hillock and caught sight of the village to which presumably these fields belonged, and stopped involuntarily. The smoke and fire, the tragedy of devasted fields and the silent desolation seemed suddenly to cry out and accuse him. He was afraid of what he would find in the village.

The houses were empty and in ruins. The roofs were smashed in and the doors torn off. Broken pitchers, plates and all sorts of pitiful domestic utensils lay scattered about. Elisha looked at the devastation in horror. It's my fault! My wicked negligence! he thought miserably. That was the only thought in his mind, he did not know why.

He was startled by a scream. A few yards further on an old woman was standing with her arms above her head screaming because she had seen him, but presently the screaming stopped and died away to a low moaning. She turned away, tottered back to the heap of earth, stones and rubble, on which she had probably been crouching until then, where she crumpled up. Then other heads and figures rose up here and there among the houses. Wherever Elisha looked they were just old men and women, only one of them was holding by the hand a single child, that stood tottering and tumbling on its fat legs, whimpering quietly. They looked at the stranger timidly and watchfully. When they saw that he was alone, possibly a wandering beggar, with wrinkled face and bristly beard, barefoot, covered with dust, unarmed, and with only a long staff in his hand, they stood still, then turned away in silence and took no further notice of him. From him they had nothing to fear and nothing to hope for. He was not worth even a glance.

Elisha stood motionless, his eyes wandering in incredulous horror from house to house, from face to face. At last he went up to the woman who had been screaming and touched here on the shoulder.

"What's happened here?"

The woman shook his hand off crossly, swallowed once or twice and said:

"Why do you ask? Can't you see?"

"Who did it?"

"They'd got us before we were awake, and what could we have done anyway?"

"Who?"

She threw up her arms and shouted: "The foreigners! Enemy soldiers and robbers. They were armed to the teeth and on horses, and they were everywhere at once."

Hearing footsteps behind him Elisha turned round. The men and women had come nearer again, and an old man asked sharply: "Don't you know that the Syrians have invaded Israel again? They did this."

"What about your men folk?"

"The King called them up. An urgent message arrived and they left the same night, and any able-bodied men who were left were either killed or captured before they knew what was happening."

"Why did you stay when the others left?"

"Where should we go? Our homes and land were here."

"And what are you going to do now?"

They merely shrugged their shoulders, some went away, some stayed and sat down on the nearest heap of rubble and took no further notice of Elisha.

"What's the name of your village?" he persisted.

"When it was still a village it was called Libna."

Elisha thought for a while.

"Which of you knows the way to the King's city?" he shouted.

Someone answered: "You have to go to Dothan and follow the main road from there."

"Is it far to Dothan?"

"Not far if you are a good walker."

"Do you know the way?"

"Yes, of course."

Elisha thought again. It was the King's fault that these poor people were abandoned to destruction and despair without any protection. His own feeling of guilt and negligence only increased his indignation.

"You come with me to Dothan, old man. I am going to see the King," he said impatiently.

The man just shrugged his shoulders again: "No, not I. You go if you like. Go wherever you like!"

Elisha shouted: "You fool! You ..." He turned to the others and banged his staff on the ground. "Listen to me! What is there for you to do here? What are you waiting for? They may come back again tomorrow, and even if they don't, you will only starve. Come with me! I will take you to the King's city."

There was no answer. After a while one of them asked gruffly:

"Why there? We have lived here all our lives, why should we go to the city?"

Another asked derisively: "Are you by any chance an envoy from the King inviting us to dine with him? Or are you rich enough to provide food for all the people here? Be off with you! We certainly have no food to spare for you!"

Elisha took no notice of him. Anger and pity had made him suddenly decide to ask them to follow him. He had no idea how he could carry out his promise, and yet all at one he felt the mysterious quiet joy, the growing certainty of success, that he always experienced when the word of the Lord came to him. He laid his hand on the shoulder of the nearest man with kindly insistence.

'Don't argue with me," he said, "and don't wait any longer. I am not a messenger from the King, but may the Lord do as much to me, if I do not take you to the King's table, so that he can look after you." He gently pulled the man to his feet.

"If you follow me, you'll be able to come back here," he shouted. "If you stay here, you're lost. Come on! Let's go! Collect whatever of your belongings you can carry. We must make haste, so that we can reach Dothan before dark."

They still hesitated, doubtful and incredulous, then suddenly one of them said:

"He's quite right. I'm going with him."

He got up and shuffled to his cottage, and one by one the others followed, and soon came back with half-filled sacks, a pitcher, a sheep skin, or a stick, whispering and excited. Elisha waited. His tired eyes showed for the first time a hint of a smile. When at last they were all ready, he set off without a word along the road leading from the village, and they followed him. Now and then one of them stopped and looked back, but they all came, men, women and the little child on his grandfather's back—a little black pitiful band, panting and groaning as they followed Elisha.

Towards evening they came across three men. When they saw Elisha they fell on their knees and kissed his hand and his cloak, for they belonged to the Sons of the Prophets. That was how the old people of Libna discovered who their leader was.

"We've been looking for you, Master," one of the three said breathlessly. "We sent a messenger to Shunem, but the people there did not know where you had gone."

Elisha said evasively:

"I was in Shunem but I left. Why shouldn't I? Where have you come from, and what do you want from me?"

"Do not be angry with us. We were looking for you because we are in danger. We come from Salsa, and Salsa does not exist any more. They attacked the village and burned it down. Don't go any further along this road in case you fall into their hands."

"Where are the people of Salsa?"

"We fled to the woods. Benhadad's men are advancing in all directions and may be anywhere. Everyone who could move at all is in the woods."

"And you have left them there?"

"We were looking for you. What else could we do?"

"Help those in need, and find your way yourselves. Enough! Let's go and find them."

One or two objected, because they were afraid, but Elisha cried: "Why are you afraid when I am not?"

Then they all followed meekly. On the way Elisha asked one of his disciples: "Were you the one who went to Shunem?"

"Yes."

"Were you at Ohad's house?"

"Yes."

"Did you tell them what happened at Salsa?"

"Yes."

"Did the King's summons come to Salsa?"

"Some days ago. The King's men were in a hurry. They rounded up all the men and took them away with them."

"And the King didn't send to Shunem?"

"That is what Ohad said. In the village they only knew what they heard from the merchant."

"They knew nothing, and I . . . I knew nothing. Was that what Joram wanted, that Shunem, that we should know nothing?"

They reached the wood and scrambled through the undergrowth and rocks further and further from the beaten track, till at last they came to a clearing. Under the trees it was already dark. Their guide uttered what sounded like a bird call, and was immediately answered from within the wood.

"Come out! Come out! We've brought help."

There was a crackling of branches here and there, and the people of Salsa crawled out. Here too there were only women, old men and a few children. They had been hiding singly, not daring to stay together or to light a fire. They came up to the guide who said proudly:

"Look, we've found the Master. He's come to lead us."

They stopped, disappointed, and a woman shouted:

"Fools! You fools! Is that what you went for? Is that what you call help?"

Another woman said: "Where is he going to lead us to? The King has taken our men away. The robbers have driven off the cattle. The corn and grape harvest have gone, and our homes are burned down. Can he give us food? Can he give us shelter? Has he any weapons? What can he do? What? I ask you!"

She gesticulated with her hands in front of Elisha's face. He stopped her and said soothingly:

"No, no! Don't blame me for your misfortunes. I can't bring your men back, nor the cattle, nor your possessions, but perhaps I can do something to keep you alive."

An old man from Libna shouted:

"He's taking us to the King, d'you hear? We're going to the King."

"Yes, we're going to the King," Elisha repeated loudly. "I want you all to come, so that he can look after you."

"It's a long way to the King's city, and even if we get there the King will not listen to us."

"And who is going to protect us from being beaten up and murdered before we get there?"

"And who is going to provide food and water for the journey?"

Elisha interrupted impatiently:

"Why are you making such a fuss? D'you know a better plan? D'you want to go on living in the woods like wild animals? Well then, if you want to stay, then stay. If you want to come, then come. I'm going on."

One of the disciples touched his arm.

"Are you sure you know best, Sir? They say that the roads and fields are full of Syrian horsemen, and we are quite unarmed. Which way do you think of going, so that we don't fall into their hands?"

"You've been living here; you ought to be familiar with by-ways and paths the Syrians don't know about. The Lord will show you the way."

He turned to the others, raised his hands above his head and shouted: "I want you to come with me, and I promise you one thing. The King will listen to you, for he will listen to me, and you shall cry out so that he hears still more, for his city is your city. It was built by your hands, by your forced labour, and your tribute. We have talked enough, it's almost evening and we have to get to Dothan. If we start from there at dawn, we can be in the King's city by evening."

Once again, grumbling and sighing, they seized their sacks and sticks and followed him.

It was already dark when they reached Dothan. The gates were shut and there was no light and no movement on the walls, but when they reached the meadow outside the gates, a voice called out of the darkness: "Halt! Who goes there?" followed by the hurried tramp of feet and the rattle of weapons.

One of the disciples ran forward and shouted: "Open the gates. Elisha is here! Do you hear? Elisha is here!"

The lights of torches appeared on the walls, and a watchman leaned over with a torch in his hand. Elisha stepped forward. Outside the gates and along the wall a deep ditch had been dug. He went as close as he could and shouted:

"It is I, Elisha! Open the gates."

"Yes, Sir . . . I'll tell the captain. We've been ordered . . ."

He jumped down from the wall and ran off. The fugitives were complaining fretfully. They had expected open gates and safety, and now the darkness and the grim preparedness of the town increased their anxiety. At last they heard footsteps returning, a little door beside the gates was opened, and a footbridge was placed across the ditch. In the doorway were two torchbearers and a little man in full armour. He bowed reverently to Elisha.

"Come in, Sir. You and your disciples are welcome. This is indeed no night to be abroad."

The waiting band crowded to the door. The captain seized a torch and held it up, asking coldly:

"Are these the sort of disciples you have now?"

Elisha answered dryly: "Yes, these are my disciples now. They come from Libna and Salsa according to my word."

"You are welcome. My house is at your disposal, as you know. For these others I have really neither room nor food. I thought you and your disciples wanted to come in, four or six or even ten, no more."

"Would you let them spend the night out here? All they want is shelter for one night."

"And tomorrow?"

"Tomorrow they are going on with me—to the King."

The captain looked at him amazed and incredulous.

"Sir, that may be very dangerous, even if there is still a road free. And the King has issued a strict command . . ."

He stopped, then suddenly made up his mind and said:

"Well, you're here. Come in. You will see for yourself that there is no more room in Dothan."

He let them in. The torchbearers shone the light into each face, but he let them all in. When they reached the market place they stopped in amazement. Dothan was not asleep. All over the square fugitives were camped and little fires were burning. Here and there amongst the crowd were goats, cows, donkeys, carts and barrows, loaded with all sorts of household goods. The crying of children mingled with the confusion of voices and the complaining of the animals.

"Has the invasion got so far?" Elisha asked the captain standing beside him.

"I don't know. A few days ago King Joram sent a message that we were to expect an attack and a siege. He ordered us to shut the gates, so that we could last out a long siege, but could I turn these people away?"

"I knew nothing about it," murmured Elisha. "No message came to Shunem."

"Will you be my guest tonight, Sir?"

"No, I will stay with these people."

"I will send you enough bread and fruit for tonight. Sorry I can't stay with you—we're very busy."

He hurried away. Elisha helped the old people of Libna and Salsa. They settled down where they could find room, then pushed their way to the well in the middle of the market place, drew water to drink and then squatted down and washed the dirt and dust from their feet, while they exchanged experiences with the others. There were refugees from Kor and Tira, from Boseth and Biblam, and from the whole countryside round Dothan. According to their account the Syrians were everywhere and had destroyed and laid waste every town and village. They did not want to stay here either, because they feared a siege. When they heard that Elisha was taking his charges to the King, more and more of them came to him asking him to take them too. To each of them Elisha said: "Anyone who wishes to may come."

Later on he sat down by one of the fires and they gathered round him, asking him questions and telling him their troubles, and he talked to them and answered them with great patience, and none doubted that he was their protector and that his word was right. After a long time, when at last they were asleep, he got up, went up to the wall and looked out over the dark land. Here and there in the distance he saw the glow of fires, and a watchman beside him muttered: "There they are, over there!"

The night was windy and overcast. Up on the wall there was great activity, sand was being brought up, stones of different sizes were being piled in heaps, torches were being dipped in tar and stacked ready, workmen were repairing damaged places. They and the soldiers came and went without taking much notice of Elisha walking round amongst them. Sometimes he was pushed aside because he was in somebody's way. Once a foreman even ordered him off the wall. Elisha did not argue, he disappeared into the shadows and walked on.

He kept thinking about the King. All this work was going on at the King's command. The call to arms had come to Libna and Salsa and Dothan, the need for men was great and messengers had obviously been sent out everywhere, but not to Shunem. Did the King know that he was at Shunem? Of course he knew, and because he knew he had not sent a messenger there. Elisha thought furiously. Once Ahab had hesitated to advance because Elisha had not yet arrived in the camp. Later, when Joram attacked Moab, he had humbled himself before the prophet and afterwards thanked him and treated him with honour, because he found water in the desert and promised victory to the unbelieving coward. Yes, that's what I did, thought Elisha. I have never been willing to believe in Israel's downfall. Every misfortune was a trial and not a judgment. This is how he shows his gratitude. He sent me no summons, no invitation, to Shunem. Why? Why? Had he forgotten all about me? Did he by any chance imagine that the voice of the Lord was silent and the prophet had withdrawn into a life of luxury, or had his prophecy become so feeble and worthless that he was no longer worth even a warning? Or was someone else proclaiming a so-called prophecy that sounded more pleasant to the King? Had the King's hatred, fear and enmity increased so much that he was handing the prophet over to the Syrians without a word, perhaps even hoping that the plunderers and pillagers would do the job that he himself dared not do?

He's throwing me away like an old gnawed bone, Elisha thought wildly. It's my fault, all my fault. Because I forgot and stayed! What have I become? Who listens to me? The poor wretches from Libna and Salsa. What can their hands or their cry achieve? I am nothing. I am getting old and have accomplished nothing. Then he heard again the whisper in the shadows and it was ice-cold:

"You are the way, the will. Go!"

Elisha stood with clenched fists. King Joram would be surprised. Elisha was coming without invitation or warning, bringing a strange band of followers, and the voice was not defeated. Then he stared into the darkness again and asked, tormented, how he was going to bring the poor people to the King, and where he would find shelter on the way? "Give me a sign," he begged with clenched teeth. "Give me a sign. Give me help. I must not fail now."

The night seemed endless. The glow of fires away on the horizon died down and vanished. On the wall it became quiet, apart from the tramping of the sentries echoing from tower to tower. Elisha was huddled against the battlements. Now and then he too fell asleep and dreamed. He saw again the heavily laden fruit trees in the garden at Shunem, Achsa's smiling face and the yearning sadness of her eyes, but the dreams seemed of things long ago like fairy tales, and turned to dark and gloomy nightmares.

He woke breathless and shivering, got up and walked up and down, came back to his place and stared vacantly out into the darkness and up at the stars in between breaks in the clouds. At last a faint breeze disturbed the drowsy silence, the first breath of the day. Dew fell, the sky became grey, and it began to get light, but it was a strange light, in which it was difficult to see. Then he realized to his astonishment that the town and the countryside were shrouded in mist, thick greyish low-lying screens of mist that concealed the meadow, the road, the trees and the fields. From out of the mist came a whispering voice, and with sudden joy he knew that he had been given the answer. He jumped up, ran down from the wall to the people sleeping in the marketplace and shouted with all his might:

"Get up! Get up! We must start at once."

He ran from one body to another, shaking the drowsy ones awake, urging on the dilatory, shouting at this one and that, until they got up and followed him out of the town, out into the grey morning, out into the mist that had come to conceal and so to save them.

It was a day of sunshine, sultry heat and wind, of thirst, exhaustion and returning fear. They made their way through the woods, and wherever they went their eyes kept glancing round restlessly and apprehensively. No one molested them, not even when at noon they reached the main road. Nevertheless they felt the presence of the enemy, for the countryside was deserted and desolate. The enemy was present in the sound of every step on the empty road, on every rock that reflected the hot glare of the sunlight, in every tree with leaves hanging limp in the noonday heat, in every quiet field. The silence and the solitude were the enemy. Perhaps Ben-hadad's men had not yet got as far as this? The refugees whispered enviously to each other that the houses that they passed were undamaged. Yet the enemy was already there. Fear and helplessness were his envoys and his horsemen. They had conquered the land before the actual spoilers arrived, for the inhabitants had gone.

In spite of all their fear they made only slow progress. Children and old people were not used to walking so far. They had brought very little water, for those who could carry anything brought their possessions with them, and the wells they came across were choked with rubble. Elisha was everywhere. He made the long journey many times over. From time to time he would carry a crying child, help an old man along, who could not go any further, or take a bundle from the back of an old woman and carry it a little way. His cloak was sticking to him, and from time to time he had to stop and mop his brow, because the sweat made his eyes smart, and rub his legs that had grown stiff and numb from fatigue and exhaustion.

One thought remained uppermost in his mind—the King! The endless journey, the heat, the thirst, and the fear were just one more crime to lay at the King's door. As they walked on further and further, he forgot more and more the enemy and the danger that threatened them. In the morning he had led his little band through the woods and accepted the necessity for detours, so that they should not be seen. Now they walked through open fields and along wide roads. The King! he thought. He must get to the King and convince him. He could not remember what he had to prove, his mind was too exhausted, but he felt a vague unspoken certainty that this journey was a trial of strength, a trial and a test. He had to place this handful of wretched peasants into the unwilling hands of the King, he had to pass the test, for it was the beginning. The night and the sign of the mist proved that the decisive hour was coming.

He walked on and on. As the sun was setting, the hill of Samaria rose before them, the steep promontory with the white specks of houses and the dark zig-zag of the fortress walls. The city was still a long way away, but they could see it at last, so they were almost there. Their steps lightened, they had won through.

They still had met nobody. They had already reached the fields and gardens of Samaria—these were empty and stripped of crops. Here and there a field had been burned, charred stubble crackled beneath their feet, and this and their own hoarse voices were the only sounds in the silence. Now they had reached the foot of the hill. In the dusk they could see smoke rising from the city, soon they could make out figures on the wall, that bobbed up and disappeared again. Now at last they must have been seen. They talked more loudly, they were in safety, what could happen now?

They panted up the last few yards, like cattle going home, but when they reached the gate, they met the same disappointment as at Dothan. Here, too, nobody appeared on the wall or in the tower above the gates. The great gates were shut and barricaded, and although they could hear the footsteps of the sentries, they could not see them, and it was clear that nobody wanted to see the refugees.

Elisha had not expected anything else. He scrambled over the tree-trunks and heaped up stones, that had been set up in a half circle outside the gates, and hammered with both fists on the door.

"Let us in! D'you hear? Open the gate!"

His voice was a hoarse croak and shouting hurt his throat. There was no answer, so he struck the gate with his staff.

"Open the gates!" he repeated. "Guards! Are you blind and deaf? Open the gates!"

The crowd behind him joined in shouting: "Open the gates! Open the gates!"

A head appeared between the battlements and a sharp voice called down: "Quiet! Who's hammering on the gate? Go away! No one may enter the city. Go back where you came from."

They turned angrily to Elisha.

"Did you hear that? Did you hear what he said?"

Elisha took a deep breath.

"Go back and fetch your captain, you dolt, and make haste," he shouted back. "It is Elisha who wants to come in."

"Elisha?"

"Elisha, the prophet," the crowd shouted, "Yes, Elisha, the prophet. Are you going to open the gate?"

It all seemed like an uncanny repetition. The running footsteps on the wall, the long wait and at last the creaking opening of a little narrow door in the main gate. They crowded round breathlessly, then fell back. In the doorway were two soldiers with crossed spears, and behind them several more.

"Where is Elisha?"

Elisha stepped forward.

"Here I am."

Between the two soldiers stood a young man in simple armour but with the King's badge on his arm. He said excitedly:

"My Lord Elisha! How did you get here at such a time, and who are these with you?"

"Refugees. Why do you ask? Are your sentries asleep, Captain, or so blind that they did not see my little band a long time ago? Can't you see yourself that they are women and feeble old men without arms? Open the gates so that they can rest."

"The King ordered yesterday that the gates should be shut. The enemy is near and the city is overcrowded. Who is to feed them all? What are women and old men to do here? They were safer in the country."

"What nonsense you talk, you stupid!" shouted Elisha. "Don't you know what is happening in the country? Where are these people to go? Their villages are destroyed. Are they to ask Ben-hadad to feed them? Open the gates at once."

The captain's face turned red.

"I respect your age, my Lord Elisha, and so I will forget what you said. The King gives me orders and I obey them."

Elisha stared at him.

"You can't do otherwise. I understand," he said scornfully. "You don't know any better, so send a messenger at once to the King and tell him that Elisha is asking to be let in, Elisha and the group with him. Tell him that, d'you hear? And hurry!"

The captain thought a minute, then answered reluctantly: "I'll do that for you. Wait for the answer."

The soldiers quickly put their spears forward and stepped back, shutting the door. The refugees heard the bolts being shot. They crowded round Elisha, some weeping loudly, others complaining: "Why did you bring us here? What will become of us? We'd have been better off staying in our ruins or in Dothan."

"Have patience! Wait a little!" Elisha cried desperately. "I'll stake my life that you will be let in."

"How will you persuade the King, when you yourself are waiting outside?"

"I will make him let us in. Have patience."

He went and sat down on the nearest rock. He had no strength left in his arms and legs, and his whole body was consumed by a burning irresistible longing for sleep and oblivion. At the same time he was conscious of a tormenting wakefulness and tension that would not give him a moment's peace.

Darkness fell. The children whimpered in their sleep. Here and there one of the old people was asleep too, leaning against a stone or a tree stump. At last they heard the sound of approaching footsteps, and a voice called from the tower into the darkness.

"Elisha, are you asleep? Elisha!"

Elisha dragged himself up.

"Here I am. I am not asleep."

"You are permitted to enter."

"You see!" Elisha cried to the waiting refugees. "Keep your spirits up. In a short time you will be allowed in also. I will not stay without you. I am going to the King and he will not refuse me."

The little door was pushed open. One man only was standing in the doorway with a single torchbearer behind him.

"Welcome to the King's city, my Lord Elisha!" he said.

Elisha listened startled. The man was standing with his back to the light. His face was in shadow, but the voice was familiar, its hardness, its sharp high-pitched tone, its sinister, restrained, artificial brightness.

"Welcome! Jehu is delighted to see the Master again."

"Jehu!" Elisha gasped. "At last! Yes, you may be delighted, but I had to shout and beg to be let in!"

Jehu's smile of malicious amusement remained.

"War, Sir. That was the order."

He stepped forward, seized Elisha's hand, bowed quickly and kissed it and stood up again.

"You want to see the King, Sir?"

"I want these to be let in, whom he abandoned in their distress, and whom I have brought here for him to care for. Must I go to Joram to get this gate open?"

Jehu looked at him with narrowed eyes. He thought a little while.

"Yes, go to King Joram and speak to him yourself," he replied.

Then after a short pause he said, as though to soften the abruptness of his answer: "Permit me to escort you to him."

They walked in silence up the steep and narrow street between the dark houses. Elisha's forehead was deeply furrowed, his lips were tight, and with every step he banged his staff loudly on the ground, with a savage effort to control the anxiety, which his reception and now the unusual silence, and the darkness of the city produced in him. He was pursued and surrounded by phantoms, the memory of that Jehu who had sat beside him by the fire listening to his words in the night before Aphek, the memory of Ahaziah with his evil haughty message, and the cunning whisper of Jehu silencing his protest. Ahaziah had become king in his father's place and soon after had fallen to his death. The house of Ahab must perish! Ahaziah died and his dynasty remained. And then the memory of the Woman, who here in this city had shamed and humiliated the prophet. It seemed only yesterday. Perhaps at this moment Jezebel was waiting to deny him access to the King again. She had Joram under her thumb as she had had Ahab, and Jehu would not talk.

Elisha was waiting for a word from Jehu, a word that would tell him more than the polite and guarded greeting at the gate, a sign that the present was as the past, a proof that Jehu was not hiding anything from him, but Jehu remained obstinately silent, and Elisha was unwilling to question him. Every question would lower him in Jehu's eyes. He was supposed to know without asking. What he did see, however, was strange and puzzling. There was no light anywhere, not a sound, not a single person, except for armed guards at every corner. Jehu continued in silence by his side, and once Elisha began to wonder anxiously whether Jehu was really acting as a ceremonial escort, or whether he was perhaps bringing a prisoner to the King to be silenced at last for ever.

He stopped and asked softly and accusingly: "Jehu, what does all this mean?"

Jehu stopped beside him.

"What are you referring to?" he asked quickly.

"This silence and emptiness. What has happened to the city? Where's the overcrowding?"

"The King's order."

Elisha said bitterly: "You talk in riddles. Why don't you talk to me as you used to?"

Jehu laughed quietly.

"King Joram is afraid of his people," he said hurriedly. "He is to blame, because he neglected the things he should have done, and let himself be taken by surprise. The city is crowded with fugitives. Who knows what they might do, if they were allowed to run loose in the streets? There are hot-heads among them, and desperate men who make trouble against the King. Joram's order is that nobody may leave the house after sunset. No lights or fires may be lit. It's to save wood and oil, and you can't sit talking for long in a dark and shut-up house . . ." Jehu shook his head and said dryly: "We're being besieged. The King must be severe."

"I didn't see any sign of the enemy on our way here."

"Then the Lord was good to you. They have invaded the country in great strength and are not far away."

"And is Joram's whole plan to sit here and wait for the enemy to knock at the gate? Or is he already waiting impatiently for him to come, so that he can open the gates and bid his enemy welcome? Perhaps he has learned from his father that he must welcome his enemy Benhadad as a brother. I knew at the time how much this treacherous brotherhood was worth."

Jehu urged Elisha on.

"I am in command of the King's troops," he said casually. "Perhaps it is too late. But now I am in command and Joram is following my plan. He has neglected so much, that he has no army ready to go and meet Benhadad, as Ahab did, but we can hold out here. The Syrians will never capture the city."

"And what about the country? What about the people?"

"The people, yes . . . but the city here *is* the people. It stands for the whole country. As long as the city holds out, Israel remains."

They had reached the great square in front of the palace. This was where the crowds had once celebrated the beginning of Ahab's campaign. The air had been heavy with a hundred scents, wine had flowed and oxen had been roasted. Tonight the square was empty, silent and dark. The only light came from the palace, and was reflected on the golden railings of the courtyard. The sentries jumped up as they passed. Jehu wore no badges and looked no different from his men, but they recognized him at once.

In the courtyard Jehu stopped once more and said in a low voice: "Joram is not very pleased that you have come, you must know. He didn't want to see you, but I forced him to."

"I know he's not pleased."

"But I am pleased. D'you know that too?"

"Since you say so, I know it!"

"Then don't forget it. It was I who brought you here."

He hurried on. Elisha followed him in silence, with Jehu's words in his ear. His pleasure had sounded distinctly like a threat.

Jehu obviously had access to the King at any time, for all the guards made way for him respectfully. Nor did he even have himself announced in the King's anteroom, but hurried through, pulled the curtain aside and went straight in.

The King's room was lit by many torches. The windows were open, the heavy wall coverings rustled softly in the draught and the torches glowed and smoked. Joram was standing by the window looking out into the night. Perhaps he had not heard them come in, for he did not move. Jehu waited at the door, and then said loudly and formally: "Sir, your servant Jehu and the prophet Elisha."

Joram turned slowly, gave them a brief glance, walked heavily over to his throne on the high dais and sat down. Now his face was in the light of the torches, and Elisha was shocked at the change in him. Joram had aged beyond his years, and his face was heavy and exhausted, lonely, haughty and lined with care. The King asked apathetically:

"What more does the prophet Elisha want from me?"

Jehu answered quickly, as though making an announcement: "Admission for some refugees that he has brought to your city, Sir."

Elisha raised his hand in protest and came a step nearer. He had been going to say something quite different, but now he said as quietly as the King had spoken: "You sent out messengers all over the country to summon your men to the army."

Joram said nothing.

"No messenger came to Shunem, where I was staying."

Joram still said nothing.

"The King knew that I was staying at Shunem, and he needed all the men except those of Shunem?"

As Joram still did not answer, he said more loudly: "Does the King not need me?"

Now at last Joram raised his eyes and looked straight at Elisha. "No, I no longer need you," he said with scarcely concealed anger.

He got up as if to avoid Elisha's answer, went to the window, turned back again and stood in the middle of the room with legs astride.

"What do you want here? A long time ago, when I succeeded my brother, I imagined that you would stay at my side in friendship and not like you were to my father or to Ahaziah. Then your word was counsel and support to me, but you left me, I knew where you went and how you spoke. I have ample evidence that you are my enemy, that your real word is only a curse aimed at my downfall. I have enemies enough. No, I do not need you, and you should be glad if I forget you."

"Is it my fault that you do not obey the word of the Lord? The curse is the Lord's answer to your conduct. I only speak the word of the Lord."

"The word of the Lord!" Joram repeated scornfully. "Yes, that is always your pretext. You believe in your Lord, because you want to believe in your own position as his chosen prophet. You speak and it becomes the word of the Lord."

Joram climbed up to his throne again and sat down, and as he went on talking he kept striking his right hand on the arm of the chair, as though he were trying to drive every word into it.

"You travel about the country. Tell me, haven't you noticed any changes? I wanted to obey your word, so I have broken down the altars which were an offence to you. For a long time my mother has had to put up with the dismissal of her beloved priests. She threatened me with the vengeance of her gods, but I did not care. I did not bother about this god or that, for I had other things to do, and why should I quarrel with my people Israel about gods? I did this because you demanded it, but as for you and your disciples, has it done me any good in your eyes? You go about making trouble just as before and telling everybody that the King is acting wickedly. You stir up the people against me, so that they refuse me service and tribute and behave even worse than in my father's and brother's time. Now at last I know what you are after, prophet! I have known it for some time. The word of the Lord is to be your sceptre. You want to rule over Israel in the King's place. That is why you will not let the King alone."

Joram leaned back and said haughtily: "I think it is clear at last who rules in Israel, and anyone who does not know, I'll show him!" He jumped up and shouted in sudden rage:

"You are betraying me, Elisha, and now you push your way in here and dare to ask if I need you! I need you so little that I do not even arrest you and leave you to rot in my dungeon!"

Elisha stood motionless during this long tirade, only his fists kept opening and closing. Now he said quietly and scornfully: "You may possibly not need me, and you may in your blindness even arrest me. Do you not need your people either?"

Joram looked up in surprise.

"Do you need your people so little that you leave them defenceless to your enemy, look on while their fields and homes are devastated, and even lock your gates when they flee to you? Do you complain that the people do not obey your orders? Look I have brought you some of your people—women, children and old men, whom you were going to forget, and I have to come to your throne to get admission for the weak, whom your arm should protect. Indeed I tell you. . . ."

"Tell me nothing, you ignorant fellow!" Joram interrupted him. "Do you know what is going on in Samaria? All this happened overnight and nothing was ready."

"Whose fault was that?"

"It is your fault and the fault of your rebels that my storehouses are empty, yet I have taken thousands into the city and feed them every day."

He jumped up, and the supple vigour of his heavy body was surprising and frightening. He went to the window, pointed out and said peremptorily: "Look here!"

Elisha looked out. The night was dark and starless, but in the far distance red stars were gleaming, little fires, hardly noticeable, but in an endless line, and still further away, in the dim distance, already veiled by the night mist, were the smoke and dull glow of bigger fires.

"Do you see them?" asked the King. "That is where they are."

"Whose fault is it?" asked Elisha again.

"Is it my fault that I believed in peace?"

"You did not believe in peace, King Joram. You simply forgot your duty. Look! You boasted that you had thrown down altars, cut down groves and dismissed a lot of parasites from your table. What do altars and groves and priests matter to you? It was easy to do, because they mean nothing to you. You said yourself that you had other things to do. You just wanted to pay tribute, to buy respite for your sins. The Lord does not accept part payments and there is no bargaining with his word. There is no common ground between you and me."

The King was still standing looking out of the window.

"There they are," he said. "Tomorrow evening they will be a bit nearer. Two or three days more and they will be encamped in the field outside the city." He turned round, leaned against the wall with his arms folded.

"I had to hear what you had to say. Now go! I did not send for you and your mob. Take them away, wherever you like. They shall not come into the city."

"You refuse them admission?"

"You heard what I said."

Joram walked aimlessly round the room and at last came back to his throne.

"I want to save the city. We cannot defeat Benhadad by force of arms, but perhaps we can by patience. Our good city shall be a fortress, not a trap. You have brought your mob here against my orders, now take them somewhere else. Take them away this very night out into the country, wherever you like. There they may perhaps find shelter and peace. How will it help if they stay here? Enough! You have heard my order. Go!"

Elisha drew back involuntarily. He looked away from the King and round the room, at the rich splendour of the wall-hangings, the luxurious wealth of the furniture, the delicate carving of the panelling, the shining marble of the floor. He looked up wide-eyed and horrified.

"I did not hear your command. I don't want to hear your cruel words. You sit here in splendour, willing to condemn the poor. I will forget all that has happened, but this decision of yours I cannot forget. And so I say, The Lord will do to you and your family what you are doing to Israel. I will not go away until you change your mind."

Joram's answer came swiftly, as though he had been waiting impatiently for Elisha's threat.

"You defy me! You dare to threaten me again! Very well, I will change my mind, and teach you a lesson. Jehu! Jehu! Fetch your men! Fetch the guard! Tell them to arrest this fellow."

Jehu was still standing at the door, silent and motionless with his hands tucked into his belt. Now he bowed low, looked up again and said submissively:

"Sir, to hear is to obey, of course! But would you not be merciful and forget your anger? The people waiting at the gate are very few in number. Are my men to see that you turn them away? Just think! They would see in them their own women and children and fathers, whom they left behind at your command. They will not understand your wisdom, but if you show pity, they will praise you. Let this handful in, I will look after them."

Joram shouted angrily: "Didn't you hear? I gave the order that your men should arrest this fellow. What are you waiting for?"

"Sir!" said Jehu cautiously and quietly. "Perhaps my men will not obey such an order. He is a great man and they revere him." He came forward and said quickly: "Take my advice, Sir. Forget what has been said here. Let these few people in, and let the prophet speak a message from you. Then his word will be as your word. This is no time to show your disagreement publicly, but your strength."

The King's face fell, and he stared at Jehu with trembling lips. It became once more quiet in the room. The only sound was the crackling of the torches, and the rustling of the curtains. Then Joram sighed and said helplessly: "You are pressing me. I gave you power and the command to defend my city, my servant Jehu. Was I too hasty? Now you are turning my own words and orders against me. Is that really your advice, and will you take the responsibility?"

"Yes."

The King kept his eyes fixed on Jehu.

"I don't want to hear any more about it today," he said flatly. "Report to me tomorrow. I rely on you. Go!"

Jehu bowed low once again, seized Elisha's arm, drew him hurriedly away and did not stop till they reached the courtyard below.

"Forgive me, Father!" he said softly.

Elisha looked at him in bewilderment.

"What have I to forgive you for?"

"What you said was true. Who else would dare to talk to the King like that? But I knew how I could make him give way. And now you will speak his message. Forgive me."

"You are very clever, my son Jehu," said Elisha gloomily.

Jehu did not answer. He raised his head and looked up once more at the windows of the King's room. He was smiling again.

10

NO one knew the truth except Elisha and Jehu, and Jehu was nowhere to be seen these days. Elisha realized, with an increasing and intolerable sense of humiliation, that the King cared nothing about him.

All that the people knew was that after a long time Elisha came back with the King's gracious permission for the fugitives to enter the city, and that was that. In their hearts they had been sure of the outcome, in spite of whatever doubts were expressed, and once again the word and reputation of the prophet had been vindicated. They knew nothing of his rejection and anger and reproach, or the King's order for his arrest that Jehu had foiled.

Elisha kept quiet and waited. When he came away from the palace, he could see only two alternatives before Joram. He could take Jehu's advice and act outwardly as if no angry words had passed; he could accept the prophet's word and invite him to attend him at the palace, as in the case of earlier wars; so he could place upon him responsibility for the royal behaviour. Or he must at last silence the rebellious prophet once and for all to prevent him from stirring up any more trouble. Elisha was waiting for the King's summons in order to refuse it. He knew what was in Joram's heart. Joram was Jezebel's son—foreign, haughty, suspicious and tyrannical. All the favour and honour that he had formerly shown to the prophet and his disciples had been nothing but calculated strategy. Perhaps now at last his patience would give out and he would take action against the prophet and so alienate the people finally from himself. No summons came from the King and nobody came to arrest him. Joram seemed simply to have forgotten that Elisha was in the town.

On the night of his arrival the enemy fires had still been far away and hardly visible, and during the day dust and mist made it difficult to see, but by sundown next day they had come much nearer. In the evening every separate fire could be clearly seen, and the men up on the wall could count them and calculate how many men were probably sitting round each fire. Two days later the Syrians had reached the city and were encamped at the foot of the hill. Their shouts and bugle calls, the clang of weapons, the neighing of horses and the clatter of chariots were clearly audible on the wall. They were hardly more than a stone's throw from the advanced posts of Israel.

Joram had done little to hinder the advance of the enemy, but inside the city he was not idle. In the early dawn his overseers collected together everyone who was not completely helpless and distributed them wherever there was work to be done. Here and there the walls were still being repaired, trenches and covered ways were being dug on the hillside. Wells, storage tanks and culverts were being made watertight. Wood, stones and torches were being brought up on to the wall. Smiths, saddlers and carpenters were busy repairing weapons and armour. Stocks of arrows, spears and bows were being carried up on to the walls and embrasures. And long lines of carts and pack animals from the country still came creaking up the hillside laden with stores and live cattle for the King's storehouses and stables.

His disciples had taken Elisha to a house in the lower town. Soon many people came to see him and listen to him, some seeking advice and comfort, others wanting nothing more than to sit at his feet and listen, and a few idle and curious onlookers, who only wanted to be able to boast that they had seen him. Most of them had to go away disappointed, for during the hours when they were free to go about the streets the prophet was hardly ever to be seen. Even the disciples in the house only knew that he went away before dawn and did not return till late at night, when the streets were already deserted and the city was asleep. In the very first week on one occasion he did not return at night at all, and did not appear till late in the evening of the next day, obviously very exhausted, covered with dust and dirt, his feet scratched with thorns. He went at once to his room. They heard him pacing up and down for a while, then all was quiet. In the morning he had disappeared again.

Nobody dared to ask questions, and so they did not learn that Elisha left the city every day. He was not sure himself why he went; he only knew that he felt stifled by the city and its houses, walls and narrow streets. It seemed alien and oppressive, he felt powerless and lost within the walls, and the word of the Lord did not speak to him there. He was not afraid of the besieging army at the foot of the hill, but the city felt hostile and menacing. The loaded carts and pack animals were still coming in through the south gate, and scarcely anyone took any notice of the old peasant with the bald head and bushy beard going out with them, with a knapsack on his back and driving a shabby donkey.

The donkey grazed during the day in a clearing in the woods. Sometimes Elisha stayed near him, sitting for long hours at the foot of a tree waiting. All round him were the little woodland noises, the fitful rustling of the trees, the crackling of drying leaves, the buzzing of insects, the call of birds or the footsteps of an animal. In the stillness confused and troubled dreams and visions rose up in his mind, a vague groping for a plan of action. There was so much to do, so much to finish. A time for decision was approaching and here he was sitting in an agony of crippled helpless inaction. There was no clear vision, no clear message, only silence.

He would get up, restless and depressed, and make a wide detour down into the valley, approaching at some point the Syrian camp, that was growing bigger every day. There he crouched among the bushes, watching and listening. Benhadad and his captains seemed unconcerned, the flanks of the camp were hardly guarded in the daytime. Elisha was able to creep close enough to hear the soldiers voices and watch their games and exercises. Once he made a still wider circle out into the country in the rear of the enemy, avoiding his supply routes. He found the country deserted. There were the devastated fields, the choked wells, the ruined cottages, but where were the people who had farmed this land? Had the enemy carried them away? Had they all fled? Where were they? Later he saw in the distance many carts moving in the direction of the camp with horsemen guarding them carelessly and confidently. Otherwise he met nobody at all.

The first rains came. The King had expected a siege and storming attacks. He had strengthened his fortifications and posted all his military strength on the walls and towers of the city, but Benhadad did not seem to be contemplating an attack. His camp just grew bigger and bigger, reinforcements kept arriving, and gradually the men on the wall realized with apprehension that he was planning to subdue the city in another way. Benhadad was taking his time and waiting for them to starve. He began to construct trenches and earthworks round the city and manned them with archers and artillery. His horsemen made deeper and deeper forays into the surrounding country. One day the carts and pack animals, that had hitherto been reaching the city, although in ever diminishing numbers, did not appear at all. Next morning Joram sent out a strong troop by the south gate to destroy Benhadad's new outposts and positions and keep at least one supply road open. The sortie was unexpected and successful. The party brought back a few carts, some captured weapons and other things, but two days later the King had to admit that he could only surprise his enemy once. His men returned from the second sortie with heavy losses. The Syrians were fully prepared everywhere in great strength, and it was impossible to make a breach anywhere. The circle round the city was closed.

When Elisha came back that evening, Jehu was waiting for him outside his house. He had been waiting some time. He drew Elisha deeper into the shadow.

"Why do you remain, silent, Father?" he asked.

Elisha looked at him with sad eyes.

"I haven't got to speak, and I have no word to give."

Jehu looked keenly at him.

"Do you regret bringing your little band here? Do you want to leave?" he asked cautiously.

"I regret that I came. Perhaps I could have achieved more elsewhere, but now I don't want to leave. What do you think?"

"Don't go out and about any more, Father."

"You haven't bothered much about what I was doing, and I haven't seen you for a long time. What do you want from me now?"

"I know what you do and where you go, and that you have been going out of the city with the carriers. Now the city is surrounded and you will be in danger if you try to go out alone. I could perhaps help you, but if you will stay, I should be glad." Jehu stopped, then went on cautiously in a distinctly harder tone: "You are witness and judge, Sir. Now that our time of trial is coming you must stay in order to see and judge."

Elisha dropped his eyes.

"I do not judge. The Lord judges," he said flatly.

"Then tell me. What does the Lord say to you at this time? So many are waiting for you to speak."

"Now is the hour of silence. The Lord does not answer according to your wish or command." Still more softly he added: "I am waiting also."

Jehu bowed formally.

"I understand. As you say, Sir. Jehu knows how to wait."

Benhadad's first attack came some weeks later, and because it had been watched for and expected for so long in vain, it came as a surprise and was only beaten off with great difficulty.

The people were wakened in the early dawn by the hoarse clangour of trumpets and the shouting of a thousand voices in the valley. They guessed what it meant, and cowered in fear in their houses and shelters. While the sentries on the wall were sounding the alarm, Benhadad's shock troops had already crept through the mist up to the advance posts at the foot of the hill and attacked them with a hail of arrows, stones and pitch-impregnated faggots.

Before the troops knew what was happening, they were overrun by the armoured men who followed the shock troops and pressed on in close formation up the hill. They were carrying long ladders, and behind them came groups of unarmed slaves pulling heavy catapults with drag ropes. Soon the first stones and arrows were falling on the walls, and anyone looking down from there might well fear that the might of Benhadad, once set in motion, was irresistible and unconquerable. Rank after rank, file after file, troop after troop, left the camp and climbed and creaked up the hill.

Joram had been relying on the watchfulness and stubborn resistance of his advance posts. It was their task to break the first assault and gain time for the defenders inside the city. That had been a vain hope. The advance posts had achieved little against the superior forces, but the hill gave some help. The ascent was steep and long, and although the advance of the armoured troops was terrifying, it was too slow.

By the time they got within range, the defenders were ready and the wall was fully manned. The first waves of attackers were received with arrows and spears, boiling water and burning torches. In a few minutes the field outside the wall was strewn with dead and wounded. The catapults certainly did considerable damage, and then the armoured troops began to set up the ladders. Here and there they succeeded in spite of all resistance, and for a dreadful time it almost seemed as if they would overcome the defenders by sheer weight of numbers. For every ladder that was set on fire or pushed down from the wall with the men on it, two fresh ladders were set up in another place.

Once a furious shout went up from Israel's ranks. One of the big catapults was set on fire by the torches. The slaves jumped clear in terror, let go of the drag ropes, and the flaming monster began to roll and went bumping and creaking down the slope, cutting a wide fiery swath through the advancing men. Later they succeeded in putting several more out of action, but even that brought no decision.

By midday the fury of the assault had hardly slackened, and the defenders began to tire and to despair. The air was filled with steam and smoke, heavy with the smell of burning wood and scorched flesh, bursting with the yelling of a hundred voices, orders, shouts and cries of pain, the crackling of fires, the whistling of arrows and spears and the dull whine and crash of stones.

They did not know what the shrill and repeated trumpet call meant, that sounded suddenly from the valley below and echoed all round the walls. They only saw that the attack suddenly stopped. The armoured troops withdrew from the walls. They were not running away. After the long hours of fighting they were retiring yard by yard in good order, without having forced a decision. The trumpet call meant that their master had decided to break off the attack for the day. They went back as if the signal meant just the end of a day's work. Soon they had withdrawn out of range, leaving behind them many dead, charred ladders, shattered catapults, and countless bows and arrows, covering the churned up earth. Yet even in retreat their power seemed disastrously menacing.

In Samaria, however, there was great rejoicing. Soon the people were streaming out of their houses and cottages up on to the walls to see the destruction and the victory. There were still many of their own dead and wounded lying about. Fires were still burning in the roofs here and there, and there was a good deal of damage on the wall itself. But that was not what they wanted to see. They looked down from the wall and enjoyed the devastation on the field, the dead and the scattered weapons. In their eyes every number was multiplied a hundred times. They were jubilant and it was some time before the King's men were able to drive the crowd back into the city. For this evening Joram gave them their liberty and the streets were filled with merrymakers. They had all shared in the victory. Many of them prophesied that by the morning the Syrians would have gone, tents and camp and all.

On the wall, however, there was feverish activity. Damage was hurriedly being repaired, there were fresh weapons, stones and torches to prepare, and sand and water to fetch. The defenders were exhausted. All available men had been in action and their numbers were dangerously reduced. There was not time to rest. The King and his captains did not believe Benhadad had departed. His next attack might well come the very next morning.

The attack did not come, either next morning or the day after.

Scouts were sent out and reported no sign of withdrawal or any special preparations. Benhadad remained there day after day waiting. From time to time news came of minor skirmishes between outposts, involving some half dozen men, but that was all.

Hunger came.

Hunger crept up on them like a suffocating fog in the night. The danger of starvation had been there all the time. It had been the real enemy from the beginning. They hardly noticed its approach, till, before they knew where they were, it was master of the city.

The market had been empty for some time. There was nothing to buy, and nobody had any stores in the house. The wealthy and the King's courtiers and favourites perhaps still had plenty, so it was rumoured, but nobody knew for certain.

The King's troops were guarding the walls, waiting and staring at the enemy, who was also waiting. On the previous day Joram had attempted a sortie with his best men. A few hours later they had been driven back with heavy casualties without ever reaching the main camp.

The King's storehouses were guarded. One day at noon a crowd gathered outside the palace demanding bread. The guards could not control them, for they were too hungry to be afraid of them. The King came out and ordered food to be distributed, meagre rations for each one, just to quieten the mob for one day at least, but what was the use? By the evening, by next day, hunger was master again. The King said that all the food in the city must be kept for the fighting men, but they were the husbands and fathers of the starving people, they passed on what they received, and it was not enough.

The only thing that did not go short was water, for it rained heavily. The water tanks were filled again, but what was there to boil? There was no corn, no flour, all the animals had gone, the donkeys, sheep and cows had been slaughtered a long time ago. Jezebel was rich, they said, and saw to it that her gods and her priests did not starve. She probably had some animals hidden away for the sacrifices. That was the rumour, but who could tell if it were true? Someone said that the day before a wealthy man had given as much as eighty shekels for a donkey's head—but who was the simpleton who got hold of it, and then sold it for silver instead of eating it himself?

Hunger reigned. Soon its victory would be complete. How could starving men defend the city? Tomorrow or the next day they would have to go out and throw themselves on Benhadad's mercy.

Elisha awoke in the early dawn. The door and window of his room were open and he shivered in the cold damp air. He struggled slowly into consciousness, for he was exhausted by the long days and nights and by hunger. He need not have suffered as much as the others, because in some miraculous way, his faithful followers kept bringing him presents of food, a piece of dry bread, a little bowl of thin soup, a handful of flour or some dried fruit. Goodness knows where they got them. They brought them in return for his help, even though they knew that he would not eat them himself. As soon as it was light he would set out with the gifts in his hands and distribute them to people who were in greater need than the rest. This went on day after day. Often he was unrecognized, sometimes a few people followed him, watching him sitting beside a feverish child or helping to dress a wound or perhaps settling a quarrel. There was a good deal of quarrelling in the streets. Suffering had made people bitter and quarrelsome. Every day Elisha went from house to house, avoiding the neighbourhood of the palace and the wealthy districts, walking about the lower town, looking, questioning, and helping. He spoke little, just a word of comfort and encouragement, as any one might do, and if they became insistent he only answered: "Wait a bit . . . hold on," and went on his way. His eyes burned, his limbs grew weary, hunger cramped his stomach, but he did not rest until the evening.

During the first few weeks of the siege he had refused to see anyone. No one remembered any more just when he abandoned his seclusion and began to go out. Perhaps it was only another kind of loneliness. Many people knew that he was in the city, and were surprised and disappointed that he did not say and do more. He had not been up on to the wall, for he had no word of encouragement for the sentries and defenders.

In the evening the older men often came to his house and sat at his feet, speaking hesitantly and cautiously and asking questions. How was all this suffering to end, and why did no help come? What about Judah's friendship and their alliance? Where was Ethbaal, the devoted father of Jezebel? Israel was isolated and would perish alone.

Elisha looked up once and said: "Have patience." Another time he said: "Wait! This may be a time of trial, but it is not yet doom." Later he said: "The Lord's will is eternal. He will fulfil his purpose." Then he was silent again, and they could understand neither his words nor his silence. Sometimes when he saw the burning hunger in their eyes, their haggard faces and emaciated limbs, he would get up and go to his room, to the hard couch that was both his refuge and his place of torment.

They revered him and so no one dared to follow him. No one saw him fling himself down and cover his eyes with his hands, so that he could pretend that the darkness was caused by his hands and the night, and was not the blindness of his soul.

For weeks something had been stirring within him. After a long period of torpor he was conscious of tension and uneasiness, but it was different from other times, when he felt the voice was about to speak to him. There was no exaltation, no illumination, no hot or icy expectation. Visions came and went before his blind eyes, and he did not know how to interpret them, a hundred paths ending in an impenetrable blank wall. His aching head was wide awake, thinking, questioning, protesting, sometimes with frantic impatience, sometimes with hesitation, because he did not dare to believe what he wanted to believe. He asked himself whether it really was the voice that was whispering within him, and why there was no illumination, no sudden happy compulsion and certainty. There were too many voices, nothing but groping and seeking, questioning and speculating, choosing and rejecting. Sometimes he felt quite sure of his path, the next moment all was confusion again. All he knew was that the day was approaching when he must speak. He was convinced that the hour was at hand. And so he shivered in his loneliness, and did not know whether it was from fear or resistance, uncertainty or impatience.

He got up that morning with an effort, went to the window and stood there breathing deeply in spite of the cold. During the night it had been raining again and the sky was grey. The streets were still empty. Water was dripping monotonously from the roofs into the puddles. He turned away again, scooped some water out of the basin, bathed his eyes and forehead, and flung his cloak about him ready to go out. There was an aching band round his head, his sleep had been short and unrefreshing, troubled by strange dreams. He was exhausted and tormented by restlessness. He made his way between the sleepers lying outside his door and in the outer room and went out. Outside he leaned against the wall again waiting, for his eyes were burning and the streets and houses were whirling madly round. Then he clenched his teeth and dragged himself away. A vague restlessness brooded and stirred within him, aimless and gloomy. He knew he must somehow find out the meaning of the Lord's will, but he could not. He walked slowly. Here he usually turned downhill, where the poor and destitute lived, but today he walked on up the hill. Somehow in the mist that clouded his eyes, in the urgency of his enfeebled legs, there was a purpose. This day was different from all the days before.

He came to the great square. There were people there already, women with whimpering children, beggars and sick people. What were they doing here so early, sitting or standing about outside the golden railings of the palace, staring and waiting? Occasionally a voice called out: "Now he is coming. He always comes at this time." Someone else shouted: "The King!" Elisha started. Had he perhaps come here because Joram came out at this time? Why today? Why not yesterday, or weeks ago, and what was to happen today? He leaned against a pillar and waited trembling. Presently a wing of the great gate opened and Joram came down the steps with his attendants. Elisha concealed himself involuntarily in order to avoid Joram's eyes. Not yet! Not yet! he thought.

There was no need to hide. Joram was obviously quite used to finding a crowd waiting for him. He walked on as if he did not see them at all, with downcast eyes, hands thrust into his sword-belt, and surrounded by guards and attendants, who cleared a broad path in front of him. The crowd pressed forward shouting: "Bread!

Give us bread! We're starving!" and "Peace! Give us peace!" More and more voices joined in, louder and louder. The faces of the guards hardened, they raised their lances to keep back the pushing crowd, and maintain a wide gap between the King and the people.

Elisha stood and stared. The King had passed by without looking up once. His face showed no emotion, he was deaf to the shouts, as though he did not want to be reminded of the distress, the hopelessness and misery. The shouting grew louder: "Give us food! Our children are dying!" Elisha raised his arms. It was as if a veil had been torn aside. At last he understood the meaning of the word he had to speak. It was as though the people were shouting to him, not to the King but to him. They were accusing him because he had not proclaimed the word of the Lord sooner, because he had only offered easy comfort and advice, and had not spoken the word they had been waiting for. The days, hours, nights, his dreams and visions and suffering, his impatience, the expectation and anger of ages, all culminated in this moment. With his head held high he opened his lips and shouted, and his voice was louder than all the clamour. The people standing round drew back in terror, and in the sudden silence they heard:

"Hear the word of the Lord to Israel! The Lord is speaking through my lips. Israel is not to blame, only the King. It is not Israel that he is going to destroy, only her King. Have patience. The doom is not meant for you. The King is guilty, the King to whom you are appealing. The curse is upon him."

The words ended in a gasp. To Elisha's ears it was the old prophecy, Elijah's prophecy. He himself had already proclaimed it to the King and repeated it to his disciples, but he had never before spoken it openly to the people. He had never publicly and unmistakably put the guilt and the curse upon the King. Now it had happened, now he had obeyed the ominous command. Had the King heard what he said? He looked up, and only then did he become aware of the breathless silence around him. The King had already reached the edge of the square beyond the crowd, but he too had stopped and turned round. Had he heard the words? Elisha moved forward with tottering steps. The Lord's command was that he should repeat the prophecy to the King's face. The crowd bowed before him and made way for him as though he himself were the King.

Before he could reach the King there was a sudden movement in the crowd. A woman had broken through the line of guards and flung herself down at the King's feet. The guards tried to remove her, but she clung to Joram's legs, shouting with drooling lips:

"King, O King! Don't you see? Help me! Give me justice!"

She pointed vaguely with her arm towards the crowd.

"She took my son yesterday for us to eat, and she promised her son for today, and now she has hidden him."

Elisha pressed forward appalled. He saw Joram's face turn ashen, as he drew back with his hand to his mouth, then answered in anger and desperation:

"How can I help you, if the Lord does not help? From my granary? From my winepress? They're empty."

With a sudden movement he pulled his cloak open.

"Look!" he shouted. "That evil man abuses me and puts the blame on me, but I am like you. I am poor, poor like you. I have no more than you."

They saw that beneath his cloak he was wearing just a long garment of sackcloth such as his foot soldiers wore.

The woman was silent. The crowd stood breathless. Elisha stepped forward:

"That is only the beginning of your punishment. The hand of the Lord will destroy you and your whole house."

Joram stared at him, his mouth opening and shutting. When he spoke his voice was bursting with sheer hate:

"The Lord have mercy on me if I do not have Elisha's head this very day!"

Elisha did not answer. He turned away as if he had not heard what the King said. He heard me, he thought wearily. He could not think beyond that: he was empty, stifled by indifference and exhaustion. The word had been spoken, it had happened, the decision had been taken. It was the end, and also a beginning. He would never speak to the King again. Perhaps this word had not been enough. He walked on. A last remnant of rational thought expected a hand on his shoulder by order of the King. He walked on, not knowing what was happening behind him. Eyes followed him, then footsteps, more and more footsteps, a wall of bodies protecting him. But the King had only uttered a threat. He had not issued the order. Nothing further happened.

Elisha walked with dragging steps towards his house. People from the square followed him whispering, muttering, asking questions and shouting, but with a different sort of excitement from before, as though Elisha's public indictment of Joram had stilled their hunger and thirst, their hopelessness and despair. Elisha neither saw nor heard them, he just walked on till he reached the house and then turned once more and looked back. The sky was clouded over and it was raining, but nobody seemed to mind. The streets were crammed with people from wall to wall. Elisha turned away without a word, stumbled into the house and went to his room. He dropped on to the bed and immediately fell into a deep untroubled sleep.

When he awoke it was evening and the room was dark. He could hear low voices in the next room. His mind was now ice-clear, and he felt as if he were acutely aware of every individual fibre, cell and drop of blood in his body. He realized quite clearly, without surprise or anxiety, what had happened and what would happen. He was not afraid of the word that had been given to him, nor of the knowledge that filled his mind. He got up, went to the door and paused. The elders, who came here every evening, were sitting outside, their faces hardly discernible in the dim light of the oil lamp on the wall. They stood up and bowed low, avoiding his eyes.

"Shut the door," Elisha ordered. "You heard what he said. He will send his men to cut off my head."

One of them said: "We have been watching here while you slept, and there are many more keeping watch outside."

Another said: "Dear Master, I will hide you. Don't stay here in this house for them to find you."

Elisha answered with a faint smile: "My Master Elijah ran away when the Woman threatened him. I will stay and face the threat of her son."

Another said: "Joram will not dare! Nobody would dare lay a

hand on you. Look, it's evening and he hasn't done anything."

"He will risk it at night," answered Elisha. "This evil also is from the Lord. That is why I will not go."

They were silent. Outside in the street they could hear the murmur of many voices. Sometime later the noise suddenly increased and then stopped. They heard the clank of weapons and someone giving orders. The voices rose still louder, accompanied by the rattle of stones and angry shouting. Then the footsteps went slowly away, and all became quiet again.

There was a knock. One of the men got up and walked heavily to the door, opened the flap and peeped out. When he opened the door, two men rushed in shouting breathlessly: "The messengers from the King! They could not get near the house. The people blocked the way, and they had to go away again."

Elisha said quietly: "Shut the door."

They sat down again and one of the elders asked: "Tell us, Master, you spoke publicly today. What is going to happen now? How much longer can the people endure their misery?" His neighbour added eagerly: "Explain your prophecy to us. You have kept silent for so long and now—What good would it do for the starving people to revolt? They would only become more easily the prey of the Syrians."

Elisha looked slowly from one to the other. No doubt several of them were asking the same question, and others were perhaps afraid that he might be angry. He was not angry. He had been expecting the question and knew the answer before it was asked. In his ice-cool mind he knew what they were thinking.

"I spoke the word of the Lord as it was given to me. The punishment is not to come upon Israel, but the King, and I did not say whether it would be fulfilled today or next year, but I did go on to say that the word speaks not only of judgment but also of comfort. The people must not revolt now but hold on, then overnight deliverance will come for Israel and a time of plenty." As they stared at him in incredulous amazement he repeated impatiently: "I tell you, a time of plenty. This misery will not last much longer."

"When?" someone asked in a whisper.

Elisha waved the question aside.

"Night is coming. Send the people down there away and go home yourselves. The time is near. Make known what I have said."

They got up without demur, said goodnight shyly and left. The sound of voices outside died away and soon all was quiet. Only the disciples who lived there remained, sitting with their backs against the wall, while two of them stood guard by the door.

"You, too, go to bed!"

"We will watch with you, Master, to see that the King does not take you by cunning."

"That is all over. He will not send again."

"Then you, too, go to rest."

"I must wait a little longer."

"Then let us watch with you."

Elisha thought a while and then said: "All right! Wait!"

He sat down on a wooden seat by the cold fireplace. Nobody spoke. The oil lamp was going out, it was getting darker and darker in the room. Elisha sat motionless. After a while he raised his head and listened. Footsteps were approaching outside.

"The King!" whispered one of them. He was going to bolt the door, and nudged his neighbour who had gone to sleep.

"Open the door," Elisha murmured. "It is not the King's men but Jehu. I knew he was coming."

Jehu was standing in the doorway peering into the gloom. He and the soldier with him were just black shadows in the darkness. Elisha did not move. He was smiling. It was wonderfully easy to smile, when he had such certain knowledge.

"Well, Jehu, has the King sent you at last to cut off my head?"

Jehu groped for Elisha's hand, bent over it and kissed it.

"My own heart brings me here, because you have spoken at last. Didn't you expect me?"

Elisha answered with gentle mockery: "I was waiting for you. I knew you were coming."

"Well, here I am! This is Bidekar, my friend and aide. I have no secrets from him."

Bidekar bowed low and said nothing. Elisha told the disciples to leave them alone.

"Sit down," he said to Jehu.

"At your feet," Jehu murmured. Bidekar stood leaning against the fireplace.

When they were alone Elisha leaned forward and asked with the same half-concealed banter:

"Why have you come, Jehu?"

Jehu's eyes glittered. His voice was restrained and he spoke very deliberately. Every word had obviously been carefully and cautiously considered.

"The word that you spoke today. How true it is! Israel is facing destruction because of the King's sin and that of his whole house. Not for the first time we are asking how this ruin can be averted. More and more people are asking that question."

"And have you found the answer?"

"You found the answer long ago, Master. Didn't you appeal to Israel over and over again to do away with the foreign gods and practices and to return to the ways of her forefathers and the commandments of her Lord?"

"That is true."

"But who was it who set up the foreign gods, and who maintains and protects their priests? Nothing will be changed as long as Ahab's dynasty is on the throne. Joram's conduct is no different from his brother's, and Ahaziah behaved as his father did. They are all alike. Look, Joram is going about today in sackcloth, pretending he is starving, but in his house sacrifices are still being offered every day to his mother's idols, and the whoredom of the Woman and her court is worse than in Ahab's time. Who in Joram's house cares about the word of the Lord? Yes, in order that the word of the Lord may be fulfilled, Ahab's dynasty must be driven from the throne of Israel. That is the answer I have found in your word."

Elisha did not answer. Jehu waited and then went on. His voice was lower, but he spoke more rapidly.

"I was alone, but I am not alone any longer. There are many others of the same mind, and they are ready to follow me. We are prepared. We want to do what is necessary to save Israel. And now . . ."

He leaned closer to Elisha and whispered hoarsely: "Tell us now! Is your word the sign we have been waiting for?"

Elisha leaned back protesting.

"No, and you know that, Jehu."

Jehu got up disappointed and defiant.

"No?"

Elisha smiled.

"No, and you should be glad that it is not the sign."

"Why?"

"There is misery and famine inside the city now and death waiting outside the gates. Can you banish the misery and hunger? Can you save the people from death?"

"I have thought about this and made my plans. We will do what has to be done and then break out at night and escape from the Syrians. Then we will send messengers to Judah and Heth and to the East, asking for help to destroy Benhadad."

"Your plan is all wrong. Listen, Jehu! You can't break out with your men alone. Furthermore Judah is related by marriage to Joram and has sent no help. Can you get help from Judah, when Joram failed? Then again, what is the use of a victory with foreign aid? Israel would only become the slaves of another power. No! The Lord alone will come to Israel's help and you must rely on his power alone. Do you?"

"No! Let us follow up the prophecy by action, Master. How can the word be fulfilled by waiting in idleness?"

"I am not waiting in idleness, Jehu. I just want to wait patiently. You heard little of what I said today. I told the people to hold on. To you I have more to say. The Lord has made Benhadad blind and foolish in his pride, so that he stays down there in the valley with his whole army. Don't you see that the prophecy is already coming true? Benhadad has left his frontiers undefended. Winter is at hand, his troops are encamped in rain and cold, consumed by fever and impatience, grumbling at the orders of their officers, and are sure to lose heart because of the endless delay. And the Lord is sending floods and falls of earth along the valleys and roads through which Benhadad brings his supplies, and the country in his rear is devastated. He will find neither corn nor animals there to feed his hungry soldiers. Do you still not see? How long can Benhadad wait? He has not risked another attack, and has missed his opportunity. Time has caught up with him, and he will creep away like a beaten cur. So Israel must hang on, for that is the Lord's will. Not by your decision or your action, but by his power alone."

Elisha sighed and said quietly: "Victory? What is the good of victory alone? A military victory cannot save you now. You must have peace if your victory is to be worth anything, peace for Israel, so that she may live. Then the word of the Lord will be fulfilled and come true."

They were silent, then Bidekar murmured hoarsely and excitedly:

"You are the Lord's chosen prophet. Your words are true."

Jehu glanced angrily at him and asked scornfully:

"Peace! A fine word! Can you achieve it? When Ahab made peace you called it treachery. What good did the peace and the pact do? It lasted a year, and now this man Benhadad is threatening us again."

Elisha smiled. He spoke more easily:

"Is it the Syrian people who are threatening Israel or just her King—this man with his lust for power, his violence, and his greed? Answer me! Has Benhadad a hundred lives, and is there no one in Syria with different ideas, no one who thinks as you do, Jehu? Isn't it possible that his days are numbered, now that he has to return home without a victory?"

Jehu jumped up and said breathlessly: "Go on!"

"I know of one man whom I treated with respect in his time of humiliation and who thanked me for what I said. Do you remember that morning outside Aphek, Jehu?"

"Hazael!"

"Yes, Hazael. On that day he said to me: 'If I survive this day, may I come and see you?' I have not forgotten it. He did survive and now occupies a position of honour, I know. Well then, when Benhadad has gone from here, I will go and find Hazael, so that he may make peace for his people and for Israel."

"Hazael make peace? He!" Jehu's eyes flashed. He asked in astonishment—and there was a hint of a threat:

"You intend to try that? Do you think you can do it?"

Elisha answered harshly and proudly: "Yes, that is what I will do."

"If you succeed . . ."

Elisha leaned forward, his eyes close to Jehu.

"You have understood."

Suddenly a note of anxiety and appraisal came into his voice.

"There are other questions, my son Jehu. You have said more today than ever before, and have opened your heart and mind to me."

"I am in your hands. I have trusted you."

Elisha leaned still closer, trying to see into Jehu's smouldering eyes, as though only there he could read the true answer and find out what was really in the innermost recesses of this man's mind.

"Don't be afraid. In any case you have already said too much to stop now. Go on! Ahab's house must be removed from the throne of Israel, you say. Go on! Who is to be King in Joram's place?"

Jehu started, then quickly lowered his eyes and answered meekly: "Whomever you in your wisdom anoint, my Father, for your word is accepted by all the people, in order that the Lord's kingdom shall be established in Israel."

"The Lord's kingdom! Where do these words come from?"

"From your teacher, Elijah, Master. . . . You taught it to me that night outside Aphek. Have you forgotten?"

"Shall it come true?" asked Elisha, deeply moved. "Shall it come true? Will you promise that?"

"If you want my word I swear it."

Elisha leaned back and shut his eyes, passed his hand over his brow.

"You have remembered my teacher's word," he said quietly and sternly. "Now remember what has been said today, for this is a pact and you have sworn. If you remain true to your promise, the Lord will be true to his word."

Jehu's voice broke in his excitement.

"When?"

"You have heard what I said. Now wait! It must be some time before the whole prophecy is fulfilled."

Elisha got up and said wearily:

"Enough! Go now. The Lord will show me his will, and I will give you the sign."

On the seventh morning after this event the city awoke to find the Syrian camp deserted.

Some beggars and lepers made the discovery first, for they had to stay outside the city walls. As they were miserable and hungry they had nothing to fear, and ventured further and further towards the camp. No sentry challenged them, nobody stopped them, for there was nobody left. They found a lot of tents full of abandoned equipment and clothing, gold and silver, and there was also food which they ate with relish. At last they came back and brought the news to the guards at the gate, who sent word to the King.

The soldiers on the wall reported later that for several hours during the night they had heard the rattling of weapons, shouting of orders, neighing of horses and the creaking of carts in the distance. They could not see anything, for the sky was overcast and the plain was shrouded in thick mist. They had remained on the alert all night, fearing an attack at dawn. But nothing happened, and when the mist cleared they too saw that the camp in the valley was deserted.

King Joram held a long council of war with his captains. Jehu urged immediate pursuit, but the King was afraid that the enemy might be playing a trick, trying to entice Israel out from the city in order to attack them in the open. It was obvious what the outcome of such an attack would be. The number of fighting men in the city had been alarmingly diminished. After long discussion Joram sent out a small band of scouts to see where the Syrians had gone.

The scouts returned in the evening. They had not been able to overtake the retreating army, but they reported that the road was littered with discarded equipment, broken down carts, and exhausted pack animals, that the Syrians had abandoned so that the rest could get away more quickly. There was no longer any doubt about the victory and the deliverance of Israel.

The people in the city had not waited for the return of the spies.

They saw the deserted camp and that was enough. They filled the streets and squares and walls, singing and dancing and shouting, the hungry, the sick, the lame, the wounded, the women, the children and even the King's men, who had been ordered to stay on the wall. They crowded round Elisha's house calling for the prophet who had told them to wait patiently and had promised them deliverance, but they called in vain. The house was empty, and shut up. Elisha and his disciples had already left the city, and amid all the singing and dancing and bustle no one had seen them go.

II

THE night was close, and even here on the flat roof of the palace the air was still. The smoke from the torches in the tall branching copper stands all round the breastwork rose in soft blue billowing clouds that drifted straight upwards, hung for a while like a pall of mist and slowly dissolved in the darkness of the night. The smoke was heavy with perfume, for the torches had been soaked in aromatic oils.

In the centre of the roof sat a group of girls with flutes and guitars, while a slave girl was dancing in the space in front of them. At the moment a single flute was playing to the accompaniment of a few softly plucked notes on the guitars, like raindrops in the vibrant silence. The wistful sensuous cadences of the flute twined gracefully and voluptuously around the same recurring note. The dancing girl was young and very beautiful, her dark skin was oiled, and in the slow rhythm of the dance the flickering light of the torches made the young flesh glisten and shine like warm polished marble, but with a mysterious and seductive mobility. She danced with her eyes open, but seemed oblivious of the night and the torches, the roof and the men, and unaware of the hot breath of desire, she danced slowly and solemnly as though performing an important and sacred rite and at the same time she was completely absorbed in enjoyment, as though by her movements she were talking to herself, subtly flattering her own body in the only language she knew.

Jezebel was reclining on a couch, her eyes closed, her head resting on her arm. She lay still and appeared to be asleep, but beneath her lowered lids her eyes were keenly alive. For a while she watched the dancing girl coldly and appraisingly, then looked from one face to another and finally back to the King, who was reclining near her. Joram's arms were hanging limply down, his chin was sunk on his chest, his eyes hot and heavy, following the movements of the dancing girl. He did not notice that Jezebel was watching him.

His Majesty the King! thought Jezebel scornfully, with malignant tenderness. He has put on weight, his cheeks are already podgy and heavy, his lips are thick, almost puffy—greedy, insatiable lips. Have I given you greed, Joram, my son? A bad gift, since I did not give you courage with it. You never dare, or only in an agony of fear, what I dared do so gaily. That is the reason for the deep lines round your mouth and the indolent hot anger in your eyes. I have not passed on to you enough of myself. I have not been very successful with you, or maybe I have succeeded only too well.

Jezebel was tired. She was feeling the strain of the sultry day, her eyes burned with the smoke and perfume, and perhaps also because of the drops that her personal physician had lately been putting into her eyes so that they should remain large and brilliant. She was tired, but very much awake and restlessly excited.

Should she choose one of these men for tonight? None of them was much good. Joram, my dear son, she thought contemptuously, my creature, like your brother, who was no good and fell from the upper window. Now you are His Majesty, the King, because I wanted you to be, because I bore you and brought you into the world, because my hand supported you and guided you, because my hand still supports and guides you. And was not the man who fathered you also my creature, a slave to my body and my will, and King with my help? I am the ruler, she thought sensuously and bitterly, but I have to use my cunning and skill to inspire you with cunning and skill, so that without your knowing it my will becomes your will. What are you thinking about, Joram, my son? I want to know.

The King's face betrayed nothing. Now it had relaxed again and his eyes wandered from the dancing girl, without expression, even bored. Was he attracted to the girl? It might be important to know that, but now not even Jezebel could read the King's face.

The music died away. With the final notes the dancing girl sank slowly and voluptuously to her knees and bent down, her outstretched hands touched the ground and slid forwards, her arms stretched along the floor and her head, breasts and body curved down in a sharp angle from the hips, till she came to rest at last in an attitude of complete surrender.

Jezebel saw the flickering reflection of the torches in the taut, dark skin and the beautiful lines of the long, slender back. She is really beautiful, thought Jezebel crossly, much too good for him. She thought with distaste of the tricks she had to employ so that her own body might retain the deceptive appearance of youth, this body that was no longer young, with flesh no longer firm and supple, this body that got tired too easily and no longer responded as it used to. Then her anger evaporated again. Her body was still disciplined and could at least be forced to fulfil whatever she demanded of it. It was still more desirable in its maturity than the beautiful young body of this girl, because it knew by experience all the arts that a human body, a woman's body, could know, and because it forgot nothing, and was able to offer all its profound knowledge and experience. Blessing and thanks to the great Ishtar! She sat up, and as the King still said nothing, she leaned over and said in a low voice with seductive, half-revealed tenderness, as though she were flattering her lover:

"My son is thinking. What is in the mind of the King?"

Joram started, glanced swiftly up at her and at once looked away again. Jezebel smiled to herself. Irritation, displeasure, a shifty look of guilt. How well she knew this reaction of Joram's! Ever since childhood, when she called him, it had this effect on him, and he still could not hide it even now. So she was surprised at his answer, for he raised one hand wearily and pointed into the distance.

"My country," he murmured with a kindly contemptuous smile, "How quickly it can forget! It has already forgotten. How long is it since the enemy's fires were burning over there, and there was famine and misery everywhere? Only a few months, yet the people have already forgotten. They have been able to sow and reap, the houses have been rebuilt, the nights are quiet, the war and devastation have become just an evil dream." He lowered his hand and his smile vanished, as though he were ashamed of what he had said, and added peevishly: "It won't be much cooler tonight."

Jezebel looked at him curiously. She knew what she wanted him to do. She had waited a long time for a favourable opportunity, and now she was glad that his words would make it easy for her. She waited a little while, then half turned away and said casually:

"My slave girl—did you see her dance?"

Joram did not answer, and she asked softly: "Do you like my slave girl? She is beautiful. Do you want her, Joram? She is very beautiful. Even on a night like this she would entertain you and give you pleasure and delight. Do you want her?"

Jezebel laughed gently. Joram did not reply, but she could see the muscles of his jaw working slightly and the blood slowly mounting into his cheeks under her gaze. She waited. Joram looked obstinately past her. Presently Jezebel stopped smiling and said quietly and coldly:

"The country is at peace. Yes, indeed; the country may well rest, but the King must not rest. He has to make use of his times of prosperity, and are you sure that the country is really so peaceful?"

Joram turned unwillingly towards her.

"The moon is going down. Do you not also want to rest?"

"No!" Then after a pause: "Did you hear what I said, or don't you want to listen today?"

"I heard. You said the King must not rest." Joram sat up and asked petulantly: "You asked whether I were sure that the country is really peaceful. Why do you ask that? Do you think I don't know?"

"You see what is visible from this roof, and that seems to be enough for you. That is obviously the way you want it, and your servants know it and keep quiet, even if they know more, so I will keep quiet too."

"You are speaking in riddles. Won't you explain your words and say what you want to say?"

Jezebel laughed again and laid her hand soothingly on Joram's arm.

"What are you afraid of, my son Joram? I simply said that the King must not rest, for he is responsible for the peace of his people."

Joram shook her hand off his arm and said surlily:

"I know. I know. I am responsible."

"I am glad to hear you say so. Then you have plans that I don't know about. I am glad. I may hear them later, or even after they have been accomplished. What does it matter, as long as you have plans?"

"Plans? Yes, of course. That is beside the point. You said more than that. What do you know that I don't know and ought to know? What do you want me to do?"

"Nothing!" answered Jezebel lazily. "It is for you to decide, for you are the King. I am getting old, Joram. Perhaps I don't want to know things any longer. I am only your mother and I worry about you, that's all."

"But . . ."

"Isn't that so, Joram? Isn't that true?"

Joram growled crossly: "No, and you know it."

"Thanks for the compliment. You are sweet, my son, and I love you. That is why I am anxious and that is why I speak."

Jezebel paused.

"The King is waiting," said Joram with hardly suppressed anger.

"You say the country and the people have forgotten. Have you also forgotten, Joram, what happened to you?"

"What are you talking about?"

"It is only a few months since the war ended, you say—not a year. Israel has survived her misfortunes, her King has survived the peril, with victory and honour certainly; but there was one man here who in the hour of greatest adversity stood up and cursed the King in front of all the people. He blamed the King publicly for all the misery and suffering. Have you forgotten, Joram?"

"No."

"Where is this man? You swore you would cut off his head. Have you punished him for his crazy curse? You let him go home, you allowed your men to give way before the rabble instead of arresting him, you let him go when Benhadad left, and you have done nothing since. Have you avenged his crime? Has his prophecy been refuted?"

Joram did not answer.

"Do you know where he is now?"

"No."

"Do you happen to know what he's doing?"

Joram still said nothing.

"I know what he's doing. He is travelling about the country plundering and destroying my groves, he and his band. He goes from one hill-top to another, and wherever he finds the images and sacred stones of my gods, he overthrows them and he has the sacred trees cut down. He stirs up the people and I know what he is saying. He keeps repeating the curse against the King and the false prophecy, that he wants to make come true by inciting the people to revolt. In the winter I thought that he had stopped, that he had learned his lesson at last and given up. It was quiet, as though he were not in the country at all, but now he is going on worse than ever."

"As long as I can remember he has been doing just that," Joram replied. "What do I care? I no longer listen to him. How many of them are there after all? A handful of deluded youngsters and an old man! There is too much fuss about them. The Lord has shown that this man does not speak his word, otherwise I should not be sitting here now."

Jezebel leaned back and spoke softly, as if she were not talking to the King at all.

"The country is quiet and the King wants to be left in peace. Very well then, I have no more to say."

"Not at all. I am still waiting to hear what you want to say."

"Oh, you won't listen to me, because you are afraid of him, my son. You may speak disparagingly about him, but I know all the same that you are afraid of him. And when you say that you no longer want to see him or listen to him, it is simply because you are afraid of him."

HTW 8

Joram turned his face towards his mother hesitantly and protested: "Aren't you afraid of him too, Mother?"

Jezebel sat up again, clasped her hands round her knees, and said coldly and calmly:

"The dungeons of this palace are very deep, Joram. Many a man has already learned that there is no way out, and has been silenced. You have only to give the word. Your men will obey your order." She raised herself still further and said scornfully: "No, I am not afraid of him. I have known him a long time. He did not dare to stand up to me, neither did his master. They both ran away from me. I am certainly not afraid of him: I am not afraid of any enemy, but I am afraid for you, because you are afraid of him."

"What are you talking about? I laugh at him." Joram laughed bitterly. "It is not the first time that you have warned me against him. I know how often he has made you angry, unpardonably, no doubt, and most annoying, and I am sorry that I ever believed his prophecy, and took his advice, but tell me what else he has achieved? An old man, a chattering greybeard, who lives in poverty and need and goes about like a beggar, when he could be comfortably off! And those who listen to him and follow him are also beggars and vagrants. Shall I make a hero of him? Shall I make him important by taking notice of him, by venting my anger on him? Am I to whip every cur that yaps at me? If I struck at him the people might remember his words and say that I am afraid of his prophecy, and struck at him for that reason."

"They would understand that the King's patience is great but not boundless, and that he cannot tolerate this insolence any longer. When they see your power, they will keep quiet and keep out of the way. Don't deceive yourself, my son. He goes about like a beggar because he chooses to. He also sat at your table, and left you, not because you wanted him to, but because he chose to. He is old, but he is also powerful. Once his followers were really only a handful; today they amount to hundreds and thousands. The boys have grown into men, they have gone forth and spread his message. He is acting according to a plan. He goes from place to place, never staying long anywhere, but everywhere he leaves someone to speak for him. Did you know that? And everyone who has a complaint, or whose claim has been refused, or has to work for you or pay taxes, comes to him and listens to his word. You are the King, and because you have to be strong and severe, there are many who bear a grudge against you, and because the gods have been kind to you, there are many who envy you. It is time to do at last what should have been done long ago."

"What should be done?"

Jezebel said kindly and soothingly: "You worry about what the people might remember and what they would say. Look! Now is the time to act swiftly and wisely. The country is at peace, the people have forgotten the sufferings of the war. During the war you were patient, because you did not want to turn the people against you. All right! Now a small band would be enough, just ten or fifteen reliable men. They could arrest him at night, while the people are asleep and nobody would know what had happened. Speed and secrecy! He will have vanished for good and the people will imagine that he has gone up in the clouds, as they still make out his master did. Nobody must know that he has disappeared into your dungeon. If you will do so . . ."

Joram stared at her in silence. Jezebel's face hardened and she said sternly:

"You asked what I wanted to say and I have told you. This is not the first time we have delayed too long. Now it must be done. You must make use of this time of peace. You must not tolerate any enemy stirring up the people against you. Who knows when another emergency may arise, and whether you will again find favour with the gods. Act now!"

"You are wise, Mother. Thank you! I will consider what you have said."

"I don't want you to consider and do nothing. I love you very much, Joram. Your mother has more experience and knows. How often have I warned you and then kept silent? Now I want . . ."

"I will do as . . ." Joram stopped, shut one eye suspiciously and asked: "As you know so much, do you know where he is now?"

Jezebel's face relaxed and she answered amiably:

"I don't send out couriers and spies, my dear. Is it so difficult to find him? Plenty of people know about him, including some of your servants. So many people here at the court know where he is!"

She sat up and looked round inquiringly. The music had ceased some time ago, the girls were lolling about with the men. Jezebel peered round patiently till she found the one she was looking for. He was sitting by the edge of the roof, alone, upright with folded arms. She looked away from him at once, for he was looking at her and the King, and she guessed that he had been watching her for some time. She leaned back satisfied and whispered smiling:

"You say only beggars and vagrants follow him. Ask your servant Jehu whether he knows where he is. Jehu is devoted to you, isn't he, Joram? It will be a fine test of his devotion for him to find the old man and deliver him into your hands! You know quite well that Jehu is one of his followers."

"Yes," answered Joram, uncertainly and angrily. "And you know that I have no better servant than Jehu. He served my father also, and has served our house since he was a boy. I have to be considerate if he... But Jehu is my friend!"

"The King has no friends, only servants, to whom he gives orders, and he has to test them again and again by his commands. What are you afraid of, if you are so sure of him? Let him prove himself. Call your servant Jehu and give him your command, so that he may prove himself."

Joram did not answer. Jezebel was still smiling. She knew quite well the struggle that was going on in Joram's mind, and was content. When Joram looked up at last there was no more displeasure in his face, but a half-concealed smile, a curious and terrifying grin compounded of fear, cruelty and an amused evil cunning. His broad fat face suddenly showed an unmistakable likeness to Jezebel's narrow thin one. He chuckled softly, musing.

"Really, you are as wise as the great serpent." He lowered his eyes, thought a while, then looked up, following the direction of Jezebel's glance and saw Jehu and his alert watchful eyes. Then he raised his hand, beckoned to a slave, and said slowly:

"Ask Jehu my servant to come here."

That's the way he spends his time, thought Jehu. He has already forgotten. When we were in danger, he went about in sackcloth, repenting of his evil ways, and now he has forgotten it all very quickly, as if it had been an illness from which he has recovered.

Jehu was sitting at the edge of the roof with arms folded and his back to the breastwork. He had chosen this spot in the hope of finding a night breeze, but there was not a breath of wind stirring, the night was close and airless. Jehu was perspiring. He stayed there because he had a view of the whole roof, with no one watching him from behind. Perhaps that had been his reason for choosing that particular spot at all.

There he lies, he thought. He has thickened up and got fat again. He is letting himself go and overdoing the gay life. He is a slave to the appetites of his fat body, always the same lusts and passions, and does not know his own weakness. A King, and yet a slave of his desires! I know better how to control myself! Does he get any happiness out of it? He never says anything. He did not speak at all during the banquet, while I was sitting beside him. I ought to have stayed with him. He broods and says nothing. None of the jesters or jugglers or women got any response from him. I wonder what he is thinking about. Perhaps he is just dozing, overcome by the hot night. How often he sits like that brooding for hours and then has nothing to say! Perhaps he is afraid. Look out, Jehu! he thought angrily, and caught his breath. It suddenly seemed as if he had spoken the words aloud. Look out! Perhaps he is afraid—afraid of whom, if not you? You don't want to show your hand too soon. This is a most unpropitious moment!

Jehu was trembling with impatience. Can I choose the time? I wait and wait. What a long time I have waited! How much longer must I wait? For years I have been preparing and keeping my own counsel, so that nobody should guess, and now I have spoken and there is nothing more to say but to give the signal. They are only waiting for the signal, and why do I hesitate to give it? Time is passing and it is still not the right moment.

Jehu took his eyes off the King and looked restlessly round the roof. My palace! he thought enviously. The King's palace! When I do give the word, at last it will be all up with this mob. I will sweep my palace clean. Jugglers, gamblers, women, foreigners—

they will all tremble before me, they will flee and perish. Great Jehu! he thought scornfully. Will that be your triumph—to drive out slaves and whores and parasites? It is easy to despise servants and slaves and now you can laugh and jeer at all this merry rabble also—at the soft yielding lips, the provoking eyes, the seductive limbs. Secretly they still make you hot and tense, but now you know how to control your body. Now you know that they are all the same, all just like the Woman. She was seductive too, with her soft and yielding lips and her beautiful eyes. She was passionate and glowing and horribly fascinating—and then next morning she was the Queen again. She dismissed you, sent you away with a laugh, and ignored you. What a long time ago it was! Today you have other and bigger plans. Think about that. You hardly dare think about it, and yet you cannot help it. She and all the others, the whole royal house, all of them! No member of Ahab's house shall remain. Their fate is in my hands, and there they lie before my eyes in voluptuous abandon—all unsuspecting.

Murder! he thought, going all hot and cold, and he found sensuous pleasure and overwhelming terror in facing the truth at last. Your plan means murder, and there is a fatal curse on a murderer and a far more dreadful curse on the murderer of the King. The King is sacred, and anyone who lifts his hand against the sacred person of the King ... Who anointed Ahab anyway? he thought maliciously. He made himself King by the sword. The elders only accepted him because they were afraid. Who anointed Ahaziah and Joram? I am the real master of Israel and have been so for a long time. It was my cunning that saved Israel when Ahab was hardly able to resist Benhadad. It was I who made Israel a nation of warriors, training them long and arduously, and I saved Israel again by persuading Joram to hold out. At that time, of course, I had already the old man's promise. He will anoint me. He knows I am the master and that I am in the right. I have been chosen, and my will is supreme. Does he know that? For the present I have to obey.

Look out, Jehu! he thought for the third time, still more angrily. Have you already spoken the word, and do you know for certain that it will be fulfilled? Are you so sure of the power behind you and do you know that success is assured? The only proof is success.

What will happen if your word is not fulfilled? The King says nothing—he knows how to keep silent. Perhaps he has already guessed what you are thinking and is just biding his time, because he has taken precautions. Look out, Jehu! He has not said a word to you tonight. And what about the Woman? She is lying there as if she were asleep, but she isn't asleep. She sees and knows everything.

And somebody may already have talked. She knows how to bewitch people and get whatever she wants out of them. There is danger in delay, danger in every hour. It is time to speak. I will give the signal this very night. The hour is favourable, it is quiet everywhere and they are all exhausted by the heat of the night. Shall I risk it? It can be done at a moment's notice, they are all ready. How long can I keep them in readiness? Some time must pass before the prophecy is fulfilled, Elisha said, and I will give you a sign. Shall I go on waiting for his sign? Words, words! And now he has gone away without saying anything. Is he making a fool of me? Oh, I shall wait, thought Jehu angrily. He knows too much. I must wait! Why did I let him get away? He was here and in my hands. I alone protected him from Joram's anger. I could have forced him into action and I let him go. If only he would redeem his promise at last! Where is he?

Jehu straightened up. Jezebel had sat up and was talking to the King. I ought to have stayed with him, thought Jehu. She is talking quietly, hardly moving her lips. Now she is smiling. What is she saying? She is getting old, he thought scornfully, then immediately had to admit reluctantly—she is still the Woman, the Queen, the evil genius, the smiling mysterious enchantress, the wicked seductive temptress, the foreigner, the sweet poison. To have her at my feet, he thought with burning greedy hatred—at my feet at last! No more standing before her with loathing and embarrassment, silent and powerless, condemned to obey! To see fear in those haughty eyes at last, and then to destroy her body and distorted face! You are smiling, Jezebel. This time there is something you don't know. I possess twice your cunning and skill. It is very sweet to await in silence your humiliation and destruction.

Elisha hates her too, thought Jehu suddenly. That is a useful guarantee for me. Where is he? Time and again messengers came in, but they had not very much to report. Sometimes they stayed away a long time and only dispatches for the King arrived from his agents and local governors. Jehu grinned. He made sure that dispatches did not reach the King too often, and so he knew more than Joram did.

Elisha had turned up in many places. Since he came back he had been travelling without rest, no longer speaking to his disciples alone, but again and again to the people, and not just appealing to them, exhorting, teaching and consoling them, but talking of revolt, the curse and the promise. He had never done this before. He had never wanted his movements known. It had been so through the winter. Now it seemed as if he intended deliberately to proclaim his power and courage throughout the land of Israel, as though he would challenge the King to take action against him. Was there a plan behind this?

You are a fool, Jehu, to go on trusting him. One day he will make himself King in the name of his God and supported by his power. They will follow him instead of you and laugh when you at last pluck up courage to speak. They shall not laugh! I am the sword. His followers are only a rabble and are afraid of the sword. Let him stir them up! He is inciting them for me, and I will make use of him. Am I not acting according to his word? He will give the sign. I shall be King of Israel by the will of his God and with his anointing—the will of my God, he corrected himself hastily, shutting his eyes, and thought fervently, the will of my God. Would he have brought me here, would he have given me success and power, if he did not intend to give me this last thing? And who will dare to defy me, when the prophet himself anoints me? He will keep his word. But will it be his last word? He is the one who can turn against me. My selection, my consecration, comes from him, and one day he may equally well deny and depose me also. Who is he to possess such power? Where does his power come from? The old man had now really achieved what he set out to do. Benhadad was dead and Hazael King in his place, Syria was weakened by discord and fear. Hazael, whom I had in my power! Was that really Elisha's doing, or had he merely forecast what could happen, must happen, and at last did happen? His God is with him, he keeps his word. Israel is at peace, as he promised. I don't want him to have such power! Does a peace that he makes help me? It is Elisha's peace or Joram's peace. But I am the sword, and what becomes of me if the sword is not needed? Think, Jehu, think hard! Do you want to be master only in order to go on obeying, the slave of the power that raises you up? Think, and be wise!

Jehu sank into a deeper reverie. The night seemed to be getting darker. He forgot Jezebel and Joram and did not notice what was going on around him. After a long time he suddenly started up and bit his lip. He had almost cried out. Into the darkness had come a sudden joyful clarity, an unexpected illumination, like a flash of lightning.

I know the answer, he thought, with a thrill of excitement. The answer has been given to me! Why didn't I think of it before? It must be like that when the word of the Lord comes to Elisha, and now it has happened to me. Is that not a convincing sign? I see my hour of destiny. I, Jehu, must achieve what he has presumed to do, and I will achieve it otherwise than he. I and I alone. I am the sword, and the sword will bring real peace. Joram will go to war, and I will rescue him, so that all can see. I can see a way that no one else has seen. Joram shall make war against Hazael. How shall I persuade him? I shall do it. And then I shall also be rid of Elisha. Who has achieved more than I? I, the King?

He started. A servant was standing before him bowing low. As Jehu did not seem to notice him, he cleared his throat and then drew back, as Jehu snapped at him: "What d'you want?"

"The King wishes to speak to you, Sir."

"I'm coming," growled Jehu hoarsely. He could not entirely conceal the shock of surprise. He passed his hand across his brow and got up heavily.

"I'll come at once."

Joram sat up. He wanted to see Jehu's face more clearly, but Jehu bowed low and kept his head down.

"Here I am, Sir, in the presence of my King."

The servility of his words pleased Joram. He flashed a glance at

Jezebel, saw her watchful, mocking eyes, and grinned.

"Rise, and listen to me."

Jehu stood up slowly. He felt an uneasy sense of danger and tried to play for time. His hands were a little unsteady, but his face showed only the willing zeal of a good servant.

"I am listening."

"Your men are now rested." Joram paused to think, then asked with subtle amiability: "Are you ready to obey my wishes?"

"Always."

"Well, then! Listen my friend Jehu! Your King is very worried."

Jehu did not answer.

"You do not ask me why?"

"I am waiting for the King to speak."

"Yes," said Joram, disappointed. "Yes, I am very worried about the disquiet in Israel. There is peace now, and the poor people are not being left to enjoy the peace. There are rebellious preachers going about causing discontent and disobedience by their words, and destruction and mischief by their deeds."

Jehu still said nothing.

Joram shouted: "I know who is responsible for stirring up all this trouble, and you know it too."

Jehu bowed, then raised his head, but did not speak.

Joram looked at him suspiciously with furrowed brow. At last he leaned back and said haughtily:

"You have nothing to say? Then listen to my command. I have put up with all this long enough. My patience is exhausted. Now you shall go and arrest this trouble-maker and deliver him up to me." And as Jehu still remained obstinately silent, he added still more loudly: "Go and fetch Elisha to me, so that I can punish him as he deserves, and the people can see my power and be silenced."

"I will go at once," said Jehu quietly and coldly.

Joram stared at him in surprise. Then a smile spread gradually over his face and he looked at Jezebel in satisfaction, but Jezebel's eyes were half closed again, her face calm and indifferent, as though she had not heard what was said. Joram knew, of course, that she had heard every word. He turned back to Jehu and asked casually, with hardly concealed scorn: "You do not object?"

"The King has issued his command."

"Not long ago you brought him into my city and even into my palace. I gave an order then and you protested."

"The King has considered the matter in his wisdom and has decided."

"Look, Jehu!" said Joram uncomfortably. "You must not keep anything from me. Why do you not speak? You have heard how this man has insulted me publicly."

"Yes."

"And I swore that I would cut off his head. I did not do so because of the war, because the people were against it, and because I was merciful. But he did not appreciate my clemency. He went on in just the same way. I gave an order, by my own decision, that the sacred stones of Baal should be removed, wherever they were likely to cause offence. That annoyed the Queen very much."

He stopped, glanced at Jezebel again, and said uncertainly and angrily:

"But he goes on repeating his curse and destroying all the sacred stones and groves. I have had enough! Now bring him here for me to punish him."

"I hear and will obey."

"Now is the time to do it. There is peace on the frontiers and your men have nothing to do."

Joram thought for a while and then added, quietly and with rather less enthusiasm:

"And another thing, when I come to think of it, it would be better done this way. I really ought to show the people what happens to rebels, so that they would fear me, but I don't want it done that way. It will be better if he disappears and is silenced. A handful of your men will be enough. You are clever. Find your victim by cunning, and see to it that no one suspects what has happened to him. I rely on you. Do you understand?"

"I understand," answered Jehu quietly. It was only by a great effort that he kept the relief and mockery out of his voice. Joram's last words had suddenly made it clear that the King was really afraid of his own order. A situation that seemed fraught with danger and unforeseen complications now suddenly offered unexpected promise. He stepped back a pace and said with contrived indifference:

"Your command shall be obeyed. I will send my captain Bidekar to carry it out."

"You won't send Bidekar at all, my friend. You will go yourself."

"I hear and will obey. But there is one thing. Everybody knows me. How can I go about unrecognized, making inquiries and arresting the rebel? It would be impossible to keep it secret."

"Yes," said Joram swiftly and with malicious joy, as if he had caught Jehu out at last. "Everyone knows that you respect Elisha and no one knows about my order. Maybe it would be better for you to go alone. Your word may be enough to bring him here. Don't you think so?"

"No, Sir. I have no authority over Elisha, nor do I know where he is."

"You don't know?"

"No."

"Then go and find him. Choose your own companions as you wish. You must start at dawn."

"I will go at once," answered Jehu again and stopped. He glanced at Jezebel, came nearer, and said hesitantly and non-committally: "Allow me one further word before I go, Sir."

"Speak," said Joram harshly. "Why do you hesitate? You know I have no secrets from my mother."

"You are punishing me, Sir, and do not even know that you are punishing me, nor indeed that I deserve punishment. Let me explain. You are taking me away from my troops—perhaps for a long time, for who knows when I shall get back? But at the moment I am indispensable."

"I do not understand. I am not punishing you. I am showing my confidence in you."

"I am not hesitating because I want to avoid my mission, not in the least. I will do what you say, Sir, but look! I have taken a liberty. I was not expecting such a command, and had made other plans. I wanted to increase your security without your knowing it. I wanted to bring you fruits that I had gathered without your command. I have given my men other orders, and now my place is with them, so that the task before us may be successfully accomplished."

"You are talking nonsense. What orders have you given? What are you talking about?"

Jehu paused before answering. Look out Jehu! he said to himself again, and suddenly a fantastic idea flashed into his mind. I know what to do, he thought fiercely. I have been shown the way! Will it be achieved tonight? When once it begins it will have to be finished. Surely he is handing me the lever that I needed. Your servant Jehu, and already your master! And you don't know it. He lowered his head and murmured:

"Ramoth Gilead! The fortress! Remember the promise given you by the miserable wretch Benhadad, who dared to attack you. He had to withdraw from your walls in shame and send envoys to make peace, to save himself from the edge of your sword. Didn't he promise to evacuate Ramoth Gilead and your fortress, which he had taken by guile and force?"

Jehu looked up and paused. Every word had to be carefully chosen to make the right impression on Joram. Presently he whispered slowly and impressively:

"Sir, you will know in your wisdom that as long as Gilead is in foreign hands Israel cannot be secure. Gilead blocks the way of the invader. That scoundrel Benhadad is gone, he has met his fate, but Hazael is in his place. We know that he is weak. He has made friendly overtures, but he has not evacuated Gilead. He is clever. He knows the importance of keeping what he has got."

He stopped. Joram said harshly: "Go on! Go on! Why do you stop?"

"Sir," said Jehu, still more slowly, as if the confession was difficult, "I have ordered my men to capture Gilead."

"What! What do you say?"

"I have ordered my men to capture Gilead." Jehu smiled apologetically.

"They are encamped at Jezreel and everything is ready. Gilead is not strongly garrisoned, my scouts have seen it. Hazael is not expecting an attack. Within a few days victory and security would have been yours and Hazael would have been powerless to avert the blow. I must admit that I have been presumptuous in giving the order on my own responsibility. Now your command is my punishment. But now that I have confessed, won't you be merciful and let me finish the task? I was doing it for your sake, after all."

Jehu stopped. He felt that he ought not to say any more. To his surprise the King was silent also, and Jehu guessed that his silence indicated indecision. In fact Joram now turned to Jezebel, as though for her advice and decision. Jehu dared not look at her. Jezebel took her time. It almost seemed as if she was enjoying the King's discomfiture. At last she said with icy severity:

"You have been disgracefully presumptuous. You deserve to be put in chains. You are the King's servant, not his master. Therefore, you must cancel your order, so that your men can see how wrong your presumption was."

Joram nodded in agreement. Then he started to speak, paused again to think, and then said more amiably than Jehu expected:

"You heard. You have acted wrongly. I will bear in mind in your favour that your intention and anxiety were right, even though it was not for you to choose and decide. Now you will, of course, carry out my command. Let your men remain in readiness."

He hesitated again. Into his face came a suggestion of the same cunning and malicious smile. "It is for the King to decide when the raid against Gilead shall take place, and it is the King's task to lead it. As for you—if you find Elisha quickly, you shall come with me and ride in my chariot. Do you hear?"

"I heard." Jehu's voice was suddenly hoarse and cracked.

"Now go and carry out my order."

"At once," Jehu managed to get out. He bowed and backed away until he was the prescribed distance from the King, turned hurriedly, stopped and looked for Bidekar, saw him amongst a group of courtiers and noticed with satisfaction that Bidekar's eyes were clear and watchful. He beckoned to him urgently, and went out without waiting for him. Bidekar caught him up on the landing. Jehu gripped his arm, dragged him away through the long corridors of the palace without heeding the surprise of the guards, and told him breathlessly and disjointedly about the King's words.

Down in the courtyard he stopped, gripped Bidekar more tightly and gasped out:

"Bidekar, send a messenger to Jezreel with the report to all the captains, tonight. Order general stand-to immediately. The King intends to march on Gilead. And send a secret message to Gilead ... to prepare ... and send a messenger to Elisha. You must find him. Tell him to hide. Joram is out for his blood. Tell him to let me know where he is hiding. It's starting, Bidekar, it's starting!"

He burst out laughing more and more loudly till his whole body was shaking.

Jezebel watched Jehu's hurried departure with tight lips and flashing eyes. When he had gone, she said scornfully:

"Well, my son, did you understand? Did your servant Jehu pass the test?"

"He obeyed," answered Joram surlily. "He didn't like my order. You wanted to test him. Well, he submitted in spite of everything. It wasn't easy for him, that is understandable. Can I ask more than that he should obey?"

"You fool!" Jezebel interrupted him with unrestrained fury. "He submitted! He is making a fool of you. He should be in prison like his teacher, in disgrace, in the dungeon, where he would starve to death and be forgotten. Don't you understand what he said? Don't you understand yet? He has set himself up above you. He has slighted his master before the whole army and given an order that was only for the King to give, the order to plunge Israel into new peril. Haven't we had more than enough misery and death this winter? How often must Israel bleed? And only when he heard your command, which he disliked so much, did he confess—hoping to escape by his confession. Your servant! He is Elisha's slave, not your servant. And you, you fool, distort and soften my words, that were a hundred times too lenient. He should be put in prison, in the deepest dungeon. And you promise him a reward for just obeying your command!"

Joram raised his hand in protest, but did not dare to interrupt her. When she stopped he said scornfully:

"Your anger distresses me. My servant Jehu loves Elisha, and I know of course that this has often annoyed you, and that your anger is aimed primarily at the rebellious prophet."

He stopped, turned suddenly to Jezebel and said peevishly and irritably: "Your advice is given in anger and is not good. How can I put Jehu in prison, my right hand man? His officers are devoted to him, the whole army admires him. They would resent it and revolt because of the injustice to Jehu. There is disquiet and revolt among the people. Shall I now stir it up in the army also?"

"Is it your army or Jehu's, my son?"

"It is my army and Jehu created it and—"

"And—?"

Joram protested: "You are angry with Jehu because of his presumption. I am angry with him because his impudent order was so right. Misery and death, yes indeed, but we must get Gilead back sometime. Gilead is the key. Jehu knows what he is talking about. It is just a matter of a sudden stroke, if we go about it the right way, over and done with in a few days—secret preparations, an overwhelming force, and Hazael unwarned. He is weak and will not be able to do anything about it."

Joram remained sunk in thought. Then he repeated loudly and angrily: "He gave the right orders. Why didn't I do it?"

Jezebel got up, drew her cloak closely round her and asked with contemptuous calm: "What are you going to do, since your servant knows better what orders to give than the King?"

Joram kept his face turned away and did not move. It was a plain insult not to rise when Jezebel did. In the end he could not go through with it and got up clumsily. He paused, took a step nearer, laid his hand on Jezebel's arm and said conciliatorily and haughtily at once:

"Why do you make fun of me? Don't worry! My servant Jehu gave the order in my name. He has taken good care not to let it be known that he did it without my knowledge. Now he has gone to look for Elisha. That will take some time, and meanwhile I shall follow up the orders. I will lead the expedition against Gilead, not he. The whole affair may well be over before he gets back. That will be my triumph and Jehu's punishment."

12

JEHU did not find Elisha's camp in the hollow until the evening of the seventh day. The search had taken longer than he had expected, for the messenger sent out by Bidekar had not returned, and Jehu was worried because he had received no word from Elisha either. The King had ordered that the search was to be kept secret, so they avoided villages and busy roads as much as possible. When they did make cautious inquiries among the country people, they received only vague and contradictory information that they could not make anything of. The prophet had been here or there, they said, but nobody was prepared to say which way he went. During the first two days Jehu took his time, for he was not at all anxious to get back quickly, but when day after day went by, and he was still wandering about aimlessly, his indifference gradually gave place to increasingly bitter impatience. He only stopped to rest when the exhausted riders could not go on any longer. He regretted a hundred times that he had obeyed the King's command at all or had imagined that doing so would further his own plans. What was going on at the court and in the camp? What was the King doing and planning, while he was riding about among the hills? At noon on the seventh day they picked up a travelling merchant, who in fear put them on the right track after they had threatened him with prison and torture.

Before long they reached the ridge overlooking the hollow, and paused, Jehu in front and his followers at a little distance behind. It had been an arduous climb, the horses were panting and snorting with tongues hanging out. The riders took off their leather hats and tried to wipe the dust and sweat from their faces.

The sun was going down. In the west the sky was a brilliant saffron paling to clear bright blue, and high above were long narrow streaks of white cloud. The air was clear for miles. On the far horizon they could see the sea, greenish blue, its wide expanse broken by glittering patches of light. There was not a breath of wind. As far as the eye could reach hills and valleys lay quiet and peaceful in the golden sunset.

Jehu peered with narrowed eyes at the hillside, the hollow, the little camp that Elisha's disciples had built down there, and the path leading from the rim of the hollow down to the plain. He could see at a glance that it would be child's play to capture the camp and its occupants. The valley was surrounded by gently sloping hills, the path was narrow and easy to block with two archers, his followers were armed and at the moment had the advantage of surprise.

Jehu clenched his fists. He suddenly saw a new possibility. During the last few days and nights he had imagined many conversations with Elisha without so far reaching any conclusion or certainty, only increasing his own vague impatience and fear. Now—suppose he did carry out the King's command faithfully! The prophet and his disciples were at his mercy here. One word from him and they would be seized and overpowered. Any of them who resisted would be killed. He would stand high in Joram's esteem and could tacitly leave the rest to Jezebel's hate and Joram's fear. They seemed to have made up their minds, and Joram might as well heap this further infamy on himself before he followed his victim. Whoever removed him from the throne would have one more reason to invoke the anger and punishment of the Lord, and would be free, uncommitted to any pact or promise or agreement. It was a great temptation and childishly easy to carry out.

Why do you hesitate, Jehu? He shook himself, conscious of a vague fear that annoyed him still more. I never thought of doing it, he thought quickly. It would be wicked folly. The hand of the Lord is over him and his word carries weight with the people. He has given me his word. I have only got to force his hand. He clenched his teeth, raised his hand as a signal to his men and rode on down the slope.

By now the people down below had noticed the approaching troop. They ran together and pointed up the hill. Jehu could see

Elisha in the distance sitting on a stone above the camp. As they ran towards him he got up and stood facing them, shading his eyes with his hand. Then he lowered his hand and spoke to the disciples. He had obviously recognized Jehu. Jehu halted his men and rode forward alone. A short distance from Elisha he stopped, dismounted and went up to him.

"Your servant, Sir!" he said formally and bowed low, for now he was angry, confused and uncertain. Then he stood up again slowly, looked at the watchful frightened eyes of the disciples and then at last at Elisha.

"Welcome!" said Elisha smiling. "What brings you here, Jehu, Captain of the King's army?"

Jehu heard the mockery in his greeting.

"A matter for you alone," he answered. "Send your young men away so that I can speak to you," and then more loudly and almost abruptly: "They may give my men some refreshment and water my horses. The journey here was tiring."

"What we have is yours. We were not expecting such a visit. But it is all right for my disciples to hear your message, for I know very well what it is, and told them of it some time ago."

"I was not sent to you with a message, Master. I sent you a message personally with a warning. Didn't you get it?"

"No."

"Then let me tell you. You and your followers are in grave danger, because of the anger of the King."

"Are you in danger too, Jehu, or do you no longer count yourself one of us?"

Jehu coloured and pointed to his men.

"Don't make fun of me, Master. I have protected you often enough. Listen! Joram has sent me with these men to arrest you and take you to him."

"Well, you have found me, so take me to the King. What are you waiting for? I have been expecting this for a long time and I have warned my disciples about it."

"You don't understand! It's not at all as you imagine. He told me to bring you back as a prisoner, so that he can shut you up for ever in his dungeon. He and the Woman intend to kill you."

Jehu came closer and said urgently: "Now d'you see? You mustn't wait any longer. You must get away into hiding, unless Joram's action is a sign that the time has come for us to act."

Elisha drew back.

"You're in a hurry," he said. "Control your impatience. How do you know whether Joram's word or deed can be a sign? The sign may come as a result of his action perhaps. But how can you be so sure? And why should I run away? I'm not afraid of Joram's anger, nor of the Woman. Listen! My Master Elijah fled from Jezebel's anger, and I know that the voice of the Lord withdrew from him because of his fear. Now I am in the same situation and the voice of the Lord shall not be taken from me. What is Joram's dungeon compared to the voice of the Lord, and what does Joram matter in comparison with Israel? I am not alone as Elijah was, and Joram may yet hear a great outcry in Israel, if he tries to do away with me. I am going to speak the word of the Lord. I am the word." Elisha laughed. "Were you trying to frighten me, Jehu? Say no more. We will set out as soon as your horses are rested. The best time to travel is in the cool of the night."

"No!" answered Jehu, disconcerted. "I should not dare to frighten you. I had to warn you. Let me speak to you in private, so that you can give me counsel, for the danger is complex, and there is much to discuss before we go."

"What more can Joram's servant have to discuss with me?"

"I am your servant. Why are you suddenly suspicious of me? Have I not kept faith with you?"

Elisha looked at Jehu in silence with wrinkled brow.

"Your words made me suspicious," he said more gently. "Very well, you are not my servant and must not be, as long as you do not forget the Lord, whose rule you have sworn to obey."

"I shall keep my word. There is so much that you do not know. You do not know what has been happening."

Elisha laid his hand on Jehu's shoulder.

"You are tired after your long journey, my son," he said soothingly. "Take your time. Rest and refresh yourself before we talk any more."

With his arm round Jehu's shoulder Elisha led him to the tents.

He told his young men to light a fire and sat quietly while Jehu ate and drank hurriedly and uncomfortably. Twilight came swiftly, night fell, the fragrant smoke from the fire rose steadily into the darkness. When Jehu had finished, Elisha motioned to the disciples, who had been waiting on them, and they moved away.

"Now tell me all about it," he said.

"Master, I have already told you. Joram is very angry. He's afraid of you. He always has been afraid of you, and you are speaking more and more violently against him. At the moment he thinks he's safe. Israel is at peace, the harvest has been gathered, now he wants to get rid of you. He has often threatened to do so and done nothing. This time there is no question about it, I know. He intends to kill you."

"And he chose you to carry out his plan?"

"That above all was a sign to me. He chose me in order to test me. He distrusts even me. That's how things are, he does not trust even me any longer. He didn't say so, but I could tell by the way he spoke. He wants to force me to choose. If I do not obey him, then he knows what to do. That must not happen. Joram has got to trust me right up to the last moment. That's why we must not delay longer."

Elisha did not answer. After a while Jehu said slyly and anxiously:

"Joram's no fool. He knows very well that I am his right hand and his defence, at least as long as I wish to be and obey him. And he has a pretty good idea that his officers and men have more respect for me than for him. Who has spent his whole life with them, Joram or I? Who knows each one of them personally, Joram or I? Who gave them your warning about the danger to Israel? I alone. I am Israel's defence. What is Joram without me? He knows that quite well. But I want him to trust me. Listen! I told the officers to obey his order, as they should, unless I sent a different command!"

"What order?"

Jehu laughed softly.

"Joram intends to attack Ramoth Gilead, to capture the fortress that your friend Hazael has not yet handed over. Gilead is to be taken by a surprise attack before Hazael is aware of it."

"And so Joram is wantonly leading Israel into war! I made peace and now he is making a new war."

"It isn't a war, only a raid, all over in a few days. Gilead is only weakly garrisoned since peace was made with Hazael. Besides Joram is only taking what Hazael promised."

Jehu paused, lowered his eyes, and continued without looking at Elisha: "That's not what I say; it's what Joram says. Admittedly it was I who suggested the scheme. I deceived him, when he wanted to send me here to arrest you. I told him I had made plans to attack Gilead and begged him to allow me to carry it through. Because he doesn't trust me he insisted on his command being obeyed, so I went. But I know that now he will carry out the plan in my place without knowing he's doing just what I wanted him to do."

"Why did you do that?"

"Joram will not take Gilead by surprise. Before I left I sent a warning to the fortress. Joram's attack will fail. At first I thought that you would send a warning to Hazael, as he is your friend. But that would have been too late. So I sent the message myself. I have men in my pay even in Gilead."

Jehu paused again, then continued softly and hurriedly: "Joram may be in a hurry. Who knows what will happen? Can you tell the flight of every arrow? Can I not aim an arrow? Who can know how things will turn out?"

Elisha burst out: "You did that without a word from me! It's treachery, not to Joram alone but to Israel and to all those who give their lives in vain. And I tell you your treachery is not the sign I am waiting for. If you go on with your scheme, the hand of the Lord will be withdrawn from you."

Jehu struck his fist on the ground.

"Your words are puzzling and confusing. You ought not to puzzle and confuse me just now."

"I'm not confusing you," Elisha answered, angrily and bitterly. "Maybe the Lord, whose word I speak, is confusing me and making my voice so feeble that you do not understand me."

"You call what I've done *treachery*! I call it strategy and sacrifice. Strategy is the weapon of the weaker side and sacrifice is justified in a good cause. You keep telling me to wait for a sign from you. I've waited and waited, and now I'm not willing to wait any longer, since you just say nothing and refuse to give the final sign. I see signs enough, they are clear enough to me."

"What signs?" asked Elisha scornfully.

"Joram's order to me. What he said to me."

Elisha laughed.

"Don't laugh!" shouted Jehu indignantly. "Your neck and mine are at stake. That is fact, not one of your dreams!" Then immediately he changed his mind, swallowed hastily and said humbly: "Forgive me, Master. I am very sorry. Your laughter provoked me." As Elisha did not speak he added with crafty flattery: "You do not answer. Listen! You have sworn a pact with me and I will keep it. I will do only what you tell me to."

"What do you mean?"

"You know what I mean. Every word you speak is rebellion and revolt as long as Joram is on the throne. The pact that you made with me was rebellion and revolt. Your power over the people is rebellion and revolt. You and I are only doing the same thing. Is it thanks to me or to Joram's fear or his foolish patience that you have been left so long unmolested? Now he is driven by fear, his patience is exhausted and so is his confidence in me, so he sent me to arrest you. Me! do you hear? Because I was a follower of yours and because I am true to you I have become suspect in his eyes. How can I wait any longer when I am faced with ruin? So I won't go back without you. You are my Master. I want to listen to your word and you want your word to be fulfilled. How can you fulfil it without me? So you must decide whether you will stand by your pact, whether you will back up what I have done, so that your word and our pact may be fulfilled, or whether you will give yourself up to me so that I can take you to the King. It is for you to choose."

"You are threatening me again. I shall ignore what you said, Jehu. It shall be forgotten. How can I be afraid of you, when I am not afraid of Joram? I told you that I am not afraid of him." Elisha looked Jehu up and down and there was sadness and mockery in his answer: "You are growing, my son. You are outgrowing my tutelage. Do you really need my word?"

"Do not belittle yourself to me, Master. You are the word of the Lord. I am the weapon of Israel, but you are Israel herself. Your word is accepted by the whole nation—and your anointing! What is my success worth without your anointing? That was our pact and I need you more than ever, now that it is about to be fulfilled."

"So that's what's on your mind!" Elisha leaned forward, put his head in his hands and stared into the dying fire. After a long time he looked up. "I will go with you," he said firmly, "not because you have seen some sort of sign, but so that my word may guide you, and so that you will not forget the true meaning of the pact. I will speak when I receive the sign." Jehu leaned forward, seized Elisha's hand and kissed it. Elisha quickly drew his hand away in protest.

"Where are you going now?" he asked.

Jehu sat up and answered impatiently: "To my troops. I must speak to my officers, so that everything may be ready. I shall go to the camp of Jezreel, and if Joram has already set out, I shall go after him. I shall send word that I am coming and that you are with me. He may be glad, as far as he is still in a position to be glad. But you will stay in the camp, not in the town, where Joram or the Woman might seize you. In the camp I can protect you. In the care of my men you are safe. Do you approve?"

Elisha merely nodded.

They set out early next morning, but only made slow progress, slower than Jehu liked. Elisha had insisted that the disciples should come with them, although they had no horses. He walked with them and stopped to rest in every village on the way. There he called the elders of the village together and spoke to them. When Jehu objected at the second stop, Elisha answered casually: "I want them to know where I'm going."

Jehu protested in vain.

"King Joram doesn't want that, I know," Elisha said. "But I do, and it is to your advantage, my son Jehu."

Jehu scowled and did not reply.

During the night at the camp Jehu had woken up several times from an uneasy sleep. Elisha was still sitting by the hearth. Jehu saw him in the cold moonlight crouching forward with the big cloak round his shoulders, dark and motionless, like a block of stone. Sometime during the night some of the disciples had come and made up the fire, and Elisha had spoken to them in a low voice. Later on he had got up and walked away, Jehu did not know where. He would have liked to follow him, but dared not, so he went to sleep again. Elisha had certainly not had any sleep. In the morning his face looked drawn and grey beneath his tan and he walked heavily. Jehu had an uneasy suspicion that Elisha was carrying out a decision he had reached in the night, and would not be turned from it by anything he could say, so he gave in and said nothing. Perhaps it was wiser to do what Elisha wanted, and perhaps it was wiser not to hurry.

Whenever the elders gathered in the villages Elisha did not speak to them very long. He would point out Jehu beside him on his horse, waiting with compressed lips and wrinkled brow:

"This is Jehu, Captain of the King's army. Joram sent him to take me to him." Then the elders, silent and thoughtful, understood the sinister meaning of the words. Those who did not yet know Jehu glanced up at him with suspicious watchful eyes, and turned back to Elisha. If he stayed longer, Jehu would lean down from the saddle and murmur: "We must go on, Master! We must go!" Elisha raised no objection. With a ghost of a smile he would repeat to the people standing round: "Yes, we must go. Pass it on." It was spoken in a friendly casual way and yet it was a definite command. He waited a little longer, and in almost every village someone amongst the elders would say: "Will you let me go with you?" and Elisha would nod consent. If nobody spoke, he would himself turn to someone—he seemed to know them all by name—and ask him: "Won't you come with me on my journey?" and nobody hesitated. Then from every place where there were Sons of the Prophets these came too. After some days, when they at last reached the plain, Jehu's little band had increased to a train of carts, wagons, riders and people on foot, travelling noisily and slowly along the road without any sign of haste, since Elisha was not hurrying. They did not know of course that the King was planning an armed raid. Elisha had not told them about that.

At last they saw in the distance the vast camp, the long lines of identical tents made of dark skins, row upon row, with broad strips of drill ground in between, the whole camp ringed with a rampart of earth with pointed towers. There it lay in the noonday haze like a flock of sheep in the fold asleep in the sun. Further on beyond the big field lay the walls and houses of Jezreel, grey and brown and white in the sunlit dust.

"Well, there it is," said Elisha to Jehu. "King Ahab waited here in his camp for me to come and speak the word of the Lord. I cursed him, it is true, but with all his wickedness he was better than his sons."

"Ahab's camp was nothing," said Jehu scornfully. "He only came here when he had no other choice, and there was a lot of fuss and discussion whenever he came. This camp is my own creation. I had the ramparts built round it and the watchtowers, and arranged the military training, so that Israel should be strong. How often I had to beg and argue before he would give me the requisite labour force! Ahab preferred to build palaces in Jezreel, where he and the Woman could live in splendour and luxury. Do you still remember Naboth and his vineyard?"

"Of course," said Elisha preoccupied, then he added bitterly: "I came to him and went away sorrowful, because he would not heed my words. He let me down, and it was at your insistence that I remained silent."

"Haven't I come now to summon you to speak? That is all I want."

"Ahab also sent for me that I might speak." Elisha looked at Jehu and said quietly: "I will speak, so that you may prove yourself, but you shall not know your final test."

"What further proof do you want from me?" Jehu asked in surprise and suspicion.

"You shall not know," repeated Elisha and said no more.

They found the camp lightly garrisoned. Joram had already set out some days before with a considerable force, many more than Jehu had expected. A message had arrived the previous day asking for reinforcements and these were about to leave when Jehu arrived. He hurriedly called together all the officers still in the camp and spoke long and excitedly to them. Once or twice he pointed at Elisha, but did not call him and left him with his followers. At last he returned with Bidekar.

"I won't let them go!" he said imperiously. "Jezreel must not be left unprotected. Of course Joram is counting on reinforcements, because what I foresaw has happened." The thought made him smile. "I must go to Gilead, and will give him my answer. You stay here, Master, because it is only here that you are safe. Joram already knows that I am bringing you. I sent him word, otherwise I could not get to him. But you are safe here and Bidekar will look after you. You will hear from me soon."

He had gone without waiting for Elisha's answer. Trumpet calls sounded through the camp. Jehu was already on his way with a small force and most of the officers.

In the evening the elders sat round Elisha. Bidekar had found accommodation for them in the camp and had posted sentries closely along the walls, so that no one could approach from Jezreel. The elders sat there solemn and bewildered, and kept looking inquiringly at Elisha. He had asked them to come with him to the King, but the King was not here, and Elisha seemed to have expected that. The King had gone. He was with his army at Gilead and Elisha was obviously not surprised. Would the King return, or did Elisha possibly intend to go on? They did not know. On the journey Elisha had been friendly and affable, even cheerfully excited and expectant. Now, although he was sitting with them, it was in solemn silence, that was like a wall between them. Now and then one of them would lean over and whisper anxiously and restlessly to his neighbour.

The camp was restless too. It was late in the evening, yet it was not quiet. Soldiers were coming and going and stopped to gaze in good humoured surprise at the elders. When they saw Elisha they pulled themselves together and went on quickly. Out of the darkness came the sounds of shouting and raucous singing, horses neighing, the rattle of weapons, the harsh scraping of grindstones and the rumbling and creaking of carts. They were preparing for something.

In the distance, in the silence over Jezreel, the lights began to go out. At last one of the elders ventured to raise his voice:

"We are waiting. You told us that the King commanded you to appear before him, but now he has gone to Gilead and you are here."

Elisha glanced up but merely nodded.

"You asked us to come with you. Do you intend to go on to meet Joram?"

"No."

"It isn't right that we should be away from home at such a time. We did not know that the King was going to war. What is going to happen next?"

"The word of the Lord will be fulfilled. Perhaps . . ."

He looked from one to the other. They did not know whether he wanted them to ask what the word of the Lord was or not. They lowered their eyes and kept quiet. After a while Elisha got up.

"Go to bed if you're tired," he said, wearily and gently. "Nothing more will happen tonight."

One of the disciples jumped up.

"Tell us what's going to happen," he begged.

Elisha stopped and hesitated. When he spoke his words held a strange persuasion.

"I am not going to tell you. Wait, as I am waiting! There will be a sign when it happens."

He turned away and left them. Along the lines of tents he went, through the main gate, past the sentries, who had orders not to let anyone pass, but hurriedly drew back when they saw him. He did not know where he was being led. He left the main road and turned into the fields, walking as if in a dream. The night was dark, the waning moon was low in the sky. He could just make out the darker shadows of trees and bushes. At last he stopped and leaned against a tree trunk, staring into the darkness. There was the camp, and over there the town, beyond that the plain and the sleeping countryside, and behind him the hills, the mountains and the river. Suddenly he seemed to see the whole country, and opened his arms as though in a wide embrace. He was filled with a sense of triumph and power, the exultant joy of fulfilment. My word and my hand! Sleep, my land of Israel in my hand, that rules over you in patience. The patience has been great, the waiting long. Now it is over. One more night, maybe, and one more day, and my word will be fulfilled.

All round him there was a strange rushing sound, the night seemed to be speaking with many voices, and he listened enraptured. Was he now to be granted the joy of hearing the voice of the Lord? His heart almost stopped in fear. The joy and triumph faded and vanished like an elusive dream and suddenly he was seized with terror. He heard many voices speaking and listened with all his senses alert, holding his breath, so as not to miss them, but the rushing sound remained confused and made no sense. Again and again he imagined that he caught a word and tried desperately to understand it, to hold it, so that it might become a sign, a message and a summons, the hint of an answer, but it vanished irrevocably before he could grasp it, like flotsam on the water. The voices of the night had no meaning for him. He clasped his hands before his face, he covered his ears in despair, he let go of the tree and ran stumbling, staggering, driven by measureless terror.

The word would be fulfilled—but what word? The elders had not asked, and now the night speaks and I ask in vain. Too much and too little! All my life I have demanded decision, and now I do not know what it is! I have taken a risk and now I must carry it through, there is no longer any way of avoiding or postponing it. And I cannot do it! He stumbled, fell and lay with senses reeling, finding a meagre comfort and relief in the feel of dew-drenched grass and soft earth, that crumbled soundlessly in his groping hands. He just lay there waiting till at last the night grew quiet.

After a long time, he got up. All round him was silence and cool darkness, within him icy emptiness and despair. He made his way back, creeping cautiously and wearily along the edge of the road, looking anxiously about, guiltily, as though he had escaped from some horrible prison and feared recapture.

Another day passed and another night. The hours dragged by like a slow trickle of sand, without reason or end. He was almost dropping with fatigue, but could not stay in the camp. He went away before dawn and did not return till night. Sometime or other sleep overcame him, and when in the early dawn a hand was laid on his shoulder he started up out of an oppressive dream. Bidekar was leaning over him, beside him a torchbearer.

"A message from Jehu, Sir."

The torch cast a reddish light and hard shadows on Bidekar's face. His voice was shrill with excitement. Elisha looked at him with dazed eyes, but got up immediately. Then he noticed that the light of the torch was deceptive. Bidekar's face was not red but pale with intense excitement and his shrill voice could hardly get the words out.

"What's the message?" asked Elisha.

"Hurry, Sir. There is bad news. The officers have heard it and are asking for you."

"Can't you speak up? What is the news?"

"Joram led the attack yesterday. It was beaten off and Joram was fatally wounded in the battle. Jehu sent the message. They are bringing Joram back to Jezreel, to the palace."

"Fatally wounded? In the battle? Was that Jehu's message? Those were his exact words?"

Elisha groped for the tent-pole and stood motionless clinging to it. There was a blinding light in his eyes, the ground rocked beneath his feet, his ears were filled with thunder, and he could hardly breathe. Dawn was breaking, it was getting lighter every minute. Bidekar was standing there with his torchbearer and it was he who had spoken. Had Bidekar noticed his weakness? Elisha raised his hand:

"Have the messenger brought here," he ordered. "I want to talk to him."

Bidekar was about to object, but changed his mind. He turned crossly to the torchbearer and rapped out: "Fetch him! Didn't you hear? Quick!" and when they were alone he said impatiently to Elisha: "There is no time to lose, Sir. Everything is ready, but there are orders to give, and Jehu—"

He stopped as Elisha looked at him, and lowered his eyes. Elisha was standing at the door of the tent, leaning forward with furrowed brow, his jaws working, staring wide-eyed towards the messenger, who was now approaching with the torchbearer, followed by two captains. The messenger was covered with dust and dirt, and so tired that he could hardly keep on his feet. He came up and bowed over Elisha's hand. Elisha raised him up quickly. His voice sounded surprisingly gentle.

"Welcome! What's your name?"

"Jair, son of Abia from Thaanach."

"You know me, Jair?"

"Yes."

"Then tell me what happened."

"My Lord Jehu sent me with the message."

"Wait, my son. That was not what I asked. I don't want to hear the message. I want to know what happened."

Jair looked uncertanly at Bidekar and the captains, who were staring at him impatiently and grimly. Elisha gestured to them and they stepped back unwillingly. Elisha led Jair into the tent by his couch.

"You're tired. Sit down," he said and sat down beside him. "Don't be afraid. Tell me what happened."

"What I said, Sir," Jair burst out surlily. "What else should I say? We waited too long, that's what it was. If Jehu had been with us from the beginning, things would have been different. They had time to prepare, they were armed, and we could not do anything. And when the King tried to break off the battle, they stormed out of the gates and attacked us. King Joram was right in the front in his chariot when he was struck by the spear. It was all we could do to get him out."

"Where were you when all this happened?"

"Quite close. Much too close, believe me."

"And you saw with your own eyes that it happened just like that?"

"Yes."

"You saw the spear and saw the King fall?"

"Yes, certainly."

Elisha leaned forward breathing hard.

"Tell me, who threw the spear?"

Jair looked at him in bewilderment, shrugged his shoulders and said gruffly and meekly: "Excuse me, Sir, I don't know the names of the defenders of Gilead. How should I?"

"Now Jair, listen carefully and tell the truth, for this is the sign. Do you hear?"

"Yes, Sir, of course. I am listening."

"Where was Jehu when this happened?"

"He was leading the chariots, as Joram had ordered. It was thanks to him that we escaped so lightly. He restored order after the King fell and some of them were running away."

"Jair," shouted Elisha. "Can you swear? Did the spear by any chance come Jehu's hand?"

"From Jehu's hand? What do you mean? No, Sir, how should he . . . ?"

"Will you swear that it happened just as you said?"

"Yes, of course—if you want me to. I saw it, I swear. Jehu turned the chariots back and grouped them round the King when he fell."

He stopped, startled and astonished. Elisha jumped up and rushed out of the tent.

"Bidekar! Bidekar! Call them together, all of them, and my disciples as well."

He turned back into the tent, taking no further notice of Jair. Soon he came out again with a flask in his hand and strode swiftly along the wide path between the tents down to the parade ground. People looked at him in astonishment and terror, for his face was alight with savage exultant joy. He stamped along as if it took all his strength to carry this burden of unbelievable happiness.

"Hear the word of the Lord!" he shouted, "Hear the word of the Lord! He has given us a sign at last. His chosen one has stood the test. The hand of the Lord has struck—his hand alone. The curse on Joram has been fulfilled."

He caught his breath and stopped. He had seen his disciples and remained staring at one of them who faced his burning scrutiny motionless and stared back. He had known Elisha for a long time and had dared to speak when Elisha himself was silent.

"You, Micha, come here!"

Elisha held out the flask to him as he approached, and drew himself up.

"Listen carefully to what I have to say to you. Gird up your loins and take this flask of oil with you to Ramoth Gilead, and when you get there, you will find Jehu, the son of Joshaphat, the son of Nimshi. Go to him and ask him to leave his friends, and take him into an inner room and pour this oil over his head and say: 'Thus saith the Lord! I have anointed you to be King of Israel!' Then open the door immediately and flee."

"I will go at once."

Micha bowed low and kissed the hem of his cloak. Elisha leaned over him and said softly: "Do what I've told you, say what I've said and nothing else."

Micha got up, looked at Elisha without speaking and ran.

In the breathless silence that followed Bidekar shouted: "You have heard. Joram has fallen and the prophet of the Lord has spoken. Jehu is our King. Acclaim him!"

The air was filled with answering shouts and the rattle of arms and the fanfares that Bidekar had obviously kept ready. "Jehu is King! Jehu is King!" They crowded round Elisha in the middle of the parade ground and bowed low. Hardly any of them heard the trumpet call from the watchtower. It was some time before they noticed it. Then they stopped, silent and someone shouted: "Listen! That must be Joram's chariot. They are bringing him back."

The sun was already high and the air was clear. They could see a cloud of dust coming slowly along the road. Bidekar turned to the captains and said: "To your posts!"

This also had obviously been prepared and everyone knew what he had to do. They dispersed quickly, soon platoons were hurrying to the walls and to the gate. Elisha was left alone with his disciples and the old people. He was completely exhausted but managed to say to them: "I have spoken the word of the Lord. Now go and make known throughout Israel what I have said."

Bidekar heard his words and turned back with a smile.

"All right. But you will stay here, Master. That is Jehu's—the King's—wish. We have to obey his wishes."

The sun was setting, the evening aglow as it only is at this time of day, before the sky pales and the mists rise. The little hill where Jehu was standing was some distance from the fortress of Ramoth, but he could see every detail even from here.

The walls of Ramoth were blackened with smoke and bore traces of the battle of the previous day, and the slope and fields even more so. There lay the big stones that they had rolled down yesterday, with smears of blood and earth on them, and the remains of the chariots with wheels or axles smashed in collision, the bloated bodies of horses, and everywhere arrows, broken spears, axes, shields, helmets and swords, thrown away by their owners as they fell or fled. The grass was furrowed with countless tracks of chariots and trampled and flattened by countless feet. The smell of smoke and corpses still hung in the air.

Behind Jehu lay the camp of Israel and beyond that the road from Jezreel to Damascus, the road guarded and dominated by Ramoth.

Here and there a bird twittered, from the camp came the sound of hammering, otherwise all was quiet. Jehu had ordered trenches to be dug and stakes driven in to protect the camp—not because he intended to stay here or feared an attack, but simply so that his men should not have too much leisure to think about their defeat. There would be no further trouble here for a long time. Jehu knew it and smiled contentedly. He had access to the fortress and those inside who were in his pay had proved themselves trustworthy. They had known about the attack and had done what he told them to. In return they had been victorious and were still in possession of the fort. That's fine, excellent, thought Jehu. Their time would come also, but then he would defeat them in a different way from that attempted by Joram. At the moment it was most fortunate that they felt safe and expected peace. A few hours more and he would strike camp and set off for Jezreel, leaving just a small force here to protect his rear from any possible surprise. They did not know that in the camp yet, only the captains were in the secret, and even they did not know everything.

Jehu looked anxiously along the road. Would the messenger never come? Did he really need the messenger, now that the hand of the Lord had shown itself so splendidly in that chance spear?

Perhaps he ought to have started that morning, perhaps it was an irrevocable mistake to let Joram set out. Was Joram already dead? What was happening now in Jezreel? He wouldn't wait for the messenger any longer. Perhaps Bidekar had bungled the plan. The messenger should have been here a long time ago—or had that cantankerous old man once again refused at the last moment to do as he had promised? He had spoken of a final test, but now there was to be no further test.

Jehu got up and turned back to the house in which he had made his headquarters. Only the night before Joram had been sleeping here. It was just a farmhouse with thick walls, small windows and a low roof, but the farmer who normally lived here was prosperous, and Joram's things were still there. It was already getting dark, the torches were alight and Jehu's captains were sitting round the table waiting for their supper. Their voices were loud and irritable. They stood up in silence as Jehu entered. He was just going to his seat when there was a shout from outside:

"Jehu, son of Joshaphat! Jehu, son of Joshaphat! Where are you?"

The voice was hoarse, penetrating and masterful. Jehu stopped. He alone knew what the shout might mean, and he could not be sure. He felt all eyes on him and tried to smile as if he knew no more than the others. The door behind him was pushed open. He did not turn round. The raucous voice shouted behind him: "Where are you, Captain? I have a message for you."

Micha was standing in the doorway. Jehu suddenly felt sure, before he had seen the messenger, that this would be the word of the Lord. He wanted to shout in exultation, but controlling himself he turned round slowly and managed to keep his voice casual and almost gay.

"To which of us do you want to speak?"

"To you Captain, alone!" And Micha held up the flask.

Jehu stared at him, suddenly embarrassed. All the others saw the raised flask and listened breathlessly. Jehu went up to Micha as though Micha had ordered him to, and said in a strangely quiet tone: "Come to my room."

He seized a torch, led Micha away and did not speak till they were alone in his room.

"Have you brought Elisha's word?"

"I bring the word of the Lord. Lower your head," and Micha raised his arm and dripped the oil over Jehu's head.

"Thus saith the Lord, the God of Israel! I have anointed you King of the Lord's people Israel!"

Jehu rose trembling. Micha seized his arm and whispered: "Listen Jehu, King of Israel!" Just a whisper, thrilling and frightening. Jehu felt a cold shiver run through him as he listened in fear: "This and no more was my message, but I have more to say, for I have never been afraid and have suffered misery and danger for speaking the word of the Lord. Thus saith the Lord through me: You must smite the house of Ahab, that I may avenge the blood of my servants that Jezebel has shed. For the whole house of Ahab shall perish. I will wipe out all the males of Ahab's house wherever they may be. And I will make the house of Ahab like the house of Jeroboam the son of Nebat and like the house of Baasha the son of Ahijah. And the dogs shall eat Jezebel in the field of Jezreel, and no one will bury her!"

Just a whisper that grew louder and louder till at last it seemed to fill the whole house. Micha let go of Jehu's arm, turned away, pushed the door open and ran out. Jehu did not move. The words still rang in his ears. Did Micha really say them, or had they come from his own lips, from the insistent secret darkness of his own wishes and plans? Micha's word thrilled him with a terrifying joy that the word of the Lord had come in this way! He passed his hands across his brow, felt the oil, straightened up and went out. When he entered the room his face was again hard and alert. The captains surrounded him, asking excitedly: "Jehu, is all well? What is it? Why did this madman come?"

Jehu stopped leaving a space between him and them and answered impatiently:

"Why do you ask? You know the man and his errand. That's what happened!"

"No, we know nothing. It isn't true. Tell us."

"He is Micha, one of Elisha's disciples. You know him. Didn't you see the flask? Well then, he brought the oil of the Lord and poured it over my head and spoke Elisha's word to me: 'Thus saith the Lord, I have anointed you King of Israel!' "

He raised his hand and pointed to the shining oil on his head. For a moment there was profound silence, then one of them stepped forward, bent down and spread his cloak at Jehu's feet and all the others did the same, and shouted:

"Jehu is King! Jehu is King!"

Jehu stamped his foot with a rattle of armour and they paused.

"All right! That's enough!" he said. "We have no time! Go and tell the men, and tell the horsemen to saddle and get ready. We are leaving."

They rushed out and Jehu remained alone, listening eagerly. He heard the trumpet call followed immediately by shouts of: "Jehu is King! Jehu is King!" He tried to walk and suddenly staggered drunkenly, his mouth opened in a wild paroxysm of laughter. He could not control himself and had to wait till it passed, but no one had seen or heard. When he recovered his breath, he groped along the wall and went slowly out into the darkness, lit here and there by fires and torches—to the waiting people.

By the time the chariot reached Jezreel Joram was unconscious, but on the way he had given orders for the city to be placed in a state of emergency, for he feared pursuit and after his defeat he was very much afraid that the troops that had remained behind under Jehu could not, or even would not, protect him. Hazael had kept a terribly strong garrison in Ramoth, far stronger than Jehu had reported and the King had believed. After his collapse nobody but Jehu could take command, he had done so without asking and had saved the army. But now Joram, weakened from loss of blood and already half delirious, began to feel a horrible suspicion, like a nightmare, that Jehu had misled him purposely and enticed him into a trap.

Joram's order had been sent on ahead of the chariots, but it had never reached Jezreel. Bidekar's men had intercepted the messenger. He resisted, so they killed him on the spot without even hearing his message. However, Jezebel had not waited for any order from the King. Two days earlier she had received a report of unusual activity in the camp, and she heard about the arrival of Elisha and his followers. Next day all the watchtowers and gates of the camp had been manned and the traders, caterers, women and hangers-on, who usually came into the camp every day and all day, were unceremoniously driven out. No one from the camp came into the town. Towards evening it was reported from the walls that small groups of armed men were methodically patrolling outside the town, keeping the walls and approach roads under observation. Jezebel did not yet know what was happening at Ramoth, but she suspected that something was wrong and issued an order on her own authority that the gates should be shut and the walls manned. Of course she knew, as well as her surprised and distracted servants did, that the order was of little use. They were defenceless; too few fighting men had been left in Jezreel. There were only the pampered palace guards, the priests and the eunuchs. Jezreel was not built for war and siege. The protection of the town was left to the great fortified camp, but the camp had suddenly become strangely hostile. It lay there silent and menacing like a malignant beast watching its prey and awaiting its opportunity.

As the King's cavalcade approached, the terrified guards ran and hurriedly opened the gates. When Jezebel saw Joram on the stretcher she was shocked. When she heard what had happened and that the army at Ramoth was now under Jehu's command, she was terrified. She questioned the men with Joram, and although their answers gave no grounds for her suspicions, she felt sure that the defeat at Ramoth and what was happening in the camp were connected parts of a single definite plan, for which only Jehu could be responsible. And now the rebel had got the army under his control.

The King was taken into his bedroom and surgeons, courtiers, and women gathered round his bed. He was delirious. Jezebel assembled her priests and ordered continuous sacrifices to be offered. She was here, there and everywhere, and with anger and threats kept demanding fresh efforts. At midday, Ahaziah arrived from Jerusalem. He had come down from the mountains into the town unmolested, but his coming did not mean reinforcements. He brought no troops with him apart from his bodyguard. He had hurried over as soon as he heard about his brother-in-law's injury. Now he was hanging around terrified and bewildered. Jezebel turned away from him in contempt.

Towards evening it looked as if the endless sacrifices and prayers were proving successful. Joram recovered consciousness. He was very weak from loss of blood, exhaustion and fever, but he was able to recognize Jezebel and Ahaziah standing by his bedside, asked for a drink and immediately fell asleep again. The doctors said that this meant that he had turned the corner. Jezebel did not believe them.

The evening passed slowly, the night wore on. Jezebel walked restlessly through her empty rooms. She had sent away her women, girls and attendants, because she wanted to be alone. Occasionally she opened the window and looked out. The news of the defeat had long since spread through the town and of course the townsfolk too knew about the strange and menacing closure of the camp. A crowd had gathered outside the palace, waiting aimlessly, staring up at the windows. Jezebel could hear the confused murmur of their voices and wondered whether this too concealed a threat. Should she order them to be driven out and dispersed, with sword and spear? The air was heavy with incense, down below in the gardens a reddish glow indicated that the sacrificial fires were still burning. The pale shadows of the priests and their attendants passed to and fro, and Jezebel could hear their weary and monotonous supplication and chanting. Behind the gardens were the lights of the town and then the darkness of the open fields. Beyond the darkness the camp fires gleamed. Nothing further had happened today, the camp was quiet, but its silence threatened Jezreel.

Jezebel was about to walk away when her shoulders suddenly sagged and she collapsed helplessly on the marble floor. Her knees refused to support her, she put her hands to her head and covered her face. Her whole body was contorted in paralysing fear and bitter helpless rage. She suddenly realized with overwhelming clarity that none of the things that she feared had so far happened. The terror and collapse was caused by her own unmistakable and unshakable certainty that what she feared would inevitably happen, that the end was near, and that she could do nothing about it. Her one consuming desire was for the danger to take actual shape at last and put an end to the agonizing suspense, and this desire only increased her fear still more.

After a long time she sat up, then struggled to her feet and clenched her fists. She was still the Queen, now she was the sole ruler, and she intended to remain so, even if Joram recovered. She went back into the bedroom. Joram was still sleeping, breathing heavily. The night passed.

Jehu and his men rode on without pause through the clear night. What a long time it seemed since the events of the evening! He had lost count of time. Expectation and doubt had been followed by anxiety, laughter and the victory, cheers and homage, the breathless haste and feverish excitement of departure. That was all over now. Forward, on and on! There was to be no sleep tonight.

Jehu's head was cool and clear, his lips were tightly pressed together, his eyes bright, his hands on the reins sure. His heart beat no faster than the pounding of the horses' hoofs behind him. The night offered comfort, secrecy and security. No one was expecting this night ride, and if people happened to hear it, they could hide in fear inside their houses and cottages and stop their ears. There was nobody to oppose him. In his clear head there was cautious anticipation and cool cunningly calculated certainty. This ride was like a military expedition, something that he was used to, and yet it was different, for this time it was his campaign. His hour had come and he knew exactly what he had to do. There was a great deal to do, and he would do it. Today, tomorrow, through the long years, he had plenty of time. This was only the beginning. Joram was still there—if he were still alive. Since the word of the Lord had been spoken, he was probably dead. Supposing he were still alive, what did it matter? He would have to die. What was he now? A bit of rubbish discarded by the hand of the Lord. The word of the Lord had been spoken, the oil had been poured over Jehu's head, what he had not yet got he would take, for it belonged to him by the word of the Lord. Tomorrow Joram and the whole house of Ahab, would be no more. He would obey the word of the Lord and destroy them. He did not know how it would happen, he had no definite plan yet, but it would happen and he would do it. Joram and Jezebel, the women, the children, the infants—he would wipe them all out. They would pay in blood for every hour of his long wait, blood for every insolent word, blood for every humiliation and embarrassment, blood for every command. Their punishment would be the fulfilment of the word of the Lord and not revenge. The priests, the servants, all the useless foreign crowd, he would hunt them out and kill them. Blood for their debauchery, blood for their evil seduction, blood for their haughty obstinacy, blood for their sinister magic, and all in fulfilment of the word of the Lord and not revenge. Who was there to oppose him? Israel was behind him, the army was Israel, and the word of the Lord was with him. Elisha? There was a pause in his greedy whirling thoughts. Elisha! Jehu smiled contentedly. Soon he would not need Elisha any more either. Already, tonight, he did not need him any longer. The long wait was over. Even Elisha did not know his most secret plans and must not know them. Jehu was King and he intended to be King alone. Who dared to question his ideas and plans, if he chose to keep his own counsel? He had been afraid of Elisha, now he was afraid of him no longer. The man of God had done Jehu's will. Jehu's will was the stronger and would remain so. He would exact forced labour from the people and impose even greater hardships on them, so that his plans should be carried through. He would build no ivory palaces, he did not want rich foods, a soft couch, women, foreign trinkets, jewellery and perfumes. He wanted roads and walls, strong camps, many chariots and weapons, and all sorts of war material. Forced labour would provide these for him. It would need time, but Jehu knew how to wait in spite of his impetuosity, he had proved that. He knew too when to strike. Ramoth Gilead—he would probably capture it sometime, but he did not intend to dissipate his forces over minor fortresses. Patience! Patience! Soon he would send secret envoys to Assyria offering loyal friendship, tribute and gifts and a firm alliance. The great King would probably be pleased at the deference of the valiant Jehu. The main thing was the alliance—the alliance against Hazael and Syria. That was the answer, the bright idea that had come to him that night when Joram in his blindness tried to test him by ordering the arrest of Elisha. Of what avail were dungeons and vengeance against the word of Elisha? The whole nation would have risen in revolt against the wicked King. He had more to do than to bother about Elisha, that was the real answer. He would do more. "Where does your danger lie, great Assyria?" his envoys would ask. "Not in Israel, that only wants peace and quiet and of her own free will sends you friendly gifts. Syria is the enemy! Hazael is the enemy!" Elisha made peace with Hazael and what was it worth? Syria must be destroyed, so that Assyria may have security and Israel peace at last. Assyria must form an alliance with Israel so that the blow that destroys Syria may be struck on both frontiers at once. There would be war and that would mean sacrifices in order to deliver the decisive blow. Nevertheless Israel would applaud Jehu, since peace would come with victory. It would take years and years, but that would not matter as long as he achieved his purpose. All else was child's play, over in a few days or weeks. Ahaziah would have to be removed from Judah. He must die, for he was related by marriage to Ahab. None of Ahab's relatives must remain. He would kill them. What about the Woman and her house? Should he send her bloody head to announce the termination of the old treaty? He would not even do that much. Let the stray dogs report her shame and downfall. The harder he struck now the less they would dare against him. Fear was a great discipline and they were going to fear him, Edom, Moab, Gad, Bashan. There was a lot to do. Jehu was King and all would be fulfilled according to his will. Was it a dream, that all seemed so easy? Forward! Forward! There is no sleep tonight. It is already dawning, the day is coming swiftly. There are the white walls of Jezreel tinged with rose in the early light.

None of the captains had asked during the night what Jehu's plans were or what their individual orders were. What was to happen had been settled long ago and Jehu's men were accustomed to silence and obedience. They all felt sure that he would make for the camp first, but when they reached the fields outside Jezreel,

Jehu did not turn aside but rode straight on towards the town. He sent a single messenger to the camp, and the men speculated in some surprise whether Bidekar already knew what had happened and what was developing now. Obviously he knew enough and had his orders. Jehu knew how to prepare an attack, they said confidently.

Jehu stopped in the middle of the field and drew up his horsemen in a wide arc facing the gate. The gate was shut, the field deserted, and nobody was to be seen on the walls, but Jehu knew that the town was no longer asleep, and there were eyes behind the turrets watching him. He wanted them to see him. Should he pretend to know nothing? Should he ride up to the gate and demand admission, as the commander of the King's army had the right to do? It was broad daylight, would they dare to refuse him admission? Once inside the gate, the rest would be easy, quickly over and done with. He knew beyond question that they would not open the gate. They had orders from the Woman. He wanted them to wait, to see his power, and wonder in terror what he was going to do. It would be some time before Bidekar's troops could get there. He turned round and saw that the first platoons were already leaving the camp and advancing in battle order. Bidekar knew his job. The eyes on the wall saw it too. Jehu smiled, and because he smiled his captains smiled also. Their King had his own clever scheme and obviously everything was happening according to plan. Behind the foot soldiers came the cavalry overtaking them and raising clouds of dust that flashed and sparkled in the early sunlight.

Bidekar was riding in front looking for Jehu. He spurred forward, dismounted, came quickly over to Jehu and bowed low. He was laughing as he said loudly: "I am in the presence of my King. What are your commands?"

"Rise, my brave Bidekar," answered Jehu happily. "Is all well?"

"All is well and ready. What are your commands?"

"Your horsemen are to join mine. Put the infantry behind them. We're waiting for Jezreel to open the gates and receive us fittingly."

"As you say."

Jehu detained Bidekar and asked quietly: "Where's Elisha?"

"I gave him my most splendid chariot and provided some for his disciples also. Those are the heavy chariots that can only go at walking pace, and I left them some distance back. I thought . . . Do you want to see him?"

Jehu hesitated. Should he let the people on the walls see Elisha was with him? The prophet's word might well open the gate. But this was a military matter, perhaps they would think it a sign of weakness, if he sent Elisha on ahead. Besides, it was too great an honour for the prophet. Let him hear in due course that this had been done without him, and see that he had no further authority now that he had spoken the word of the Lord.

"No, not yet. It may still be dangerous here. The prophet of the Lord must not come into danger, do you hear? Tell him so and put a few guards round him. Assure him of my warmest regard and gratitude."

"It shall be done at once."

Bidekar swung himself on to his horse and rode back to his men. He gave a signal and they shouted as loudly as they could:

"Jehu is our King! Jehu is our King!"

Jehu stood up in his stirrups and raised his helmet in salute. Then he looked at the gate again. Had they heard the shouts? It was time that something happened. He caught his breath. They had heard! The gate was opening slowly, were they going to let him in? A single horseman appeared and the gates shut again behind him. All eyes were on the rider, one of the young servants of Joram in court dress, riding gracefully and skilfully, but as he approached with all eyes on him and saw the serried ranks waiting in menacing silence, he seemed to feel embarrassed. When he stopped in front of Jehu, his voice was tense and he spoke more hurriedly than custom demanded:

"Greeting, Jehu! I bring a message from the King. What brings you here and is it peace?"

Jehu's hands tightened automatically on the reins. The King—then Joram was still alive. What did it matter? What was he? A bit of rubbish discarded by the hand of the Lord. But what would the others think? He is alive! Jehu clenched his teeth and let the messenger wait. At last he turned to his captains:

"The fool," he said with amused contempt. "He doesn't know who is King."

They laughed. Jehu had found the right tone. They were surprised at the message and also a little depressed. Now it all seemed a joke. Jehu turned to the messenger:

"What have you to do with peace?" he rapped out. "Fall in behind me."

Before the messenger knew what was happening two men seized the halter of his horse and dragged him away.

"Wait," said Jehu disdainfully. "We have plenty of time, we can wait. Soon the next one will come. They are very inquisitive over there."

They laughed again, but someone behind him muttered: "Did you hear? He spoke in the name of the King." Then he corrected himself. "In Joram's name. Is he still alive then? He was bleeding to death."

Another broke in: "He may have spoken by command of the Woman, so that we should not know. And even if he is alive, how long will he live?"

They stopped laughing. Nobody spoke.

"Here he comes!" cried Jehu angrily. He had overheard the conversation behind him, but pretended not to notice it. The gate opened again, and from a distance it looked almost as if the same messenger was coming out again. He looked just like the first one, except that he no longer capered or behaved affectedly. His hesitancy and nervousness were obvious even at a distance. He seemed to be very much afraid, for he halted further away and shouted:

"Captain Jehu! The King is waiting for your answer. What brings you here, and is it peace?"

This time Jehu did not keep him waiting. He gave a signal. Two horsemen rode up to the messenger and brought him between them up to Jehu.

"Here is your answer, fellow. What have you to do with peace? Go and join your friend."

They led him away. Jehu stared at the gate again. His patience was exhausted, his gay confidence of victory had vanished. How much longer should he wait? He knew he must not wait long, his position as King was still new and insecure. If he did not carry his purpose through quickly, they would soon forsake him and even turn against him, since Joram was alive. So far they had trusted him, although he had kept quiet about his plans. Did they realize yet that he was actually just as powerless as Joram on his sick bed? Joram could not resist an attack, he had neither men nor weapons in the town, but as Jehu had not forced the gate with one swift blow, he could not now mount an attack either, for he had neither catapults nor ladders. Joram had taken all the heavy equipment to Gilead, and even if Jehu had time to fetch it, he knew that he dare not besiege Jezreel—his men would soon desert him. He could feel their eyes on him and guessed that they were already weighing him up. He was still hesitating, wondering what command to give, when he started and shouted with relief:

"They are opening the gates. Get ready!"

Both wings were slowly and ceremoniously opened and a troop of horsemen with lances and pennons came out escorting two carriages. Jehu's face was suddenly contorted with fury. The horsemen were Joram's bodyguard and he could already see the heavy figure leaning back in the first carriage, holding himself up with obvious effort. Joram had come himself! And in the other carriage was Ahaziah. Jehu felt icy fear clutching at his heart, and then uncontrollable savage rage of disappointment. What Joram was doing was sheer madness. But this madness might save him. He was showing that he was still alive, that he was not afraid of Jehu, that he could match the rebel's courage with his own. Then Jehu's eyes flashed. The Lord has delivered him into my hand, he thought. That was what it meant....

Joram ignored the waiting troops, the half-circle of horsemen, the close ranks of infantry and the waiting chariots. He kept straight on up to Jehu and when he got near enough waved a greeting with his heavy hand and gasped out: "Jehu! Jehu, my servant! Is all well and is it peace?"

Jehu leaned far forward, pointed with wide sweeping gesture to the troops, and shouted shrilly and wildly: "What peace? Your hour has come, wretched man! The whoredom and witchcraft of your mother are worse than ever! This is the end! You and your house must go!"

Joram goggled at him in fear. Had he really imagined that Jehu was coming in peace? Perhaps he had only just understood what was happening.

"Treachery, Ahaziah, treachery!" he shouted. With a despairing gesture to Ahaziah he urged his driver to turn and flee.

Jehu stood up, and what happened next was not the result of a premeditated plan. He suddenly saw with blinding clarity and irresistible certainty what he had to do, what he had always wanted to do from the very first. He stood up, snatched his bow from his shoulder and took aim with deadly accuracy. His arrow whistled through the air, and before his hand had dropped or the bowstring stopped vibrating his cruel eyes saw that it had pierced Joram's heart. He saw Joram collapse and his carriage stop. Ahaziah drove off in terror, the whole cavalcade scattered and fled.

"After them! shouted Jehu. "After them! Quick!"

At his command the troops surged forward. Nobody noticed the old man get out of his chariot, push his surprised guards aside, and run panting and stumbling across the field, only to arrive too late. The bow and arrow were already poised as he shouted in a breaking voice: "No, No! Not your hand!"

It was too late, the arrow had already done its work. Too late! They ran past him without hearing or recognizing him. Nobody heard as he raised his hands helplessly and sobbed out:

"Oh, the treachery, and the curse! That was not how it was meant to be. Not by your hand!"

He collapsed in angry impotent despair, beating his breast and groaning. Then more and more softly he whispered: "Oh, the treachery! Oh, the curse on him who raised his hand!"

13

THE square round the well was deserted. Beersheba was still asleep, the people and the animals, the brown cottages and houses. Far away the first cock crowed.

Micha awoke reluctantly. He was cold and his limbs were stiff and sore with lying on the hard stones of the well. He raised himself awkwardly and looked round with leaden eyes drunk with sleep. He glanced from stone to stone, from house to house, and slowly back at the three soldiers asleep rolled up in their cloaks at the foot of the well.

He looked at them pensively. They belonged to the King's bodyguard, but for this journey Jehu had made them dress like servants. Micha did not know whether they were armed or not. They followed him silently and respectfully like servants and never left him. From the first day Micha had wondered whether they had been sent to protect him or to watch him. It was true that Jehu treated with great honour the messenger who had poured the oil on his head. He often sent for him and made him repeat the prophecy aloud, and showed him all sorts of favours. And yet—Micha shut his eyes despondently. It was all useless, the bitter disturbing truth within him could no longer be stifled. Jehu was not acting according to the word of the Lord, but just doing as he liked, his favours were a bribe and so became an increasingly heavy burden. And now this honourable mission with its flattering message was not really a favour, but a malicious test, even if it did not turn out to be something worse and more dangerous. Had not Jehu often spoken laughingly of Joram's clumsy ruse? How he tried at last too late to arrest Elisha, and sent him, Jehu, so that he might prove his loyalty by his obedience? Jehu was cleverer and not so easy to see through. "I wonder where Elisha is," he would say confidentially. "What is he saying, now that his prophecy has been fulfilled? Why does he avoid me? My heart longs to see him. Go and find him for me, Micha. Go yourself and persuade him to come to my court, for I wish to honour him fittingly. Go soon. I will give you a good escort."

Micha was breathing hard. Did the King really not know where Elisha was? He knew about everything else that went on in Israel. During the first few weeks he had posted his spies everywhere to keep him informed. Or was Elisha no longer in Israel, perhaps? Did Jehu really know nothing about him, and so was suspecting danger? Yes, Elisha out of the country might well mean danger for Jehu. So what was he scheming? And why the escort? Oh, the meaning of that was clear enough, and had been clear from the day he was sent out. To ask such a question was just a cowardly evasion and transparent self-deception. Jehu could find no better messenger to go in search of Elisha, but the messenger was only a pledge and hostage in his hand, and Jehu did not readily give up a good hostage.

Didn't you know that, Micha? Oh yes, I knew it a long time ago, he thought bitterly. On the other hand he knew also why, after wandering about aimlessly for a long time, pretending to search diligently, he had now come here. He had to admit to himself what his secret plan and his answer to Jehu had been from the first. He looked at the soldiers again and smiled. They were asleep. Yesterday he had deliberately kept them walking without rest till late in the evening. He too was tired, but he was still tougher than Jehu's famous bodyguard. He hoped they would go on sleeping soundly for a long time.

He got up and crept away on tiptoe, keeping one cautious eye on the sleeping men. They were still snoring and heard nothing. Micha crept across the square and walked on, keeping within the shadow of the houses, then almost immediately turned off and stopped, trying to remember which way to go. It had been here, he thought, it must have been one of these houses. But were they still alive and living here? Dare he inquire for them? He walked on slowly, looking this way and that, turning round every few minutes to listen. It was still quiet. After a few steps he stopped again. Hanging up there was the sign of a potter and in the little courtyard beside the house an old woman was milking a goat. Micha walked up to the fence.

"Peace be with you!" he said diffidently.

The woman started in surprise.

"What? What d'you want?" she asked gruffly. She rubbed the back of her hand across her brow and repeated in a rather more friendly tone: "Well, what d'you want? You startled me, I didn't hear your footsteps."

"I'm hungry. Would you please give me a drink of milk?"

"Wait till I've finished."

She resumed her work. After a few minutes she suddenly stopped and looked up. She got up with an effort, put her hands on her hips and looked at Micha suspiciously.

"You! Where have you come from? How did you get here so early?"

"I come from Israel. I am on a journey," answered Micha evasively. As she did not answer he added reluctantly: "I have come from the King's city."

"That's where you come from, do you? Wait! Let me see your face. Are you by any chance—?"

"Aren't you Jochabed, the wife of Simon the potter?"

"So it is really you. You are Micha," said Jochabed grimly. "I didn't recognize you at first. It was a long time ago. This time you are not asleep! Did you sleep at the well again?"

Micha made an effort to smile.

"Yes, I did sleep there. The Lord bless you. I am glad to see you. I was looking for you."

"You have been long enough giving yourself that pleasure. Not that I mind! And now you have chosen a bad time to come."

"I have been travelling about in many places far from here, but today I am looking for you."

Jochabed said nothing and did not return his smile.

"Won't you ask me in, now that you know who I am?" Micha pleaded.

"Go away!" Jochabed answered harshly. "This is not an inn.

Simon brought you here that time, and it caused us worry and annoyance, and now . . . No, go away !"

"I am hungry," Micha urged. "My feet are weary and sore. Let me rest a little while in your house, and then I will go away."

Jochabed kept her eyes on him. Once or twice she seemed about to speak, then shook her head helplessly in silence. She seemed agitated.

"No, no, wait ! I'll ask Simon. I know what he will say, but I'll ask him. Stay where you are. I'll call him."

She hobbled to the house, opened the door softly and shut it firmly behind her. Micha waited, vexed and disappointed. He had spoken diffidently to the woman, and in return she made him wait like a beggar. He would speak differently to Simon. He glanced round impatiently and anxiously. It was gradually getting lighter, but the sky was still dark and it was beginning to rain. The rain would soon waken the soldiers. At last Jochabed came back with Simon. He too shut the door cautiously and carefully and remained standing on the threshold.

"Come closer, Micha," he said quietly.

Micha came into the courtyard and said loudly: "I am very glad to see you again. Do you still remember bringing me into your house a long time ago?"

"I remember. The things you told us then are not easily forgotten."

"I was only a child then. Today I can tell of greater things that I have seen and done."

"That may well be," said Simon drily.

"I was then of no importance, a servant, but since then . . . the hand of the Lord has raised me up. I have come from Israel, from the court of Jehu our King. Look ! It was this hand that poured the oil on Jehu's head and these lips that proclaimed the prophecy that he fulfilled. It has happened. Do you know just what has happened?"

"Ahaziah the King of Judah has been killed. In Israel Joram and all his house have been killed and others besides."

"All, all of them. Jehu had Joram's body thrown into Naboth's vineyard, and the Woman was thrown out of the window by his men. His horses trampled her to pieces so that only her skull and feet and the palms of her hands were left. Her body lay outside Jezreel like dung on the fields. The prophecy has been fulfilled. I saw it. Do you want to hear what I saw?"

"No," said Simon quietly. "I don't want to hear it."

Micha stopped in surprise. Then he remembered and said softly and urgently: "No, perhaps this is not the time. Simon, you took me into your house when I was with my Master Elijah, and we were afraid of being pursued by the Woman. I . . . Now I am afraid of pursuit. I came to you to ask you to hide me. You are a righteous man and fear the Lord."

"Who is pursuing you?"

"Jehu's guards. They came with me. I left them asleep. I . . ."

"But that's nonsense! You said the hand of the Lord raised you up. You poured the oil on Jehu's head and now his guards are pursuing you? That's too much! Tell the truth. What are you looking for here? You were not looking for me, that's not why you came. Tell me what you really want, and then go."

"You don't believe me," Micha answered crossly. "You know nothing, that's it. Listen! Elisha himself sent me with the oil and the message to Jehu. Elisha himself, do you hear? But when Jehu fulfilled the prophecy, he went away and has not been seen since. The King is inquiring for him. He wishes to honour the prophet whose word I brought him on that day, and he sent me out to look for him. I'm looking for Elisha. Do you happen to know where he is?"

Jochabed put her hand to her mouth. Simon glanced at her and turned back to Micha.

"I don't know where Elisha is, how should I? You are on the wrong track. Go away and look somewhere else."

Micha came a step nearer.

"Listen!" he said excitedly. "You don't believe me. You ask who is pursuing me. I trust you, and I will tell you everything. . . . I don't know whether they are really looking for me, but they will certainly do so. You must help me and hide me. Jehu really sent me to find Elisha for him. It was supposed to be an honour. He sent a fitting escort with me. And I told you just what he said. I swear those were his words—he says he wants to honour the prophet. But I'm afraid. I don't trust him any longer. I escaped from the escort and they will look for me. I must get away from them and find Elisha alone. I'm afraid. I don't know. Elisha must decide. He's the only one who may be able to help, his words may perhaps stop what is going on. But perhaps he's also in danger. Jehu does not know where he is at present, perhaps he only wants to get hold of him to silence him. I can't go on any longer. I must see him and get his advice. I must tell him that I . . . Listen! I am done. Tell me where Elisha is and hide me till night. You helped my master, help me now for Elisha's sake."

"I don't know where Elisha is," said Simon stubbornly, "and you . . . go away!"

"You will not help me?"

"I can't help you."

"Oh, you will regret your harshness," said Micha wildly, and turned in despair to go.

The door behind Simon creaked as it opened. Jochabed cried out, Simon drew back terrified, and Micha stood rigid. Elisha was standing in the doorway, leaning exhausted against the doorpost and looking from one to the other.

"You mustn't conceal me from this man any longer, my brother Simon," he said quietly. "I have nothing to fear from him and I want to talk to him. Come in, Micha."

Elisha walked with uncertain steps to the couch and lay down again. He pointed without speaking to a low stool by the wall, and Micha sat down stiffly and hesitantly. Now that he was alone with Elisha he did not know how to begin.

"I have been ill," said Elisha after a while. He had his arms bent under his head and was staring at the ceiling. "I was on my way, and could not go on. Simon took me in here."

"Were you going to the King?"

Elisha turned his head slowly and glanced at Micha in contemptuous surprise.

"No, I certainly was not going to the King."

"He's looking for you."

Elisha did not answer. He was breathing heavily, but evenly. For some time Micha sat silent, angry and abashed. Suddenly Elisha asked sternly: "What do you want of me?"

Micha burst out: "Did you hear what I said to Simon?"

"I was wakened by your talking. I guessed it was you. I don't know how long you had been there. You were asking Simon to help you, and he pretended to know nothing about me. He is still afraid. Then I came to the door. What do you want from me?"

"An answer," said Micha passionately. Then he remembered and continued more calmly: "Elisha, you went away when the word of the Lord was at last fulfilled. Everybody came to welcome Jehu on the day of his victory, but you went away without a word, and since then.... It will soon be spring, and Jehu does not know where you are. Wherever I went looking for you, no one could tell me. They asked me 'Where is he? What is he saying now?' and I could not tell them, because I was asking the same questions. And so is the King. He sent me out to find you. He is always asking me what you are saying now."

"Tell him Elisha is saying nothing."

Micha leaned forward and asked guardedly: "Are you keeping quiet because the word of the Lord has been fulfilled?"

Elisha did not answer. He might not have heard the question at all. Micha jumped up.

"Let me tell you," he said scornfully and bitterly. "The word has been fulfilled to the last detail. Joram is dead! The Woman is dead! All her followers at the court are dead! Jehu did not waste a single day. He pursued Ahaziah and killed him. He got hold of Ahaziah's brothers and killed them—forty-two people! He sent messages everywhere, wherever there was one of Ahab's family—ostensibly friendly messages, but the elders understood and were afraid and killed them all. They brought their heads to Jehu. He had the bloody heads of the King's sons piled up in two heaps outside the palace for everyone to see. Seventy heads! And whoever else he found he killed. Jehu fulfilled the word of the Lord in blood. Ahab's house perished in blood. And Jehu did more. He issued a proclamation saying: 'Ahab served Baal little, Jehu intends to serve him better. Gather together all the prophets of Baal and all his servants. Let none of them be missing, for I wish to offer a great sacrifice to Baal.' People were amazed and did not understand, but he was saying all this with his tongue in his cheek, so that he might destroy the worshippers of Baal. He sent out through all Israel and they all came. When they were assembled in the temple of Baal, so that it was crowded to capacity, he himself put on his royal robes, and while the sacrifices and burnt offerings were being prepared, he had the temple surrounded and said: 'If any man escapes, the man responsible shall answer with his life.' None of them escaped. They were all killed. Then all the graven images and sacred stones were brought from the temple of Baal and burned or smashed or used for building. Jehu has destroyed the worship of Baal in Israel. Nobody would dare to sacrifice to him. He is ruling Israel with blood and fire and the people groan and tremble at his harshness, for no one is safe from his hand."

"Did you come to tell me this? I know what he did, and I know what he's doing."

"And you say nothing?"

"I say nothing."

"Master . . ." said Micha anxiously. "Elisha ! Has the word been fulfilled?"

Elisha was still staring at the ceiling.

"I don't know," he answered quietly.

Micha buried his face in his hands.

"You must know!" he cried. "Answer! I am in despair. I see nothing but blood, blood on my hands, blood from my lips, the bleeding bodies, the bloody heads of the children. He had them all killed that he disliked, everyone who was even suspected of loyalty to Joram. Was that the word of the Lord, and has he fulfilled it? Is that how it was to be fulfilled? He has desecrated it. It was my fault, all my fault! Listen! I tell you I have served you badly. I did not do what you told me to do. You sent me to anoint him and you said I was to open the door and flee. But I stayed. You said I was to say what you told me to say and no more, but I said more. I spoke the word as I believe it, the word that I have always heard from childhood. I demanded vengeance from him. I demanded blood in the name of the Lord, revenge and death, because I remembered the misery that I have suffered for my fidelity, and the many others who died in prison for the Lord's sake. Do you hear? I demanded this in the name of the Lord. Jehu acted on what I said, and it's all my fault. I was blind and dense. Jehu did not do it for the Lord's sake. How do I know whether my word was the Lord's will anyway? I no longer know anything. He let it happen, and yet it was evil. Look, Jehu keeps me in luxury because I spoke in that way. He keeps asking me to prophesy. I'm his shield, my word is his justification. And he smiles! His smile is blood, there is blood on his greedy hands, his shadow is the fear of death, he oppresses the people with forced labour and taxes more cruelly than ever before—and it is all my fault. I can't bear it any longer."

He threw himself down sobbing and buried his face in his arms. Elisha raised himself up and looked sternly at the prostrate figure.

"Don't exaggerate the importance of your guilt, and boast about it. Your confession only makes my own guilt more obvious. I sent you. What difference does it make if you did not do and say just what I told you to? Whatever you said came in the first place from the word I spoke. My word was wrong. It's my fault."

Micha raised his head bewildered and surprised.

"Don't you understand?" Elisha went on. "Must I say it again? What I did and said were both wrong. It's my fault. Didn't you know?"

"No, no! It was I who spoke that day," Micha passed his hand across his eyes and said angrily: "So you knew—the prophecy has been fulfilled. You said you did not know. And although I spoke your word, it was not your word alone. Elijah said the same. Was Elijah's word not the word of the Lord then? Was Elijah's word wrong?"

"Elijah's word was true. The truth is great and dangerous. Truth is one thing; what we are able to perceive another. Does the bloodshed frighten you? Do the pile of heads and the suffering upset you? There are other things to weep for. Look, Elijah's word also caused bloodshed, the brook was red with blood that day. Didn't you see it? He was not guilty in the sight of the Lord, for his word was the word of the Lord. What Elijah did was done only for the

Lord's sake, he wanted no more than that, nothing for himself, he obeyed the Lord's will implicitly. Then because the Lord in his great patience willed it so, he laid his mantle on me—me!—so that his word might be fulfilled. And I wore his mantle unworthily. I was to be the instrument only, and I presumed to choose an instrument myself, and I chose badly. I chose Jehu, whom I feared. I raised him up because he humbled himself before me. I trusted his oath that I knew was unreliable. I had to test him and wanted him to pass the test. I knew in my heart of hearts that he was only being cunning, and all the time I feared his treachery. He cared only for his own power. That was all he wanted. What does the word of the Lord matter to him? A cloak for his ambition, a disguise for his hate. Baal's followers were to him just Jezebel's followers, so he killed them. Soon he will be exactly like Joram. Today it is quite clear. I see it, you see it. How easy, how shamefully easy it is to see now what should have been clear from the first."

Elisha leaned back with his eyes closed and went on quietly: "Today I know better, to my bitter cost. This knowledge is my terrible punishment. In me too there was hate, hate, ambition and impatience. How often they had insulted me and people like me, for so many years. I wanted to vindicate my word to them, to fulfil Elijah's prophecy in my own way. What is truth worth if it does not become reality? That is what I thought. I prophesied punishment and revenge. I wanted to bring the curse and ruin upon them at last and was hard and merciless. And I denied and forgot. However could I forget! That is my great fault, that I forgot."

"Forgot what?"

"His truth, the greatness of his truth. His will is both judgment and mercy, severity and patience. He wants more than coercion. He wants obedience by your own free will. Elijah knew that. I forgot."

Micha sat up. He was trembling all over.

"Why do you confuse me?" he cried in terror, "Punishment and destruction at the hand of the Lord was my Master's prophecy for the wicked dynasty, and you said his word was true. And yet it isn't true? But it has come true!"

"At the hand of the Lord, you said. But why do you weep and blame yourself if it is the Lord's doing? Is it just because it has come true, and you are horrified at the reality? If it was the hand of the Lord, you ought to be glad that it has come true. But it was *not* the hand of the Lord. Oh yes, I too wanted the hand of the Lord to show itself. I waited for the sign and failed at last in patience and sinned by presuming to decide. Wasn't it the hand of the Lord that struck Joram at Gilead? Certainly it was. I wanted it to be so and acted too eagerly. The message from Jehu was enough for me, it was the sign from the hand of the Lord. Joram was dead, the hand of the Lord had struck him. But now he was alive, so the blow had not been the sign from the Lord at all. A threat and a warning perhaps, but even in the blow there was mercy and forbearance, and so it was not the final sign. But I did not wait until its meaning was made plain to me, I spoke and acted swiftly, because I had wanted to do so from the first. Joram fell by Jehu's hand, by the hand of an ambitious servant, not by the hand of the Lord. But I had chosen and anointed him . . . and Jehu is King."

Micha sprang up angrily.

"I won't listen to any more. Why did I come here, and why did I ask you? You are wrong. My Master taught me that everything that happens, both good and evil, is from the Lord. Jehu is King. The guilt and horror and grief that I felt as I saw what was happening was probably only weakness and fear on my part. It has happened, and so the Lord must be with Jehu. Isn't his triumph also his justification?"

"No."

"Don't you believe that any longer either?"

"Micha," whispered Elisha bitterly. "We know so little about the Lord. I have lived for him and know so little. He is within me. I feel his power, his guiding hand, I know the restlessness he puts within me, the constraint and the revelation—but not his secret, the ultimate truth of his being, which remains his mystery. How could I? I can only form my own picture of him, and surely he is the source of every such picture, since he created everything including me. He is everything that I am and can do, and yet is no part of me. He is within me and yet inaccessibly high above me, for

I am his creature and he is the creator. He speaks, but with a different voice from mine. He is the word that is not spoken by any lips, without beginning or end. By his grace we are able to see proof of his power, but it is a long way from this proof to God himself. No, it cannot be as simple as you would like it to be, that just whatever happens is evidence of his purpose. No! Perhaps our fathers once said so, but that was just their primitive idea of the God they were seeking, the little that man was able to see of him, not what he really is. Now I am beginning to understand something beyond that. He is the sole creator of all things, and that must include evil. He has created it and allows it to happen. But above all created things is God himself, the spirit, the law, the mysterious law. Am I confusing you? It bewilders me, it is ancient and yet very new and difficult to express. His law is inexorable, that is his covenant with his chosen people. But his patience also is eternal and inexhaustible. He is timeless, his purpose must be fulfilled. Only to me, his human servant, is it important that it should be fulfilled here and now. Do I then know the full mystery of his purpose? Perhaps it is in his mercy that we are not allowed to know the final answer. For what lies beyond the fulfilment? Thus I begin to understand what his 'evil' is—not just a punishment, but a trial. It's a touchstone by which you may prove yourself and come to perceive his law within you again and again, in eternal repetition! Look! What has happened? What does it matter in his eternity that a servant rebels against his master and kills him? Less than the smallest wriggle of a worm ... The important thing is the great evil that he created to test us, and which I failed to withstand. I presumed—I, his creature. I tried to be as he is and make my own decisions. So now let me remain silent."

Micha went closer to the couch.

"All right, be silent!" he said venomously. "This is a late and evil hour to refuse to speak! You made it happen. Your prophecy was the cause of the evil, and in view of that you intend just to keep quiet. It is easy for you to say 'it's my fault', very easy to say now. Why did you go away and say nothing? Jehu was anointed according to your word, and the people are still asking for a message from you. Perhaps you could put a stop to it and disown it. Because you do not speak, they imagine that this is how it is to be, and submit in silence. What has happened? Nothing! The wriggling of a worm! Oh, yes, when I came here I was very worried. I was afraid of what he might be going to do to you. I wanted to warn you and also to summon you to do something. I wanted your help and your decision. But upon my soul, now I shall go and announce to the whole nation that Elisha has done wrong, that his evil prophecy has brought disaster upon Israel, and that now he just hides away and ignores it all. He confessed his guilt to me and comforted himself with the thought that the evil is only a trial, that may be left to happen, so that others may prove themselves. You let it happen!"

"Micha!" whispered Elisha. "My poor son! Go then and speak, if that is how you see it. What is your accusation in comparison with the guilt of which I accuse myself? What is there worse to fear than my own condemnation?"

He got up wearily and laid his arm round Micha's shoulder, as if he were leaning on him for support, and at the same time trying to hold upright the one who was drawing back.

"Look! I went away because I saw the evil I had done and my life was forfeit on account of my sin. I sought and really wished for death. And when the Lord smote me with illness I really imagined that this was the end according to his will and was ready and glad. I swear to you I was ready and glad, for it would have been easier. But he did not want it so, there was again mercy in his judgment, infinite and awful mercy. Here I am and have to endure it. He laid me low, so that I should learn, and all that I have learned is that I should seek him. I travelled a long way in my weakness, yet I know that this was but the first step. How should I speak now, when I only know my guilt and not his word? I must keep quiet for a long time—that is his will. I will walk according to his will and seek him in silence, so that I may find him again, so that I may really find him at last."

"Where will you go?"

"Back," murmured Elisha, "back where I came from—and where Elijah went."

He dropped his arm from Micha's shoulder.

"Goodbye, my son Micha, God be with you! I have no other answer to give you. Go!"

Micha stared at him. His lips opened and shut, but he said nothing. Suddenly he bent down, as though a hand were pressing the back of his neck, kissed Elisha's hand, pushed it away, ran to the door, flung it open and rushed out.

Simon was still standing on the threshold outside the door. When Micha flung it open and ran past him, he drew back terrified and looked anxiously at the door. When he saw it close and remain shut, he turned and hurried after Micha. He had not understood much of what was being said in the room, but during the long wait he had noticed three strangers, who were obviously Micha's companions looking for him. They had walked along the street once or twice looking here and there. Simon had pretended not to see them, and they had not questioned him, then at last they had gone back to the well.

The street and the square were already busy. Traders had put up their stalls, women were standing gossiping by the well, children were playing about, shepherds and farmers were going out with their goats and sheep. The strangers were standing at the entrance to the square. Simon quickened his pace. He saw them walk towards Micha and bow before him, but their faces were suspicious and menacing. Simon went cautiously nearer to hear what Micha said.

"You were looking for me. You were asleep when I woke. I went to look for him and did not find him. He isn't here. Let's go."

"Where?" asked one them.

Micha looked from one to the other for some time. Was he still undecided? Simon was frightened. Then when Micha spoke it sounded like a command:

"Back to the King. I don't want to search any more."

They seemed to hesitate and then simply said: "As you will."

They took Micha in the middle and set off with him across the square towards the road leading to the gate. Simon breathed more freely as he watched them go, then turned and walked slowly back to his house. Outside the closed door he stopped again and listened, but heard nothing. He was just going into his workshop when he heard Jochabed's voice.

"Simon!"

She was standing outside the little stable looking at him anxiously and inquiringly. Simon went up to her, stroked her hand and said softly: "It's all right! He's gone."

"I was afraid."

"You needn't be afraid. He's gone and will say nothing."

"Yes . . ." said Jochabed uncertainly. She was still waiting, but Simon said nothing more. She looked up hesitantly, pointed up at the sky and whispered in astonishment: "Look!"

Simon followed her eyes and smiled. The day was brightening, the clouds were thinning and lifting, and now between them, flooded with gentle light, there appeared a wide strip of blue.